For testimonials from law enforcement,
visit Carolyn Arnold's website.

ALSO BY CAROLYN ARNOLD

Detective Madison Knight

Ties That Bind
Justified
Sacrifice
Found Innocent
Just Cause
Deadly Impulse

In the Line of Duty
Power Struggle
Shades of Justic
What We Bury
Girl on the Run
Life Sentence

Brandon Fisher FBI

Eleven
Silent Graves
The Defenseless
Blue Baby
Violated

Remnants
On the Count of Three
Past Deeds
One More Kill

Detective Amanda Steele

The Little Grave
Stolen Daughters

The Silent Witness
Black Orchid Girls

Matthew Connor Adventure

City of Gold
The Secret of the Lost Pharaoh

The Legend of Gasparilla and His Treasure

Standalone

Assassination of a Dignitary
Midlife Psychic

A totally chilling crime thriller packed with suspense

CAROLYN ARNOLD

The killing is just getting started...

ON THE COUNT OF THREE

A Brandon Fisher FBI Thriller

HIBBERT & STILES
PUBLISHING INC.

Hibbert & Stiles Publishing Inc.
hspubinc.com

This is a work of fiction. Names, characters, places, and incidents are the products of the author's imagination or are used fictitiously. Any resemblance to actual events, locales, or persons, living or dead, is entirely coincidental.

Names: Arnold, Carolyn, 1976
Title: On the Count of Three / Carolyn Arnold.
Description: 2021 Hibbert & Stiles Publishing Inc. edition. | Series: Brandon Fisher FBI Series ; book 7

Identifiers: ISBN (e-book): 978-1-988353-73-9 | ISBN (4.25 x 7 paperback): 978-1-988353-74-6 | ISBN (5 x 8 paperback): 978-1-988353-75-3 | ISBN (6.14 x 9.21 hardcover): 978-1-988353-76-0

Additional formats:
ISBN (5 x 8 paperback): 978-1-989706-68-8
ISBN (large print editon): 978-1-989706-38-1
ISBN (audiobook): 978-1-989706-39-8

ON THE
COUNT
OF THREE

PROLOGUE

Op-Ed columnist Pamela Moore passed away today after a violent home invasion left her for dead. Pamela was..."

The reporter droned on, sensationalizing Pamela's redeemable qualities while shoving all her faults, misgivings, and mistakes into a closet of obscurity. But it was a fine representation of Pamela's real life: she had spun perspectives to make a headline. More than that, she had been so obtuse that she had painted his family as *idyllic*.

She knew nothing!

His heart was thumping in his ears, his mind replaying the reporter's words: *left her for dead.*

As if he'd done that on purpose.

He clenched his fists and focused on his breathing, on slowing his heart rate. Sometimes he wondered why he put himself through watching the video over and over. The incident had taken place just over three years ago.

Still, he settled into his chair to journey back in time. To listen to what the newspeople had said about his victim, her masked assailant, and what had looked like a home invasion gone horribly wrong. It reminded him of what he'd done right and where he'd failed.

Pamela's fiancé came on the screen. He was the picture of calm put-togetherness in his pressed suit, standing in front of the camera with a microphone to his lips. He, too, was singing her praises and calling for justice.

But poor Pamela. There would be no justice for her. Her case was as cold now as her body in the ground.

He focused on the TV again and listened.

"Sadly, police have no suspects at this time but say the man who did this is considered to be especially dangerous. They don't believe that robbery was the motive, and they warn women to remain vigilant."

Her confirmed death and the reporter calling him *especially dangerous* were takeaways he rather enjoyed. He leaned forward, a smile playing on his lips as he stopped the recording and rewound the VHS tape. He was determined to dwell on the good that came with the botched murder of Pamela. He'd learned from his mistakes and his second murder had gone much better. While they say practice makes perfect, he didn't greedily indulge. No, he only took out those he deemed worthy of his attention. It was enough to quiet the darkness inside him. But there were times that the burning need to take a life was all-consuming. He called that side of him the Night.

It was an authentic part of himself, having lingered in the background for some time, calling out to him, taunting him to listen to its petitions. And now, as a man of thirty-seven, he was no longer afraid or leery of this facet of himself. He entertained the blood-filled fantasies of the Night when it was prudent, and no more would he be robbed of the fulfillment that came with taking someone's last breath. His preferred killing method assured that now.

The VCR whined down to a *thunk*. He got up from his recliner and ejected the tape. He returned it to its cardboard sleeve and put it back under a floorboard near the TV set. It was safe there.

He laced up his boots and headed out to the shed—where he was holding his latest victim. The Night purred within him, yearning to be satisfied. His heartbeat pulsed beneath his skin, anticipating what was to come.

He reached the shed and entered. The woman was naked and fixed into a guillotine that he'd crafted with his own hands. The woodworking skills his dad had taught him turned out to be useful after all. The blade was suspended and ready to be called into action. There'd be no escape for her; any movement would upset the delicate balance of the apparatus. Ah, yes, he'd finally concocted the perfect murder weapon, one his victims couldn't come back from.

He creeped closer to her, the floorboards creaking under his steps.

Her long, straight hair cascaded from the crown of her head around her face. She cried out in dry, heaving sobs, "Please…no." As if she knew what was coming.

He ignored her pathetic protest, went over to his tripod, clipped his cell phone into place, and started recording.

"Smile for the camera." He swiped her hair back, and she arched her head up the small amount the restraint around her neck would allow.

Terror streaked through her eyes. "Please…don't…do… this." Her mouth gaped open and shut, open and shut.

"You know why you're here," he said.

She wept, but it came out weak and pitiful, lacking conviction—merely gasps for breaths and hiccups in her throat. "I… Please forgive me."

He smiled. She was right on schedule: three days out here and she'd lost her fight to live, hope extinguished and her survival instinct gone. This was when they became boring to him. He much preferred when they clung to hope without reason.

And now, there she was, requesting absolution. But he was neither a priest nor a redeemer.

"We'll start on the count of three," he said in a singsong voice. The Night pulsed beneath his skin with a heartbeat of its own.

"No, no, please!" the woman screamed.

It pierced his ears, but he smiled, moving into position next to her. "One…" He reached out for the chain that suspended the blade. "Th—" His phone rang. His body quaked, the tremors of the Night snaking through him.

He grabbed a roll of duct tape from a nearby utility shelf and slapped a piece across her mouth. He normally didn't have to worry about their screams out there, but he wanted to answer this call. The ringtone told him it was his girlfriend, Roxanne. She fit into his life plan—at least for now—and he didn't want to mess things up with her.

He kept his eyes on the woman as he answered his phone. "Hey, sweetie."

He listened as his girlfriend prattled on about their plans for the following evening—dinner, then a movie. Nothing new there. She said maybe dancing afterward, but they'd never make it to a club. She'd be ready for bed by ten, and he'd tuck her in. She was as predictable as drying paint and about as exciting. But she played along with his sexual fantasies without contention, and she'd do anything to make him happy.

"You'll pick me up? My place at six o'clock?" she asked.

"I can do that. I'm looking forward to spending some time with you."

"Love you," Roxanne told him.

"Love you, too." He hung up, smiling, and let the expression carry for his victim to see. He set up his cell phone to record again and walked toward the woman. "Let's pick up where we left off, shall we?"

She was screaming behind the tape and bucking her head wildly. She was clearly trying to slide back, as if she could worm her way out of the guillotine.

Yes, fight. It makes it so much more fun...

"One," he roared above her. "Two..." He wound the chain around his fingers. With a flick of his wrist, he released it. "Three."

He smiled at the camera as the woman's head fell to the floor and rolled. It settled faceup, her eyes looking right at him. He'd heard that the mind went on living for minutes after decapitation.

He got down next to her head, swept some hair out of her face. He then put his hands over her eyes and lowered her lids. "Sleep well."

CHAPTER ONE

APRIL, PRESENT DAY, THREE YEARS LATER
WOODBRIDGE, VIRIGINIA

I sure as hell hoped there was no truth to the idea that the way a day started set the tone for everything that followed. Or I was screwed. My day had started at five o'clock—before the alarm—with me waking up to my girlfriend Becky's arm lying across my chest and my leg dangling off the edge of the bed. My phone was buzzing and dancing across my nightstand, its lights flashing like some sort of crazed disco ball. It was like trying to rouse the dead to get Becky to move, but eventually she groaned and rolled over.

My boss, Supervisory Special Agent Jack Harper, didn't even say hello, just got straight to business. "We've got an urgent case. Wheels up in twenty."

I barely grunted, but he must have taken that as agreement because he said, "Good. See you there."

I sighed and tried telling my still-asleep appendages that it was time to move. Easier said than done. I staggered out of bed, tripped on the corner of the comforter that had spilled mostly onto the floor, and narrowly avoided slamming my nose against the doorframe. Making it to the hallway unscathed had been cause for celebration, not that I had the time to revel in the accomplishment.

I was in and out of the shower in less than two minutes. Even though I ran a comb through my hair, it was as unruly as my attitude this morning. The red tufts didn't want to lie down in the back. Becky came into the bathroom and sat on the toilet while I brushed my teeth.

"Mor…ning," she said, the word fragmented by a yawn.

I continued brushing, my gums taking the brunt of my frustration. Since we had become exclusive about two months ago, I'd pretty much kissed my privacy goodbye. We didn't live together, but she was taking over my house. Her toothbrush was even in the holder.

"Where are you off to this time?" she asked.

Becky knew all about my job as a special agent with the Behavioral Analysis Unit, and as a police officer in a nearby county herself, she respected that a job in law enforcement didn't always have set hours. And with mine in particular, I could receive a call to move at any given moment. Sadly, serial killers—the type of criminal we primarily hunted— didn't adjust their schedules for our convenience.

"Did you hear me, Brandon?"

I peeled my eyes from her toothbrush and set mine in the slot next to hers. The layers of sleepy fog were finally clearing, and I realized just how brief Jack's call had been. "He didn't actually say…"

"Text me once you land? Let me know you got there— wherever *there* is—safely." Becky wiped and flushed. She inched up next to me, and I stepped back for her to wash her hands.

"Sure, but I've gotta go." I spun for the door, and she grabbed me, pulled me back, threw her arms around my neck, and kissed me.

I let myself sink into the moment for a second or two but then untangled myself from her arms. "I really have to go."

And I ran from my house—straight out into the dark morning, the pouring rain, and a puddle a few inches deep.

My socks were still soaking wet as I stood under the hangar looking out at the government jet on the tarmac. Its door was open. That was the good news. The bad news was that I was late, and Jack had very little tolerance for tardiness.

Fat drops of water bounced off the pavement a good four to six inches and pounded the metal roof overhead as if we were under fire. Given the whole "April showers bring May flowers" adage, the city should be blooming beautifully by next month. Not that that helped me right now.

It was a good fifty yards to the plane, and looking up at the black sky, I didn't see a break coming soon. But the longer I took, the later I'd be, and the more furious Jack would become.

I took a deep breath. *Here goes nothing…*

I put my go bag over my head and ran out from the hangar. Pellets of rain hit my skin like shards of ice, but I kept pushing forward, comforted by thoughts of the dark roast coffee they'd have on the plane. I ran up the stairs and boarded the plane, mentally savoring the robust flavor while bracing for a verbal lashing.

Jack was standing next to the coffee maker, which was near the doorway, and my colleague—and ex—Paige Dawson was seated at one of the tables, sipping from a cup.

Paige was just another example of the universe's warped sense of humor. Of all the beds I could have fallen into, it had to be hers. And then I found myself on her team with the BAU a couple of years later. Nothing like being in a pressurized cabin with an ex-lover. At least we were amicable—for the most part. We'd be far more than that, truth be told, but the Bureau wasn't a fan of mixing business with pleasure, and Jack would have no problem enforcing the policy. He wasn't a fan of emotions in the first place, and his people needed to walk a fine line between intuition and emotionally charged observations.

I understood where the man was coming from, though I constantly struggled to meet his standards. He'd served in the military before the BAU, and then a divorce saw his ex getting custody of their son. His tough-guy persona wasn't for show; it was him. And his salt-and-pepper hair distinguished him as a man of the world.

"You're late." Jack looked right through me.

"There was traffic and—"

"*Both of you* are late." Jack's gaze went past me, and I turned to see Zach Miles, the fourth member of our team.

I beat *him* here? Maybe this day had a silver lining after all.

"I'm sorry, Jack." Zach brushed past me, and I took that as my cue to get that first cup of coffee.

I dropped my bag on the floor and rummaged in the drawer for a pod of dark roast. There was only light. I picked one anyhow.

So much for my day looking up.

I held the pod, staring at it, as if by doing so, it would change the flavor. But there would be no point in complaining. As the machine gurgled to life and sputtered out the brew, I expected to hear Jack's voice over it all, laying into me and Zach for being late. But no one was speaking. If it had just been me who was late, I'd still be getting an earful from Jack and being teased by Zach. I know that for a fact because I'd been in that situation more than once.

I grabbed my coffee and joined the rest of the team at a table. Jack gestured a go-ahead to one of the crewmembers, and they closed the cabin door.

Jack tossed three folders onto the table, one in front of each of us, and held on to a fourth for himself. "We've been called by Miami PD to look into the case of a missing woman."

My mind froze on *Miami*. I grew up in Sarasota, about 230 miles from Miami, but I considered the whole of Florida my old stomping ground.

"Miami?" It felt like my collar was tightening around my neck.

Jack narrowed his gaze on me. "Yes. Is there a problem?"

"No." *Only that if my parents find out how close I am to them, they'll want a visit.*

It wasn't that I had a bad relationship with them, but my pops and I never quite saw eye to eye. No matter what I accomplished in my life, he wasn't impressed.

The plane started moving, and I looked out the window beside me to the hangar, longing to return there. I'd at least still be in Virginia, a suitable distance from Pops, a long way from Florida, and—

"Wait, you said Miami?" I asked, an idea sparking in my mind.

Jack pursed his lips. "I think that's clear by now."

"There's an FBI field office right there," I said, sitting up and stretching out my neck. "Why aren't they—"

"We've been specifically asked for," Jack cut in. "Now is there anything else or can I continue?"

"There's nothing else," I said, apologetic and remorseful, not sure why I was provoking the man.

"There's reason to believe that a serial killer has abducted the woman." Jack tilted his head to the case files in front of us as the plane rocked violently, speeding down the runway. "Look it over and we'll discuss. We've got a meeting with the locals when we land."

I opened the file and immediately wished I hadn't. The pictures on top were of two decapitated heads. Today was about to get a whole lot worse.

CHAPTER TWO

Zach lingered over the case file, stretching out the time it would normally take him and defying his genius IQ and speed-reading abilities. Today his emotions, rather than his brain, were taking the lead. His mind was on his fiancée, Sheri, and a vow he'd made regarding his future family, the one he'd almost lost hope of realizing. He'd told himself that if the day ever came that he had a wife and children, he'd leave the BAU. Now the promise—spoken many years ago and only to himself—sank in his chest like a heavy weight, sucking air from his lungs, haunting him. He had a feeling the day of reckoning was finally here.

But these people—Jack, Paige, and Brandon—were also family. It hurt to think of leaving them. Brandon's lips were moving slightly as he read. Paige was leaned back in her seat, her legs up, knees to chest as she studied the file. Jack was looking back at him.

"Did you want to give everyone an overview?" he asked.

Paige and Brandon set their files on the table. Paige put her legs down.

"The missing woman is Jenna Kelter, niece of Miami's mayor, Walter Conklin," Zach began, willing his mind to focus on the case. "Apparently, he's Kelter's only living blood relative, but she was reported missing at two o'clock this morning by her husband, Gordon Kelter. It's believed that her disappearance is connected with two prior murder cases given the similarities in victimology."

"They must be quite apparent to jump on this so quickly," Brandon said and looked at Jack.

Jack nodded his head toward Zach.

Zach went on. "Now Jenna Kelter was charged with DUI vehicular homicide four years ago. The other two murder victims—Kent West and Marie Sullivan—shared the same charge. Eighteen years ago, West drove off the road and into a building, killing three of his college friends who were in the car with him. Within that year he was charged for three counts and sentenced to twelve years, which he served. Sullivan's accident was seven years ago. She killed a husband and father and served four years."

"And Kelter?" Paige asked.

Zach heard her question, but his mind drifted to Sheri again and the surprise she'd had for him the night he'd proposed. It was a secret he'd been keeping from his colleagues these last couple of months, a secret that would change his and Sheri's lives.

"Zach?" Paige pressed and glanced at the others.

"Uh, yeah." He snapped out of it and refocused. "Her accident was five years ago, took about a year to go to trial. She was given and served four years in prison. She was just released this past Thursday. West and Sullivan were abducted three days after release from prison, and their heads showed up three days later." He listened to himself recap the case so robotically, so matter-of-factly. Since when did macabre crimes become so mundane, spoken about as if reciting something of no importance? These were people's lives he was talking about, and yet, he'd become calloused to that fact over the years. What would another eight years with the BAU do to him? Do to his future family?

Brandon cleared his throat, and Zach turned to him. "You said they were abducted three days after release? Kelter was reported missing on Monday morning, but her husband last saw her on Sunday," Brandon said, pulling from the file. "Exactly three days after her release."

"That's right," Zach confirmed.

"Is there any indication where West, Sullivan, and now possibly Kelter were abducted?" Paige asked.

"Unfortunately, not," Zach started. "I would say that it seems our unsub may have an interest in the number three. It's present in the timing of the abductions, when the heads are found, and the occurrence of the murders. West was killed six years ago, Sullivan three years ago, and now, there's Kelter."

"I agree," Jack said.

Zach swallowed roughly, knowing already that this unidentified subject would be one for the books. The case would likely only get darker from here, and far uglier. It was the ugly that Zach had become stained with while working for the BAU, and he feared it might never wash off. But he'd have to learn to bury it if he was going to make a fresh start.

"It's believed the decapitations were the cause of death," Zach continued, "and the rest of the victims' bodies were never found. The medical examiners working the West and Sullivan cases both described the cuts to their necks as being smooth and clean. Neither wagered a hypothesis on what was used to sever the heads." He found himself falling into a rhythm. "Their heads showed very few signs of decomp, but there was some insect activity. The presence of blowfly eggs indicated that West's head was decapitated within twenty-four hours of discovery. Same for Sullivan. But neither's time of death could be pinpointed further than that."

"That's discouraging," Paige lamented.

"That's what we're dealing with," Zach said, sounding cooler than he'd intended. He was still battling with the reality of his personal life. It had all happened so quickly; he'd gone from being single, to engaged, to an expectant father. He'd known for a couple months, but it still struck him as surreal most of the time.

But he was at work now. He had to get a grip and focus on this case. Kelter's life depended on it. He took the photos of West's and Sullivan's heads from the file. "As you can see from the pictures, both were wrapped in plastic bags, surrounded by tissue paper, and placed in boxes."

Paige pointed out a paragraph from one of the case documents. "West's head was left on the steps of Miami-Dade County Courthouse?" Her gaze met Zach's. "Rather brazen."

"Well, if you keep reading, you'll see that video captured the box being dropped off at three thirty in the morning. It wasn't discovered until start of business by a young defense attorney named Brianna King."

"We've got this picture." Jack held up a black-and-white photo of a person in a hoodie, but the quality made it hard to make out if it was a man or a woman. "It was taken from the video that Zach just mentioned."

"But obviously it hasn't gotten the locals anywhere," Brandon said.

"Obviously," Jack said drily, and Brandon's cheeks flushed red.

Brandon jutted out his chin. "And the other head was dropped off..." He consulted the file, seeming eager to discover the answer himself.

What he was looking for was buried much deeper than where he was looking. "Sullivan's head was delivered to her attorney's office—Hanover & Smith, LLP," Zach said. "It was signed for by the woman at the front desk."

"Brazen again," Brandon said, and he and Paige nodded to each other. "No lead there, either, I take it."

Jack shook his head. "No video either. Now, Sullivan's head was delivered by Miami Messenger, a local delivery service, but Miami PD found nothing there. The law office often used the service, but they didn't have any record of a delivery scheduled for the time and date in question. The delivery people were interviewed at length; their backgrounds checked out, and they were cleared. All we have is the description of a nice-looking man with brown hair."

Brandon drank some of his coffee. "Do we think that the killer is delivering the heads themself? Then again, it could be someone they are working with or someone they pay to drop them off."

"Far too early to answer that question," Zach started. "But it's possible that our unsub could like to see the reactions to their work firsthand."

Brandon winced. "Very risky."

"Did anything stand out about the delivery boxes?" Paige asked.

Zach shook his head. "No. They were just standard white boxes with lids. Similar to the kind used in bakeries for cakes. They could have been purchased from any office supply store or postal outlet." He paused a moment. "You also might have noticed from the photographs that the victims' eyes were shut. They were glued—standard adhesive, nothing traceable. Again, no lead there."

"The unsub could've felt remorse or judged with their eyes on him," Paige wagered.

"Or the unsub wanted to be the last thing their victims saw," Brandon offered.

Zach's mind wandered again, his thoughts going to all the death encased within one investigation. Beyond the murders, there was the loss of life caused by the various car accidents. The world of the BAU was drenched in bloodshed. How could he possibly turn off the job as he played with his pure, innocent child? The images, the massacre, would always be there, burned into his brain. But if he was being honest, that was the least of his concerns. One day the job could claim far more than his sanity.

CHAPTER THREE

The coffee in my gut was a churning, acidic whirlpool. The victims had been alive when their heads were severed. Now give me bloody murder scenes any day of the week. But decapitations? No thank you. Maybe it all started with that "neck bone connected to the head bone" song as a kid? Even kids know a head should always be attached to the body! I ran a hand through my hair, basking in the fact that my head was still there.

My repulsion wasn't because I was still wet behind the ears. I'd seen my fair share of serial killers' handiwork since I'd come on board with the BAU about three years ago: Some who tortured, some who raped, some who mutilated bodies. Even one who wore his victims' skin, but the latter desecration had been done *post*mortem.

And here I was, not even in Florida yet, and my pops's voice was in my mind. He'd have no sympathy for what I faced every day on this job. He'd never been a fan of the BAU; he would have been happier if I'd enrolled and served in the Navy as he had. To him, serving God and Country was more in line with patriotic duty. That was all fine and good, and I had no doubt it was because of him that I'd hoped for an assignment in counterterrorism when I finished at Quantico. But that wasn't meant to be. And I'd adjusted. The work I did with the Bureau made a difference regardless of Pops's opinion. We brought closure to devastated loved ones, got justice for innocent victims, and on the best days, even saved lives.

My gaze fell to a photo of Jenna Kelter, and I stared into her eyes. She was the image of a thirtysomething girl next door. She was a brunette with hazel eyes and a cute smile. We needed to save her, and the fastest path there was to figure out what sort of killer we were dealing with. I considered this killer's actions thus far and drew a preliminary conclusion. "Our unsub is intelligent, organized, yet adaptive," I posited. "They have the patience to wait until circumstances fit their needs."

Paige nodded. "That could also indicate they'd watched their targets beforehand."

"Even if they were familiar with all the victims' routines before prison, what's to say their schedules resumed that within three days of release," I opined.

"Well, they obviously knew where to strike to get them alone. None of the families or their friends saw the abductions." Paige pressed her lips, a little smugness coming from her.

I flipped through the pages, looking for details on their bail hearings. "I'm assuming Kelter got out on bail?" I'd read enough of the file to know that she didn't have any prior DUI offenses, so the bail amount would likely have been set low.

"She did. And her trial came quickly because she didn't dispute the charges," Zach said. "According to the file, she'd expressed remorse."

"How much time passed from when she made bail until the trial?" I asked, pressing on.

"Six months."

Everyone's eyes were on me. "Was she given a tracking bracelet?"

Zach shook his head. "It wasn't believed necessary."

"Well six months would be long enough that Kelter could have adhered to her basic routine before the accident," I started. "The unsub could have familiarized themself with her habits and schedules during that time."

Paige was nodding. "But like you brought up a moment ago, were the three days before their abductions enough time for them to resume their previous schedules?"

"We can't afford to overlook the possibility that it was. We'll need to find out if the victims had any reoccurring activities on their calendars," Jack said. "Getting back to the two murder victims. What do they tell us about our unsub beyond the fact they are seemingly organized and intelligent?"

"Killers who dismember often lack empathy and don't always experience emotions," Zach offered.

"By delivering the severed heads to such public places, it indicates our unsub seeks attention," I added. "Whether our unsub is doing so themself or not, it's still making a splash."

"I'd say they're the type to feed on media coverage," Paige started, "to bask in what they've done. They likely take pleasure in witnessing people's horror at finding the packages."

"Given this profile, it's quite possible that Kent West wasn't their first victim." Zach tapped his fingers on the table, and uneasiness was coming from him in waves. I locked eyes with Paige. I wasn't alone in noticing Zach's unnatural mannerism.

Zach went on. "Before they killed their first victim, they probably spent a lot of time fantasizing about doing so. This level of violence doesn't just build overnight. And given the restraint the killer shows in pacing out their timing…"

"But are they?" Paige asked. "As you just said, there could be more victims than we're aware of yet. Either way, the fact that they're holding victims for days implies the unsub is process-focused."

"That could indicate the unsub is torturing them, but we have no proof of that," I said.

"Just holding them is mental torture," Paige served back. "The victims would have clung to the hope of escape or rescue only to have that light extinguished."

"I'd side with them being more *act*-focused," I challenged. "The killer may want to make a bigger statement."

"The killer clearly feels something about DUI vehicular homicide," Jack surmised. "And there must be something special about these three cases in particular that attracted our unsub's attention. We'll need to gather all the facts about the West, Sullivan, and Kelter cases."

Paige scribbled something in her notepad.

"Now, we all know there are at least five psychologies behind mutilation." Jack held his left hand out in front of him, his fingers curled except for his index, which was stretched out. "One, defensive." He pressed the pad of his right index finger to his left one. "Two, aggressive." He uncurled his middle finger and pushed down on it. He continued to count off on the rest of his fingers and his thumb as he went. "Three, offensive. Four, psychotic. And five, organized crime."

"We can rule out *defensive* right off the top," I said, squaring my shoulders. "Usually in that situation, the killer's mutilating a corpse to hide evidence or make identification difficult."

"Agreed. The faces are not marked and are easily identifiable," Zach clarified. "But there's the matter of the rest of the remains. Does the unsub separate the head from the body for the purpose of their 'display'?" Zach attributed finger quotes to the word *display*. "Or do they do it for convenience of disposal? And if the latter, do they cut up the rest of their victims' bodies? We really need to know what he's doing with the bodies before we can completely dismiss a defensive motivation."

"Based on the heads, we could rule out an aggressive mindset," Paige said, gesturing toward Zach. "There's no sign of physical torture before death there."

"And without the rest of the bodies, we don't know if the killer's using them for some sick, sexual purpose," I said, sarcastically thinking that Pops would be so "proud" if he heard me now.

"I agree," Jack said. "It's too soon to exclude offensive motivation. It's also far too early to know if our killer suffers from psychotic episodes," Jack added. "Delusions, hearing voices…"

"Given the specific victimology, I'd say we can pretty safely rule out organized crime," I said, grasping at the one motivation we could realistically check off the list.

"Really, our unsub could be decapitating their victims for any number of reasons," Zach summarized pointedly, pulling the pin on the grenade.

Paige let out a sigh and leaned on the table. "Then where the heck are we?"

As if on cue, the pilot announced that we would be beginning our descent into Miami International Airport.

I pointed to the speaker and smirked at Paige. "Well, I can tell you one thing for sure…"

She smiled, narrowed her eyes at me, and shook her head.

CHAPTER FOUR

CENTRAL DISTRICT POLICE STATION
MIAMI, FLORIDA

The last time detective Kelly Marsh had seen Jack Harper was nine years earlier at her granddad's funeral.

She fished out an antacid from her pants pocket and popped it into her mouth. Not that they were helping at all. The first four hadn't anyhow.

She'd followed her inclination to bring Jack down here, but him actually coming was another thing entirely. Seeing him would bring her past back in vivid color, and she wasn't sure she was ready for that. But she knew that if Jenna Kelter stood any chance at all, Jack was her best shot. And after all these years, he'd listened to Kelly when she called him—even though she'd woken him up in the wee hours.

Her sergeant hadn't been as kind. Ramirez had laid into her about waking him up with "something that could wait." But she knew how to play him. He liked the spotlight, and he'd want to look good in it. If he didn't do all he could to ensure the safe return of the mayor's niece and something happened to her, he'd be the one needing to explain himself to the media. She had worked it from that angle and quickly had gotten approval to call in the FBI.

She glanced at the clock on the wall; it was just approaching ten in the morning. And to think this case got started just eight hours earlier, and now she was setting up a conference room for Jack and his team.

It had been pure luck that the officer who Mr. Kelter had spoken with was aware that Kelly was obsessed with the West and Sullivan cases and recognized similarities in Kelter's background.

She stepped back from the whiteboard, taking in the photos of West, Sullivan, and now Kelter that she'd hung up with magnets. She'd pulled the details of their cases from memory and jotted them down by each photo—their ages, dates and locations of their accidents, names of the fatalities, dates sentenced, dates released, dates of disappearance, dates their severed heads had shown up, and where they'd been delivered. The particulars were like CliffsNotes of all the information she had. Beneath Kelter's photo and particulars, she added, *Presumed next victim.*

Her stomach clenched and then tossed. The similarities were there in front of her in black-and-white. And she felt somewhat responsible. She wished she could have seen Kelter's disappearance coming and prevented it, though that wasn't being logical or fair to herself. There were a lot of people who had been charged with DUI vehicular homicide in the past seven years, so it would be impossible to keep tabs on them all. And there'd been no murders matching this killer's MO, even in ViCAP, the FBI's Violent Criminal Apprehension Program, which tracked violent crime. She'd begun to think that maybe the killer had gone quiet.

But it wasn't like she'd given up on solving West's and Sullivan's murders. Though, if her sergeant had a say, she would have. He thought she was simply obsessing over her first case, which had been West's murder, but she knew better, and it had her butting heads with Ramirez. Especially after Sullivan's murder, when Kelly first suspected Sullivan's murder was connected to West's. But Ramirez hadn't wanted to hear it, and he hadn't wanted her investing time in their cases when there were always new ones to solve. As he had so clearly reminded her, she was from Homicide, not Cold Cases.

Oh, even the memory had her seeing red. She clenched her fists, allowing her nails to dig into her palms. Surprisingly, it had a calming effect on her—most of the time.

Thinking that West and Sullivan might finally get justice assuaged her guilt-ridden conscience. Ironically, with the thought of being freed of this burden, she wondered what the next chapter of her life would hold, but then she found herself musing about the past. The one Jack's presence no doubt would churn to the surface.

He knew her history. How she had seen her mother shoot her father when she was only six years old. How her mother had gone on to serve a fifteen-year sentence for manslaughter. How her granddad had left the military to raise her and her brother. How they'd left their home in Detroit to move in with him in Virginia. How her brother, Chet, started acting out and ran away at seventeen, not to be seen again. And how her mother's actions had changed the direction of Kelly's life again when she had taken off after being released from prison. In fact, it upset more than Kelly. It had nearly killed her granddad. He'd hired a private investigator and moved to Miami on a tip that Kelly's mom had been seen there.

That had been eleven years ago when Kelly was twenty-two. She'd followed him south when his health had taken a dive. The man literally had ended up dying of a broken heart. A military general reduced to a broken spirit.

But there was some good to come out of the trauma she'd experienced in her life. She'd heard her calling to enter law enforcement. Her father had been abusive, and her mother had acted in self-defense; still, the charges hadn't been dropped. It was probably why Kelly had made it her life mission to put only the guilty behind bars—for her mother, for the falsely convicted. Kelly's drive to be the best was why she'd enrolled in the FBI Academy. But becoming an agent wasn't meant to be.

It was all these memories that she wished she could suppress, purge. But upon seeing Jack, she was sure they would come flooding back. It seemed all it took was the *thought* of seeing him.

She grabbed a rolled-up map of Miami from the table and was uncurling it when someone shadowed the doorway.

"I see you're getting everything ready." Sergeant Ramirez's voice was like nails on a chalkboard, but that was because she had very little respect for the man. At least he'd done the right thing by letting her call in the FBI. But one right move didn't compensate for the fact he was a prime example of shit rising to the top. Well, that and connections. He was in deep with the police captain and the mayor. It didn't seem to matter that Ramirez placed more emphasis on closure rates than justice. He failed to realize the two were not always synonymous. Was early retirement for the man too much to ask for?

Ramirez was smirking his sardonic, know-it-all smirk. "Don't think for one moment I don't know you played me, Marsh. And I don't know if I buy into this theory of yours that a serial killer is behind Kelter's disappearance, nor do I care."

She squeezed her fists tighter, her nails just short of drawing blood.

"I *do* care that Miami PD's reputation comes out of all this in pristine condition. Am I understood?"

"Clearly." *Agree, be amicable, and maybe he'll leave me the hell alone.*

"You wanted to be FBI, didn't you?" Another smart-alecky smirk and a comment he knew damn well was true. "Guess you get your chance to play agent. But remember, you represent Miami PD. If you fuck up—and I mean, no matter how small—your ass is out the door." With that, Ramirez left.

She watched after him, staring at the now-vacated doorway, still clenching her fists until shots of pain registered in her brain and she extended herself mercy. She opened her palms to find fingernail marks deeply embedded in both of them.

She turned around to face the whiteboards, trying to get her mind off Ramirez and back on the case. Still, she couldn't help but wonder what she'd done to deserve him. The pompous, sanctimonious piece of shit that he was, with his threats and his—

"Detective Marsh?"

A smile spread across her lips. She'd recognize that voice anywhere.

CHAPTER FIVE

Jack." Detective Marsh turned around. She was grinning. And she was a looker. Her brown, blown-out hair fell a few inches past her shoulders, and she was probably about five-and-a-half feet tall. She had a runner's body, almond-shaped eyes, rosebud lips, and a sun-kissed complexion.

She looked from Jack to the rest of us. "This must be your team."

Jack smiled at Marsh like a proud father. "It is." He gestured for us to introduce ourselves.

"Special Agent Brandon Fisher," I said, holding out a hand to her. She had a solid grip and wore fluorescent-green nail polish. Her eyes met mine, and hers lit. Who said brains and brawn couldn't coexist? I pegged Marsh as a powerhouse.

She made the rounds with Paige and Zach, then returned to Jack.

"I heard about your mother," Marsh said. "I'm sorry I couldn't make it up for the funeral."

Jack held up a hand. "Not necessary. We all have jobs to do." He paused. "So why don't you tell us what you can about Kelter?"

She nodded. "Her husband reported her…"

I was aware that Marsh continued to talk, but I was stuck on the fact that she and Jack obviously shared a history. For a man who would have us believe he didn't have a personal life, evidence to the contrary stood in front of us. Marsh's instant reaction to his presence alone should have told me that much. A large grin? Jack rarely initiated those from anyone.

"Her husband won the lottery?" Paige's question cut through my thoughts.

How much had I missed?

Marsh nodded. "Just before Kelter's accident. He netted sixteen mil after taxes."

I whistled. "And we're sure he didn't take her out?" I asked in jest. It earned me a dirty look from Jack and an obvious analysis from Marsh. I shrugged off the disapproval.

"I think that's an angle that deserved attention," Marsh admitted. "The husband was interviewed at length already. Here's the thing, though, if he wanted to keep the money, why not disappear when she was in prison or take her out before she went in?"

"How can you be sure he's not involved with her disappearance?" I challenged, despite the fact that she'd defended my position and raised a couple of good points. I wanted to know when she'd had time to interview the man *at length*, but I didn't poke that one.

Marsh locked eyes with me. "It's still early, but his alibis checked out and I haven't uncovered any reason to believe he's involved."

"Kelter fits the mold of this killer's previous victims," Jack stated. It almost felt as if he were standing up for Marsh.

"Exactly, and what motive would Mr. Kelter have had to kill West and Sullivan?" Marsh pressed her lips and raised her brows.

"You sound confident in the husband's innocence," I concluded.

"I haven't seen reason not to be." Marsh was quick to jump on that, mirroring everything about this case so far. We were rushing on this faster than we normally would. It had to have something to do with Jack's relationship with Marsh.

"Tell us about the suspects in the previous cases," Jack directed Marsh.

"Obviously nothing got us anywhere or I wouldn't have called you, but"—Marsh walked in front of the board and stopped next to Kent West's photo—"our best lead was the video showing the person in the hoodie dropping off the box containing West's head."

If that was our *best* lead, we were running on the wrong side of luck.

"Speaking of the person in that video, we'd like to watch the footage," Jack said.

"Of course." Marsh pointed to the same black-and-white photo we'd looked at on the plane. "All it gives us is approximate stature. We never see their face."

"Like they knew where the cameras were," I chimed in.

Marsh nodded. "We can't even tell for certain if it's a man or woman, really, but it's most likely a man, based on gait."

"And even if we figured out who that is—" I flicked a finger toward the picture "—what's to say it's even going to get us anywhere? That might not be our killer." I was resurrecting the conversation from the plane, but it was worth bringing up again.

"Truth is, we don't know." Marsh pressed her lips together. "We don't even know if the same person delivered Sullivan's head to the law office." Marsh put her fingertip to a checklist of the evidence under West's photo. From what I could gather, nothing there was anything new to what we'd read in the file. Marsh continued. "As far as suspects go, it's a dead end. But we interviewed *a lot* of people: vagrants, the families of West's DUI victims, students and teachers at the college who knew West, the woman who found West's head."

"Brianna King, a defense attorney who was on her way to court," Zach squeezed in.

"Yes, and a good friend of mine," Marsh volunteered. "If you'd like to speak with her, I can arrange it."

Jack gestured for Marsh to continue.

"When I asked West's family if they were aware of anyone who might have had issues with him, they told me they'd received a bunch of hate mail."

"That could be helpful," I said.

Marsh winced. "Unfortunately, they threw it out when West went to prison. They didn't think they had anything more to worry about." Marsh stepped forward, toward Marie Sullivan's information, and stopped beside it.

I skimmed the particulars of the accident, refreshing my memory, and then turned my attention to the evidence collected at Sullivan's crime scene. I read until I got to the mention of duct tape and asked Marsh to expand on how it was used.

"There was just a trace of adhesion found on her face and it turned out to be duct tape. I think the killer may have put it across her mouth to keep her quiet."

"Makes sense," I reasoned.

"Though tape was never found on West," Jack noted.

"No, but that doesn't mean it wasn't used. It just means we have nothing to prove that it was," Marsh said. "The strongest suspects in the Sullivan case were her ex-husband and Abigail Cole. Cole's husband died when Sullivan struck his car."

"He was just out getting ice cream for her," I said, shaking my head, unsettled by the fragility of life and my intolerance for drinking and driving. I'd been doing a good job so far of keeping my personal feelings on the matter to myself, but the loss of life was so senseless. The accidents never had to happen.

"He was," Marsh confirmed. "She was pregnant and had a craving. More tragic still is that Abigail ended up losing the baby."

"Poor thing," Paige said, compassion in her eyes.

Marsh nodded and added, "That about covers the basics. I've asked for the evidence boxes from the West and Sullivan cases to be brought up, but I haven't seen them yet. I might have to go get them myself."

All this loss... My gaze sweeping across the board. It was hard to let go of my personal views on drunk driving completely. I felt for West and Sullivan but also had empathy for the victims killed in the car crashes West and Sullivan had caused. Their actions had stolen loved ones from friends and family. By extension, Kelter had done the same. But regardless of the heartache these three people had caused, none of them had deserved a violent end.

The thing with Kelter was that we didn't even know for sure if she'd been taken by West and Sullivan's killer. We had gotten here so quickly after she supposedly went missing. What's to say she hadn't just run off? Or who's to say that someone else—namely Gordon Kelter—hadn't put together the similarities and was banking on them to get away with making Jenna Kelter disappear? Sixteen million bucks in his pocket and no need to share a penny with anyone. Everyone was dismissing the possibility too easily in my opinion. The spouse is always first suspect if something happens to their mate. Whether his supposed alibis cleared him or not, I still wasn't convinced he was innocent.

"I know we touched on it, but playing devil's advocate," I began, "maybe Kelter's husband had her kidnapped or killed."

"As I said," Marsh replied, "we have no reason to believe he was involved or orchestrated any of this. And why wait until now? As we've established, he had the money before she went to prison."

"And why would Mr. Kelter go to such lengths?" Paige asked. "He could just file for divorce like most people."

"He also has no criminal record and no motive," Marsh reminded me with a pointed look.

"You mean, besides the millions he won in the lottery that he might have wanted to keep to himself." When something got in my head, it could be a little hard to shake it. Maybe I was a little antagonistic and hardheaded, but those characteristics also had their benefits in my line of work. "Paige, you can't be naive enough to just dismiss the possibility. People have killed their spouses to get out of marriages before."

"I also said that his alibis clear him," Marsh countered.

"I remember, but—"

Jack gave me a mild glare. "At this point, we just need to find Kelter. The who, the why, and the how of it, we'll figure out as we go." Jack's voice had an edge to it, but he clearly had a soft spot for Detective Marsh. "I'll have Nadia look into other DUIs in Miami involving fatalities in the last eighteen years. That will cover from the time of West's accident to now. We'll see if we can find any others who were involved in similar situations and if they were threatened or harmed in any way."

"And who's Nadia?" Marsh asked.

"Nadia Webber is our analyst back at Quantico," Jack told her. "When we need anything researched, she's our go-to."

Marsh nodded. "Going back to what you said, Jack, I've already looked into that and nothing stood out."

Jack raised a brow. "You looked for victimology similarities?"

"You don't need to ask that," she replied with a smile. Jack returned it.

I must have entered the twilight zone…

Marsh pointed to a stack of paper on the table. "Backgrounds were pulled on anyone tied to the West and Sullivan cases, as well as Kelter's accident."

She *was* good, but I wasn't sure how much I liked her just yet. I had a feeling she might make me look bad.

"I have financials coming through for Kelter now," Marsh said. "Her phone records should also be in soon, and her number is being monitored. If her cell turns on, we'll know about it."

"Impressive." Jack's smile lingered. "Have the financials and phone records sent to Nadia Webber." Jack handed Marsh a card. "Her e-mail's on there."

"Okay," Marsh said, glancing at the card.

Jack continued. "Brandon and I will go talk to Ava Jett, the widow of Kelter's victim. While we're getting a feel for the situation there, Paige and Zach, I want you to go talk to Kelter's husband. See if you can get an idea of what her schedule looked like. If we work backward, maybe we can figure out where our unsub latched on to her."

"Will do, boss," Paige said.

"Just a word about Gordon Kelter," Marsh started. "He has a pile of hate mail for us. I just haven't got around to picking it up yet."

Paige and Zach nodded, simultaneously and evenly, like those bobblehead dolls.

"And I'll interview Kelter's friends," Marsh said. "If that works for you, Jack?"

He nodded. "Sounds good. Find out—"

"What I can about Kelter's schedule from them?" Another smile and Jack was mirroring the expression—again.

Okay, this *was The Twilight Zone.* Since when was Jack not only *okay* with being interrupted but *happy* about it? If I did that, his eyes would shoot laser beams at me and he'd pin me with a scowl.

"Just so you know," Marsh went on, "I did look into the backgrounds of West and Sullivan and couldn't find anything they had in common either socially or professionally. Their age difference may have had something to do with it."

"We'll need to look outside their social circles," Jack said, and Marsh nodded.

"Before we go," I started, "about Kelter's husband…" Jack's glare halted my words, but I took a deep breath. "I've got to just put this out there. Marsh, if you connected the past cases, who's to say Gordon Kelter—or someone else who wanted to see Kelter disappear—hasn't done so, as well?"

No one had anything to say to that.

CHAPTER SIX

Life could change in the blink of an eye—or so they said. Zach didn't even think it took that long. Life could be over in a flash. All one really had to do to realize that truth was take a good look around.

With this case, the accident victims probably had figured they were starting any other ordinary day. They probably didn't have even a fleeting thought that they wouldn't return home that night.

The local FBI office had supplied the team with a couple of SUVs. Zach and Paige were in one of them, stopped at a red light, and he was watching the people crossing the street. They had no idea how vulnerable they were, how fragile life was.

Paige looked at him from the passenger seat. "You okay over there?"

"Why wouldn't I be?" But he knew why she'd asked. They always filled the space between them with animated conversation about whatever case they were working, but this ride had been pretty quiet.

"Zach?" Paige pointed to the light that had turned green.

Zach pressed the accelerator, hoping Paige wouldn't push him and would just leave him to his thoughts, no matter how depressing they were. Then again, death was a fact of life. The Grim Reaper showed no favoritism, snatching whomever was in his path. There was certainly nothing fair about the timing or selection process.

"I'm having a hard time seeing," Paige said.

He looked over to see her squinting behind her sunglasses.

"You have an optical migraine coming on?" He'd had them before, and they were horrid—zigzag vision often accompanied by speech problems. Usually an antacid and a few Tylenol helped right things. "Do you need me to pull over?" He started looking for a spot.

"No." Paige smiled. "I was referring to the smoke in here." She waved her hand as if to clear the air. "You're so deep in thought."

He settled back into the seat.

"What is it?" Paige asked. "You have something serious on your mind."

Zach looked over at her, wishing he could become invisible. But if he was going to open up to someone, she was a good choice.

He gripped the steering wheel and twisted, his knuckles whitening. "I guess now is as good a time as any."

Paige shifted her body, angling more toward him, frowning. "Now, you're worrying me. What is it? You and Sheri okay?"

"We're good." By keeping things cryptic, maybe he could derail the conversation before it got going.

"*Good?* Why am I having a hard time buying that?" Her eyes scolded him. "If you're having problems, I'm here for you. Is she upset that you had to go out of state last minute?"

"No. She knew what she was getting into." Zach slid her a gentle smile.

"Well, then you're a lucky one, Zach."

He was, and he knew it. Maybe that's why he felt like garbage for viewing his future child as an unwelcome burden. Even acknowledging the thought made him shrink.

"Some say that we make our own luck," he added lightheartedly, hoping they'd find a new path to venture down discussion-wise. Opening up to someone was losing its appeal.

"If we do, I suck at it." Paige gave a self-deprecating laugh.

"Oh, someday you'll meet Mr. Right," he teased, glancing at the road, then back at her.

"Should it bother me that you went right to my love life?" She thrust out her arm and twisted an imaginary blade.

He was smiling.

"It's a good thing I like you." She laughed. "Let's talk about something other than my love life."

"The case?" he asked, hopeful.

Paige slapped his arm. "Don't think I'm letting you off that easy. *Spill.*" The last word was said with stark seriousness.

Maybe it was best to lay the groundwork for what would follow. "Sheri is pregnant."

"She's…" Paige's face lit into a large grin.

Zach would have laughed at her animated reaction if his stomach wasn't tied up in knots. How was she going to react when he told her his plans to leave the BAU?

"At a loss for words?" he asked.

"Yeah… Well, kind of. You just got engaged. I take it this wasn't planned?"

"Nope." And he wasn't sure what shook him more, seeing himself as a father or working in a cubicle.

She nudged his shoulder. "But you're happy about it, right?"

He found himself going still—his body frozen, his thoughts suspended. His lungs expanded with air, and he looked at her, hesitant to admit his innermost feelings, as if voicing them would confirm that he was a bad person.

He'd been shocked when Sheri had told him she was pregnant. Not because commitment scared him; it didn't. He'd just proposed to her after all. But a baby meant *real* change. Turn-your-world-upside-down change. That was more what he was afraid of. Then again, it could be a matter of him not wanting to let go, of not knowing how he'd balance this job and a baby.

"It was a surprise," he said. "That's all."

"Oh."

That one tiny word was a sucker punch to the gut. The way her eyes were scanning him, she was reading him. His anxious energy, his grip on the wheel, the subtleties behind his words, his reaction to the news—it obviously wasn't lost on her.

"You're afraid," Paige added. "Babies are a lot of work."

He chuckled. "You talk like you know firsthand."

"Kids aren't in my future, but that's me. I think I'm missing the mommy gene." She gave a small smile. "But for you and Sheri, this is exciting. It will be the start of a fun and interesting chapter in your lives."

She had no idea. He breezed through a yellow to red.

"Why do I have the feeling there's more?" Paige asked.

Because you're a damn good FBI agent.

"Here goes." He paused. "I promised myself a long time ago that if I got married and started a family, I'd take a desk job." His gaze flicked to Paige's. His heart was pounding, but his breathing was shallow.

"Oh." A few beats. Then, "Ohhh. You're leaving the BAU?"

"Please don't say anything about this to anyone. Obviously, I don't need this getting to Jack before I talk to him."

"So you are leaving…" Paige slumped. "You *can* work the job and be a father, Zach." Bless her for trying, but her reassurance rang hollow.

"Like I said, I promised myself a long time ago—"

"Yeah, I heard you," she interrupted. "Do you hear yourself? A *long* time ago. You're allowed to change your mind."

"You know about my brother-in-law, Greg, don't you?" he asked.

She nodded, somber. "He was shot in the line of duty." Her brow pinched as if she didn't get why he was bringing him up.

"Right. Because he was a cop." Zach's chest tightened. "He left my sister alone, pregnant and with a two-year-old to raise."

"So you worry that would happen to you?" she asked gently.

"I'm not worried about me. Greg's death nearly destroyed my sister. I wouldn't want to do that to Sheri or leave our child without a father."

"And you think if you get a desk job, that will guarantee that won't happen? You know, for a genius—"

"I know I could die at any time."

"Then what's the issue, Zach? Life is for living. And you have someone who loves you. Soon you'll have a son or daughter looking up to you."

He pulled on the collar of his shirt, which was becoming more restrictive the longer the conversation went on. "I just…"

Paige reached over and squeezed his forearm. "Just promise me you won't rush to any decisions."

"You should know me better than that." Saying the words, he felt like a hypocrite. He struggled to envision his future with a family *and* working with the BAU.

He pulled into the Kelters' drive, welcoming the reprieve speaking to Gordon would bring. At least his mind—and Paige's—would be focused on the case.

CHAPTER SEVEN

Marsh held some sort of power over Jack, and I was determined to find out why. Not only had they been happy to see each other but every word that came from her lips seemed to make Jack proud. And in contrast, everything I said was frowned upon. Literally.

"How do you and Marsh know each other?" I asked.

Jack and I were in our assigned SUV but hadn't left the station's parking lot.

His window was down, but he still reeked of the cigarette he had before getting into the vehicle. "She went to the FBI Academy."

I stiffened. *That's all?* I swallowed the urge to say the words out loud, and instead asked, "Did she pass?"

He started the car and pulled out onto the road. "Yep."

"You were one of her instructors?" I clenched my jaw. Getting Jack to open up was like pulling at weeds with deep, entrenched roots.

"I was." He took a turn as indicated by the GPS, heading for Ava Jett's house.

"I knew her grandfather well," he offered, just when I thought the conversation was over.

"How did you—"

Jack looked over at me. His hardened expression said it all. Our little question-and-answer session had come to an end. We sat in silence the rest of the way to the house Ava shared with her son, Nathan.

She came to the door wearing fluffy slippers and a housecoat. Her eyes were bloodshot and puffy. She clearly regarded Jack and me as an inconvenience. "Who are you?"

"FBI, ma'am," Jack replied with his credentials in hand.

Her gaze went to me. "What's this about?"

"We'd like to talk with you about Jenna Kelter," I said.

Ava sniffled and pulled out a bunched-up tissue from one of her robe's pockets and dabbed her nose. I stepped back. Getting sick wasn't on my to-do list.

"The last person I want to talk about is her. She took my Lester away from me—the only man I've ever loved," Ava said. "I got the life sentence, and she walks away after four years? Tell me how that's fair." Heat simmered in her tear-filled eyes. "Every day I wake up, and he's not beside me. The only way I can sleep at all is because I take these." Ava pulled out a sleeve of pills from the same pocket that housed the tissues and held it up for a few seconds. Pain emanated from her, creating a swirling, dark energy that cloaked her. The tragedy was still very raw, even though her husband had died five years ago.

I could only imagine what she'd been through. An accident was one thing to accept, but to know that it was the result of a drunk driver was another. In my opinion—black-and-white as it may have been—the driver was pretty much on par with a killer. They'd made a choice to get behind the wheel intoxicated. Maybe I should have more compassion or leniency for these convicted drivers. I was guilty of getting behind the wheel with a mild buzz before. Back when I'd just turned twenty-one. There'd been a gathering and some coolers. When friends had wanted to pick something up at the corner store, I hadn't hesitated. I'd hopped in the car without thinking about the fact that I'd been drinking. It wasn't until I slowed at a stop sign that I realized my head was a bit foggy. From that moment on, I swore that if I was going to be drinking, I wouldn't be driving.

I met Ava's eyes and said, "We're sorry for your loss, Mrs.—"

"No, please don't call me Mrs. Jett." Ava shook her head. "It hurts too much. It only reminds me of what I've lost."

"*Ava*, we can only imagine what you're going through," I said again, gently.

Ava shook her head. "You can't unless it has happened to you." Ava gestured at her getup. "You probably think I'm home sick from work? But this is what my life looks like when I'm not at work ever since…" Her voice cracked.

"Let's sit down." Jack's directive was tempered with sympathy. Maybe I was rubbing off on him a bit.

When I'd first joined his team, he was more than a little rough around the edges. Not to say that he didn't care about the victims or the loved ones left behind, but you'd never see a tear bead in his eyes. He was just better than most at hiding his emotions. He was a product of his background. He'd seen a lot of loss and devastation in his lifetime, and he'd had to grow a thick skin or risk going crazy.

Ava led us down the hallway toward the back of the house. We passed a kitchen with stacks of dirty dishes on the counter, before reaching the living room.

I moved a few T-shirts and a pair of jogging pants off a couch cushion to make room for Jack and me to sit. Ava sat on a sofa chair with no visible sign of being embarrassed at the state of her home. Besides the wardrobe cyclone, a couple of dishes—complete with pizza crusts—sat on the coffee table, along with a bowl of cheese curls. Envelopes were also fanned out, their faces stamped *Past Due*.

Ava swept them up and stuffed them into one of her robe pockets. "Why do you want to talk about the woman who murdered my husband after all this time? Do you think we can get her more prison time?"

"She's missing." Jack laid it out there with a cool, calm detachment.

Ava's eyes twitched and then widened. "And why would I care?"

"We believe she's in danger," I added, though not expecting too much compassion after how she'd worded her earlier question: *the woman who* murdered *my husband.*

Ava crossed her arms and sank back into her chair. "I hope you don't expect me to get upset over that, either."

"We don't expect anything," Jack replied.

Between her rigid body language and her vacant stare, I'd say that however dark Kelter's fate might be, Ava would be okay with it. But the question was, had she acted on her hatred for the woman? Was she involved with Kelter's disappearance in any way?

I took out my phone and brought up the pictures of Kent and Sullivan that had previously been supplied to the media. She didn't recognize either of them.

"Who are these people? What do they have to do with the woman who murdered my husband? Do you think they took her?"

"No," I said, pocketing my phone again.

"I don't understand," Ava said, her brow pressing down in confusion.

She struck me as genuine, but there was a way I could confirm whether she was being honest or not. "How long have you lived in Miami?" Surely, if she'd been in the area six or seven years ago, she'd have heard about Kent and Sullivan. Decapitations didn't make the news headlines often, thank God.

"We just moved back two years before..." Ava cleared her throat.

"Before...?" I wanted clarification.

"Before the *accident.*" She curled her lips in disgust, as if somehow the word didn't do what happened to her husband justice. "Lester was born here and loved the weather and the culture. Guess it's poetic in a way that he also died here. If you can call being murdered poetic."

Ava's gravitation toward the word *murder* for her husband's demise confirmed she saw the car crash in much the same light as I did: while his death may not have been planned and executed, it was preventable. This viewpoint would only bolster her hatred of Kelter. And maybe she honestly didn't know about West or Sullivan, or have anything to do with their murders, but that didn't necessarily clear her for Kelter's disappearance.

I pressed on. "The man was Kent West and the woman was Marie Sullivan." The hook was baited.

"*Was?* So they are both dead?" Ava's mouth opened, closed, opened again.

"Uh-huh. Kent was murdered six years ago, and Sullivan was murdered three years ago." I gave Jack a brief sideways glance, and he nodded subtly.

Ava's chest rose and fell with rapid breaths. "Did this Kelter lady kill them, too?"

"Not exactly." Then I saw the error of my ways. I'd said *murdered*, and she didn't seem to see any distinction between the true meaning of the word *murder* and a *DUI fatality*.

Ava's head tilted toward Jack. "What is it, then?"

"We believe the same person who killed them may have abducted Mrs. Kelter," Jack explained. "Is there anything you have to say about that?"

Jack knew how to play the cards he was dealt, when to withhold and when to be forthcoming. In this case, coming forward so honestly would accomplish a couple of things. It would give us her true reaction and could reveal whether her lack of concern regarding Kelter's welfare was sincere or surface bravado. It was one thing to talk tough and another to follow through. And being faced with the fact that we were linking Kelter's disappearance to two previous murders might shake her to talk. Then again, it could have the opposite effect.

Looking at Ava, her face was stoic, giving away nothing. If we wanted to get any more from her, it might take a more direct approach in our questioning.

"Would you happen to know where Mrs. Kelter might be?" I asked.

Ava looked at me, and I watched the revelation that she was a potential suspect strike. She gulped. "Why would I—"

"Just answer the question," Jack told her.

"I…" Ava rubbed at her throat where her skin had become blotchy. "I don't… I haven't seen her since she was sentenced in court." Her chin trembled, and her hands were shaking.

"So you wouldn't mind telling us where you were yesterday?" I prompted.

"As in the *whole* day?"

A wide net to be sure, but without a sense of when Kelter actually disappeared, there was no other choice. "Sure." I gestured to her, implying that she should begin explaining.

"Easy." She paused. "I was working three shifts, three different diners." Ava provided us with the times and locations of where she waitressed. "They're nothing like the office job I used to have, but I quit after Lester…"

I couldn't see Ava shedding a tear if Kelter was killed, but I could see the fear in her eyes. Was it because she was guilty of something, or just a nervous reaction?

CHAPTER EIGHT

Hope was a double-edged sword. It could empower and destroy. In some ways, hope was worse than closure. Especially when bad news came on the tail end of sparked optimism.

Zach hoped that his and Paige's assurances wouldn't serve as harbingers of such destruction to Gordon Kelter, but staying positive would be necessary, even if statistics pointed out that the odds weren't good for Jenna Kelter returning home safely.

The Kelters' bungalow was bright yellow and terracotta orange. They walked along the concrete path leading to the front door. It was patterned to look like square tiles. The whole place certainly looked low-end except for the beaming silver Mercedes in the driveway. Paige pointed to it.

"If it weren't for the car, I would have guessed Gordon blew his lottery winnings," she said. "Then again, maybe that represents what's left. Personally, I'd be running from this neighborhood and settling into a house with an ocean view." She stretched out her hands. "The Biscayne Bay out my back door. Ahh, that'd be the life."

Zach smiled at her. "Not sure how far sixteen mil gets you in this city, but it should definitely get them out of this zip code. Maybe he's been waiting for his wife to get out of prison."

"Patient man, if that's the case." A mild breeze blew a wisp of her red hair across her face, and she swiped it away before she stepped up onto the front landing. It had an overhang but there was only room for one of them to stand under it. Zach remained on the staircase. Paige knocked, and they waited.

Gordon answered the door, his gaze sweeping over them. "FBI?"

Zach nodded, and Gordon stepped back to let them enter. The place felt cramped between the bold choice of red-painted walls and oversized furniture.

Zach wiped his shoes on the mat. "Mr. Kelter—"

"Gordon is just fine," he quickly corrected.

Cool, calm, and casual, like his wardrobe: He wore a loose-fitting T-shirt and baggy shorts. Strange, given the circumstances: his wife missing and the FBI being in his home. In fact, there was no indication the man was stressed or upset about his wife's disappearance at all. No worry lines creasing his brow. No rushed movements or rapid blinking. No aversion to eye contact. It was possible Brandon's theory about the husband could hold more merit than Zach had originally thought. Then again, Gordon's alibis had been confirmed already.

For what times, though? They didn't know *when* Jenna went missing. And if Gordon was behind her disappearance, what's to say he didn't feed Marsh the wrong times intentionally?

"I'm Agent Zach Miles, and this is Agent Paige Dawson."

"Here—" Gordon led them to a living room at the back of the house "—sit where you'd like." He'd said it like there were numerous options, but there was a couch and a recliner—the latter of which he sat on. Zach and Paige took spots on the couch.

Toward the back of the room, there was a small table being used as a desk, a computer and a monitor sitting atop it. A browser window was open and showed what looked like a menu with a background image of lobsters. Zach made a mental note of the restaurant's name from the header of the page. *Magical Bar & Grill.*

Gordon shot up to his feet. "I should have offered you something to drink. Do you—"

"I'm fine, thanks." Paige turned to Zach.

"Me too," he said.

Gordon dropped back into his chair with a *whoosh*.

"You got here quickly. I just reported her missing. Guess that's what happens when it's Walter's niece who's in trouble." He tapped the arms of the chair. "He's the mayor."

Gordon's dislike for the man was clear in his tone of voice. "We're not here because of him. We're here because—"

"Walter always gets his way, and he probably only '*cares*'—" He added finger quotes, then slowly lowered his hands, Zach's statement finally sinking in. "You're not here because of him?" Gordon's features darkened, and he swallowed roughly.

Zach shook his head.

"Tell me she's going to be—" Tears filled Gordon's eyes, and he covered his mouth, let his hand fall. "I'm trying to hold myself together. Keep my head."

"You're dealing with a difficult situation right now. It's understandable for you to feel emotional," Paige told him.

Gordon blew out a breath and nodded. He palmed his cheeks. "I thought maybe someone kidnapped her for a ransom… You know, to get to my money. But if that was the case, the cops would be here, tapping the phone line. I've seen those movies before." Gordon's shoulders lowered; he was shrinking by the second. "The FBI… You investigate…"

"We're here to bring your wife home safely," Paige offered up the first sprinkling of hope gingerly.

Zach looked at her, but obviously Marsh hadn't filled Gordon in on her suspicions about Jenna being abducted by a serial killer. Though it was probably for the best at the onset of an investigation like this.

"So you will save her?" Gordon directed this to Zach.

He hated making promises he couldn't keep. The one he made to himself flashed to the front of his mind, but now was not the time to dwell on it. "We'll do everything within our power to find her and bring her home alive."

Gordon's eyes widened. "You're here because you think some killer has her? And the odds aren't good, are they?" He ran his hands down his face, elongating his features. "You can tell me. I can handle the truth."

"Every case is different," Zach said. People often asked for the facts, but they never really wanted to know them.

Gordon sat back in his chair and rocked a few times. Silence fell over the room with the exception of a humming ceiling fan.

"Would you run us through your wife's schedule yesterday?" Paige requested.

"I told Detective Marsh everything I know. Don't you have access to her files?"

"We do," Zach told him. "But it's best that we hear it straight from you. There may be small things that you didn't mention before or that stand out as important now."

"Well, it was Sunday, so she wasn't up to much."

"Was it normal for her to have low-key Sundays before she went to prison?" Paige asked.

"Pretty much."

"So yesterday Jenna…" Paige prompted.

"She read in the morning—" Gordon nudged his head toward the back of the house, and Zach figured he was referring to an outside patio or deck "—and went to church for the twelve o'clock mass. That's what she told me anyway."

"You're wondering if she told you the truth?" Zach latched on to Gordon's doubts. They didn't know for sure that a killer had Jenna. Maybe she had left her husband. Though Zach didn't want to entertain the consequences for Jack with the FBI director if that turned out to be the case.

As if Gordon were reading Zach's mind, he said, "If she left me, that would be easier to take than thinking of her in danger."

"What church did she attend?" Paige asked.

"A Catholic one," Gordon punched out, then added, "St. John's. They're on Northeast First Avenue."

"I take it you're not religious?" Zach asked.

"Oh, heavens no." He slapped his hand on the arm of the chair for emphasis.

"Do you know if she had any plans after church?" Zach inquired, preferring to hear Gordon's answer directly and not just run with what was in the file.

"She told me she was going out for dinner with girlfriends."

"Do you know with whom specifically?" Zach asked.

"No," Gordon said quickly.

Gordon appeared ticked off by the fact that he didn't know, and Zach would wager Jenna hadn't told him who she was meeting up with. The marriage wasn't as solid as it might appear at first impression. Though Jenna's serving time in prison wouldn't have helped with that situation. "Who did she normally hang out with?" Zach asked.

"The few I know of are Carrie, Leigh-Ann, and Stella."

"That's Carrie Hayes, Leigh-Ann Marble, and Stella Bridges?" Zach pulled from memory.

"Yes."

"Did she typically go to church with them?" Paige inquired.

"I know Carrie and Leigh-Ann attend. Don't know about Stella."

"Did Carrie or Leigh-Ann typically pick her up for church?" Zach asked, trying to see if he could establish a pattern from before prison.

"She drove herself before the accident, but after that a friend started picking her up."

That made sense because with Kelter's conviction, her driver's license would have been permanently revoked. Zach leaned forward. "Do you know which friend?"

"I don't know," Gordon said, defeated. "If she told me, I wasn't listening."

"Going back to the three women you mentioned, was it usual for her to go out with them on Sunday?" Paige asked.

"Yes, but it was different things all the time—drinks, dancing, catching movies." Gordon was biting on the inside of his cheek, and his face was flushing a bright red.

So much for low-key Sundays...

"Did she regularly do anything or go anywhere besides church on Sundays?" Zach asked, trying to see if Kelter had any sort of fixed schedule on Sundays.

"Don't think so," Gordon stated. "I don't even know if she went out with all three women or one or two of them or mixed it up."

"Okay." Zach nodded.

"Besides dinner, did she have any other plans with her friends yesterday?" Paige asked.

Gordon's eyes flashed pain and betrayal. "She told me they'd be going to the movies."

"Did she say which one?" Zach inquired. There'd been mention of the movies in the interview notes but not a specific one.

Gordon's mouth contorted into a squiggle, and he hitched his shoulders. "She might have, but I was angry that she was going out at all, so I wasn't really listening to her." Regret flickered in his eyes. "It's been over four years since we've spent any real time alone together, but I started feeling badly for yelling at her about leaving and tried to call her to apologize."

"And when was that?" Zach asked.

"Maybe a few hours after she'd left. She wasn't answering her phone. I called Carrie and Leigh-Ann. They said they hadn't heard from her. Hadn't seen her at church, either."

"What about Stella? Did you try her?" Paige asked.

Gordon shook his head. "I don't know her number and neither did Carrie or Leigh-Ann. I asked them."

It was possible that Jenna's friend Stella—or another friend who Gordon didn't know about—had picked her up and the two of them went somewhere. It was also conceivable that Jenna had gone missing right from her front walk. "What time did she leave the house?"

"Eleven thirty."

"Did you see anyone pick her up?" Zach asked, hoping Gordon would give them something to go on.

Gordon clamped his mouth tight and shook his head. "Too angry to care at the time."

"Fair enough," Zach said. They would reach out to Stella Bridges to see if she had picked up Kelter and check Kelter's financials. If she took a taxi or driving service, something could show there. At least they'd narrow down the list of options. While her financials would be coming in soon, it might prove faster to just ask Gordon if any unexpected charges had come through. If they were lucky, it might provide them with some clarity on when and where she went missing. "Have you seen any charges from yesterday show up on Jenna's card?"

Gordon nodded. "One. I noticed it just minutes before you got here. It was dated yesterday—a purchase at some bar. I can't believe she'd lie to me after all we've been through. Tells me she's going out with friends, but they don't see her? Who was she with? What was she doing?"

Zach wasn't about to make any guarantees the marriage was sound, but he offered Gordon what he could. "It's possible that someone stole her credit card. What bar was it?" His gaze went to the computer monitor.

Gordon's followed, and he nodded. "Magical Bar & Grill. It's on the river. I looked it up. I have no idea what she'd be doing there," Gordon added.

"And there's nothing saying that she was there," Paige stated.

"Nice of you to say, but I think she's cheating on me." The words were sour, despondent.

"Well, let's not assume that," Paige told him.

Gordon shot her a glare. "And why not? She told me she was going to church but didn't. She's been gone for years, why should I assume I know who she is anymore?"

Tingles ran up Zach's back and neck. Sure, Gordon was under stress, but his moods rolled over faster than a hooker. "Did you have any reason before seeing this charge to believe she was cheating on you?" Hopefully, he'd encourage some rational thinking. He certainly hoped that Gordon hadn't entertained these thoughts before. Otherwise, what were they doing here? Jenna could have just run off.

"Not that I can recall. But remember, she'd been in prison for four years."

"That must have been difficult for you," Paige empathized.

"You have no idea."

"Yet you stuck by her." Paige smiled at him.

"She's my wife, Agent," Gordon responded with a lick of heat. "And if the blame for her accident rests on anyone's shoulders, it's mine."

Interesting twist in the conversation… "Why do you say that?" Zach asked.

"If I hadn't come into the money, she wouldn't have been out celebrating at Henry's."

Zach knew from the file that Henry's was a restaurant and jazz club. "But she was the one who got behind the wheel," Zach reasoned with delicate caution.

"When you come into a bunch of money, it makes you feel invincible, like you're untouchable. The rules no longer apply to you." Gordon paused for a moment and rubbed the stubble on his jaw. "That's how she explained herself to me. No matter how you paint the situation, it was the money." Gordon added the latter part with contempt, as if he loathed having won the lottery. "Stella's just lucky Jenna dropped her off at home before the accident. The passenger side of the vehicle was demolished."

Zach recalled reading about that in the file. When questioned by police, the friend, Stella Bridges, had admitted to being drunk herself. "Were Jenna and Stella close?"

"I'd never heard of Stella before that night, and to date, I still haven't met her. Ask me, she's an enigma. Apparently, she is to Carrie and Leigh-Ann too. They don't have her phone number, as I told you."

Paige shrugged her shoulders. "Even if the three of them hung out from time to time, it doesn't mean Carrie and Leigh-Ann were close with Stella."

"Was it common for Jenna to drink until she was drunk?" Zach recalled Gordon's earlier mention of Jenna drinking with friends on Sundays before she'd gone to prison.

"She had a weakness for red wine. One glass led to a bottle, led to two bottles," Gordon replied.

"And did you drink with her?" Zach asked, resisting the urge to raise an eyebrow.

Gordon reached beneath the collar of his T-shirt and pulled out a chain with a bronze sobriety chip dangling from it. "Ten years sober. And I've had no draw to go back to the stuff." He dropped the medallion against his chest. "I can't believe she was at a bar yesterday. She just got out of prison," he added with a hint of disgust.

"That doesn't mean she was drinking alcohol—that is, if she was there," Paige reminded him.

"I'm still wondering if I'm being played. Maybe she just ran off on me."

Gordon had certainly charted the gauntlet of possibilities, from a kidnapping for ransom to his wife leaving him. He seemed to have lost sight of the other likelihood, the reason the FBI was here: someone had abducted her, and she was in grave danger.

"Detective Marsh told us that Jenna received hate mail that you'd have for us," Zach said rather abruptly. He felt for the man, but he wasn't here to pat Gordon on the shoulder and tell him everything would be okay.

"Yes. Give me a minute." Gordon left the room and returned with a three-inch stack of envelopes. From the looks of it, quite a few hadn't even been opened. He extended them to Zach, who snapped on a pair of gloves before taking the mail from Gordon.

"You really think she was targeted because of her accident?" Gordon asked, dismissing the idea of Jenna leaving him again. The man was really grasping to make sense of why his wife hadn't returned home.

"We think it's possible," Paige confirmed.

Gordon paled. "We had some guy come to the house once. He was banging on our door, yelling that she was a killer. He never came back and he didn't destroy any property, so I never reported it."

It was unlikely Zach's next question would get them anywhere, but Gordon's answer would be worth noting. "Do you remember what he looked like?"

Gordon quirked an eyebrow. "This was not long after the accident first happened, so no."

"Understandable," Zach said, though he couldn't truly relate, seeing as he had an eidetic memory. He pulled out his business card, hesitating as he considered if he should ask Gordon what he was about to. The truth was, they could get the information themselves, but it would take longer, and if Kelter had been taken by a killer, especially the one Marsh feared, they were running out of time. "We're going to need you to call your credit card company and find out the date and time the charge was actually made at Magical Bar & Grill."

Gordon took Zach's card. "Sure."

"Please let me know what you find out. As soon as you can?" Zach added, feeling a little bad for asking Gordon to do this. The poor man had enough to deal with.

Gordon's gaze was fastened on the card in his hand, and his eyes glazed over.

"Mr. Kelter?" Paige prompted.

He lifted his head and sniffed. "Yeah..."

"Just stay strong. We're going to do our best to find your wife and bring her home safe. And you've been a big help." Paige got to her feet.

"I'm glad you think so, because I feel like..." His chin quivered.

The man's shock was giving way to grief. Zach and Paige offered to call friends or family for him, but Gordon told them he'd be fine. Then they saw themselves out.

"What do you think?" Paige asked as they walked to the car.

"For starters, I think their marriage was far from perfect."

"Oh, I don't doubt there are skeletons in the Kelters' closets," Paige said. "I know I tried to reassure him, but maybe she *did* run off."

"Well, that'd certainly be better for her than our initial suspicion."

Paige nodded. "And marginally better for Gordon. Horrible for Jack, though. I wouldn't want to be the one explaining all this to Hamilton."

The FBI director could be vicious. "That makes two of us."

They loaded into the SUV and buckled up. Zach passed off the mail to Paige once she put on a pair of gloves, and they headed back to the station.

"If we run with a theory that Kelter had a lover on the side, we're probably going to have to assume that relationship survived prison, too. Not impossible, but unlikely," Paige said.

"If it was love, it would have lasted. They say that love stands the test of time," Zach waxed poetic.

Paige stuck a finger in her mouth. "Gag me."

Zach changed lanes, signal and all, and still got honked at for his trouble. "In all seriousness," he began, "we have her phone records coming to us, but if she was in this other relationship, it might not hurt to check her visitor logs from the prison, too."

"Look at you." Paige smiled at him.

With her expression, Zach appreciated how delicate and fickle the balance of life truly was. They'd just left a man who wasn't sure if his wife would ever come back to him alive, and they were experiencing moments of lightness. Not necessarily wrong, but not altogether fair. That was life. And in their world, the darkness met the light all the time. Thank goodness, because otherwise the darkness would consume them.

CHAPTER NINE

Pinch me.

That's what Kelly was thinking as she walked up to the door of Kelter's friend, Carrie Hayes. Not because she was going to interview someone. Throughout her career in law enforcement, she'd questioned more people than she could count. Rather, she still couldn't believe that Jack was here. *In Miami.* It had been so long since she'd seen him, and he looked exactly the same, except for maybe a few more gray hairs and lines around his eyes.

If her granddad were still around, he would have loved to see the two of them paired up and working a case together. He had loved Jack like a brother, not that he'd ever said as much. But Kelly could tell by the way he had spoken about him and the way his eyes had lit up when he did. Her granddad had loved regaling her with stories about serving in the military with Jack. It was also clear he'd had a profound respect for Jack, and during Kelly's venture through the FBI Academy, she'd come to see what her grandfather had seen. Jack's character was aboveboard, and he didn't just aim for perfection but somehow attained it.

Kelly rapped her knuckles on Hayes's door.

The sound of footsteps was followed by an unlocking dead bolt and a twisting handle. A woman peeked through a small opening. She regarded Kelly with curiosity.

"Mrs. Hayes? Detective Kelly Marsh, Miami PD." Kelly held up her badge. "We spoke on the phone."

The woman opened the door wide and motioned for Kelly to enter.

"Thank you for agreeing to talk to me on such short notice," Kelly told her.

"Anything for Jenna." Hayes reached around Kelly to lock the door again and proceeded to rub her arms as if fending off a chill.

"Is there someplace we could sit and talk?" Kelly took in the modest home. From the front door, she could see the living room off to the right, and the slew of baby toys that littered the floor. A baby was in an activity jumper, sucking enthusiastically on a pacifier.

Hayes followed Kelly's gaze and smiled. It was apparent that Hayes was a proud mother.

"And who's this?" Kelly asked, showing interest, and a trickle of maternal instinct flushed through her. But her clock was running out if she was going to build a family the old-fashioned way. To start with, she didn't have a lead on Mr. Right.

Hayes walked over and cupped the back of the baby's head. The fine hair wasn't much more than fuzz on a peach. "This is Ruby."

"Ah, how nice." Kelly finger-waved at Ruby, who spit out her pacifier and smiled. Kelly's heart melted a fraction.

"You said you had questions about Jenna," Hayes said. "Is she all right? Gordon called here yesterday looking for her, but I haven't seen her since Friday night."

"And what was Friday night?" Kelly took out her notepad and pen.

Ruby was still fixated on Kelly. Her large blue eyes soaking up the visitor.

Kelly sat on the couch, and Hayes dropped onto the floor next to her daughter. She played with her little fingers, and Ruby didn't seem to mind.

"There was a little gathering to celebrate her release from prison. Not many of us there. Just me, Leigh-Ann—that's another friend of ours—and Gordon."

Kelly nodded. "Where was the gathering?"

"Just at some restaurant."

"It might matter which one," Kelly pressed.

"Henry's. Really it was probably in bad taste, seeing as…"

Kelly nodded, filling in the rest of what Hayes had likely been thinking. *Seeing as that's where Kelter had gotten drunk the night of her accident.*

"None of us drank or anything," Hayes continued. "We wanted to support Jenna."

"Did she decide to quit drinking?" Kelly would be more surprised if she had. She'd seen it far too often: someone suffered through rehab only to return to the streets and use.

"She didn't say as much." Hayes put the pacifier back in her daughter's mouth. Ruby spit it out again. "It's just we didn't want to encourage it. Just with all she'd been through."

"I get it. Completely understandable." Kelly paused a moment. "Was she her normal self that night?"

"As normal as I can remember."

It sounded as if Hayes hadn't seen Kelter in years. "Did you visit her in prison?"

Hayes broke eye contact and focused on Ruby. "I did a couple of times, but I hated going there."

Kelly nodded. She'd had her fair share of experience with prison—and at way too young an age. Her granddad would take her to visit her mother, but the encounter had always been bittersweet. Mostly bitter. The system sucked the life from her mother, and Kelly watched her become a shadow of her former self. Though who could blame her? The institution's energy was one of broken dreams and the devil.

"Jenna must have been happy to get out," Kelly said.

"She was, but I think she was also nervous about the future."

"Why's that?"

"She wasn't happy with—" Hayes stopped when Ruby started fussing. She pressed up and down on the jumper, but Ruby wailed. Hayes stood and took her daughter out, holding her and bouncing slightly to soothe the child. Ruby eventually laid her head on Hayes's shoulder and put her thumb in her mouth, her eyelids fluttering with tiredness but her stubborn will fighting off sleep.

"She wasn't happy with…?" Kelly prompted.

"She and Gordon were having issues. Not that she actually came out and told me as much. The truth is, she and I used to be a lot closer years ago."

"Before she went to prison?"

"Even a few years before that."

"Why do you think your friendship grew apart?"

Hayes pointed to her baby's back and then laid a flat hand on it and rubbed in circles. "Do you have children?"

Kelly shook her head.

"Then I wouldn't expect you to fully understand," Hayes said gently, "but when you do, they become your whole world. Jenna didn't get that."

Kelly looked at the resting baby. She wasn't old enough to factor into a shattered friendship between Hayes and Kelter. "You have other children?"

"One, yes. Devin. He's in kindergarten," she added. "But Jenna never really got that he became the most important thing in my life the moment he was born."

"Some women aren't made to be mothers." Kelly's friend Brianna was a prime example. She'd made it clear to Kelly on numerous occasions that she had no interest in having kids—ever—and Kelly believed her. Brianna had no patience for crying babies and never made a fuss over any that Kelly had seen. Her friend's main goals in life centered around her career, not settling down and having a family.

"I get that, but with her…"

Kelly let the silence ride out.

"She didn't even come to my baby shower." Hayes swallowed roughly. Her eyes filled with tears, but the intensity of her gaze told Kelly she was angrier than she was hurt at this point. "I thought we were best friends. And if she doesn't like babies, fine, but the least she could have done was support me."

"I can understand your being hurt."

"Well, I tried to let it go. The Bible teaches forgiveness, but as you can tell, I'm still having a hard time with that one." Hayes withdrew her hand from Ruby's back and ran it down the side of her own face, to reference the evident emotion.

That one... It was Kelly's first clue that the fissure between the two friends was more than a missed baby shower. It sounded more like Hayes had a problem with forgiveness overall. "What was your reaction to her being convicted?"

"Mortified and shocked. She killed a man." Hayes's nose crinkled up with disgust. "It took a lot out of me just to celebrate her release."

"Why's that?"

"I lost a family member to a drunk driver," she admitted quietly. "It's very hard to forgive."

"It's always hard to lose someone you love." Kelly wasn't going to get caught up in a moral debate about drinking and driving.

Hayes pressed her lips together and swayed Ruby in her arms.

Kelly moved on, saying, "She told Gordon that she was going to church yesterday—"

"Which I find appalling, as well. Jenna hadn't been to church for months before the accident even. She stopped not long after becoming friends with that woman... What was her name?"

Kelly's insides were swirling. Gordon had told her that Jenna used to go to church every Sunday. So if Jenna hadn't been going to church, where had she gone? And was that where she'd inadvertently attracted her killer?

"Oh, I'll remember. Just give me a few minutes. She's some fancy surgeon or something. I think she owns a ritzy place right on the water's edge."

Ruby was fast asleep in Hayes's arms when Hayes blurted out, "Stella Bridges." Ruby stirred and started to cry. Hayes did what she could to calm her daughter, but her tactics weren't working. Kelly thanked Hayes for her time and saw herself out.

Stella Bridges was the friend Kelter had been celebrating with the night of the accident. Maybe she could shed some light on what Kelter was up to on her Sundays when her husband thought she was at church. Visiting Kelter's other close friend, Leigh-Ann, would have to wait.

CHAPTER TEN

Oh, I don't doubt there are skeletons in the Kelters' closets.

That's what Paige had said to Zach when they had finished speaking with Gordon. It was quite likely she'd hit that one right on the mark. Gordon had called Zach when he and Paige were at the station dropping off the hate mail. He'd confirmed that Kelter's card was charged at Magical Bar & Grill on Sunday night at eleven o'clock. Now, maybe, it had been stolen as Paige had suggested, but it was also possible Kelter had used the card herself. And if she did, was she even missing? And if she *was* missing, what had she been doing the rest of the day? They were questions that needed answers, and Zach and Paige were hoping to get at least one of those answers at the restaurant.

Zach got the door for Paige, and she dipped her head in thanks.

"No matter how much society tries to convince us that it is, chivalry isn't dead," she said, tossing out a smile.

He tried to be a good man, Lord knew, but sometimes it wasn't easy. He had his own skeleton in the closet by keeping his plans for the future secret from the woman he loved. He'd told Paige, but Sheri was the one he should be talking to. He could have snuck in a brief call to her when he was at the station, but he'd convinced himself it wasn't the time.

Inside Magical, there a sleek bar with black and chrome stools lining the back wall, which contrasted with the fishermen's nets and lobster traps holding plastic lobsters hanging from the ceiling. Meant to create atmosphere, they were more successful at catching dust. The place was clearly confused about what direction it wanted to go: traditional bar or family restaurant.

Laughter and conversation made for a robust cacophony, the smell of seafood was strong in the air, and the place was teeming with tourists and locals alike. There was a line to be seated, and looking around the place, the bar was packed, too. Their cook must be better than their decorator. Then again, being waterfront on the Miami River with a full-service patio didn't hurt.

"It will be a forty-minute wait," the hostess told them as they approached the front stand.

Zach moved closer and flashed his credentials. "We need to speak with the owner or manager."

The woman's brown eyes widened, and she blinked. "Okay." She backed away with a raised finger in the air to indicate she'd just be a minute.

A moment later, the hostess returned with a man in his thirties. His face hadn't seen the sharp end of a razor in at least a day, and he had dark, shoulder-length hair. The man fixed his silver eyes on Paige and gestured for her to follow him. Zach supposed he was invited along, too.

The man led them through the restaurant and kitchen to an office. It was a simple space: one laminate desk with a monitor. There was a swivel chair behind the desk, its leather arms worn down, likely from scraping against the pullout keyboard tray. A broken, crooked chair was positioned against one wall but would have been better off in a dumpster.

The manager closed the door. His gaze darted between the two of them, and sweat beaded on his forehead. "Tina said you're with the FBI?"

The kitchen was hot and Zach's own pits were wet, but this guy was hiding something. Was it serial murder, abduction, or something else entirely?

Zach introduced himself and Paige using their formal titles. "And your name?"

"I'm Tommy Warner."

"We have questions about a woman who may have dined here last night," Zach said, running on the assumption that she'd been the one to make the charge.

"Do you mind if I—" Tommy looked at his desk chair, then at the busted one. "Sorry, I don't have a place for you to sit."

"We're fine to stand," Paige said.

Tommy dropped into the swivel chair. "What woman are you here about?" He spoke causally enough, but the death grip he had on the arms of his chair gave away his anxiety.

Zach regarded Tommy more skeptically. He was in his thirties—statistically the age range when serial killers committed their first murders. He also held a manager's position, and one would assume he'd be both responsible and intelligent enough to hold such a job—another aspect that suited their unsub.

"We'll get to that," Zach said. "But first, were you working last night?"

"I'm here seven days a week." Tommy wiped a cheek against his shoulder as if scratching an itch. "The owners are more like silent partners in all this. They hire people to run the business while they soak up the sun, golf, do whatever it is they do."

He'd detoured slightly from Zach's question, but it could have been due to nerves and unintentional. "Seven days a week doesn't mean you're here twenty-four hours a day," Zach pointed out. "Were you working last *night*?"

Tommy picked at the frayed leather on the arms of the chair. "Yeah. I was here from ten in the morning until three this morning."

And now it was noon. The guy pretty much *did* work twenty-four hours a day. Maybe he was cagey because he never slept.

"That's a long shift," Paige empathized. *Cue good cop.*

The man shrugged. "It's okay. You get used to it."

Zach pulled up a family photo of Jenna Kelter on his phone and held the screen up for Tommy to see. "Do you recognize her?"

Tommy leaned in. "Uh-huh. She used to be in at least once a week. Name's Jenna if I remember right?" Zach nodded, and Tommy continued. "She was normally in on Sunday nights, come to think of it. Before last night, I hadn't seen her in a long time."

Well that answered one question. Jenna *had* been the one to make the charge. Thanks to Tommy, they also knew that she normally came here on Sundays, though Gordon had never heard of the place. Maybe she normally paid cash. If so, had Jenna intentionally kept the place from her husband for some reason? Zach's heart ticked up a few notches. He was about to dive into territory he'd rather avoid, but he plunged ahead anyhow. "Was she here alone?"

"Yes and no. She came in by herself, but she wasn't ever alone. Some guy buddied up to her for a while."

"Did you recognize him, as well?" Paige asked.

"Maybe from another time he came in?" Zach added. Another man didn't mean Jenna had been cheating and had left Gordon. It could just mean that their unsub knew when to find Jenna at this bar.

Tommy shook his head. "Don't remember seeing him before last night. Doesn't mean he hasn't been here before but he's not a regular."

"You said this guy buddied up to her for a while? Did it seem they knew each other?" Zach took a jaunt down the path he didn't want to travel.

Tommy smirked. "I don't think so. And he was laying it on thick. Even used a lame pickup line about heaven missing an angel or some shit."

Paige snuffed out a laugh. "How did she react to that?"

Tommy stared at Paige for a few seconds. Neither of them said anything.

"You really don't know? That lady—" Tommy pointed to Zach's phone "—is a lesbian."

Now that was a curveball that hit Zach in the head. Paige, too, judging by her agape mouth.

Tommy leaned forward. "You didn't know?"

"She's married—to a *man*," Zach said. Not that it necessarily meant anything these days.

Tommy pointed a finger at Zach. "Now *that* surprises *me*."

"This might seem like a stupid question, but how do you know she preferred women?" Paige asked.

"Remember how I told you she used to always come in on Sundays? Well, it was with a woman, and let me tell you, they were more than friends."

"Did this woman show up last night, too?" Paige asked.

"Uh-huh." Tommy swept his tongue over his lips. "They were making out at the bar like a couple of teenagers, giving every man in sight a hard-on."

Comments like that right there led to the misconception that chivalry was a thing of the past. Zach cleared his throat. "What can you tell us about that woman?"

Tommy remained silent.

"What's her name?" Zach asked, taking another stab.

Tommy winced.

"Now's not the time to clam up. This woman—" he shook his phone, referring to Kelter's photo "—is missing, and we believe she might be in danger. This friend of hers might be able to help us find her." He'd stick with the theory they were here to chase down unless indisputable evidence pointed in another direction. Though with every ticking second, Zach feared that whatever Jack's personal connection was to Kelly, it might have been clouding his judgment and had him taking on this case prematurely.

Tommy studied Zach. Seconds ticked off. "Her name is Stella."

The same Stella that Kelter had been celebrating with the night of her accident? "Last name?"

"I don't know that. But I do know where she lives." Tommy proceeded to give them directions and added, "It's some wealthy oceanside community. The chick's loaded. She's some world-renowned heart surgeon or something. She's got looks and money, but she's a ballbuster. Hates men. Apparently always has."

The Stella who Kelter had been with the night of her accident was a heart surgeon...

"Did Jenna leave with Stella?" Zach was being swayed further toward Kelter leaving her husband, despite feeling like he was betraying Jack somehow. Kelter could be laughing it up with her lover right then.

"Yeah, I assume so. I had to go back to the kitchen for something, but when I returned to the floor, both of them were gone."

"What time was that?" Paige asked.

"Around eleven."

The time of the charge to Kelter's card confirmed his intel. In case Zach's suspicions about Kelter's "disappearance" were incorrect, it was best they leave here as armed as possible. "You wouldn't happen to have security video we could take with us? One that maybe captures the entire bar area?"

"Yep. We do."

Zach stepped back. No request for a warrant and no line about the cameras being around for show. "What about one in the lot?"

"Can't help you out there."

Zach nodded. One out of two wasn't bad. At least they had indoor footage.

Tommy pulled the keyboard tray out all the way. "Just give me a few minutes." He clicked the keys, moved the mouse around, grabbed a USB drive out of a desk drawer, and popped it into the computer. A few more keystrokes and Tommy handed them the data stick. "Here you go."

Paige took it from him. "Thank you."

"Anything I can do to help law enforcement." Tommy's sentiment fell flat, but Paige smiled anyhow. Likely that good-cop role resurfacing. It brought Zach back to how strangely Tommy had been acting when they had first shown up… Before he'd ask Tommy for an alibi, there were a couple other things Zach wanted to cover.

"Just a few more questions," Zach interjected.

Tommy looked at him. "Sure."

"What time did Jenna get here last night?"

"Somewhere between eight thirty and nine."

"And Stella joined her at what time?" Zach asked.

"Say nine thirty?"

"All right, just one more thing before we go. Where did you go after your shift, and can anyone attest to it?"

"You think I'm involved somehow?" Panic streaked across Tommy's face.

"It's just part of the job," Paige stepped in, smoothing things over. "We have to ask."

"I got home at three thirty this morning by the time I got things sorted here," Tommy offered, not seeming impressed by the need to account for his whereabouts. "My roommate can vouch for me, if that's necessary. Ron, one of my employees, can confirm I was working until three."

Paige nodded. "Is Ron here now?"

Tommy shook his head.

"We'll need his number," she said. "And your roommate's contact information, too."

Tommy scribbled both on a piece of paper and handed it to Paige. "Now, if that's all, I should get back to work."

"We'll see ourselves out," Zach said.

His stomach rumbled as he and Paige walked through the restaurant to the exit. He could normally pass on seafood, but the aromas of butter and garlic were killing him. It was lunch time, though, and breakfast was long gone. But eating would have to be quick, and it would probably come in a paper bag delivered through a drive-thru window. They had another lead to follow.

CHAPTER ELEVEN

Jack wasn't taking the news about Kelter's relationship with Stella Bridges well—at all. He'd smoked two cigarettes since we'd found out, and he smelled like a human ashtray sitting next to me at the conference room table.

Paige and Zach had filled us in on their visit to Magical Bar & Grill and had dropped off the security video. Now they were following their lead to Stella's front door while Jack and I stayed back at the police station. They were having all the fun so far, but at least we had a "movie" to watch. It would provide us some visual context to the manager's testimony and might even provide us with some useful information.

Jack was breathing heavily, and it didn't take a profiler to know that he was mad. Probably more at himself than anyone else. I'd be angry with myself if I were in his position, too. After all, he'd broken his own rule about letting emotions factor into the job. There was no way around it: Jack's connection to Marsh had pushed him to act prematurely. Nothing else could explain his swift—and unprecedented—reaction to a missing person report. Twenty-four hours hadn't even passed before we all hopped on a plane down here. I hoped it wasn't going to bite Jack in the ass, but attempting to make him feel better would be useless. For one, Jack didn't take to coddling, and two, I respected him too much to try.

He was pawing through the hate mail on the table, though not really looking at it. I'd never seen him so fidgety before. It was as if he was in a holding pattern until we received an update on Stella Bridges.

"We might find a lead among the different letters," he deadpanned.

I hated seeing this man in place of the almighty and confident Jack Harper.

I nodded. "Makes sense."

The silence might as well have been thunder, and I itched to fill the silence. "While you were out earlier, I verified Ava Jett's alibis and pulled the background on the manager from the bar. He had a bit of a rap sheet, but no offenses in the last eight years. Before that, he had two charges of drug possession and served minimal jail time. Nothing to indicate that he is a cold-blooded killer." I looked at Jack, expecting some snarky response about paperwork not necessarily showing a person's true colors, but he gave me nothing. I cleared my throat and continued. "If he's behind any murders, nothing points that way on paper."

"Did his alibis check out?" was all Jack asked.

I nodded.

"That leaves us with the video." He gestured to the laptop in front of me where the opening image of the video was frozen on the screen.

I fast-forwarded to 8:50 and saw Kelter take a seat at the bar. By nine, a man sat on her left and tapped her on the arm. Her facial expression and body language indicated that she wanted him to go away. She leaned away from him and kept putting her left elbow on the bar, erecting a barrier between them. The guy refused to take the hint. He tapped her shoulder a few times, and it only made Kelter wriggle farther from him.

After about thirty minutes of that, throughout which I was impressed by Kelter's self-control, a woman came up to Kelter and kissed her on the mouth.

"Stella Bridges," I said.

The man watched them for a while but then left without looking back. And any heterosexual man wouldn't have blamed him if he had.

Jack and I continued watching until the two women staggered out of the bar, arm in arm.

I stopped the video, my stomach roiling for Jack. He got up and headed for the door. Some people drowned their stress and regrets in booze, but Jack smoked his away.

I felt so bad for him that a very small part of me almost wished we were wrong to suspect Kelter had left her husband.

CHAPTER TWELVE

Cold air blasted from the vents, but the hot sunshine coming through the windshield was the victor. It was like winter and summer were competing, or maybe even trying to coexist. Zach entertaining the idea that he could be a father and a field agent felt much the same. Regardless, people had been choosing between career and family since the start of civilized society. It wasn't like he was the first person to deal with this, so why should he consider his circumstances anything special? If only he didn't love his job so much, it would be far easier to keep family in first place.

Zach and Paige were on the way to Stella Bridges's house. It was possible they'd find Kelter there, but if not, it would seem Bridges was one of the last people to see Kelter before she disappeared.

"I can't imagine what poor Jack's thinking right now," Paige said.

Zach hadn't wanted to bring the matter into the light again, but now that Paige had… "He's likely feeling like he jumped the gun."

"But the director wouldn't have approved the investigation if Jack was jumping the gun, right?" Paige looked pensive, as if she was unsure whose side she was on. Did the blame rest on Jack for making the wrong judgment call or on the shoulders of the FBI director who had approved the investigation? Did it even matter?

Zach went to pull into Stella Bridges's drive, but another car cut him off and butted in ahead of him.

Paige leaned forward and lifted her sunglasses. "Is that Marsh?"

Both vehicles stopped and parked in front of a wrought iron gate. Beyond it were well-groomed lawns, palm trees, and magnolia trees. Tucked deeper into the property was the house, its roofline all that was visible from where Zach and Paige sat.

They got out of the SUV, and sure enough, Kelly was walking toward them.

Despite the silver-mirrored lenses of her sunglasses, she was squinting, the skin pinching around her eyes. "What brought you guys here?"

Paige pointed toward the house. "Stella Bridges was with Kelter last night at a place called Magical Bar & Grill."

"Well, that's good. It gives us a lead on the timeline." Kelly glanced at Zach and let her gaze trail back to Paige. "What is it?"

"Jack didn't call you?" Paige asked.

"Noooooo." Kelly dragged out the word.

"We think Kelter might have left Gordon for Stella," Zach laid out, not bothering to ask Kelly what brought her to Bridges's front door.

"They were lovers?" Kelly raised her brows, skeptical.

"It would seem," Zach said.

"No." Kelly shook her head rapidly. "There's more to this. I just know that Kelter's been taken by a serial killer."

Zach appreciated Kelly's conviction, but he wasn't convinced just yet. "Until we *actually* have evidence of that…"

"Kelter could be inside," Paige stressed.

"No." Kelly shook her head. "I'm not buying that. The victimology lines up with West and Sullivan."

They could stand there all day arguing about how they could look at things, but it wasn't going to get them anywhere. "We need to talk to Stella to find out what's going on," Zach said.

"Sure, but I'm hanging around." Kelly walked up to the intercom, Zach and Paige flanking her. She reached out to push the intercom button, but Paige stayed her hand.

"You never told us what brought you here," Paige said.

Kelly drew her hand back. "Jenna's friend Carrie told me that Jenna hadn't been going to church for years before her accident. She said she'd stopped not long after becoming friends with Stella Bridges. I was hoping to get some insight into their friendship, thinking maybe Stella might know where Jenna actually went on Sundays. From there maybe figure out when and where she was abducted."

Paige turned to Zach. "Seems another skeleton came out of the closet," she said.

Kelly didn't question Paige's comment and rang the intercom.

"Who is it?" a quiet woman's voice said over the speaker.

"Miami PD and the FBI, ma'am," Kelly announced. "We'd like to speak with Stella Bridges."

"May I tell her what this is regarding?" the woman asked.

"I'm sorry, but that's between us and Ms. Bridges."

After a moment's pause, a buzzing sound cut through the air, and the three of them loaded back into their vehicles. As Zach drove down the serpentine drive, he admired the landscaping. Mature palm trees and lush gardens provided hues of green and splashes of reds and yellows. The lawn was immaculately manicured and had been cut on an angle.

The end of the lane curved around a fountain with a stone sculpture in the center, which depicted a woman draped in flowing cloth holding a tilted amphora. Water poured out of its spout into a circular basin.

Zach parked at the top of the drive, taking in the building. It was two stories with a spread-out floor plan. A second-story balcony was perched above the doorway and decorated with furniture and oversized potted plants. Zach assumed it was more for show than use. It was nice, but if this were his place, he'd never leave the front of the house, which overlooked the water.

He appreciatively breathed in the salty air that carried on a gentle and somewhat cool breeze as he walked to the door that faced the road. It was black with an arched top, and it towered over his six-foot-four height by about two feet. He'd expected that the woman from the intercom would be at the door waiting to greet them, but it remained closed. He searched for the doorbell, but Paige got there first.

Footsteps were approaching from the other side, and the door slowly swung open. A woman stood there tying the belt on a sheer wraparound that draped her small frame. Beneath the coverup, she wore a patterned blue bikini. Sunglasses were perched on the top of her head. Piercing gray metallic eyes studied them. Even if her profession didn't give away her intelligence, her discerning gaze did.

"What do you want?" she asked abruptly as she walked around them and closed the door. She smelled of coconut oil and sun-kissed skin.

Zach flashed his creds. "FBI Agent Miles. This is my colleague Agent Dawson." He tilted his head toward Paige, then gestured to Kelly.

"I'm Detective Marsh with Miami PD, Central District, Homicide." Kelly showed her badge.

Stella squared her shoulders. "And what brings you here?"

"Do you have someplace we could sit down?" Zach eyed the sunken living room and the wall of windows beyond it. The view of the water was breathtaking.

Stella put her hands on her hips, a diamond tennis bracelet dangling from her left wrist. "Tell me what this is about first."

"You're friends with Jenna Kelter, correct?" Kelly asked before Zach could speak.

"Okay, I'll play along." Stella reached into one of the pockets of her wraparound and glanced at her cell phone. "Sure, we're *friends*."

"Is she here, ma'am?" Zach asked, drawing a hot glare from Stella. There was the ballbuster Tommy had mentioned.

Stella let her phone drop back into her pocket and crossed her arms. "Why would she be here?"

Paige jumped in first. "You had drinks with her last night at—"

"Magical Bar & Grill," Stella finished. "The question is how do *you* know that?" she snarled, obviously feeling as though her privacy had been violated.

"We're investigating Mrs. Kelter's disappearance." Kelly dumped the news on Stella, but the woman didn't seem worried in the least.

"Disappearance," Stella scoffed. "That's ridiculous. I saw her just…"

"Last night," Paige reiterated. "Did you leave the bar together?"

Stella nodded. "We came back here, made love, and fell asleep together. When I woke up to use the bathroom just after two in the morning, she was gone. I figured she just went home."

"Before prison, did she normally spend Sunday nights with you?" Zach asked, risking Stella's wrath again.

Stella nodded.

"Does she usually slip out in the wee hours?" Kelly asked.

Stella nodded again. "She slinks home and sneaks into bed with Gordon."

"And he's never questioned where she was?" Zach asked.

"Not that she told me."

Interesting. Gordon must have been obtuse to the fact his wife returned home on Monday in the wee hours. Otherwise why report her missing when he did?

"I'm assuming she normally drove herself around," Paige started, "but she doesn't have a license right now. Do you know how she got to Magical Bar & Grill or how she would have gotten home? Maybe she took a cab?"

"A cab?" Stella spat with disgust. "No. Well, I wouldn't think so anyway. She knows how to reach Dominick."

"Who's Dominick?" Kelly asked.

"Well, he's not my driver per se, as he's not on my payroll, but he works for a local driving service, Checker Limousine, and I always request him when I need a ride. Not that he was around to drive us home from the bar last night. Dominick dropped me off at the bar. I called for him to pick us up, but when we stepped outside one of Checker's cars was already there. I thought it looked like Dominick's vehicle, but he wasn't behind the wheel. I told Checker to disregard my request for a car."

That had Zach's attention, and a lead weight balled in his gut. "Did you ever have this driver before?"

"No, but we were too wasted to care. We just wanted to get back here."

Tingles were running wild up Zach's back. "Did you get a good look at this driver?"

"No. Again the booze. I just know that it was a man." Stella shook her head, her regret tangible.

Their unsub could work at the same company, but before Zach jumped to any conclusion, he needed more information. "You said it looked like Dominick's car?"

"Same make and model. A white Chrysler 300." Stella said that as if it was enough to jump to the conclusion she had. The driving service could have had more than one white Chrysler 300.

"Did the driver mention Dominick at all?" Zach asked off the cuff.

"Actually, he did. He said that Dominick wasn't feeling well." Stella shrugged, then her eyes widened. "Do you think he did something to her? Maybe he showed up in the morning and took her?"

"It's too soon to know," Zach told her.

Stella's eyes were filling with tears, and she began to tremble.

"Let's sit," Zach suggested.

Stella flicked a look to Paige and Kelly, then back to Zach. "What happened to her?"

"Let's sit and talk." Zach stepped toward the couch.

"In that case, let's move this outside. Follow me." She led them to a back patio that surrounded a large in-ground swimming pool. Twenty lounge chairs lined the pool. An open textbook was on one with a towel tossed over the back, and on the table next to the chair was a glass with some fruity-looking libation. Stella grabbed the drink on her way past it, and she continued to guide them to a larger table with chairs and an umbrella.

Stella sat in one of four chairs there and crossed her legs. Paige, Kelly, and Zach took the other seats.

Stella steeled herself, deep breath in, shoulders drawing back, head held high. "Okay, hit me."

"All we know for sure is that Jenna's whereabouts are currently unaccounted for," Paige said diplomatically.

"So you have no idea if she's all right or not." Stella made the bleak conclusion and sniffled.

Kelly turned to look at Paige, then to Stella. "We have reason to believe—"

Paige glared at Kelly and cut in, "We don't know if she's all right or not, and that's what we're trying to determine."

Kelly's posture stiffened as she glowered at Paige.

But Stella's gaze stayed on Kelly. "What do you believe?"

"It's too early to say," Paige insisted.

Stella pointed a manicured finger toward Kelly. "I'd like to hear it from *you*."

"I believe she's in danger," Kelly admitted.

Shaking her head, Stella pulled out her phone. "This is all a misunderstanding, you'll see." She pushed a button and held her phone to an ear. Moments later, she said, "Jenna, baby, call me when you get this message." She set her phone on the table. "She just has her phone off. That's all."

"Her husband hasn't seen her since eleven thirty yesterday morning and reported her missing around two in the morning," Zach said, presenting the facts as delicately as possible. "As far as we've figured out, you're the last one to have seen her."

Stella cleared her throat and lifted her head high.

"She told her husband she was going to church when she left yesterday morning, but her friends said she wasn't there," Zach started. "Do you know where she might have gone? Who might have picked her up?"

"Well, we were going to get together earlier in the day, but something came up at work. I didn't get to see her until nine thirty at the bar." Stella sounded regretful. "I'd sent Dominick to pick her up at her house and when I told her I was caught up with work, she said she'd go see a movie then come back here."

"And that's what she did?" Paige asked.

"Yeah, as far as I know. She got restless waiting around here for me and headed to the bar at eight thirty. I told her I'd meet her there. I went straight from work." Stella slid her gaze to the detective and tears beaded in her eyes. "I can handle the truth. It's obvious there's more to Jenna's disappearance than you're telling me. The FBI doesn't come around asking questions about people who may or may not be in danger. And you said you're in Homicide." Stella gave Kelly a pointed look.

Zach had heard enough to redirect his suspicions down their original path: Kelter had been abducted and was quite likely in the hands of a serial killer. Could Stella really handle that theory? No doubt she had to deal with unpleasant situations with her chosen career all the time. She'd likely given notice to family members on many occasions. "We think it's possible that Jenna was taken by a serial killer," Zach confessed.

"I see." Stella was staring at the tabletop, her eyes glazed over.

"We'll need the information on the driving service you use, please," Kelly requested.

"Checker Limousine." Stella went on to rattle off the company's number from memory. "You don't think she was taken from here?" She sat up straighter and uncrossed her legs. "I thought I had the best security money could buy."

"She easily could have gone missing after she left here, or even after leaving the driver's care," Zach said to comfort her. "Do you have surveillance cameras on the premises? Maybe at your front gate?"

"Absolutely, and I can give you the security company's information. Maybe you'll see something that will help find her." Stella paused and stared at her phone. "I just can't believe this is happening… She was going to leave Gordon for me. We were going to be—" Stella spun her phone on the table.

"We're going to do everything we can to bring her home safely," Paige said. It was the same thing she had told Gordon.

Stella picked up her phone and dialed again. "I just can't accept what you're telling me."

Zach's heart ached watching this woman gripping on to hope so tightly, beyond reason and logic. As a surgeon who surely had faced life's unfairness numerous times throughout her career, she should know that endings weren't always happy. She simply didn't want to—

"It's ringing!" Stella jumped to her feet.

Zach looked at Kelly, who was on her phone already, probably getting someone on tracking Kelter's phone immediately.

"Come on, baby, answer…" Stella was perched on the edge of her chair, tears pooling in her eyes again. "Hello? Jenna? Jenna, are you there?"

"Here." Zach tried to take the phone from Stella.

"Someone answered…" she said. "Someone…"

Zach got the phone to an ear just in time to hear a single expletive before the call was cut off.

CHAPTER THIRTEEN

Everyone, everything had a purpose. And Roxanne served his. She was loyal—to a fault—and naive. She was exactly what he needed, and she'd do whatever he asked of her. In return, he was a doting boyfriend when it suited. To instill loyalty, one sometimes had to give to receive. And that's what he was doing at La Casa de Jose—listening to Roxanne rant about a coworker. He couldn't help it if his mind wandered. He hated leaving his latest victim unattended, but sometimes exceptions needed to be made.

She is safe and secure.

He'd repeat that mentally until it stuck and he believed it.

Cutlery crashed to the floor. Dishes smashed. He looked over his shoulder to see a red-faced busboy scurrying to clean up the mess he'd made. An older man came out from the back, flailing his arms, talking in Spanish, and gesturing toward the front where people were waiting to be seated.

"I suppose someone could be having a worse day than I am," Roxanne said.

"That's a good way of looking at it." He turned back to face her and smiled but felt the expression crease away in increments.

Safe and secure...

He pulled out his phone and pressed the button to wake the screen, but it was black.

"She thinks she's God's gift to man, too, you know? It's like every man wants her." Roxanne sucked back her cola through a straw. "One guy turns her down, and I have to hear all about it. How he must be out of his mind to turn 'this' down." She rolled her eyes.

"Sounds like *she's* out of her mind."

"Right?" She sucked back more cola.

He held down the power button until the phone's logo came on the screen.

"Can't you put that thing away?"

Red-hot lava shot through his veins. How dare she tell him what to do!

But he couldn't afford to lash out the way he wanted to. He'd only create a scene, and what worked best for him was staying under the radar. He pocketed his phone and reached for her hand.

"When you go back after lunch, tell her you have work to do and don't have time to listen to her problems," he suggested.

Ironic how he could have been giving the same advice to himself…

"I do," she blurted out. "But she either doesn't listen or doesn't care. Who knows which… But it doesn't stop her incessant yakking." Roxanne mimicked talking with her hand. "Oh, I'm sorry. Now *I've* been talking nonstop." She fussed with her straw, lifting it up and down, up and down. "How's your day going?" Roxanne's eyes were focused on him, but she'd moved on to fidgeting with her cutlery, which was wrapped in a paper napkin. She finally ended up tearing off the paper napkin ring.

"Hon?" she prompted when he didn't respond.

His leg started bouncing under the table. The Night was whispering to him, demanding more attention be paid to its needs. He pressed on a smile. "My day's been great so far. I slept in, too."

She sighed. "I would kill to sleep in."

She had no idea how exhausting kidnapping and killing were. How both deserved a nice, long snooze afterward. And the last twelve hours had been *exhausting*... He really should drug his prey, but there was something more exciting about live bait.

"Please don't do this to me." She screams and thrashes as I fix her into the guillotine.

A shiver snaked through him. The Night wanted to be heard, longed for another victim. *Now.*

He stamped down its hunger and reached out to tuck some of Roxanne's blond hair behind an ear.

"Is everything okay?" Roxanne leaned toward him across the table.

His leg bounced faster. "Why wouldn't it be?"

Roxanne was staring at him, not saying a word, and he had an idea. There was something he could do that might tame the monster within him.

He glanced over a shoulder and saw no indication that their food was on its way. He tugged on her hand. "Let's go."

"Go?" she squeaked out. "We've already ordered."

The woman could be dumb as a stump at times. "Not go. *Go at it*," he said impatiently as he stood and pulled her to her feet. "Come with me." He slipped an arm around her waist, and she let him lead her.

He opened the door to the men's restroom and stepped aside for her to go first. She hesitated and stopped. "Someone might be in here."

Then I'll have to kill them...

"Less talk." He nudged her inside and followed close behind. He took a quick look under the stalls and confirmed they were alone. He flipped the latch on the door and turned on her. The thunder of the Night was pounding in his ears, in his chest, through his veins.

He slammed her up against the far wall, grabbing at her and kissing her neck. She writhed and moaned. Her hands were reaching out for him, but he slapped them away. He kept going at her as if she were his last meal.

He nibbled on her ear, teeth sinking into flesh. She cried out but then reined herself back. He kept kissing her, nibbling her, his incisors piercing skin. And she kept writhing.

He pulled back and put one hand to her forehead while he took his other and worked to lower his zipper. "You know how the fuck I like it. Keep still," he ground out.

She did as he said; she always did. Though, this time, her eyes widened and were looking right at him, looking *through* him.

"And close your fucking eyes." He clawed at her waist with both hands, inching up the fabric of her skirt. Then he went at her center, pushed aside her panties, and thrust himself into her. She gave no audible reaction as he entered her, but her breath hitched and she tightened around him. Still and silent—just the way he liked it.

With his hands on her hips, he drove into her until he had release. The power tearing through him was sedating the Night.

He let go of her and stepped back. She clutched the fabric of her shirt, bunching it to cover her cleavage as if she were modest. Tears beaded in her eyes, and she licked her lips before biting down on the bottom one.

Seeing her like this reawakened the Night. He rushed over to her, cupped her chin, then crushed his mouth against hers. He'd do her again if he could. Anything to quiet the Night again. This time it was louder, its lust for blood insatiable.

His phone rang, breaking his concentration. He let Roxanne go, answered the call, but said nothing.

"Hello? Jenna? Jenna, are you there?" the caller blurted out.

Blood rushed to his head, panic swelling in his chest. He tightened his hold on the phone and looked at it. Why was this person saying Jenna's name? A sick feeling ran through him. He must have charged and grabbed Jenna's phone and not his own…

"Fuck!" He hurled the phone across the room, and it shattered. "Fuck, fuck, fuck!" He slammed his fist into a paper towel dispenser. A piece of plastic from the lever lodged into his hand and blood trailed down his arm. He felt no sting from the injury. He plucked out the shard and tossed it to the floor.

"Babe?" Roxanne's eyes were wide, her gaze bouncing from him to the wall to the floor, back to him. She backed away from him a bit more. "What is it?"

His breath came in choppy, heaving gasps. The Night was wrapping its hold around his heart and squeezing, taunting him to act. To act *now*. He reached out and grabbed her throat. Her hands went to his, trying to pry him loose. It was so tempting to silence her forever. He squeezed, and her eyes bulged.

But no, I can't do it this way. I'll be caught.

He let his arms drop, zipped up his pants, and got out of the restroom as fast as he could.

He ran smack into their waitress outside the restroom door.

Startled, she burst out, "What the hell?"

He brushed her aside.

"You've already ordered. Where do you think you're go—"

The waitress's voice faded to obscurity as he hurried through the restaurant. He reached the front door and stepped out onto the sidewalk. His nostrils were flaring, working to fulfill his lungs' desperate need for air.

There was no doubt the cops would be tracking Jenna's phone. He started into a jog, cradling his hand. Everything he'd worked to accomplish could have just come shattering down around him.

CHAPTER FOURTEEN

It seemed our killer had a taste for Cuban cuisine. Kelter's phone was traced back to a restaurant by the name of La Casa de Jose. Though, that was assuming the man who answered Kelter's phone was our unsub. Part of me was willing to take that leap given the man's reaction to the call. Profanity followed by a dropped call—and according to Tech, a lost signal. I was stuck on one glaring detail: our supposedly intelligent unsub had answered Kelter's phone. Then again, criminals usually screwed up and made mistakes at some point—even the smart ones.

La Casa de Jose was a few blocks from the courthouse, and Jack, Marsh, and I were en route there now while Paige and Zach were checking in with the driving service Stella used.

"The guy is probably long gone by now." Marsh squirmed in the back seat like an anxious and impatient child on a road trip.

"If he has any brains at all," I added.

"Dumb slip-ups are how some of the best get caught," Marsh countered.

"If they were the best, they wouldn't get caught," I volleyed back, being a wiseass because I knew full well she was right. I'd just been thinking the same thing. "How couldn't he have noticed that he had the wrong phone?"

"He could have the same one." Marsh's suggestion came quick and had Jack looking over at me with a smirk. He was in a hell of a good mood ever since Kelter went back to being a victim, as horrible as that sounded…

"So you're telling me that he never noticed that the lock screen image was different?" I asked.

"He could have just turned it on and shoved it into a pocket," Marsh said nonchalantly, and I detested how easily she made me look bad in front of Jack—again.

Jack pulled into a parking spot near the restaurant, and the three of us headed for the door. The hostess smiled at us when we entered.

"Hello," she greeted us, a friendly smile on her face. Her expression faded when Jack and I held up our creds, and Marsh her badge. No doubt law enforcement netted the same response worldwide.

"I'll get the owner," the hostess said, tucking her chin to her shoulder, her cheeks flushed. "I'll be right back."

From appearances, the place did pretty well. There weren't many empty seats. A waitress delivered a couple of entrees to a nearby table and eyed us with curiosity. She looked over a shoulder at the same time the hostess was returning with a Latino man in his early sixties. Silver hair on his head, thick eyebrows, and a mustache to match. He was wearing a blue polo shirt and tan slacks under a knee-length white apron.

"It's about time you got here. I called at least an hour ago," he said.

I slid a sideways glance at Jack, who was probably as lost as I was, but he was looking at the man. Why had he been expecting us?

"Well, we're here now," Jack said, playing along. "And you're—"

"Jose Garcia, the owner." Jose waved for us to follow him through the restaurant. "Come see what this moron did. We have him on tape, too, if that helps you get this guy."

"We'll definitely want to see the tape," I chimed in.

"Of course, of course, but first—" Jose stepped into an alcove off to the right and back of the seating area where the restrooms were. He opened the door to the men's room and gestured for us to go inside. "Look what he did."

The room was small—two stalls, a urinal, and a sink. On the wall was a busted paper towel dispenser. Its lever was on the floor, and there were a few drops of blood on the tile surrounding it.

Please don't tell me that he'd called the police over that.

"You see it, yes?" Jose said excitedly. "He destroyed restaurant property."

Wow. He *had* called about that.

I backed out of the room, and so did Jack and Marsh. I almost hit my head on a fragrance dispenser mounted on the wall. It cleared my height—if barely—but apparently, I was a little jittery and I jumped back anyway. I shook it off and focused on how this seemingly inconsequential destruction of property might give us a lead through forensics.

Marsh and Jack made eye contact, and she nodded, pulled out her phone, and stepped away. I gathered she'd be calling in the Crime Scene techs.

"Where's she going?" Jose called out. "Is she calling those people who dust for prints and stuff?"

"She is," Jack told him, and Jose's posture relaxed. "Has anyone else been in the restroom since the man who did this?"

"Only me and Leslie, one of my waitresses. She went in after the man stormed out of here. There was a lady picking up stuff off the floor. Trying to cover up what they did, I guess."

Hairs rose on the back of my neck. "A lady?"

"Yes. I think it was his girlfriend."

"Is she here now?" I tucked my head out of the alcove and glanced at the patrons.

"No, she left," Jose said.

Maybe we were reading the situation incorrectly and the

woman was Kelter. I hesitated to ask, but we needed to know. "What did she look like?"

"Blond, trim, wearing a short skirt."

I nodded. Kelter was a brunette, but women changed their hair color all the time. And reverting back to the theory Kelter may have left Gordon, she might take steps to alter her appearance. Though, none of this blended with Kelter and Bridges's affair.

"And the man? What did he look like?" I asked.

"Anything distinguishing about him?" Jack added.

"He had a small, round scar on his neck. That's what Leslie told me." Jose tapped his neck below his right ear. "Right here."

"Do you know where he went from here?" Jack asked.

"He went outside and headed west, but I couldn't catch him." Jose put a hand over his heart. "I'm not as young as I used to be. On his way out, he nearly ran over Leslie."

Marsh returned. "They'll be here soon. We should clear the restaurant."

Jose's eyes widened. "Clear my— Wait a minute. You didn't come here about my paper towel dispenser, did you?"

I shook my head.

"You are cops, though?"

Obviously, the hostess hadn't filled Jose in completely. Jack pulled out his creds again. I was close behind, and Marsh was a fraction of a second after me.

"FBI? ¡Dios mío! Oh my God!" Jose staggered back, his hand still over his heart.

"Whoa, easy there." I quickly caught the older man's arm and held him steady. He shook me off as if he was embarrassed by my assistance.

"What's going on here?" Jose's gaze flicked toward the restroom door and then he looked back at the three of us. His eyes flicked to Marsh's badge. "You're a cop."

"Detective Kelly Marsh," she told him. "Miami PD, Homicide." And then off she went to start clearing the restaurant.

Jose's mouth gaped open and shut like a fish's. "Homicide?" His gaze trailed after Marsh, who was talking to a waitress with a short blond bob. He didn't seem concerned about the loss of business anymore.

"We're investigating the disappearance of a woman," Jack explained.

"You think the man who broke my dispenser took her?"

"He's a person of interest," I said, committing to nothing.

Jose's face paled. "Oh."

"We'd like to see that video you mentioned," Jack began, "and to speak with Leslie."

"I'll get her first, then the video." Jose walked off, and a moment later, a petite woman in her thirties approached. She had a tan complexion, and her long black hair was wound in a bun. The pocket of her half apron was stuffed with a notepad and a pen.

"Hi?" she said, clearly wary. "Mr. Garcia said you wanted to talk to me?"

Jose was nowhere to be seen. Hopefully, he was all right given the shock he experienced when we told him why we were here and he was just getting the video.

I addressed Leslie. "We'd like to talk to you about the man who—"

"You mean the slime who raped that woman in the restroom, then ran off?"

"Raped her?" I asked incredulously. If rape was suspected, why was Jose more concerned about his stupid paper towel dispenser? Sometimes the way people thought just didn't make sense.

"Uh-huh." Leslie fell quiet for a few seconds and frowned. "Not that she said as much, but she was silent, almost catatonic, when I found her. There had been life in her eyes when I took their orders, but after, they were dark, like the light had gone out. She kept covering her neck with her hand, but I could see that it was all red and blotchy. I don't know exactly what happened in that restroom, but I think that man raped her. And the restroom smelled like sex."

She flushed. "Mr. Garcia seemed blinded by rage over the damage. He couldn't see that something wasn't right with her. He kept going off on her. Eventually she put a twenty on the table and left. We couldn't force her to stay."

"Did she say anything to you?" Marsh asked, joining us again, obviously overhearing enough of our conversation to jump right in.

"Just that her boyfriend got some bad news and had to leave."

Bad news, all right… This man had to be our killer. Though knowing that didn't get us any closer to finding him.

Leslie's nostrils flared. "I've seen it before in family. She's being abused one way or another." Any sadness she'd been showing disappeared and was replaced by anger. Her hand balled into a fist. "If I ever see him again…" She blinked and relaxed her hand as if cluing into the fact that her words smacked of a threat in front of law enforcement. "Anyway, is there anything else I can do to help? If not, I should get to closing out my tables."

"Actually, we have a few more questions for you," I said. "Has he been in here before today?"

"I've seen her before, but not him."

"Does she normally pay cash?" I asked. We might not have a credit card trail to follow from today, but maybe a past visit would yield one.

"I think so?" Uncertainty strained her voice. "I'm guessing you'd like me to say she paid by credit card. But even if she did, I couldn't tell you when."

"Do you think they'd been seeing each other long?" I asked to get a feel for the significance of their relationship.

Leslie hitched her shoulders. "I'm not sure. He seemed to be zoning out on her when she was talking to him. That normally happens after being in a relationship for a while."

The door of the restaurant opened, and I peeked out from the alcove. Two techs from Crime Scene were speaking with the hostess at her stand.

Jose returned, pointing to the techs, and Marsh left to greet them. "Happy they're here," Jose said and held out a USB stick to me. "That's the surveillance footage."

"We wouldn't mind taking a look at it now," Jack said.

"Sure. Follow me." Jose turned toward the kitchen.

"May I get back to work?" Leslie asked.

Jose stopped walking and looked back at us.

"We'll come get you if we have any more questions," Jack told her.

Jack and I were about to go with Jose when Marsh approached with two male CSIs. One of them was long and lean and probably a few inches over six feet, while his partner's cherubic appearance made him look like a junior high student. He was all of maybe five six. It was easy to identify the lead over his number two.

Long and Lean pointed a finger toward the men's room. "This the one we need to look at?"

"Yep," Marsh confirmed.

No introductions were made, and the investigators beelined toward the restroom door.

The three of us stepped back to allow them access. After they went inside, Jose said, "You want to see that video now?" and resumed heading toward the kitchen.

Jack and I started after him when Marsh grabbed my arm. I stopped and faced her. So did Jack. "I'm going to stay with the techs, watch how they make out here," she told us.

Jack nodded, and I would've sworn that I detected a subtle smile. He was impressed by her tenacity and need to stay on top of things. I wasn't sure the CSIs would have been. I wouldn't have appreciated the hovering, but then again, she wasn't in my good books anyway. It took effort for me to garner Jack's approval, and it came to her so easily.

CHAPTER FIFTEEN

My God, I am so careless, so stupid…

He was pacing the boardwalk, trying to clear his head by breathing in the fresh, salty air, but it wasn't working. He was agitated, and the Night was furious. He had been such an idiot grabbing the wrong phone and then leaving Roxanne behind.

Stupid, stupid, stupid.

And that wasn't even considering the fact that his prints and DNA would be all over that restroom. He looked down at his injured hand, at the dried blood, wishing he could feel, but he was numb. The Night was taking over.

He cupped his head with his hands, his fingers digging into his scalp, and walked in a circle. Passersby stared at him, doing double takes as if they knew something was off with him. Well, they'd be right. One mistake could be what took him down.

He dropped his arms and took in a deep steadying breath. *Focus on the facts.*

He'd been careful not to leave a trace of himself during past kills and didn't have a record. So even if they dusted for his prints, could they track him down?

He balled his hands into fists, expecting—even desiring— some pain from the injured one, but nothing.

It will be all right, he consoled himself. Yet the Night roared—getting louder, more persistent, and wishing he'd act more often. It tempted him by reminding him how killing soothed his soul. He couldn't deny that. It was as close to a religious experience as he could hope to get. The study of the Bible and making confessions had been his mother's thing, not his. If there was a Heaven and Hell, he'd be headed for burning damnation. But in this life, killing was a heavenly blessing. How he longed to have it rain down over him…

The police could be on to him. He had to bury the impulses deep within, ignore the taunting to act. It was time for damage control, and he had to find out what the police knew. The uncertainty was driving him mad.

What if he hadn't been as careful as he thought he had? His prints and DNA could be in a police database somewhere, ready to come back to bite him.

And Roxanne… The cops could have gotten to her, but she was his puppet, weak and malleable. Or did that make her a liability? Maybe they could make her talk. He had tried to choke her. What if she feared for her life and told them everything? He had to know what was going on, but his phone would be with his victim.

He paced some more, looking around. He spotted a pay phone and paused at the sight of the relic.

Well, what do you know? God provides after all.

He hurried over to the phone and fed some change into the machine. He waited as her line rang a few times. Then her voice mail picked up. His entire body froze despite the warm breeze and the hot sun.

"I'm so sorry about earlier, baby," he said. "Please call me." He hung up, slush running through his veins. The cops could be interrogating her at this moment. They could be tracking her calls. He had to leave. Now. He turned to hurry off and came face-to-face with a little girl and a man, who he assumed was her father. She was laughing and skipping but stopped doing both abruptly before colliding with him. She stared up at him while the father's brow hardened.

"Sorry about that," he said to the father and pressed on a smile.

The father eventually nodded and returned the expression before leading his daughter away.

"Great day to be outside," he called out after them, swallowing the bile that came with the sentiment.

"That it is," the father replied as he and the girl carried on down the boardwalk.

He watched after them for a bit and was taken back to his childhood. He was curious as to when the Night had actually taken root, but just like always, when he tried to figure it out he couldn't pinpoint the exact moment. Maybe it had been there from the start of his life and had fused itself into his consciousness over time. What he *did* know was that life used to be good. That was, until Michael had moved in. As his mother had liked to claim, Michael was the other name for Jesus. As if Michael was the family's savior. Only he didn't save the family; he destroyed it. Even Mom and Dad's marriage fell apart not long after.

He clenched his hands into tight fists. Michael had been anything but a savior for him. Because of Michael, his dad had started looking at him differently. The vacations to Disney World had stopped, and the presents on birthdays and at Christmas had dwindled. Really, Michael had killed the good within him and encouraged the Night to take over.

Who really had the right to judge good and bad, right and wrong? Wasn't it all about perspective?

He smiled as he hustled down the boardwalk. He should thank Michael for helping him evolve into his true self. He had to protect the Night just as he would his own soul; it was as real as flesh and blood. No matter the cost, he had more work to do.

CHAPTER SIXTEEN

It was the hunt that fueled me to become better at my job with every passing day, with every new unsub we needed to stop. Pops would never be able to understand that or appreciate the spike in adrenaline that accompanied a lead like the one Jack and I were on the verge of now. We were about to see our killer's face for the first time. Maybe I was rushing to conclude this man was our unsub, but the pieces were falling together: he had Kelter's phone, he had a violent reaction to the call, took off from the restaurant, and had a submissive partner. Though I wasn't about to share my conclusion with Jack just yet. Surely, he'd poke a hole in my theory and tell me I was relying too much on coincidence.

Jose's office was off the back of the kitchen. It had two workstations with computers and trays full of paper. Both desks had hutches plastered with photographs, charts, telephone lists, and business cards. There were a couple of chairs for visitors tucked in a corner. Jose moved them opposite his desk.

"Sit," Jose told us, and we did as he had directed. He proceeded to angle the monitor so that Jack and I could see it, and then he leaned back in his chair. Its frame creaked with the movement. He inserted the USB drive into the computer and started the video.

The quality was grainy and black-and-white. The camera pointed toward the front door, showing the dining area, but the restroom alcove was off screen. Patrons were lined up at the hostess stand, and three waitresses were serving. A busboy hurried to clean a table and dropped some plates and cutlery. Jose came out of the kitchen and laid into the guy.

"Not one of my finest hours," Jose said without any evidence of being embarrassed. He pointed to a table. "That's the couple."

The woman was facing the camera while the man's back was to us. But as we kept watching, the man got up and coaxed the woman to her feet. He had his arm around her as they walked toward the camera, in the direction of the restrooms.

The man was average in all respects and dressed casually in jeans and a T-shirt. Nothing about him screamed that he was a serial killer, but rarely did killers look like killers. It would have certainly made our jobs easier if that were the case. Assuming he was our unsub, he'd fall into the same category as many sociopaths who didn't seem suspicious to neighbors, friends, and family.

The man carried himself with authority and determination. He took evenly spaced steps and held the woman close to his side as he led her to the restroom. Her shoulders were slightly lowered, and her arms appeared rather limp as she submitted to his direction.

She was slender and attractive with curly hair that reached past her shoulders and was dressed in a short skirt—just as Jose had told us—and a blouse. The contrast of their personal styles was obvious, so either it was a mismatched date or the woman worked in an office and was on her lunch break.

They were about to walk out of the camera's view when Jack said, "Pause it there."

Jose got to it a bit late, and their backs were to us.

"Rewind it just a bit," Jack directed.

Jose did as Jack requested, and then the man and woman were facing us. I prepared myself to peer in the eyes of a man who could have been the killer we hunted, and my heart raced. It beat even faster when I looked at him. I'd seen him before, but I couldn't remember where. I'd share as much with Jack, but he preferred solid data to something that hinted at déjà vu. There was something else I would tell Jack. "Do you see that white fragrance dispenser on the wall behind him?" I asked.

Jack nodded.

"I just cleared it, like him. I'm six two, so—"

"He's six two," Jack concluded, obviously resigning to the evidence pointing toward this man being our killer. His eyes lit, and I took that as him being impressed with me. It only lasted briefly before he asked Jose, "Can you print that off for us?"

"I think so." Jose's fingers danced across his keyboard and a printer hummed to life.

Jack pulled out a card and handed it to Jose. "And send the video there." Jack indicated the card.

Nadia would be able to work with the video and try to get a hit with facial recognition software. Hopefully she'd have more luck with that than I was with recalling why he looked familiar. I was racking my brain, and nada.

Jose took the card from Jack slowly, as if it could bite him. His gaze drifted to the desk briefly.

The silence in the office was punctuated by the clanging of pots in the kitchen.

"Is that woman in danger?" Jose asked, pointing at the screen.

A good question and one we hadn't had a chance to discuss. It was rare for serial killers to turn on the people they were close with, but it wasn't entirely unheard of. We weren't even certain this was our unsub, but if it was and this woman had upset him enough...

"Mr. Garcia," I said, "would you leave us to talk privately for a moment please?"

Jose looked at Jack, who nodded, and Jose got up and left the room.

"She could be in danger," I said to Jack. "It's plain to see she's submissive and compliant. I think Leslie was right when she said the woman seems abused. And if she was raped, she didn't call out for help or say she needed any assistance afterward."

"Your point, Brandon?"

"My *point* is that she must be useful to him in some way, but what if he starts to see her as a threat? His answering Kelter's phone has to have thrown him off. What if it actually accelerates his need to kill? She was a witness to what happened when he was in the restroom; she'd know that something was up with him. Maybe she's starting to question the type of person he really is. He could fear she's talking to the cops."

"She probably has no idea he's a killer. And that's assuming he is." Jack regarded me with a serious expression.

"Even if he's not our killer, something's off with the guy. He punched a towel dispenser and then ran. Seems a little excessive if the guy just happened upon Kelter's phone."

"The waitress suspected he'd raped the woman he was with. Maybe he was afraid he'd be caught for that," Jack countered.

My gut clenched, and the skin on the back of my neck tightened. There was no doubt in my mind that he was our unsub. "I've seen him before," I blurted out.

Jack narrowed his eyes on me. "What do you mean you've seen him before?"

"Just that. I can't remember where yet, but it will come to me. He's our unsub. And yes, I *feel* it, but I also believe the proof is in front of us." I pointed to the screen. "And I think she's in danger."

"Hmm."

"Say more than that. Please."

"She could be."

My mouth was open, ready to defend my viewpoint further. I snapped it shut, still not sure his agreement was what I had wanted. It was bittersweet actually. With his confirmation, there was no denying that now we had two women to save and no idea where to find either of them.

CHAPTER SEVENTEEN

It was hard to know who was following the strongest lead—Jack and Brandon or him and Paige. Then again, maybe both trails would take them to the same person. But Zach found it hard to believe the killer had delivered West's and Sullivan's heads personally. Even if the unsub had wanted to feast on people's reactions, it could be done through the media, with far less risk of getting caught. As far as Zach figured, the driving service Stella Bridges used factored in somehow. Whether it led them to another suspect or not remained to be seen.

Zach and Paige stepped inside the office of Checker Limousine, and it smelled of motor oil and rubber. No one was at the front desk.

Zach led the way through the office until they found themselves in a service bay. A Crown Vic and a Chrysler 300 were being serviced. There wasn't a stretch limo in sight.

"Can I help you?" A rotund man came toward them wearing stained coveralls and holding a rag.

Zach and Paige showed him their credentials and introduced themselves.

"Well, I'm Dwayne Spencer, the owner here." Dwayne rested his hands on his hips, the rag dangling from one of his hands.

"We'd like to speak to your driver Dominick," Zach said.

"Whatcha want with Dom?"

"Is there someplace private we could talk?" Zach's gaze went to a set of metal stairs leading to an office space that overlooked the garage.

"There's nothing much you can say that will shock me, and I hide nothing from my guys." He jerked a head backward, and one of the mechanics who had his head under a hood looked over as if on cue.

"We'd like to ask him about his shift last night," Paige interjected.

Dwayne looked at Paige. "What about it?"

Apparently, they'd have to give the man something to pry him open. "We're investigating a case he might be able to help us with."

Dwayne wrung the rag in his hands. "That's not good news."

Zach regarded the man, unsure what he meant by that. "Why's that?"

Dwayne stuffed the rag into one of the pockets of his coveralls. "Well, I tried to reach him this morning. Left him a message. I figured he was sleeping in, but..." Dwayne's brows scrunched up. "Is Dom all right?"

Good question. Now Zach wasn't so sure. "We don't know yet. Why were you trying to reach him?"

"Just wanted to ask him if he was up for overtime next week."

Zach nodded. "You said you figured he was probably sleeping in this morning? Does he normally work nights?"

"Uh-huh, that's right."

"Did he return the car after his shift last night?" Paige asked.

Dwayne looked at her. "He must have because it was in the lot when I got in this morning."

Zach frowned. "So he worked his entire shift?" It didn't make sense given what Stella had told them.

"Yeah, as far as I know."

"Who would know for sure?" Paige asked.

"Larry!" Dwayne bellowed over his shoulder.

The mechanic Zach had noted earlier trudged over. He was gangly, and his face was black with grease. "What's up, boss?"

"Did anyone fill in for Dom at any point last night?" Dwayne asked.

Larry's bottom lip came up over the top one, and he shook his head. "Not that I'm aware of." Larry shifted his gaze to Zach.

"Did you see Dominick when he returned his car from his shift last night?" Zach asked Larry.

"No. I was upstairs with Cindy figuring out a booking error."

Dwayne looked questioningly at Larry. "Is it all figured out?"

"Yes." Larry looked peaked. "But it wasn't so much a booking error..."

Dwayne's face flared red. "Explain."

"And it involved Dom," Larry said sheepishly.

"What happened?" Dwayne growled.

"Call came in about two thirty this morning to go out to Stella Bridges's place, but Dom didn't confirm pickup or drop-off."

Dwayne threw his hands in the air. "You sent another driver, I hope. The last thing we need is her pissed off at us."

Larry looked down at the concrete floor and scuffed the tip of his boot against it. "It wasn't caught until about three this morning—"

"Around the time Dom would have returned his car," Dwayne interrupted. "So you could have questioned him in person."

Dwayne was busy staring down his employee while the hairs were rising on the back of Zach's neck. Someone, whom Larry hadn't requested, had filled in for Dominick and didn't know to confirm pickup and drop-off? Or didn't want to? "How does confirming pickup and drop-off work?" Zach asked.

"The driver just calls into the office," Larry answered.

Paige glanced at Zach, then addressed Larry. "When was the last time Dominick *did* confirm a ride last night?"

"After he'd dropped Miss Bridges off at Magical Bar & Grill. It was nine thirty."

Dwayne's body stiffened. "You haven't heard from Dom since nine thirty last night?"

Larry stepped back, putting more space between himself and his boss.

Dwayne mumbled something incoherent, then said to Larry, "We'll talk later."

"Is it normal for Dominick to miss calling in his pickups and drop-offs?" Paige asked.

"No, and I was going to talk to Dom about it today," he added with a glance at Dwayne.

Zach had a bad feeling about this. Either Dominick was involved with Kelter's disappearance and went off the grid, or his mysterious fill-in had done something to him. "Do you show a pickup at Magical Bar & Grill at about eleven last night?"

"Miss Bridges called but canceled," Larry told them. "Said that one of our drivers was there already."

"And do you know who that was?" Zach asked.

"I assumed it was Dominick. His vehicle's GPS tracking system showed him there."

Stella's assumption it was Dominick's car in the bar's lot had been right.

"And he drives a…" Zach prompted, just to be sure.

"A white Chrysler 300," Dwayne finished.

"Did the GPS also show his car at Miss Bridges's for the two thirty call?" Paige asked.

Larry took a rag from his back pocket and wiped his forehead.

"Well?" Dwayne turned to look at him. "Did it?"

"I…don't know."

Dwayne pointed at the second-floor office. "Go find out. Now."

Larry ran off to carry out his boss's orders.

GPS might be able to put the car there, but it couldn't prove that Dominick was behind the wheel. "Do you have any video surveillance that might show Dom dropping off the vehicle?"

"The cameras in the lot are dummies to discourage vandalism and theft," Dwayne admitted.

Zach nodded, disappointed, but thankfully, they still had an avenue to explore with Bridges's security company.

"What's standard procedure when a car gets returned at the end of shift?" Paige asked.

Dwayne shrugged. "They just return it to the lot."

"What happens to the keys?" Zach wanted to know.

"Each car in my fleet is assigned to two drivers, and they hold on to the keys. There are two shifts per vehicle. Dom's is from seven in the evening until three in the morning. The other driver is Antonio Luna. He starts his shift at five in the morning and finishes at three thirty."

Zach checked his watch. It was two o'clock. "We're going to need you to call him back so we can talk to him and have the vehicle looked at."

Dwayne slid his gaze to Paige and crossed his arms. "I've been real cooperative, but I'd like to know what's going on now."

"We're still investigating, but it's possible your vehicle was used in a crime last night," Paige said.

Dwayne shook his head wildly. "No. No, there's no way. There wasn't any damage to it or I would have heard. Now, I can't stop you from talking to Antonio, but if you want to search my vehicle, I'll need to see that warrant. It's bad enough that I'd need to pull it from service. The last thing I need is word getting out that one of my cars was used for something—" Dwayne rolled his hand "—sinister. My business will be ruined."

Zach wasn't going to point out that if the vehicle was used in a crime, it would probably boost business. Sadly, macabre sells.

Before he had a chance to respond, Larry hustled toward them, all flailing arms and legs. He was panting when he reached them.

Dwayne looked disgustedly at his employee. "What is it?"

"The GPS in Dom's car went offline after last showing at Miss Bridges's at about eleven thirty."

"Dom disabled it?" Dwayne's nostrils flared. "And no one noticed this until now?"

Zach ignored Dwayne's last question and said, "Let me guess, he's never done that before."

Larry shook his head.

There was no doubt in Zach's mind that this had something to do with the anonymous driver who had been at the bar at eleven last night. "We appreciate your help." Zach let his gaze go to both men. "We'll be back with a warrant to search the car. For now, call it back and make sure no one else touches it, including the two of you."

Both men just nodded, and Zach and Paige headed back outside. When they reached the sidewalk, he turned to her. Her dire expression said what he'd been thinking: Dominick could very well be in danger.

CHAPTER EIGHTEEN

The techs found a shoe print and some fingerprints, as well as blood on the lever, some drops on the floor, and this." Marsh held up a small evidence bag that contained a piece of black plastic.

Marsh, Jack, and I were standing outside the restroom while the CSIs were still working inside.

"It's part of a phone," Marsh continued. "The only piece that was found. It was in the back corner of one of the stalls."

"So he smashed the phone and the dispenser. He was obviously blinded by rage from the phone call," I said. This only supported my conclusion that this guy was our unsub.

"He may have rushed out of here, but someone cleaned up," Marsh said.

"Jose said that Leslie had found the guy's date picking something off the floor," I reminded them, not sure if Marsh was around when the owner had said that.

"Her cleaning up after him tells me something else," Marsh started.

"Yeah. She could know more than we thought," Jack said and looked at me. "She might not just be in danger; she might be involved."

"Well, we've never been able to establish how and where the unsub abducted his victims," Marsh reasoned. "It's almost as though they vanish into air. No drugs showed on the tox screens for West or Sullivan. It's possible they were coerced at gunpoint or under threat, of course, but if a woman was working with the unsub, she'd be a lot less intimidating and threatening."

"They could have been persuaded any number of ways," I said. "We've lent credibility to the killer knowing the victims' routines, so he could have gotten close to them, built up trust." I wasn't ready to fully roll over to the girlfriend being involved just yet. "Organized killers are often in long-term relationships. The partners are usually oblivious to their mates' true natures."

Marsh ground her hands into her hips, the evidence bag dangling from her grip. "Sure, but there have been—and still are, I'm sure—partnerships among serial killers."

"Statistically, they are more likely to work alone," I rebutted, feeling a bit like a jerk, but I didn't care for a detective assuming the role of profiler and trying to show me up in front of Jack—again.

"*Statistically.*" Marsh paused. "But there are always exceptions to stat—"

Jack held up a hand, and Marsh stopped speaking. "None of this is getting us any closer to our unsub—or Kelter."

"Or the unsub's girlfriend," I added. "Think about it this way. If she had any idea what her boyfriend was up to, why would she pick up pieces of the phone *and* stick around? She would have hightailed it out of here, too, but she didn't."

"Yet she refused to wait for the cops." Marsh punctuated her stance with pressed lips and raised brows.

"She was afraid. Understandably so," I said. "And assuming she was in the dark about her boyfriend, she'd think he destroyed his own phone."

Marsh's eyes widened. "She wanted to smooth things over." Then she smirked. "She could be planning to get him a replacement, and if she does and she activates the phone, we can track her down."

"Wouldn't she need his cell provider and account information to do that?" I took pleasure in poking the tiny hole into Marsh's suggestion.

"Nope. Just a SIM card," Marsh replied without missing a beat.

"But she picked up all the pieces of the phone but the one you hold in your hand," I said.

"Either she didn't know that *or* she took them with her so we couldn't lift prints." Marsh raised her brows, stressing the fact she still hadn't released the girlfriend as a potential partner to our unsub.

"Doesn't explain the other prints left behind. Why not wipe everything down, including the towel dispenser?" I asked.

Jack paced a few steps and tapped his shirt pocket. "We just need to find the two of them."

He was obviously as frustrated as I was, and we might need to rely on forensic evidence to lead us to them. Then again, the man ran off. Was it simply a matter of escaping or was he unconcerned about the prints and DNA that he left behind? Or had the call thrown him off so much that he never even considered what he was leaving behind?

I took the evidence bag from Marsh and looked closely at the contents. "It's the bottom corner of an iPhone," I said, holding mine up next to it.

Marsh pursed her lips, and she quirked an eyebrow. "You do realize how many people have iPhones, don't you?"

"I never said that fact would lead us to him," I served back. "I was just making an observation. But you said they got some prints." I squared my shoulders and stared Marsh in the eye. "Any off this?"

"A partial thumbprint off *that*, yes." Marsh bobbed her head toward the evidence bag I was holding.

So he got the call, smashed the phone to the ground, punched the dispenser, and ran out of here. "You mentioned shoeprints and blood, so the girlfriend didn't try to clean up anything besides pieces of the phone?" I asked to confirm.

Marsh shook her head. "Doesn't look like it."

"See, right there," I said, starting to feel cocky. "She wasn't worried about the blood being tied to her boyfriend. If she had knowledge of his crimes or worked with him—"

"She would have been," Marsh finished.

"Right." I was a little stunned we agreed.

"And he wasn't worried about leaving trace behind because—" Marsh scowled "—he's not in the system."

"My earlier thoughts were leading me there," I confessed. "Let's hope she gets him a replacement like you mentioned."

"Doing so would fit with the kind of woman she seems to be—submissive, loyal, probably always wanting to make things right," Marsh reasoned.

"Well, if she sticks to the script, we're golden," I said.

"Yep. And she will." Marsh sounded confident, and it was abrasive.

"Guess we'll see."

"She will," she repeated. "And when it's activated, we'll have the bastard."

"We'll be closer," Jack corrected and looked at me. "Get the picture of him over to Zach and Paige."

"On it, boss." While I was sending off the message, Jack's phone rang. He answered, and as the seconds ticked by, I could feel that something was wrong. It only took one look at the set of Jack's jaw to tell me someone was dead.

CHAPTER NINETEEN

The dead body in front of Zach didn't match the picture he'd just received from Brandon, but it looked a lot like Dominick Banks.

Zach had spotted the body through the sidelight of the split-level bungalow Dominick rented. The corpse was supine on the floor and naked. His eyes were shut, and bruising marred the man's throat. He and Paige had gotten the building manager to let them inside, and they were waiting for the others inside the house while officers cordoned off the outside. Crime Scene and a medical examiner had been called, too.

"It's Dominick Banks. We found him just like this," Paige told Jack, Brandon, and Kelly once they arrived.

"Theories?" Jack requested.

Zach filled them in on his and Paige's visit to Checker Limousine.

"Get that warrant," Jack directed. "We need to look at that car."

"We've already got Nadia on the paperwork," Paige replied.

Jack nodded. "Do you think Banks was involved in Kelter's abduction?"

"He could have been partners with someone, but if so, they had a falling out," Zach reasoned.

"That's an understatement," Brandon lamented.

"Our unsub could have seen Banks as the easy way to get to Kelter," Brandon suggested, then added, "Though, he's never killed to get to his intended target before."

"That we know of," Marsh served back.

"If our unsub killed Banks to gain access to Kelter, it was a smart move on his part. Kelter would have gotten into the car, no questions asked," Paige said.

"Stella Bridges said she never saw the driver?" Jack sounded skeptical.

"She'd been drinking with Kelter," Paige replied. "She wasn't worried about who was behind the wheel."

"I can't believe she's drinking again," Brandon mumbled, and everyone looked at him. "She gets out of prison for DUI vehicular homicide and sidles right back up to a bar? One would think she'd have learned her lesson."

"Hence the driving service, Brandon," Paige said.

Regardless of Paige's counter, Zach could respect Brandon's viewpoint.

Silence draped over the room until Jack broke it.

"Different MO, but given circumstantial evidence— Banks's connection to Kelter—I think it's safe to assume our unsub is Banks's killer," Jack said.

"I agree," Zach chimed in.

"And you said Banks hadn't been heard from since nine thirty last night?" Jack asked.

"That's right," Paige replied. "But Banks's car was outside Magical Bar & Grill at eleven when Bridges and Kelter wanted to leave. The GPS in the car verifies this; the tracker wasn't disabled until after eleven thirty."

"After showing up at Bridges's house," Zach emphasized. "This guy's brazen. He obviously knew the vehicle was being tracked but didn't worry about it until he went to leave Bridges's."

"Okay, but when and how did Banks end up here?" Brandon asked, pointing at the body.

"That's a loaded question," Zach started. "Paige and I found out Banks's last confirmed fare was nine thirty, when he dropped Bridges off at the bar." Zach went on to explain the business's process of confirming pickups and drop-offs. "By eleven his car is in the bar's lot with a different driver. That means—"

"He was likely killed between nine thirty and eleven," Brandon concluded.

"Right, but that doesn't mean he dropped the body off right away. All we know is Banks's car was back in the Checker's lot by five in the morning," Zach said.

"That also gave the unsub time to drop Kelter off wherever he's holding her," Paige said. "We assume he must have picked her up at Bridges's at two thirty when there was a call placed with Checker."

"But you said the tracker was disabled after eleven thirty?" Jack asked. "And the last confirmed fare was nine thirty?"

Zach nodded.

"We need to get the GPS records from nine thirty to eleven thirty. That might help us figure out where he was killed. I don't think it was here." Brandon's gaze went to the floor. "It doesn't look like there was a struggle."

"And given the violence of the attack, that's surprising," Kelly tacked on.

"Uh-huh," Brandon replied.

Zach smiled at the fact that they agreed. A sibling rivalry seemed to exist between them, both fawning for Jack's affection. Both driven, both capable law enforcement officers. Little boys and girls really lived inside all of us—our bodies just got larger.

"If he wasn't killed here, then where?" Paige asked.

"That's something we need to figure out. Looking at the Checker car might help. We also have to speak with that other driver who has the keys," Jack said.

"We intend to," Zach told him.

Paige nodded. "We pulled his background before coming here. Not a blemish."

"And before either of you ask, his DMV photo doesn't match the man from the restaurant," Zach added.

"Though, he could be working with him," Jack countered. "You should go drag him in—"

"I was told someone was just dying to see me." A woman with a pleasant smile stepped into the living room carrying a bag. Her long black hair was pulled back into a ponytail, and she was easily in her late forties, maybe older given the experience in her chocolate eyes. But it was also clear she took care of herself. She was slender, and her dark complexion was glowing.

"It's true," Kelly said, tossing out a smile.

Zach had worked around medical examiners and coroners long enough to know they all acquired morgue humor. It bordered on macabre and inappropriate, but it was one of the ways they dealt with the death they encountered every day.

The ME's gaze flicked to each of them, and she smiled, the expression lighting up her eyes. "I'm Lillian Paul. My friends call me Lily." She held out a hand to Brandon first.

"Spec—" He cleared his throat. "Agent Brandon Fisher."

Zach smirked. Brandon had a thing about including his full title whenever he introduced himself. Maybe he was finally realizing how obnoxious it could come across.

"Ah, I'm sure you're *special*, too." Lillian winked at Brandon. She certainly was friendly, and it would be easy to think of her as Lily. She shook everyone's hand, then looked at Kelly. "Did I beat the CSIs again?"

"Yeah."

"Hold up, we're here." Two CSIs came into the room, introduced themselves, and got to work. Processing would take them awhile, longer than Zach—or any of them—had the luxury of standing around for, but it would be nice to be brought up to speed on something. Time of death, for one.

Everyone but the CSIs stood to the side of the room while they processed the area around the body.

"Do we have an ID on the vic?" Lily asked no one in particular.

"We believe him to be Dominick Banks, thirty-five," Kelly began. "We also believe he was murdered by a serial killer we're tracking."

Lily screwed up an eyebrow. "A serial killer?"

"I know you don't like to get caught up in hypotheticals—" Kelly rushed out.

"I prefer science because it's based on facts," Lily said. "And to make an unbiased conclusion about any crime, I need to assess things as I see them." The medical examiner had a reverential way she went about soaking in the scene, and Zach respected that. He also had a mind that worked well with facts, statistics, and logic-based reasoning, but he'd come to appreciate that sometimes those things were mere barometers and didn't exclusively stand on their own. There were always exceptions and anomalies. And as a profiler, all too often their initial assumptions were proven false.

The CSIs backed up from the body and told Lily she could "have at it."

She snapped on some gloves and touched Banks's face. Her fingertips pressed around his throat, nose, and eyes. "His eyes have been glued shut."

"Just like previous victims," Kelly blurted.

"This man was strangled," Lily said. "Does that align with previous MOs?"

Kelly shook her head. "In those cases, COD was decapitation."

"Oh. Then why do you think the same killer did this?" Lily gestured toward the body.

Zach provided Lily with a brief overview and added, "Our killer doesn't shy away from making public spectacles of his victims. Their heads are usually delivered or dropped off in boxes. Here, it's not as public, but Banks has been put on display." Zach was thinking specifically about the fact that the man had been stripped naked. "He might have been left in his home, but I could see the body clearly through the front sidelights. A display," Zach reiterated.

"The killer wanted him found," Brandon offered.

"Seems that way to me," Zach agreed.

"The others were decapitated, and the rest of their bodies were never found." Kelly let her comment hang, then clarified her point. "Our unsub has never been about hiding the identity of his victims. He's always left their teeth intact and never mutilated their faces, making identification easy. Really, if you think about it, our unsub leaving the whole body here isn't much of a leap. It is a display as Zach said." Kelly glanced at Zach.

"When was TOD?" he asked Lily.

"He's in full rigor," Lily said, pressing her hands to the body. "All I can say right now is he died at least twelve hours ago."

Zach consulted his watch. *3:30 PM.* "Our assumption Banks was killed sometime between nine thirty and eleven could still work." He turned to Lily. "Could you give us a better indication on TOD?"

"Possibly." Lily put on a pair of gloves and snapped some photos of Banks. She then proceeded to make a small incision in the abdomen and pierced a thermometer into Banks's liver. She said, "Can one of you get the temperature in here?"

Kelly walked over to the thermostat and called out its reading.

"All right." After a few more seconds, Lily removed the thermometer and scribbled the reading in a notebook. Her face contorted as she figured out the math. "This man died anywhere between fourteen and twenty hours ago."

Zach sighed. He'd been hoping for something a little more precise. Then again, depending on where Banks had been killed and the temperature of that environment...

"Well, I think we can discard one assumption we'd made," Kelly began. "Banks's murder isn't an indication that the unsub is escalating. Banks was dead before the killer was spooked by the call to Kelter's phone. And you know what that means?" She let her gaze land on each of them. "We said before that our unsub never killed anyone else to get to an intended victim, but we can't know that for sure. And if that's the case, how many other victims are we looking at?"

"I want the answer to that." Jack pulled out his phone. "I'm having Nadia see what she can find for murders in Miami similar to this one. Maybe something will pop that will connect the murders and lead us to our unsub."

Zach looked at Lily, who'd gone back to working on the body.

Jack was talking to Nadia in the background.

Lily rolled the body. "Oh."

Zach moved in closer.

"He didn't die in this position. See the lividity." She pointed to where the blood was pooled on the side of his right arm and torso, giving the skin there a purplish hue.

Zach hadn't seen it before now because that side had been facing the fireplace. Lividity was a telltale sign of the positioning of the body in the first couple of hours after death. If Banks had died faceup, lividity would show on his lower back, buttocks, backs of his arms, and elbows.

"As we'd considered earlier, he wasn't killed here," Zach concluded.

Jack hung up. "We know for sure now?"

Everyone nodded.

Zach added, "And wherever Banks was killed, his body was kept on its side for a couple of hours after death."

"That tells me that the killer didn't drop off the body until after situating Kelter," Brandon said. "The killer could have kept the body in the trunk until then."

Zach nodded. "Could be, and there's a lot less eyeballs in the wee hours. There'd be a lot less chance of being seen and getting caught."

"Our unsub has to be strong to cart a dead body around," Kelly said. "Even if it was just from a vehicle into here."

"I agree," Zach responded.

"Going back to our conversation about the killer wanting to create a display," Brandon started. "It would have just been easier to dump Banks's body somewhere. He wanted it to be found. Otherwise why take him to his house?"

"All right, we have a lot of angles to explore." Jack clapped his hands once. "Brandon and I will talk to the neighbors, see if they saw or heard anything. Zach and Paige, you two get back over to Checker Limousine, talk to the Antonio guy, and get CSIs working over the car. Also get those GPS records."

Zach nodded. "Consider it done."

"We'll meet up at the station after we're all finished and regroup," Jack went on.

"I'd like to get a map started and see if we can establish an activity radius for this unsub," Kelly volunteered. "I'd hoped to have had it finished before you arrived."

"Sounds good."

For the first time, Jack didn't smile at the detective's initiative. It was probably only temporary. He likely just wanted to get this case solved and find Kelter before it was too late. It was starting to feel like for every step forward in the case, they took two back—if not more.

CHAPTER TWENTY

Dwayne Spencer was standing with hands on hips when Zach and Paige entered Checker Limousine. "I was hoping the evidence would lead you somewhere else," he said.

"I'm afraid not," Paige replied.

Dwayne's face paled. "What is it?"

In ideal circumstances, the next of kin was the first informed, but sometimes exceptions had to be made. Zach made eye contact with Dwayne. "We found Dominick, and he's—"

The man's mouth fell open. "He's…?"

"We're sorry to inform you, but Dominick is dead. He was murdered." Zach laid it out there, sticking to the cold, hard facts but delivering them with kindness.

Dwayne put a hand to his forehead and spun slowly in a circle. "No, this can't be happening. It doesn't make any sense. Why would anyone want to kill him?"

"We were wondering if you'd know," Paige said gently. It was a logical counter, but it was unlikely that Banks had known his killer.

He shook his head. "No. He was a nice guy. He was always on time, did his job. Never got any complaints from him. The other guys, they bitch all the time."

"We're sorry for your loss." The sentiment, which was intended as genuine, stuck to Zach's heart like a burr. He'd spoken that line so many times over the years, he wondered if the repetition had dulled its meaning.

Dwayne nodded his head slowly. "The car's in the back."

"Before we go…" Zach's words had the man halting and looking at him. "We need to know if any of these men look familiar." Zach took out his phone and brought up an array of men's photos that included their unsub. He extended the phone to Dwayne.

Dwayne regarded him and the phone with hesitation. Eventually, he reached for it.

"Take your time," Zach told him. If Dwayne did recognize the unsub and *how* he knew the guy was useful to the prosecution of the case, he could be called to testify. That's where the photo array versus a single picture came into play. The response wouldn't be prejudiced, and Zach wouldn't have burned a witness.

Dwayne pinched his fingers to the screen, enlarging and shrinking the image. About a minute passed before he gave the phone back to Zach. "I've never seen any of these men." He rubbed above his left eye. "Did one of them kill Dom?"

"We're still investigating," Paige replied, drawing the man's gaze.

"You obviously think one of them did," Dwayne said sadly.

"We do." Paige made the admission on an exhale, and it had Zach turning to look at her. This case was wearing on her. Her eyes were slightly bloodshot. Her hair, which normally fell in soft curls, was lying rather limp, and Zach felt it had little to do with the humidity. Her shoulders, which were typically high and back, were lowered and hunched forward, too.

"Well, I hope you find the son of a bitch because Dom didn't deserve this." Dwayne's cheeks reddened as his anger surfaced.

"We'll do our best to bring Dominick justice," Zach said.

The front door opened, and two CSIs entered. One was in his late fifties with a thin frame except for a small beer belly. The other was in his thirties with a mustache and a pleasant smile.

"And so it begins," Dwayne lamented.

Zach and Paige introduced themselves to the investigators.

Beer Belly held out his hand. "Ken Trevors, and this is Alan Bury."

Alan gave a mock salute in greeting.

"Now that everyone knows everyone, follow me." Dwayne took off through the door to the back. Sadness and anger emanated from the man as the four of them followed him into the garage.

"Well, this is it." Dwayne pointed to the only white Chrysler 300 in the garage.

Zach pulled out the search warrant and handed it to Dwayne, who took it and stuffed it into his back pocket without so much as looking at it. "I'm sorry, but the car needs to be kept out of service until it's been fully processed," Zach said.

"And depending on what we find," Ken chimed in, "we might need to take the car with us."

"Do whatever you need to. The keys are on the front seat." Dwayne sounded defeated and waved a hand toward the second-floor office. "Antonio's in my office. Should he have a lawyer present?"

"There shouldn't be any need for that," Zach told him. "We just have a couple questions for him."

Dwayne nodded and led the way to the office. The space was what one would expect for being over a garage. No surface would pass the white-glove test. Dust was everywhere, the level of grime indicating it hadn't been cleaned in months. A simple executive desk shared the space with a couple of file cabinets, a swivel chair, and a few molded plastic chairs with steel legs. A man was sitting in one, slouched down, reading a book. He closed the mystery novel when they shadowed the doorway. Zach had a feeling the man wouldn't care for the genre as much once murder touched his reality.

"Agents, this is Antonio Luna," Dwayne said. Zach was impressed by how well the owner was holding himself together given the news that had been unloaded on him.

Antonio stood and tucked the book under an arm. Zach and Paige gave Antonio their names.

Dwayne cleared his throat and locked eyes with Zach. "Can I tell him?"

Zach nodded. "If you'd like to be the one to do so, that's fine."

"Dom was murdered." Dwayne served it quickly, and Antonio gasped.

"Are you being serious right now?" Antonio asked, eyes wide and darting.

"Unfortunately, yes," Zach replied.

"Why? What happened? Do you know who did it?" The stream of questions rushed from the driver.

"Let's just sit down and talk for a bit." Zach sat in one of the chairs across the room from where Antonio now stood, and Paige took a seat beside Zach.

Dwayne jacked a thumb toward the door. "Should I go or…?"

"Can he stay?" Antonio rushed out.

"He can, if that's what you want," Paige responded.

Antonio nodded, sitting back down, and Dwayne rounded his desk and sat in the chair there.

Paige crossed her legs and leaned in toward Antonio. "We just have a few questions."

"Whatever it is, I'll do my best to help." Antonio held his book flat in his lap with both hands gripping the spine.

"Was anything different about the car when you picked it up for your shift today?" Zach asked, starting there.

"Not that I noticed."

"What about a different smell to the car? Were there any dominant scents in the air?" Zach's question was a reach. Everyone had their own distinct smell and no doubt the car would absorb a cacophony of fragrances from the fares, but maybe, just maybe, their unsub had left a distinct odor behind.

Antonio scrunched up his brow. "Umm, I'm not sure."

"Where was the car parked when you picked it up?" Paige asked.

"In its usual spot in the lot. Nothing stood out to me at all. I just got in and got to work."

"So you worked your whole shift from behind the wheel?" Zach queried.

"Of course."

"No need to go in the back seat or the trunk?" Zach was just being proactive. They still didn't know where Banks was killed, but they'd ruled out his home. To transport the body, the unsub could have put it in the trunk as Brandon had suggested. It could explain the positioning of the lividity. Crime Scene could verify all this, assuming they did find forensic evidence.

Antonio glanced at his boss, then looked at Zach. "No, I just stayed in the driver's seat. Oh, I set my lunch bag on the floor of the front passenger's side."

"Okay, good to know," Zach said, not even sure if it would factor in, but best to be armed with more knowledge than less.

"How well did you know Dominick?" Paige asked.

Antonio shook his head. "Not very well. With his shift starting a couple hours after mine, we rarely crossed paths. When we did, we'd say, 'Hi, how you doin'?' and things like that, but no real conversation."

Zach nodded and pulled up the photo array on his phone again. He caught Dwayne's eyes as he did, and angst etched the owner's facial features. Zach walked his phone over to Antonio. "Do any of these men look familiar to you?"

Antonio studied the images. "Can't say that they do." He squinted. "I'm guessing that's not what you want to hear."

"All we want is the truth." Zach gave Antonio a tight but hopefully reassuring smile.

"We were told that a driver filled in for Dominick last night around eleven," Paige said, flicking a look at the owner.

Dwayne's posture stiffened, but he remained silent.

"What do you know about that?" Paige turned her attention to Antonio. "Did Dominick have people step in for him before?"

"Not that I'm aware of." Antonio's gaze skipped to his boss, and Zach wondered if the answer would be different without Dwayne in the room. "But that's not a part of my job to know," Antonio added.

"It is important that you tell us the truth," Zach said, essentially reiterating his earlier statement.

"The truth is, I don't really know." Antonio frowned.

"Okay, that's fine. Thanks for your help." Zach pulled a card from his pocket and handed it to Antonio. "If you do think of anything at all, call me."

Antonio took the card and tucked it between the pages of his book. He tilted his head toward Dwayne, and with that, he got up and left the room.

Dwayne leaned back and clasped his hands over his stomach. "He seems to be taking Dom's death better than I am."

Zach hadn't thought either man was handling it well. "We all process loss differently," was all Zach said.

"I suppose." Dwayne took a pen and tapped its tip against the top of his desk.

"We're going to need something else from you," Zach said, pulling a second warrant from his pocket and handing it over to the owner. "We need access to the GPS records for Dominick's car, as well as the call log from his shift."

"We've been quite open with you, but you want more still." Dwayne's jaw clenched. "Very well. I'll get it together for you." He rolled toward his desk and started clicking away on his keyboard.

Zach and Paige excused themselves and went to check on how the CSIs were making out with the car.

Ken was sealing up some lifted prints on a piece of clear plastic the size of an index card. "It's a print gold mine in there."

If their unsub had been there, he hadn't bothered to wipe the vehicle down. Though that would have been more suspicious. Not that prints would necessarily get them anywhere in identifying their unsub anyway. Zach wasn't holding his breath. It was either panic and not thinking clearly that made the unsub leave the trace behind, or he didn't fear it leading to his identity.

"That's half to be expected," Paige said.

"We're just getting started here. Sorry there's not much more to say at this point." Ken pressed his lips together and ducked his head and arms back into the car.

Zach looked around for Alan and found him leaning inside the trunk. Zach moved toward him, but neither he nor Paige said anything to disturb him. Alan was collecting something from the carpet with a pair of tweezers.

"Should we go?" Paige asked.

"Let me just grab the reports from Dwayne." Zach trudged back to the owner, his steps heavy. Forensics played an important role in solving murders, just as profiling did in finding killers. Sadly, both felt like they took far too long sometimes.

CHAPTER TWENTY-ONE

The face from the restaurant video was haunting me, even with the fresh download of Dominick Banks's crime scene. I knew that face from somewhere, and not knowing where was going to drive me mad. It was sort of like when you tried to remember the name of a movie or an actor and it wouldn't come to you. Or even worse, when it's just the glimpse of an image or the trace of a thought and you couldn't even come up with the right words for Google to find the answer for you. Until I figured out why he looked familiar—whether he made me think of someone I'd seen in my life or someone who came up within the confines of the case—it was going to eat away at me.

The four of us, plus Marsh, were in the conference room back at the station. She was standing in front of a map of Miami that was attached to a whiteboard with black magnets in the corners. Small, colored magnetic pins were scattered on the map. Marsh was prepared to school us on geography.

Jack and I had briefed everyone on how we'd made out with Banks's neighbors, which hadn't been great. In fact, they hadn't produced any leads. No one saw or heard anything. It was like the unsub we were after was a ghost.

"I've read the GPS report from Checker Limousine. It shows the car going to Magical Bar & Grill at nine thirty, like we figured it would, but it didn't leave until eleven when it went to Bridges's, where the car showed at around eleven thirty. From there it goes dead, just as they told us at Checker," Zach said.

"Banks was killed in the bar's parking lot," I said.

"Looks like," Zach replied.

"So our unsub obviously dropped off Banks's body after he'd disabled the tracker and before he returned the car. It was sometime during the wee hours, as we thought. That's probably why none of the neighbors saw anything," I reasoned. "They'd be asleep."

"Okay, the call log gave us a little more than we'd expected," Paige said. "There were a few pickups on Bridges's account, starting with a pickup at Kelter's house at eleven thirty yesterday morning." Paige glanced at Zach and Marsh. "There was also a pickup at a movie theater at three forty-five yesterday afternoon."

"So Kelter did go to the movies," Zach said.

Paige nodded. "It would seem so. She got to Bridges's at four fifteen. Next call charged to Bridges's account was a pickup at her house at eight thirty."

"About the time Bridges said that Kelter got restless and went ahead to the bar," Marsh chimed in.

"Yes." Paige pointed her finger at Marsh and smiled. "Then the pickup for Bridges at the hospital and the drop-off at nine thirty at the bar."

"Good," Jack said. "And how did Crime Scene make out?"

"They were still working over the vehicle when we left to come back here," Zach replied. "The lead CSI said they'd be at it for a while. They might even bring the vehicle in to examine in more depth."

Jack turned to Marsh. "All right. Tell us what you have."

Marsh pointed to a red pin on the map. "That's La Casa de Jose." She pointed to another pin. "Miami-Dade County Courthouse, where West's head was left." Another pin. "Hanover & Smith, LLP, where Sullivan's head was delivered."

"All in the downtown area," I said. "Within nine city blocks."

"It would indicate he is comfortable in the area, possibly lives or work around there." Paige reached for the water pitcher and filled her glass. She took a quick sip and added,

"Hanover & Smith represented Sullivan specifically, but both trials were heard at Miami-Dade County Courthouse. I'm sure Kelter's was, too."

Marsh nodded.

"Could there be something to that? Maybe our unsub has a past connection to the courthouse?" Paige wondered aloud, glancing at Marsh.

"Likely a broad sweep," Marsh said. "All DUI offenses for the area would be tried there."

"I was afraid you were going to say that." Paige blew out a breath that had her bangs flying up.

There was something to Paige's statement. "He liked the courthouse for his first platform," I said, "but didn't return there with Sullivan's head. As we know, her head was delivered directly to her lawyer. He took a more brazen approach. He wasn't content to just drop her head off, he wanted it hand-delivered. I think he wanted to make more of a splash, an impact, with his second victim."

"Having the entire city see the report about the head on the courthouse steps wasn't enough to satisfy him?" Marsh argued, testing my patience.

I was about to rebut when Zach said, "I think Brandon might be right. The courthouse steps weren't intimate enough, *personal* enough."

Bathed in validation and loving the feeling, I went on. "By delivering Sullivan's head to the lawyer's office, was it also meant as a threat to the lawyer? We know that Kelter had received hate mail and so had West, so who's to say that the lawyers didn't get any directed at them?" I leveled my gaze on Marsh, curious if she'd ever looked into the matter.

"I think we're getting off topic here. Let's stay focused." With that, Jack brought any warm and gooey feelings I had to an end. He got up and traced the nine-block perimeter with a finger. "So we can see our unsub gravitates to this area, but where do the victims live?"

Marsh pointed out three blue pins and rattled off the surnames as she went along. "All three are outside of the activity radius."

"Where's Bridges's place on the map?" I asked.

"Here." Marsh put a fingertip to a green pin. It was outside the activity radius, too.

Jack got to his feet and paced. "Where were West's and Sullivan's accidents?"

"West's was at the corner of Northeast First Avenue and Northeast Second Street." Marsh pointed to a yellow pin on the board. "That's only two blocks from West's campus."

"It's also to the west on Northeast First Street," Zach said. "Whereas Kelter's church is to the east."

"Yes, that's correct," Marsh said. "West and his friends had been drinking at Club One on Northwest First Street and Northeast Second Avenue." This time a purple pin.

Marsh was nothing if not a slave to color coding. Red for disposal sites and the restaurant where our presumed unsub had been. Blue pins for victims' homes. Green for Bridges's residence. Yellow for accident sites. Purple for the victims' drinking spots.

Speaking of…

"Both West and Kelter were drinking in the downtown area," I noted.

"Yes. Even Sullivan had drinks at Rendezvous, here." Marsh indicated the intersection of West Flagler Street and North Miami Avenue. "And her accident was here." A yellow pin marked West Flagler and Northwest First Avenue.

"Near the courthouse," I observed.

"Yes. Kitty-corner," Marsh confirmed.

I focused on the map, willing myself to come up with something brilliant. My gaze went to the green pin for Bridges's home and the yellow pin for Kelter's accident. They were a fair distance apart. "I thought Kelter had dropped Bridges off the night of the accident."

Marsh traced out a route on the map that went from the bar to Bridges's to the accident site. "Everything related to the accidents happened within this radius." Marsh moved her finger around the map, circling everything from the college campus in the north to Southwest First Street in the south and Northeast Second Avenue in the east and Northwest First Avenue in the west, extending out to include the victims' and Bridges's homes.

"So we're just looking at a bit of a larger activity radius," I said.

"About thirty-three square blocks," Zach said, having counted everything that quickly.

My gaze was fixed on the map, and my mind was on the locations of the accidents. "They were close enough that maybe—"

Jack raised his brows. "What were close enough?"

I could have just said the *accidents* were close enough and went on to share my point. But with everyone staring at me, I had swallowed the word *accidents* as a jagged lump. "I have a hard time calling them accidents." The back of my neck stiffened, prepared for a debate.

"What else would they be?" Paige narrowed her eyes. "Do you think they were intentional?"

"I think they could have been prevented."

Paige groaned. "You can't relate to drinking and getting behind the wheel or even thinking about doing so? Maybe a friend has stopped you from doing it in the past?"

I glanced at Jack and the others. None of them were about to jump in. Jack must have had a reason for letting Paige and me talk this out.

"So?" Paige's eyes challenged me.

She didn't know I'd driven under the influence briefly when I was younger or how it had changed my perspective on drinking and driving. But with her steady eye contact, another memory surfaced. It had been my first case with the BAU, and it had taken us to Florida, as well. I'd gone out with Paige, and we'd met up with an old friend of mine. We'd had some wings and beers, and she'd had to reinforce that I wasn't fit to drive.

Jack took a seat, leaned back, and clasped his hands. It was apparent he wasn't going to stop us anytime soon.

I felt my cheeks heat. "There's a difference between thinking about it and actually doing it."

"And what's that difference?" Paige paused, jutting out her chin. "A good friend who is there to help you realize that you shouldn't drive? What if a friend like that isn't around? What if everyone you are with is tipsy? There wouldn't be any sound judgment in the bunch of you. Is it plausible, then, that you'd get behind the wheel?"

Now I knew how defendants felt on the stand. "It's plausible, but I don't see myself doing it."

"*But* it's plausible. So let's say the person has a little less resolve than you do or they really don't think they're feeling it. They get behind the wheel—" Paige walked her fingers across the table "—and off they go." She swept her hand across the surface. "Then they get into an accident. Do you consider them a horrible person? A monster? Or do you extend some mercy and see them as a fallible human being who made an error in judgment?" Paige's cheeks were red and her jaw tight.

"I view them as making a horrible *choice*."

"Ah." Paige pointed a finger at me. "But is it really a choice? Are they even thinking about whether or not they should drive?"

"They sure as hell should be," I shot back, my temper fully ignited.

"If they were sober enough, aware enough to make a choice, then yes, if they get into an accident and kill someone, that's a different story. But with most people who get behind the wheel intoxicated, it's not premeditated."

"If they know they're going to drink, they should make transportation arrangements ahead of time." I bit back saying that that's what designated drivers were for. "That's all I'm saying."

"You're missing the point," Paige said with a groan.

"All right. That's enough," Jack barked. "You both feel strongly on the matter, and I've let you get it out."

I was having a hard time getting a satisfying breath despite heaving for air. My nostrils were flaring. My core was overheating. A pulse was throbbing in my cheek. And my gaze was locked on Paige.

"But it doesn't matter how either of you feel." Jack shot to his feet. "What matters is how our killer views drunk drivers." Jack glanced at me. "I'd say he probably views them the way you do, Brandon."

For some reason, hearing that made me feel somewhat victorious. Though what did I win? I was right, and Paige was wrong?

Jack turned to me. "So why do you feel so strongly?"

I detected judgment and responded quickly. "Because it's wrong."

"No personal experience with the matter?" Jack pressed.

I certainly wasn't about to share my personal history, even if it proved helpful. And I didn't see how it would. Saying it had happened to a friend wouldn't fly in this room, either. "No. It's just something wired into me, I guess."

"Well, I doubt it's as simple as that for our unsub," Jack said. "Something in his life triggered him to take things as far as he does." He took a few steps.

"I'd say that's a good assumption," Marsh replied, cutting through the tension in the room.

Paige and I kept looking at each other but we'd both glance away to hide it. Why was *she* so opinionated on the matter? Was the matter personal to her or was she protecting someone?

"It probably wouldn't hurt to take a closer look at the families affected by the people West and Sullivan killed to see if we find this guy," Jack stated. "We have a picture now, so maybe they'll recognize him?"

I know I certainly did, but I still couldn't pinpoint why. I looked at the printout of the still from the restaurant security video. I got up and walked to the board.

"What is it?" Jack asked.

"I recognize him."

Paige snickered, and I cut her a glare.

She held up her hands and smiled. "What? We all do."

If we were alone, I'd call her a smart-ass. "I meant from somewhere other than the restaurant."

"Close your eyes," Zach directed me.

"I don't want to—"

"Do it."

I closed them.

"Now answer my questions quickly," he instructed. "Does his face look familiar to you?"

"Yes."

"Does it have to do with La Casa de Jose?"

"Yes."

"Because of anything else?"

My eyes sprung open. "I've got it. You're a genius, Zach."

"So I've been told." Zach smiled.

I brought up the video from Magical Bar & Grill and fast-forwarded to where the man had come up to Kelter at the bar. I pointed proudly to the screen. "That's him."

"The man who was trying to pick up Kelter," Jack said, looking deflated that he hadn't pieced it together. "I didn't—"

"We were focused on Stella Bridges," I assured him. My gaze drifted to the black-and-white photo on the whiteboard of the person in the hoodie. I kept my focus on the image while my mind pulled up mental replays of the videos from Magical Bar & Grill and the one that captured the drop-off on the courthouse steps. My heart sped up as I made a conclusion. "I think our unsub delivered West's head himself."

CHAPTER TWENTY-TWO

The room went silent after my epiphany—not one of them challenging what I'd deduced. They must have seen it too.

"We can place our unsub at Magical Bar & Grill," I said.

"At nine, Brandon," Paige began. "But Banks dropped Bridges off at nine thirty."

"Around the same time our unsub left his stool," I said.

"How could he know he'd catch Banks?" Marsh asked.

"I don't have all the answers." I shook my head. "But we know from the GPS records that Banks's vehicle was in the bar's lot from nine thirty until eleven. Our unsub left not long after Bridges came in."

"I know we figured earlier that Banks was likely killed in the parking lot, but no one saw a thing?" Skepticism licked Paige's tone.

"I don't know how he pulled it all off yet," I admitted. "The restaurant doesn't have security video outside, but maybe we should take a physical look around the lot? We might find something useful."

"You're assuming the car and Banks were in the lot. He could have dropped Bridges off out front," Paige suggested.

"I'm just talking out a theory," I said.

"Brandon," Marsh started, "you were going to say something a bit ago about the geography of the accidents? Before the debate about drinking and driving?"

I stared at her, trying to remember. "Oh right. All the accidents happened in a close vicinity. I was wondering if West, Sullivan, and Kelter were all treated at the same hospital."

"West and Sullivan were treated at the same hospital. I assume the same holds true for Kelter," Marsh said. "Looking at the hospital didn't lead anywhere with West and Sullivan, but I can look into it again and with Kelter."

"It's probably a good idea," Jack said.

It was hard to fight a smile. "Look into EMTs, doctors, nurses," I added. "Maybe we'll get lucky and one of them is our unsub."

"I've got it, Brandon," Marsh said. "All the accidents took place between eleven and three in the morning, too. I know there are years between the accidents, but it could possibly put the unsub on the same shift."

"We could expand our search for this guy to anyone whose job could have brought them to the scene," Zach reasoned. "City workers? There'd be need for redirecting traffic, possibly shutting off power. Reporters?"

"Actually, Marsh, I'm going to get Nadia to see if she can find any name that comes up more than once for the occupations we've mentioned." Jack began. "Why don't you go speak with Bridges's security company and see if you can get the footage from this morning."

Marsh nodded. "I can do—"

The door to the room burst open, and a man walked in with three men tailing him. Two of them wore earpieces.

The man in the lead was broad shouldered and barrel chested. He wore a tailored suit, and given its styling, I'd say it didn't come off any rack at a department store.

"Please, Mayor Conklin," the man in the back said. "If we could just—"

Conklin spun and jabbed a meaty finger toward the man, making him flush. "I demand an update on my niece's whereabouts. I heard that someone answered her phone, that you have a suspect."

Jack got to within six inches of Conklin. "We're working on tracking him down."

"And who are you?" Conklin challenged.

"Supervisory Special Agent Jack Harper and this—" Jack gestured to Paige, Zach, and me "—is my team, from the FBI Behavioral Analysis Unit."

"What do you know? It wasn't smoke and mirrors. You did get them down here." Conklin's facial expression soured as he looked at the man without an earpiece. We were all looking at him.

Marsh stepped in. "This is Sergeant Lucas Ramirez."

Ramirez held out his hand to Jack. He didn't reach for it, and the sergeant squirmed.

"And I'm Walter Conklin, the mayor of Miami." He didn't bother with formalities, likely seeing how well that had worked for the sergeant.

"I could tell right away that you are the one in charge here," Conklin added, as if trying to smooth over his earlier brashness.

"What matters is finding Jenna," Jack said, unmoved.

"See?" Conklin's face lit up, and he pointed at Jack as he looked at Ramirez. "That's what I'm talking about—a man who takes action." Turning back to Jack, he said, "Now, who is the man who answered my niece's phone?"

"As I said, we're working on tracking him down." Jack remained firm.

"You're all doing that while sitting around here?" Conklin's gaze went to the table and an open box of donuts.

"Have one if you'd like," Jack offered calmly.

"No thanks." Conklin patted his flat stomach. "Are you close to catching him? To getting Jenna back?"

"Are you close to your niece?" Jack asked him, completely sidestepping the mayor's questions.

Conklin hesitated, then said, "Sure. She is family. But I'm not sure why my relationship with her matters right now."

"If you really care about her, you'll leave and let us do our jobs."

Score one for Jack.

Conklin straightened out his tie and stepped away from Jack.

"Mayor Conklin, let's go talk in my office." Sergeant Ramirez walked over to the mayor.

Conklin held his ground, chest heaving. His eyes were fixed on Jack. "I appreciate you being here and doing all you can." Conklin made the comment through clenched teeth and then let Ramirez guide him out of the room.

Jack closed the door behind them and spun, fixing his gaze directly on Marsh. "I see that Ramirez and the mayor are tight."

"Don't get me started," Marsh snarled. "But if you're thinking he's how the mayor found out about the call, I'm sure you're right."

CHAPTER TWENTY-THREE

Kelly had shot a man in the line of duty once. It had been a domestic call that had gone south, and it had come down to her life or that of a man who'd pulled a gun on her. She hadn't given it any thought; she'd just reacted. The bullet had caught him between the eyes—instant death.

The brass had ordered all the required steps to get her back to active duty, but the psych evaluation proved the hardest to pass. She'd met with a shrink for weeks but hadn't been able to get clearance because he'd claimed she was suppressing her feelings. What the good doctor couldn't appreciate was that Kelly had felt nothing—not regret, not fear, not a sense of her own mortality. *Nothing*. It wasn't until she played things up as if she had been traumatized that she had received approval to return to work. Deceiving the doctor wasn't something she was proud of, but it had been necessary.

She'd learned that her true feelings about having killed someone were a secret best kept to herself. People would either look at her with sympathetic eyes as if she were in denial or think she was a psychopath. While she could live with them questioning her sanity—it never hurt to keep people guessing—she didn't need anyone's pity. She'd done what needed to be done. Simple as that. And, sure, she'd dreamed about the incident periodically, but it was always a black-and-white replay of what had happened. Maybe a doctor would argue that the lack of color was an indication that she'd been traumatized or something, but she took it as her being at peace with it.

But now her finger was itching to pull the trigger again. Ramirez had really crossed the line this time. Sharing sensitive case information with someone outside the department? He should have his badge stripped. But nothing would happen to the man. He was untouchable, and he knew it.

Jack's phone rang, and he answered on speaker. "Talk to us."

"Hey, guys and gal," the female caller said.

"Two gals," Kelly spoke up. "Detective Kelly Marsh."

"Oh, Nadia Webber. Nice to hear your voice," Nadia replied. "I received Kelter's financials that you forwarded to me, by the way. I also have her phone records."

"Did you get anything helpful from either?" Jack asked.

"Not sure if it's useful," Nadia said. "I saw the charge at Magical Bar & Grill, but there are also a couple of purchases that were pulled from Kelter's bank account." Nadia gave us the name of a restaurant and a theatre.

"Well, that confirms the movie," Paige said.

"And the phone records?" Jack prompted Nadia.

"Not much there as her phone was just reactivated. There were calls to Bridges and Checker Limousine."

Jack nodded. "Okay, what else do you have for us?"

"I ran the man's and woman's faces through facial recognition software but didn't get any hits. I also looked into murder cases and MOs in Miami similar to Banks's, and no luck there."

"What about the families of the accident victims?" Jack asked Nadia. "Did you dig into their backgrounds?"

Kelly felt a splinter of betrayal. Or was it disappointment? She'd provided reports, but maybe that wasn't enough for Jack? Her cheeks heated.

"I did," Nadia said. "None of their immediate family members had criminal backgrounds, but all of them had hardships after the accidents. And I'm talking about more than dealing with the loss of a loved one. Abigail Cole, whose husband was the victim of Sullivan's accident, lost her unborn son and has a pile of credit card debt. Ava Jett, whose husband was killed in Kelter's accident, lost her job and had to refinance her house. The parents of the three boys that West killed had their share of marital problems between them—counseling, divorce."

"Wait a minute," Brandon said, looking at Jack. "Go back to Jett. She told us she *quit* her job."

"She could have been embarrassed that she was fired," Kelly offered.

"These people lived through hell, that's for sure," Brandon said.

Was that him agreeing with her? She might need to sit down before she fell down.

"But she still lied to us," Brandon added.

"If our killer was tailing West and Sullivan, it's possible their families saw our unsub and didn't even realize it. We have to figure out where he latched on to his victims," Jack stated. "Brandon and I will go talk to Gordon and see if he recognizes the man from the restaurant. I'd like to get a feel for him myself. Paige and Zach, I want you to talk to Stella Bridges about the same." Jack turned to Kelly.

"I'll go talk with West's parents and do the same," she volunteered. "Sadly, Sullivan had no one in her life she was close to who could help."

Jack nodded. "Go to the Wests' after you finish with Bridges's security company."

"And what do you want me to do?" Nadia asked.

"You look into anyone who overlaps in *any* way when it comes to West's, Sullivan's, and Kelter's accidents—doctors, nurses, reporters."

"You got it. Anything else?"

"Not now." Jack ended the call and stood. The rest of his team followed him out the door.

Kelly didn't blame them. She'd follow Jack all the way to Virginia in a heartbeat. Or farther if he asked her to. There was something about being around him that sparked hope inside her, hope that she could change her life, that there was far more she could accomplish. But to do so, she'd have to leave Miami PD. It was both a liberating and terrifying prospect.

A sliver of guilt pierced her heart at the thought of her mother. Could she leave Miami when her mother could still turn up? But when was it time to let go of the past? It was clear her mother didn't want to be found. Kelly shook the personal thoughts aside and stood.

Ramirez darkened the doorway. There was no sign of the mayor or his small entourage.

Kelly went to go around Ramirez, but his words stopped her. "They've already gotten further than you did in the last few years."

She clenched her hands, fingernails digging into her palms. Her granddad taught her to choose her battles wisely, and she had to show restraint until she had another job offer.

"What? Nothing to say? Cat got your tongue?" Ramirez pushed her buttons mercilessly. "I told you at the start of all this that if you embarrassed the Miami PD, you'd have to answer for it."

Oh, how she wanted to lay into him about how he never even had thought the cases were connected until she'd put them together, but fighting with him wasn't worth the energy. "I've got to go." Kelly brushed past him.

"Where are you off to?"

If he thought she was going to share details of the case so he could pass them along to the mayor, he was dumber than he looked.

"I asked you a question, Detective," he pressed.

"To help the FBI," she tossed over her shoulder as she continued down the hall, feeling Ramirez staring at her back. It was the only view he deserved. Well, that and a few hand gestures…

Hammond Security was set up in a strip mall, and as Kelly walked in, a handsome man greeted her from behind the counter. She held up her badge, and his smile disappeared. "I'm looking to speak with the manager."

"You've got him," he said all businesslike, but he was also blatantly checking her out. His eyes traced over her face and slid down her form.

"Detective Marsh with the Miami PD, Homicide." She jutted out her chin. "And you are?"

"The—"

She angled her head. "Besides the manager." The guy was cute, but she wasn't here to land a date, and she'd never been a fan of mixing business with pleasure.

"Jordan Hansen." He flashed a devilish grin. He wasn't the guy a girl took home to momma.

That's if you have *a momma who's actually around…*

Kelly needed to clear her throat, but she refused to do it. She wasn't going to show how uncomfortable he was making her. "I'm here about your client Stella Bridges. She was going to call ahead and—"

Jordan smiled.

Kelly tilted her head. "Why are you smiling?"

"She did call, and I've got the video queued up and a copy already on a flash drive for you."

"Oh." *What do you know? Cute* and *efficient.*

"This way." Jordan led her to an office, and she admired the view from behind—*of his behind*. Nice rounded cheeks, strong legs, broad shoulders. She felt her face flush. She really needed to make more time for a love life—or at least a sex life. A woman has needs, and she'd been ignoring hers for far too long. Obviously. She was salivating over a stranger during an active murder investigation.

There was a flat screen TV on the one wall, and the video was frozen. The time stamp in the bottom corner was for that morning at 2:35. Kelly recognized the view as looking at the road from Bridges's front gate. There was a vehicle heading in, but it was too dark to make out much more than shadows through the windshield. She turned to Jordan.

"Ms. Bridges told me what you'd be looking for specifically," he explained.

"And what did she say?" Kelly was feeling suspicious. Of what, she wasn't quite sure.

"Just that she had a feeling you were interested in the driving service she uses. She told me the type of vehicle to keep an eye out for and the approximate time it might have been at the gate."

Heat coiled in her chest. It was one thing for Bridges to help arrange this cooperation; it was another if she was discussing aspects of the case. "Did she tell you why?"

Jordan shook his head, and worry lines creased his otherwise smooth brow. "Not the details."

Kelly let out the breath she was holding. She gestured to the TV. "Can you play the video?"

Jordan closed the door to his office and proceeded to do as she asked. She watched as the gates opened and the car went in. Approximately five minutes later it was coming back out.

"You said you had it on—"

Jordan took her hand and turned it palm side up. He dropped a USB stick into it.

"Thank you," she said through partially gritted teeth and tucked it into her pocket.

"If you need anything else…"

Her back was to him and she was headed out the office door, but she could tell the cocky son of a bitch was smiling. She put a little more sway in her hips, then slipped into the department car and cranked the AC.

CHAPTER TWENTY-FOUR

It was apparent Marsh didn't care much for her boss, given the shades of red she had turned when Ramirez had walked in with the mayor. On this matter, we certainly agreed. He'd overstepped. Regardless of the mayor being Kelter's uncle, the sergeant had no right to share an ongoing investigation with a civilian, regardless of whether that man held a public office or not.

All of this was running through my mind on the way to Gordon Kelter's. I had no idea what to expect once we got there, though Zach and Paige had given me the impression that Gordon was rather subdued while being all over the place emotionally at the same time. Apparently, he was taking the brunt of the accident on his shoulders and was experiencing some guilt.

Gordon answered the door in a pair of shorts and a plain white T-shirt. Jack and I held up our creds, and he stepped back inside. We followed.

Gordon ran a hand through his hair, which was in desperate need of washing. "Please tell me you have an update?" He cut right to the chase. He didn't even seem to care who we were.

Jack covered that much first, and then answered Gordon's question, albeit in a roundabout way. "We might have a lead. Now, it might mean something, or it might not." He was ever cautious, always careful not to spark hope when there wasn't any. One thing I both admired and disliked about Jack was his ability to just lay things out as they were. No flourish, no bullshit.

"Do you have someplace we could sit down?" I asked, eyeing the flickering lights coming from a room in the back of the house.

"This way." Gordon took us toward the lights and dropped into a sofa chair. Jack and I sat on a couch facing him.

"We think it's possible the person who took your wife may have known her routine from before she went to prison. They could have been banking on the fact she'd resume it once released. We understand her Sundays were a variance of a few things. Is that right?" Jack asked, despite already knowing about her quiet mornings—or at least the one she'd had yesterday.

I studied Gordon as he leaned an elbow on the arm of his chair and tilted his head into his hand. "It's been so long since she had any routine except for whatever it was behind bars."

"Try to think back to before she went to prison," Jack told him.

"Just what I told the other agents, I guess," Gordon said with a shrug. "She liked to read in the mornings, go to church in the afternoon, and then out with friends afterward."

"And how did she normally get there?" I asked.

Gordon looked at me. "She drove herself before the accident. Afterward, she'd get a lift from a friend. Don't ask me who."

That aligned with what Zach had told us. "Did you ever go out with her on Sundays?"

"You mean to church?" Gordon waved his hand. "No. Way." Two words spoken so slowly that they came out like their own sentences.

I recalled that Zach had mentioned Gordon's disinterest in attending, but he could have done other things with her on Sundays outside of the house. "Okay. What about anything else? Brunch out, maybe?"

Gordon closed his eyes, and the wrinkles on his brow smoothed out. He opened his eyes, and they reappeared. "We'd go to brunch at Charlie's Diner sometimes."

"And did you go there with any sort of regularity?" Jack asked, stealing Gordon's gaze.

"I suppose. Um, probably every other week or so."

If our unsub was tailing Jenna, it's possible Gordon saw him at one of these brunches or at some other time. I pulled out my phone and brought up a photo array that included our suspect. I walked over to Gordon and handed him my phone. "Do you recognize any of these men?"

Gordon dropped the arm he'd been resting his head on and looked intently at the screen. He took his time and it was rousing hope within me, but he eventually lifted his gaze to meet mine. "Sorry. I really am." His eyes glazed over, and everything fell quiet. I could feel helplessness and sadness washing over him.

I put my phone back into my pocket. "We are doing all we can to find your wife."

Gordon sniffled. "And…one of those men took her?"

"We believe it's possible, yes," I admitted, partially worried that Jack wouldn't be impressed by the honesty, but I felt backed into a corner. Showing the man an array of pictures sort of made the reason for our interest obvious. We *were* thinking one of them took his wife.

Gordon let his eyes go from me to Jack, back to me, and they stopped there. "I heard that a man answered her phone this afternoon."

He must have heard it from the mayor, or who knows, maybe Ramirez himself. I glanced at Jack to take this one, as my temper was starting to ignite.

"Where did you hear that?" Jack asked calmly.

Gordon didn't take his eyes off me. "Does that matter?"

"It does when it relates to an open investigation," Jack said coolly. I imagined his aggravation was more directed at the sergeant than poor Gordon here.

"I just want some answers. You can understand that." Gordon's cheeks flushed, and he pursed his lips.

Jack nodded. "I can. But please understand that for us to do our jobs, we need to stay focused on certain things." All trace of coolness was gone from Jack, but Gordon's nostrils flared.

"A man answered my wife's phone," Gordon seethed.

"I promise you that we're following any and all leads in the case." Jack was firm and held eye contact with Gordon.

Gordon looked away first. "My wife isn't a *case* to me," he spat. An errant tear fell down his cheek. "She needs to be a person to you, too."

I felt for the man, I really did, but there had to be some disconnect between us and the victims' families or we could be railroaded by emotions that weren't even ours. Not getting personally involved in cases is the first rule of working in law enforcement.

"We're sorry that you're going through this," I offered, meaning it.

Gordon sniffled again and bobbed his head. His eyes were full of tears.

Jack stood, and I recognized the poor timing of Gordon's grief.

"Can we call someone to come be with you?" I asked.

"Nah, I'll be fine." Gordon took a deep, staggering breath, the inhale pulling the life energy from the room. Even keeping my personal wall up, I felt the downward tug.

"We'll be in touch the moment we have anything more," I told him, and Jack and I saw ourselves out.

Jack pulled out a cigarette—*lucky me*—and lit up. For a guy who was all about burying—and even denying—his emotions, smoking was his release from feeling anything, his gateway to nirvana. I feared what might happen if Jack ever quit. Heartbreak, anger, and regret just might destroy him.

CHAPTER TWENTY-FIVE

Stella Bridges's maid told Zach and Paige that Bridges was on shift at the hospital. It had shocked Zach, considering the woman's emotional state. She had to be in turmoil. He sure wouldn't want to be under her scalpel.

Stepping through the hospital's automatic sliding glass doors, Zach took in the ten to fifteen people who sat in the waiting room. There were men and women, adults and children, people of various nationalities. What they held in common was the weary look on their faces and the slumped, rounded shoulders of someone in pain. He settled his gaze on an elderly gentleman and the two women flanking him. They were probably his grown daughters. One held the man's hand, the other had an arm around him. He appeared disconnected from their contact, his eyes glazed over as he stared across the room at seemingly nothing. Likely hoping for good news but worrying the worst was going to come. Zach guessed that his wife was in surgery.

One of the daughters met Zach's eye and, in response, squeezed her father's hand. She was clearly his protector. No matter the outcome, the man would get through what was coming next because he wasn't alone; he had a support system.

Paige nudged Zach's arm and pointed toward the admissions counter. She led the way, his legs moving slowly behind her as he kept watching the family of three. They all looked like they hadn't slept for days. It was quite possibly true, as stress could do that to the body. It worked overtime on the mind, playing out scenarios, most of which would never even come to pass.

"We'd like to speak to Dr. Bridges please," Paige told the female nurse at the desk.

When the nurse glanced at her computer, Paige looked at Zach. She mouthed, *Are you okay?*

He nodded. He was fine. He would be anyhow. He just had to stop thinking about that family, about how their lives could potentially be changed forever depending on what happened in that OR. Again, an assumption.

"Dr. Bridges is in surgery at the moment," the nurse said, and Zach looked over at the family again. One of the women was resting her head on the man's shoulder.

Was Stella Bridges operating on their loved one?

Paige slowly drew her gaze from him to the nurse. "Do you know when she'll be done?"

"Could be another half hour—longer if there are complications."

Paige tapped the counter. "Okay, we'll be over there." She scanned the waiting room. "Let us know when she's out."

The nurse nodded.

Zach leaned forward and nudged his head toward the father and his daughters. "Is Dr. Bridges operating on their family member?"

The nurse's gaze followed Zach's direction, then looked at him, lips pressed into something between a frown and scowl. "I'm sorry, but that's confidential information."

"Of course. Sorry." What had he been thinking even asking that? He wasn't usually so drawn to the lives of strangers, but the sadness emanating from them was like a magnet that kept pulling on him.

He started toward the waiting room, and Paige touched his arm. He stopped and turned to face her.

"I'm asking again. Are you okay? And don't lie to me." Paige scanned his eyes.

He just wanted to say he was fine and move on, but he couldn't get the words out. "Life is short."

"Uh-oh."

"What?"

There was the hint of a smirk on her face. "You're going dark on me again. Yes, life is relatively short, and things can change at any moment. But isn't that all the more reason to live as fully as possible every day?"

He couldn't refute that logic. "I get that, Paige."

"You sure? Because you have a wonderful fiancée and a baby on the way. You are blessed." She smiled softly.

"You're right." With the words came an overwhelming desire to be the best husband and father the world had ever seen.

"Have you talked to Sheri yet?"

He angled his head. "When was I supposed to do that? Before or after Banks's murder?"

"You have time now. Jack's not around, either."

He appreciated that she didn't counter with the fact he could have called Sheri in the hours before Banks's murder. He'd been beating himself up over it, despite giving himself a pass because the conversation could be a lengthy one.

"Go," Paige urged. "Do it."

He held eye contact with her.

"I'll come get you if Bridges comes out," she added.

"Okay." He moved toward the exit, preferring to make the call outside. Over a shoulder, he said, "Thanks."

"Of course."

He saw Paige take a seat near the family of three before he slipped outside. He pulled out his phone and was about to call when he noticed the video option. He'd just left her this morning, but he'd love to see her face. Why the heck not?

He pulled his ear buds out of his pocket, set them up, and hit the video call button.

Sheri answered on the third ring. She smoothed down her hair and her shoulders were heaving as if she'd run to the phone. Regardless, she was smiling at him and he smiled right back.

"Did I catch you at a bad time?" he asked.

"Never, baby. I'm just looking like a mess, that's all."

"It's after eight at night, so go for it."

She simpered and angled her head. "Thanks."

He laughed. "That's not what I meant."

"Then start saying what you mean," she teased him.

"I *meant* it's time to relax, let the hair fall down, take the bra off, put on a pair of pj's."

"Why should I be surprised that your mind went straight to the bra."

"Not really the bra so much as—"

Honking horns blasted from the street.

"Where are you?" she asked.

"Miami," he said, being smart.

"Brat. And more specifically?"

"The hospital," he said. Her brows pinched, and she looked worried. "Nothing to be concerned about, just working the case."

"Phew." Sheri blew out a breath. "You shouldn't tell a girl you're at the hospital unless there is something to worry about."

"People worry too much." He thought of the father and two daughters, of himself. The hypocrite his statement made him. Why did people worry anyhow? Logically, it didn't do an ounce of good or change any outcomes. "How are you and Jamie?" Jamie being the name he'd love to name their baby if it was a boy, though the name was unisex.

"You mean Catherine?" she countered with a smirk. They'd already placed their individual orders with the universe. She wanted a daughter, he a son.

"Sure," he caved.

"We're both good. Say hello." She held the phone to her belly, being a goofball.

"Hello, Jamie."

The screen returned to her face, and she was studying him.

"What? You're not going to say anything to that? Correct me or anything?" He'd expected *some* sort of a reaction from her.

"You're a brat. I'm used to that." She turned serious for a second. "You don't usually call when you're on a case."

"Not true. I've called you from hotels lots of times."

"Yeah, at the end of the day. But you're still working now. Obviously, Jack's not around." She smirked. He'd explained to her before that Jack wasn't a fan of personal calls during working hours.

He shook his head. "He's not. I'm following a lead with Paige."

"And you're waiting for something?" she guessed.

"For *someone*. Thought I'd call."

Silence fell between them, a rarity, and he felt the need to fill the space. He was the one who had called her after all. "There's something we need to talk about."

"Uh-oh, why don't I like the sound of that?"

He held up a hand to save her any more anxiety. "Nothing serious. Well, it is serious, but it doesn't have anything to do with us or our relationship."

"I never really thought it did." Her eyes peered straight through him.

He stepped farther to the side of the doors. A woman walked past him and into the hospital holding a screaming baby in her arms. Zach rounded the entrance and watched as the woman went inside toward admissions, his eyes blurring out of focus, his mind on how to say what he needed to say. He didn't want her to talk him out of a choice he needed to make. Maybe it hadn't been a good idea to call Sheri about this.

"What is it, Zach?"

His eyes came into focus, and Paige was waving her arm at him.

"I've got to go."

"You can't go now," Sheri pleaded.

"I'm sorry, hon, but I've got to go."

"You better call me tonight."

"I promise." The pledge was out, and he could have kicked himself. Now he'd have to find a way to call for sure, and she'd want to pick up where he'd left off. They blew each other kisses and ended the call.

Paige met him with a solemn face. "Bridges is good to talk to us. She told us to go on ahead to her office and she'd meet us there. I have directions."

Zach looked over to where the father and daughters had been sitting before. They were gone now. "What happened—" He couldn't bring himself to finish. A sick feeling swept over him.

"To?"

He flicked a finger toward the now-empty chairs.

"Ah, that man and his daughters?" Paige's eyes dimmed, and he didn't care for that or the fact that Bridges would be catching up with them in her office.

"Bridges operated on the man's wife, didn't she?" he guessed. "The mother?"

"She did." Paige frowned and shook her head.

A horse may as well have kicked him in the gut. How had he let himself become so tangled up with the dilemmas of people he didn't even know? Modern-day thinkers preached the belief that all humankind was connected, but for the most part, Zach didn't buy into that. Sure, actions had consequences and one person's actions could affect others, but that was as far as the ripple went. Or was it? Maybe there was some merit to believing we all had more of an effect on one another than we liked to believe.

"They've gone to see..." He couldn't bring himself to say *her body*.

Paige rubbed his arm. "They did. Come on."

"What happened?" He wished he could just let it go.

Paige pressed her lips together. "There were complications. That's all I overheard."

The part she wasn't telling him, the part that didn't need saying, was the devastation that would have flooded the family—the crying, the tears, the shock, the anger.

"Let's go," Paige said and led the way.

. . .

Framed diplomas and certificates lined the walls of Stella's office. Sleek lines, neat and orderly; not a piece of paper out of place or any personal effects—photographs or knickknacks. Though given Stella's home, she didn't strike Zach as a collector of bric-a-brac.

Stella wasn't there yet, and usually he'd take an opportunity like this to scour the space, even if more out of curiosity than anything else. His mind was always hungry for the next challenge. Right now, all he could absorb was loss and emptiness.

He sat in one of two chairs that were positioned across from a desk. Paige was reading one of the framed items on the wall when Stella entered the room.

She came in with the energy of a wet rag. She swept her hair back, twisted it, and held it in place with an elastic band. She didn't say a word to either of them and dropped into her chair.

Paige said, "Sorry to hear about your patient."

"Thank you." Stella leaned on the left arm of her chair. "It's never easy, no matter how many times it happens."

"What happened?" The question slid out of Zach without him thinking too hard about it, but he set his gaze on Stella. There was a brief resistance in her eyes, but the barrier disintegrated.

"Normally it's a routine operation, but there was a complication. I did my best, but it wasn't enough," Stella said grimly.

"Sometimes things happen, and there's nothing that can be done," Paige said. While she sounded sympathetic, she kept glimpsing at Zach. She sat beside him. "We have a question for you actually."

"You know, yeah, things happen. Life's not fair. Yada yada. It doesn't mean we have to like it. It doesn't mean we even have to accept it." Stella opened a desk drawer, took out a bottle of aspirin, popped a couple of pills in her mouth and swallowed them dry.

Zach imagined this was a rare side of the put-together surgeon, but the failed surgery only would have compounded the anxiety she was already feeling with her lover missing, not to mention likely taken by a killer.

"I know I'm ranting, venting, whatever you want to call it." Stella stopped abruptly. Seriousness rained down on her features. "To me, what happened in that OR is unforgivable."

Paige leaned forward and cocked her head. "Why do you—"

"This one isn't on me. It's on that family. I had limits to what I could do in there and what I couldn't."

"We all have limits," Paige said, somewhat impatient.

"No, I had limits placed on me. I operate on all types of people. Different races and religions. Today it was the patient's religion that interfered with my doing my job." Stella paused. "Did you see them in the waiting room?" She was looking straight at Zach, and he nodded. "Can you believe that couple had four daughters? All of them alive. Only two came here, though."

He was trying to piece together Stella's initial comment with her question, but he was failing. How did the patient's religion connect to what happened on the operating table, and by extension, to the couple having four daughters?

Stella continued as if reading Zach's mind. "The family was torn apart by religion. The only reason I even know about the other two daughters is because of the patient's medical records."

"Sorry to hear that," Paige said.

"Uh-huh. It wasn't my place to bring it up, but I talked to the two daughters who were here, when their father wasn't around. They told me they aren't in communication with their other sisters anymore."

Zach was familiar with several religions that cast out nonbelievers. To him, the thought of cutting off ties with family over something relatively trivial like a difference in beliefs was hard to accept. One would think the blood connection was enough to forever stitch families together. Then again, why was there so much pressure placed on family? If someone had a friend who suddenly gained different interests and common ground disappeared, the relationship would dissolve—often with no hurt feelings. Still, none of this explained why the operation had resulted in the woman's death. "How did the patient's religion factor into her dying?"

"She lost a lot of blood on the table," Stella said. "Not that I should be saying any of this to you. They don't believe in blood transfusions. I did all I could to staunch the bleeding and to replenish with nonblood alternatives, but they had signed instructions not to transfuse…" Stella sat up straighter. "Anyway, please give me some good news."

Zach wondered if it really was adhering to the patient's wishes that had resulted in her death or if Stella's mind had been preoccupied with Jenna's disappearance. But no good would come of him attacking the surgeon. "We're still working the case, but we have a lead." Zach had found his voice and his strength—thankful for both.

"Is it the man who answered her phone?" Stella perked up. "Did you find him?"

"We're working on it." Paige pulled up the photo array on her phone and extended it to Stella. "Do you recognize any of these men?"

Stella held Paige's phone but was looking back and forth between them. "Was it one of these men who answered Jenna's phone?"

"We'd like to know if you've seen any of them before," Zach added.

"Not exactly forthcoming," Stella lamented, but her gaze dipped to the phone. Her eyes snapped back. "Yes. I know him." She handed the phone back to Paige, and Zach caught that their unsub's face was on the screen.

"How?" Paige asked.

"Well, I don't really *know* him." Stella rubbed her neck. "But I've seen him before."

"Where?" Zach was quick to ask.

Stella drew in a deep breath. "Jenna wanted to go to Lester Jett's funeral, so I went along to support her."

"And that's where you saw him?" Paige interjected. "At St. John's Catholic Church?"

Zach recalled from the file that's where Jett's funeral had been held, and it seemed Paige had too.

Stella looked at Paige and nodded. "Jenna and I got to the church in plenty of time for the service, but she couldn't bring herself to go in. She was afraid that someone would recognize her. It was foolish of her; she was dressed in black and wore a black veil that covered her face. We sat outside the church until the service was over. That man, he came out of the church afterward. Sort of a dark creature if you ask me."

Zach nudged forward on his chair. "Why's that?"

"Well, just as he was coming out, Jenna knocked her purse off the bench we were sitting on and spilled the contents onto the ground. He helped her pick everything up, but he never said a word to either of us."

Zach wasn't sure what that meant, if anything. It did put their unsub at the church, though. It would definitely be worthwhile to follow that lead. Maybe someone there would know his identity.

"That's the only time you saw him?" Paige asked.

"Yeah. I just remember him because he was so…quiet. He lent Jenna a hand, sure, but he was…" Stella squirmed as if shivers were racing down her spine.

"Okay." Zach stood and so did Paige.

"That's all you wanted?" A line formed in the middle of Stella's brow, as if surprised they were leaving already.

"We'll update you once we learn more," Paige assured her.

"Guess that's all I can ask." Stella's gaze fell to her desk, and Zach and Paige saw themselves out.

In the hospital's parking lot, Zach turned to Paige. "Jack and Brandon are going to want to know this."

"Maybe the answer we've been looking for will be found at St. John's," Paige replied.

Zach found irony in Paige's statement. Many people went to church for answers—to their problems, to the world's—but the BAU would be going to church to potentially find a killer.

CHAPTER TWENTY-SIX

He trudged through the woods, appreciating the gentle breeze in the otherwise sticky air. It was after eight at night and the sun had sunk in the sky and lost its power. He should be in the city, putting his hands on Roxanne—around her neck and squeezing tightly if the Night had its way.

She hadn't returned his call from earlier in the day. She was either mad at him or the cops had her in custody. She could lead them to his apartment, but he was hinging all bets on her loyalty. A tall order when there was no communication between them right now. He'd just like to speak with her, know for a fact that she hadn't told them anything.

He'd staked out Roxanne's work for a while around the time she should have left, but he hadn't seen her. It was possible he'd just missed her, or she could have gone to her apartment after the incident at the restaurant. She could just be shutting him out, making him work for reconciliation. He could have gone by her place, but he had to err on the side of caution in case the police had her under surveillance.

"Ahh!" he yelled into the night air, his voice not even echoing back to him out here.

At least she had no knowledge of this place. He'd been smart enough to take precautions over the years, including holding back his real identity. After all, he had secrets to protect. Speaking of, he wondered if the police had found the driver's body yet.

He'd been careful with the man, too, acting at the opportune time and moving swiftly. It had been a sweet execution actually. He'd pushed himself beyond his comfortable limits by returning the vehicle to the driving service. It had been a risk, but a necessary one. If the authorities caught on to him, he wanted to make it crystal clear that he was the one calling the shots. No, the Night was in charge.

Shivers tore through him. The urge to kill again bubbled within him like hot lava, crusting the surface and about to explode. Just like a dormant volcano coming to life, there'd be no holding back the Night.

He reached the shed and stopped his steps to deeply inhale and exhale a few times. If he acted tonight, he would be ahead of schedule. A part of him wanted to slow down time and just go with his normal flow. But the Night within him was roaring, demanding that he kill her now. It wanted to make a statement. It wanted to ensure that this act was carried out in case the police did find him and try to stop him.

Not knowing where Roxanne was had him teetering on the brink of insanity. He had to try her phone again before he went through with the Night's plans for the evening. To act now, so soon, went against his usual way of doing things. He didn't want to rush or act impulsively, to be forced by someone else's agenda.

He pulled out his phone and called Roxanne. She answered on the fourth ring, just before he figured he'd be shuffled to voice mail.

She didn't say anything.

"Roxanne?"

"What do you want?" she snapped.

She was pissed. No question there. "Did you get my messages?" He'd left a few by that point. "I told you I'm sorry."

"Just because you apologize doesn't make everything better." She sniffled.

He smiled. She was trying to present a strong front to him, but her emotions were besting her. "You know I love you. I didn't mean to—"

"You left me at the restaurant after... I was so humiliated."

She didn't even say anything about the fact that he'd tried to strangle her. Her self-respect truly was nonexistent. "Did the cops harass you?" A good question, he'd thought. A way to show interest and concern for her while gathering the information he longed to know.

"No, I left before they..." She left the rest unsaid, but what she'd told him brought some relief.

"So you weren't questioned about the damage to the restroom?" It wasn't his top concern, but he had to take the safe route and he wanted to make absolutely sure she was telling him the truth.

"No," she stamped out with some heat. "I told you. I left before they got there."

"I am sorry," he said demurely, knowing when to let things go. He'd push her more when they next met in person. Control was easier to achieve when the power of touch could be utilized.

"You..." She started sobbing.

This had to be about him trying to choke the life out of her. He rolled his eyes but mustered up the sweetest tone he could manage. "I lost my temper, I admit that, but sometimes that happens. You get angry sometimes, too."

"I'd never—" She started sobbing.

"How about we have dinner?" he suggested. "Tomorrow night. Let me make this up to you."

I should win a boyfriend-of-the-year award.

"I don't know."

"Please, give me a chance," he petitioned. They'd had their spats in the past, and this wasn't the first time he'd tried to kill her.

Roxanne was sniffling on the other end of the line.

"You've forgiven me before. Please just this once more."

After a few seconds, she said, "Fine. I'll forgive you."

"Oh, thank you." He looked heavenward and shook his head. He might not believe in God, but it surely felt like Roxanne had been a gift from above.

"Maybe we can even stay in tomorrow night?" Spoken as a mischievous flirt.

He grinned. "Sounds nice."

"I could make us something."

"I'll be there. What time?" He'd hand that decision to her, give her the feeling of some control.

"Say seven thirty?"

"I'll see you then."

"Looking forward to it." She was smiling when they said their goodbyes.

As he hung up, the realization of what he'd just done hit him like a sledgehammer.

You're such an idiot!

He paced in a circle. What if Roxanne had lied to him and the police had carted her in? Or maybe they had her identity and were tapped into her phone. They might be able to trace his call here. Even if they couldn't pinpoint his exact location, they'd have an area to search. He had to act quickly or risk failure. His heart racing, he jogged to the shed where his victim was bound.

Tonight was the night whether he wanted it to be or not. He'd forced himself into this position, or maybe the Night's insatiable hunger for blood had been maneuvering things all along.

CHAPTER TWENTY-SEVEN

It had happened hours before, but Kelly hated the way Brandon had looked at her when he basically implied she'd dropped the ball with the lawyers. She'd had no reason to ask if they'd received hate mail, and the lawyers were still breathing. Regardless, his implication was nattering at her. She prided herself on being on top of everything, being one step ahead. This case was beating her enough in that regard. She'd never have seen Banks's murder coming even if she'd had a crystal ball.

She was driving to Clark and Mariella West's home to see if they recognized the unsub from anywhere. It was gratifying to now potentially have the face of their son's killer, but her experience in life told her celebrating prematurely would just doom her.

That had been the case with her mother's release from prison. The date had been circled on Kelly's calendar from the moment they learned she was getting out, and she'd counted off the days. She'd been twenty-one at the time and working through the FBI Academy. She had been having the time of her life, too. The future was looking bright. She had no idea the ground was about to fall out from beneath her.

Kelly had gone to the prison with her granddad. By that time, her brother was twenty-seven and they had no idea where to find him. She had hoped he'd come to the prison, but he never showed. Her mom came back home with her and Granddad, but she wasn't there for long. Not even a week later, they woke up and her mother was gone.

Granddad tried to tell her that her mom was having a hard time adapting to life on the outside. Kelly always thought her mom had given up way too easily. As such, her mother's abandonment had been harder on her than seeing her mother shoot her father. Maybe because she had been six years old and too young to appreciate the finality of it.

Kelly returned to the Academy and used her pain to fuel her drive to become the best FBI agent the Bureau would ever know. She got as far as graduating. The rest didn't seem meant to be, and it was another dream that came raining down like spent fireworks.

So, yeah, she'd learned some time ago not to get excited about anything in the future, and she was determined to remain grounded in the present. It was a lot less painful way of living. The disappointments couldn't touch you as deeply when you didn't have expectations.

Kelly stepped onto the West's front porch and rang the doorbell, her past weighing heavier on her than she'd have liked. It had to be because Jack was around, messing with her mind, bringing memories and emotions to the surface that were otherwise long buried.

The Wests did well for themselves. Clark was a wealthy investment banker, and the couple lived in an upscale neighborhood. One that no doubt had a committee that met about everything from how short to keep the grass trimmed to allowances on Christmas decorations. Lots of ambitious people clawed their way to make it to a place like this, but it didn't appeal to Kelly. She preferred the freedoms associated with middle-class living.

The door opened on the two-story house. Mariella West, now a woman in her sixties, had retained her pleasant face and trim figure. She stepped back without saying a word.

Kelly went inside the house and wiped her shoes on the mat. "Sorry to have to come so late." It was nine o'clock at night.

"Nonsense, dear. Thank you for calling. If it were midnight and you thought you found our son's killer, you'd be welcome." Mariella's voice fluctuated with emotion— trepidation, perhaps. The poor woman would be lost in a world where hope and defeat took turns holding power.

Clark West came in from the grand sitting room and held out his hand to Kelly. He was a slender man, about six to eight inches taller than his wife.

"Good evening," Kelly said to him. A few seconds of awkward silence fell between them.

"This is nuts, us standing here in the entry," Mariella said. "Let's go sit down, shall we? Do you want anything to drink?" She was already winding her way into the sitting room, Kelly and Clark following.

"No, thank you." Kelly smiled and sat down on a chair she'd been in before. "I shouldn't be here too long."

"You've reopened Kent's case?" Clark leaned forward on the couch where he now was sitting beside Mariella. He'd always been the type of man to wear his emotions on his sleeve; the corporate world had never corrupted him. Kelly respected the hell out of that. Even with the loss of his only son, he'd remained dignified and pleasant. While she was aware that the Wests had gone to marriage counseling after Kent's death, there was no sign of any issues between them. At least they were united in wanting to nail their son's killer.

"There has been a development," Kelly said, wishing to avoid answering Clark's question directly.

Mariella reached for her husband's hand. It had been six years since their son's murder, but the impact was still tangible.

"This is because of that woman who's missing? That's why you're looking into his murder again," Clark said, and Mariella looked at her husband. He turned to her. "It's all over the news. The mayor's niece. She was convicted of DUI vehicular homicide like Kent was." His eyes glistened.

The Wests looked at Kelly, their eyes large, their souls longing for answers and closure.

"Do you think it's the same person who killed Kent?" Mariella's chest hitched visibly. "Is this a serial killer?"

"You heard correctly about the mayor's niece," Kelly said. "She is missing, and she does have a record like Kent had. Unfortunately, I'm not at liberty to comment any further as it is an open investigation."

"But so is our Kent's. I mean, you're here." Mariella squeezed her husband's hand.

"Yes, in a way it is," Kelly said, providing them a clue without confirming outright that their son's killer may have Kelter. "We've never been able to figure out exactly where Kent was taken, and we're trying to ascertain that, as well as how, but we do have a lead in the case."

"*We?*" Clark gripped on to that.

"I'm working with the FBI."

Mariella gasped and smiled broadly. "They're really going to figure this out this time." She looked at her husband, eyes wide with expectation and excitement.

"It's probably best if we maintain realistic expectations. It has been six years since Kent's murder." Kelly paused, hating that there was no way around saying that dirty word. It was one she rarely gave a ton of consideration to unless she was sitting in front of a victim's loved ones.

Clark patted the back of his wife's hand. "We understand."

Kelly brought up the photo array that included their unsub and gave her phone to Clark. "Take a close look at these men, and let me know if you recognize any of them."

"You think it was one of these men?" Mariella's face softened with sorrow while her eyes lit slightly with hope.

"We think it's possible," Kelly told her. "We also believe that the man who killed your son was familiar with his schedule so he knew when to abduct him. Our thinking is that you may have unknowingly seen this man lurking around."

Mariella and Clark looked at the pictures, taking their time to pore over them. A few minutes in, Mariella started sobbing. She reached for a tissue from a box on an end table and blew her nose.

"I'm so sorry." Mariella bunched up the tissue, and her chin quivered.

"There's no need to be sorry, Mrs. Kent. None at all." Kelly's heart went out to them, but she sheltered herself from taking on their pain.

"I don't recognize any of them, either." Clark handed Kelly back her phone. "I wish I could say I did." He wrapped his arm around his wife and took her hand.

Kelly dipped her head and frowned. "I wish I had better news for the both of you. Please know, the FBI and I are doing whatever we can to bring justice for Kent."

"Thank you for always caring about him," Clark said solemnly. "He was never just another case to you, and we're very appreciative and grateful for that."

Kelly swallowed the emotion that balled in her throat and stood. "If you need anything, you have my number."

She'd seen the Wests many times over the last six years, and as sweet a couple as they were, the next time she sure as hell hoped it was with the news that she had just arrested their son's killer.

CHAPTER TWENTY-EIGHT

I hated this feeling in the pit of my stomach that told me we were going to be too late to save Kelter. Based on the unsub's previous killing record, we still had time—technically. But that could all change, and who knew the repercussions of that phone call. It could have made him completely unpredictable. All of this was hypothetical, but the fact remained that Kelter's SIM card hadn't yet fired back to life. I'm sure I wasn't the only one losing hope that it would.

It was eleven at night when I finally made it up to my hotel room. Given the hell of a day it had been, it felt far later. The team and Marsh had all eaten together while bringing one another up to speed. From there, we went our separate ways with our marching orders for the next morning. Jack and I would be visiting the church; Zach and Paige would be attending Dominick's autopsy and checking in with Forensics to see if there were any updates; and I wasn't sure what Marsh would be up to.

I dropped my bag on the bed and rooted through it for my running shoes and workout gear. I emptied my pockets onto the nightstand and felt my phone vibrate softly. That meant I had a missed call or new text message.

It was from Becky.

Where are you? Are you okay?

Crap. I'd told her I would let her know where I was and that I'd gotten there safely. I should just fire off a quick text to update her and let her know I was fine. Something inside me felt fettered, as if responding would be more out of obligation than desire. But she was just showing interest in me and was worried about my safety.

I keyed in a quick reply.

In Miami. Nightmare of a case.

I tossed the phone on the bed, and that's where it would stay while I put in some time at the hotel gym. Even a solid fifteen minutes of cardio followed by a shower would help to purge me of this day and bring sleep swiftly. Exercise worked better than any sleeping pill on the market. For me, at least.

It took me mere minutes to transform from FBI agent to gym rat. I grabbed a hand towel from the bathroom and set out to kick my own ass. While my favorite exercise activity was boxing and I had a punching bag hanging from the ceiling in my bedroom, most hotels didn't offer one. But anything that got the heart rate up was good by me. I was a bit of a cardio junkie.

After I'd finished my workout, which had gone from an intended fifteen minutes to forty, my body was humming. I was wiping the sweat from my face and neck, about to leave the gym, when Paige came in.

"Hey," we said to each other.

It probably counted as the shortest conversation we'd ever had—if you could call a greeting a conversation. I turned around. Only God would know why, but I wanted to pick up our debate from earlier in the day and clear the air.

Paige was stepping onto a treadmill.

"You'll want to watch the grooves in the belt," I warned. "It's a little worn."

She looked at me, tilting her head. "Good to know." Her eyes were saying, *What else?*

"So Jack asked me why I was against drinking and driving—" I paused when her eyes met mine.

"Why are you bringing this up?" She hit the "start" button on the machine, and the belt started rolling at a slow speed.

I took that as a signal she was curtailing the conversation. And sure, I could walk away, but I wanted to know why she defended drinking and driving. Call it more curiosity than stubbornness. "The matter of DUI is personal to you," I said.

Paige put her feet on the side rails and hit STOP. "Just because I have strong feelings..." She let out an exasperated sigh. "You think you know me so well."

I tossed my towel over a shoulder. "Prove me wrong."

Paige rolled her eyes and stepped off the machine. Given the heat coming from her, I thought she might be close to decking me. But her face softened when she said, "I had family who grew up in rural Georgia."

"You're from Atlanta, though?"

"Yes, *I* am, but stick with me."

"Okay, you have family in rural Georgia. Go on."

"There was a farmer who lived in the area. He never had a sober day since his wife died. He drove a pickup truck and went into town with a bottle of whiskey on his passenger seat. The cops knew all about him." She paused, and I was tempted to cut in but resisted the urge. "He never got so much as a single bumper scratch," she continued.

"We both know it only takes once."

She leveled me with a glare.

"Who was he to you?" I braved.

"My uncle."

I nodded, taking pride in the fact that I did know her as well as I thought I had.

"Now don't get smug." Her eyes carried a glint of irritation, but she was smirking.

"I'd never dream of it."

She shoved my shoulder and smiled.

I gestured toward the treadmill. "Sorry to interrupt your workout."

"Yeah, I'm sure you are."

By the time I reached the door, she was back on the machine and running flat-out, but then I thought of something else. I turned around and walked up next to her.

"Are you…kidding me?" She was already a little breathless.

"What's the deal with Jack and Marsh?"

She looked sideways at me. "Do you really think…I know all there is to know…about Jack?"

"I do." Paige and Jack were pretty close and went a good way back themselves. Their camaraderie implied they talked and shared their secrets with each other. Maybe that was part assumption.

"Argh." Paige slowed the treadmill, and I waited for her to catch her breath. "Kelly's grandfather served with Jack in the military. That's all I know. Don't ask me about ranks or anything specific."

Ah, so that was how Jack had known Marsh's grandfather. Still, it didn't explain everything. "There has to be more to it. They read each other's minds." I sprang my hand open next to my head, indicating how it blew my mind.

"I don't know if you can handle all of it."

"Don't patronize me. Come on," I said. "Talk to me."

"No, you know what? If you want to know about their past, talk to Jack or talk to Kelly." She was obviously feeling closer to the detective than I did, referring to her by first name and all.

"I tried with Jack. You know what he's like." Then I realized she didn't. "Never mind. You don't. He *talks* to you."

Paige laughed. "Jack talks when there's something he wants to say. Funny, eh?"

"Now you're being a smart-ass."

"Huh." Paige tilted her head from side to side.

"Fine. You're not going to tell me. I will just get one of them to."

"Okay." She sped up the treadmill again and waved at me. "Bye-bye now."

"Night."

I went back to my room, kicked off my shoes, and let my clothes fall to a heap on the floor as I headed for the shower. The hot water felt incredible, and I lingered under the spray for a while, letting it wash away the stress of the day. It may not have been as nice as the showerhead I had at home, but it did its job.

When I was done showering, I changed into a pair of shorts and a T-shirt, ready to crawl into bed. I picked up my phone and checked the time—just after midnight—and I noticed Becky had replied to my message.

Nightmare day of my own. Can we talk?

It was sent about an hour ago; immediately after my message to her. She might not even be up now. I sent a quick text to see, and my phone was ringing seconds later.

"Hey." She sounded exhausted.

"Bad days all around, I guess." I hoped for her sake she couldn't trump mine. After all, I was working with a brownnose cop on one hellish case. "Ladies first."

"It's my brother, Sam." She sighed, and I felt for her. She'd only mentioned her brother a couple times in passing, and it was never paired with good news.

I dropped onto the bed. "Let me guess. He wants more money?"

A deep exhale came over the line. "When else does he reach out? And he's trying the whole guilt-trip thing again."

"Because it's worked for him in the past. You have to learn how to tell him no and mean it." I found myself getting agitated just thinking about this guy. I'd never met him, and if I ever did, I couldn't be held responsible for my mouth running off.

"Easier said than done. He's family," she said defensively, as if I were slime for telling her to stand up for herself. I never understood why women shared their problems if they didn't want solutions.

After a moment of silence, she said, "Since we're on the topic of family… Are you going to see your parents while you're in Florida? You probably should."

Maybe Becky's response had come from disliking my advice, but now that the roles were reversed, I could understand Becky's cool reception. "I'm working a case."

"When it's over," she clarified.

"I'm in Miami. They're in Sarasota." If the job excuse didn't cut it, surely the distance would.

"You're closer there than you are when you're in Virginia." She said it with a smile that traveled over the line.

I found myself smiling, too. "Can't put anything past you."

She laughed, and I loved the sound. I missed her more than I'd realized. Maybe I was overreacting to the whole being-exclusive thing, to waking up on a slice of my king-size bed and to her toothbrush in my holder. There were worse things in life.

"What's the case?" she asked, her voice turning husky as the late hour seeped in.

Speaking of worse things…

"A woman's missing, and we think a serial killer might have her." I couldn't share all the gruesome details with her. It was an open case, but she was a police officer, and I felt comfortable sharing the basics with her. I knew she'd keep them to herself.

"Any leads?"

"Two steps forward, one back."

"Playing it vague, I see."

I detected another smile. "I have to withhold some things," I said.

"Uh-huh. So how long do you think you'll be gone?"

That question made an imaginary restraint tighten around my neck as if I were being yanked back to Virginia by a leash. "Not sure."

"Well, keep me posted and call when you can. I like hearing your voice."

"You're such a sap," I said.

"You know you love me. Let me hear you say it again," she requested lightheartedly.

It felt like I had been backed up against a wall. "If I say it too much I'll wear it out."

"Huh." She paused, the silence building over the line. She then added, "I think we need some time together. I feel like we're growing apart."

Hearing her say that speared my heart. As much as I wanted to fight the speed of this relationship, I did care about her. I even loved her. "Everything's fine," I promised her. "When I get back, we'll spend some time together, do something fun." I wasn't going to touch on the fact we needed to talk as just saying that would create unnecessary drama.

"I'd like that." Her words were hopeful, but her tone was flat.

"And I do love you, Becky." The sentiment slipped out.

"There you go. Now that wasn't so hard. I like hearing it," she said, sweet and sexy. I imagined the small line forming between her brows the way it did when she was being seductive.

"But if I said it all the time, you'd get tired of it."

"Without sounding like a *sap*, we could always try it."

"I love you, I love you, I love you, I love you, I love—"

Becky laughed, interrupting me. "You're such a brat."

"Me?" I gasped, playing it up. "I didn't even get it out a full five times, and you shut me down."

"Fine, you win," she consented. "You don't have to say it *all the time*."

"Just know that I do." And I meant it.

"I love you, too. Oh, and you should at least call your parents."

"And you should tell your brother to take a hike." I was smiling when I hung up. I could certainly do a lot worse than Becky.

I should have just plugged my phone in to charge, but I was tapping it against my thigh. Was I seriously considering calling my parents now? Sure, they might be night owls, but that wasn't the point.

"Urgh." I dialed their number.

Pops answered on the fourth ring, and he sounded groggy.

"Pops, it's—"

"Brandon? What are you doing calling so late?" My mother had hopped on another extension.

"You were asleep?" I asked them.

"We were," Pops answered gruffly, obviously displeased to be pulled from his slumber.

"Sorry. I thought you guys stayed up late." We weren't in touch every week anymore, but apparently there was more distance between us than I'd realized.

"We haven't for a while now," Mom said. "What's up, sweetie?"

"Just called to talk." Maybe it was best not to mention that I was in Florida. There would be less obligation that way.

"Call back in the morning, hon," she said, her voice muzzy from exhaustion.

I didn't have the heart to point out that it technically was morning. "Tomorrow night would be the soonest. I'm working a case."

"You're always working a case." Pops's judgment was clear.

"I'm in Florida working a case." I slapped a palm against my forehead. What had I been thinking saying that? Was it about standing my ground or peacocking my importance, letting Pops know I was around but not available? Elusive, just out of reach.

"Then get over here for a visit," she said. "But tomorrow."

"As I said, I'm working. And I am in Miami."

"Still, you're in Florida. Finish up your case and come by."

"He's too busy being important," Pops said to Mom.

I rolled my eyes.

"Have you taken any vacation time since you joined the FBI?" she asked me.

Fine, I'd shock them both. "I'd love to see you, Mom."

"Then you're coming?" Mom sounded hopeful and awake now. I felt bad for making her both those things.

"I'll do my best."

"You talk to that boss of yours or I will." Mom's mind was set, and I imagined her facing off with Jack. I'd like a front-row seat for that event. My bet would be on Mom.

"I'll see what he says," I started, "but I'm not even bringing it up until this case is solved."

"And how long's that gonna take?"

"I don't know." I was starting to wonder if Pops was still on the line, but the sound of his breathing gave him away.

"Well, we're going to hang up now. You get some sleep, and hurry up and solve this case. Then you come see us," my mom said. "Night. Love you."

Click.

I stared at my phone as if it had betrayed me, and now I felt as awake as Mom had sounded. I reminded myself it was best not to dwell too much on what had just happened and try to get some sleep.

I put my phone on the nightstand, turned out the light, and got under the sheets. I'd expected thoughts of visiting them to keep me awake, but rather, it was Mom's closing words, *Hurry up and solve this case,* that had me tossing and turning. If we didn't hurry, Kelter was as good as dead.

CHAPTER TWENTY-NINE

Death was everywhere. Nothing had changed except for Zach's perspective. Sometimes it felt as if happy endings were very few and far between and fate was nothing but fickle and random. Even the poor woman who went in for heart surgery hadn't survived a "routine" operation. He hated thinking of life in such a negative way, but ever since he realized this could be his last case, he was looking at everything differently. The fact that he and Paige were on the way to an autopsy wasn't cranking up the positivity. And he hated feeling that way, even on a small scale. He had so much to be thankful for—good friends, Sheri, their baby.

Zach crept the SUV forward and tapped his hand on the steering wheel. This morning's traffic was a nightmare. They'd hardly moved in the last fifty minutes, and it would be nice if he and Paige got to the morgue before nightfall.

Move forward two feet. Wait ten minutes... Move forward two feet. Wait ten minutes...

Paige reached for the radio knob. "Would you mind?"

"Not at all. Maybe some music will make all this less painful." He gestured out the windshield at the BMW whose bumper was inches in front of them.

She tuned in to a rock station and turned the volume low enough to easily talk over.

They rarely listened to music while working a case, even on the road, but sometimes diversions for the mind worked wonders for a case. And music was fine with him anyhow, as he had a lot to think about. Where was he going to find the strength to leave the team?

"How did you make out with Sheri last night?" Paige asked. "What did she say when you told her you are thinking about leaving the BAU?"

"I didn't tell her." He'd called Sheri last night, just as he'd promised, but left the topic of work off the table. He had a feeling she'd try to talk him into staying or, worse, feel responsible for him considering a desk job. The last thing he wanted was for her to shoulder that responsibility. If he left, that would ultimately be his decision and all on him.

"Oh." Paige paused. "Have you made up your mind?"

He was relieved Paige didn't get into how he should have bared his soul to Sheri. "Not yet."

"There's still a chance you'll stay, then?" A subtle smile. "I still think you should talk it out with her."

"It's really my call." He glanced over at her, and she pursed her lips. Her gaze chastised him.

"You're going to be married. It's best to—"

"It's my career, Paige, not Sheri's." His words came out sharper than he'd intended. He'd been naive to think she was going to let the matter go.

"Of course it is," Paige said.

Zach wasn't sure what to make of her response. Was she agreeing with him or harboring underlying judgment that he should discuss the matter with Sheri? He couldn't bring himself to worry about what Paige was thinking too much; he had enough going on in his mind as it was.

They got to the morgue and met up with Lily. Dominick Banks's corpse was lying on a metal slab, naked and prepped for autopsy. Lily was in a full apron and had on a hat with a face shield.

"You two ready for this?" Lily asked them, almost as if she didn't think they'd been through the process before. Zach had lost count of how many autopsies he'd attended.

"Ready as we'll ever be," Paige said.

Her response pretty much mirrored Zach's feelings on the matter. It wasn't his favorite thing to watch, that was for certain, but it was a necessary step in an investigation. Sometimes small things came to light under the scrutiny of an ME during a preliminary and throughout an autopsy that helped collar killers. It was best that they were present so they could respond to any potential leads sooner rather than later.

"I've already conducted a preliminary and collected some evidence from the body," Lily began. "Given the shape of the contusions on the neck, I'd say he was strangled by hand. Based on their size, I was able to approximate the span of the killer's hands and from there estimate height." Lily held her head a little higher when she said, "Six three or thereabouts."

That lined up with their unsub to within an inch.

Lily continued. "Usually I fill in detectives on fibers and trace after I've finished up, but did you want to know now?"

Zach bobbed his head. "Now would be good."

"All right." Lily glanced at the body, seeming eager to get started on the autopsy. She looked back at Zach. "A fiber was pulled from the deceased's hair. It will be going to the lab, but I'd say it was a carpet fiber."

Banks had been lying on his hardwood floor. "From where?"

Lily smirked. "That's for you and the lab to figure out, but I'd say that it came from a low-pile carpet."

Zach's gaze went to the lividity showing on Banks's side and the fact that he hadn't spent his first few hours of death supine. Zach deduced that the killer likely had to conceal the body while returning it to Banks's home and staging it. Unless he drove around town with Banks's corpse in the front passenger seat playing out *Weekend at Bernie's*. "Could it be carpet fiber, say, from the trunk of a car?" Zach asked.

Lily looked at him and nodded. "Sure, I would think that's possible."

Zach turned to Paige. "The unsub did put him in the trunk after he killed him."

"If that's the case, he would have needed to be there for a couple of hours," Lily said, "for the lividity to form the way it did."

Zach nodded. "Can I see the fiber?"

"Be my guest." Lily grabbed a small plastic evidence bag from a table. Inside, the fiber was tiny and charcoal gray.

"Thanks," he said.

"Don't mention it," Lily replied, putting the bag back on the table.

"What else? You mentioned trace?" Paige asked. "Did you pull DNA from under his nails?"

"Possibly. I'm not sure yet. I can tell you that he didn't fight back, though." Lily's face fell. "But there's something else."

Paige glanced at Zach and back to the ME.

"I don't see this often, thank goodness. It turns my stomach like nothing else. I can handle mangled corpses of any shape or size, but this…"

Zach could imagine that Lily had seen it all in her career, and for this finding to upset her, it had to be revolting.

"There's evidence that the body was sexually assaulted." Lily put a hand over her stomach. "And I'm talking about…"

"After death?" Paige blurted out.

Lily pressed her lips together, pointed a finger at Paige, and nodded.

None of them said a word for a few minutes. Necrophilia was a whole other layer of their unsub to unravel. What had pushed him to that? Zach was aware of the textbook answers: the love maps that formed early in life. Role models in a child's life helped teach what was and wasn't accepted sexually, what was considered normal and healthy and what was considered deviant.

"See? It turns the stomach." Lily let her hand fall from where she'd been rubbing her gut. "I don't know what it was done with yet, but there was a pointed sculpture taken from the deceased's home. It is being tested."

"A foreign object?" Zach asked. Typically, that could indicate erectile dysfunction or castration, but their unsub had a girlfriend.

"Yes. Now, if you don't mind, I'd rather just dig in." She motioned her head toward the cadaver.

Zach gestured for her to go ahead, despite being queasy himself now.

Lily sliced into Banks, making the Y-incision with skill and precision. She lowered her face shield and armed herself with a bone saw. "Too bad we're nauseated. I'm about to serve up a couple of ribs." She attempted to smile at her joke, but the expression fell short.

"Oh, it's too early for ribs anyway," Paige said, playing along.

Zach and Paige stayed and watched the entire autopsy, but compared with the news Lily had delivered before starting the process nothing enlightening was found. They thanked Lily and headed back to the SUV.

"What do make of all that?" Paige said, buckling her seat belt.

"Safe to say our unsub likely had a very traumatic childhood," Zach said. "He experienced abuse in some way when his love map was forming."

Paige nodded. "You think he was sexually abused?"

"Dr. John Money first came up with the love map theory in the eighties," Zach said, probably unnecessarily because when the theory was first proposed had little relevance to its implications.

"Well, I'm aware that all of us learn what relationships are from those closest to us—mostly from our parents."

"Right. That was Money's theory. Our parents, to start with, provide us with an inner gauge of how relationships should work, the appropriate conduct and so on when it comes to sexuality," Zach explained. "Our love maps are formed as children and continue to develop as we grow older. When a child is sexually abused, it taints their view on sex, love, intimacy, and lust. Statistics show that such children are at risk of developing bizarre sexual fantasies later in life."

"Like necrophilia," Paige replied.

"Just one of the ugly possibilities."

"Probably one of the ugliest."

"Not going to argue with you there. That and the fact the violation was done with an object gives us insight into our unsub."

"Yeah. In his case, I'd say he's distancing himself from the assault."

Zach nodded. "Now that we've discussed that, let's move on."

"Amen to that!" Paige steepled her hands as if praying.

Zach drove them to the lab, and a guy named Barry gave them some of the forensic findings. Not that any of them were helpful to tracking down their unsub's identity. Prints lifted from the Cuban restaurant were processed and met with no hits in the system, not even matching ones lifted from the Checker Limousine vehicle. Not that it surprised Zach. Their unsub hadn't been prepared at La Casa de Jose; he could have worn gloves when driving the car. The results from the DNA taken from the restaurant would take longer to get back, but Zach wouldn't be holding his breath for any solid lead there, either.

While the fiber that Lily collected still needed to be processed, as did the suspected violating statue from Banks's home, the carpet in the trunk of the Chrysler seemed to be a color match for what she'd taken from Banks's hair. Maybe they'd be able to connect Banks to the trunk. What they really needed was a connection to their killer. He needed to be stopped before someone else paid with their life.

Zach's phone rang when he and Paige were coming out of the building. "Agent Miles," he answered and held his breath as the caller relayed their message.

CHAPTER THIRTY

Jack and I walked inside the St. John's Catholic church that Kelter used to attend and where Stella had claimed to see their unsub. Wide aisles led to the pulpit where a large crucified Jesus was looking down over the space. No doubt to remind everyone who saw him that humankind was imperfect and in need of saving. I wasn't sure I bought into that propaganda. A greater being, sure, but not one that required us to line the pockets of priests and attend church every Sunday. Ironically, for a place claiming to be about love and acceptance, it made shivers run down the back of my neck and an unsettled feeling grew in the pit of my stomach.

A door opened to the right of the pulpit, and a woman in her sixties came out. "Can I help you?" Her demeanor was pleasant enough, but she didn't exactly make me feel warm and fuzzy.

"We're agents with the FBI—" Jack paused as the woman signed the cross. "I'm Jack Harper and this is Brandon Fisher."

"I'm Regina Brown. I'm Father Ryan's right hand. How can I help you?" She might have been small enough to stuff into a suitcase, but she had the fire of a bobcat in her eyes.

"We understand that Jenna Kelter is a parishioner here," I said.

"Yes. Horrible what happened with the accident and all." Regina clasped her hands and angled her head. "What can I help you with?"

"Have you ever seen any of these men before?" Jack pulled out his phone and brought up the photo array.

Regina scrolled through the pictures and pointed to the photo of our unsub. "I've seen him."

Good news that she remembered his face, but... "Do you know his name?"

"No. I only saw him the one time."

And crash and burn...

"When was that?" I asked, suspecting what her answer would be.

"He was at Lester Jett's funeral. That was easily five years ago. He gave a generous donation, too."

"Are you responsible for tracking the donations?" I asked.

She nodded. "One of the many hats I wear."

"So the man in the picture made a donation at the funeral?" Jack asked.

"Uh-huh. That's right. He sought me out and said the funds were to go to the Jett family, but he wanted the money routed through the church."

Okay. Now I was listening. What would make our unsub donate money to the Jett family? Another aspect of what Regina had said earlier struck. "How much was this *generous* donation?"

"Thirty thousand dollars."

I tried to fight my jaw dropping. Lost the battle. "Whoa."

Regina held out her hands as if to say, *See, I told you. Generous.*

Jack looked at me, the vein in his forehead throbbing.

"Ahem. That's certainly generous," I deadpanned, going for the polar opposite of my initial reaction to the amount, though it was difficult. Thirty—*three zero*—thousand dollars. Murders *three* years apart. *Three* days out of prison. Killed *three* days after that.

"He wrote a check, then?" Jack tucked his phone back into his pocket.

Regina nodded. "A certified one. I probably only remember that after all this time because it's not every day I process a check that large."

The donation might have been made about five years ago, but it could still give us some info that might help in tracking him down. Though I couldn't figure out why our killer would leave such a trail. "Could you send us a copy of the check?" I asked.

"I can," Regina started, "but it will take some time to pull the records."

I nodded, appreciating that this could be the break we were waiting for, but I was still in shock at the amount. What prompted our unsub to give so much money? Did he know the Jetts well? People typically didn't cough up that much cash for friends, let alone strangers.

While the donation might have raised some questions, it told us our killer had money—either still had or had five years ago.

"It was horrible what happened to that poor woman. Mrs. Jett," Regina clarified. "Having her husband ripped from her life like that. And to think, we've lost two members of our church that way…to drunk drivers. But those drivers live in their own torment. No amount of prison time could help them live with themselves."

I was aware Regina had continued speaking, but I was stuck on her words, *We've lost two members of our church that way.* Maybe she was just mistaken and was referring to Kelter's disappearance? It would have been all over the news by now. I was surprised that she hadn't brought it up, actually.

"Who else besides Mr. Jett?" I asked, curious.

"Abigail Cole."

The woman who was made a widow because of Marie Sullivan's accident.

Jack and I looked at each other.

"I take it that's news to you." Regina arched a brow.

"You could say that," Jack admitted.

"The records show that Cole's funeral took place in a home," I said, remembering having read it and rather proud that I had. Some things stuck, whereas others fell through like water through a sieve.

"Ah, yes. That poor dear lost her way. But she was baptized here."

I went on to inquire about the three families affected by West's accident, but Regina had never heard of them. So we couldn't tie all of the victims from the DUI accidents to this church. Two out of five families was still something.

Regina hadn't heard of Kent West or Marie Sullivan either. Maybe we just had to dig deeper. We certainly needed to figure out if the seeming connection to this church mattered in the grand scheme of tracking down our unsub.

Regina pointed to Jack's pocket. "That man, the one in the photo you showed me, what has he done?"

"We can't discuss details of an open investigation," Jack replied.

"Ah. Then I'm going to guess it has to do with Mrs. Kelter's disappearance." Regina tilted her head and smiled knowingly at Jack.

Jack held firm. "We can't say."

"Fine, then. Anything else?" Regina clasped her hands, her expression hardened.

"We'd like to talk to the priest," Jack said.

"I'll see if Father Ryan can see you now. Stay here." She turned to leave.

"Before you go—" Jack pulled two cards from his pocket and handed them to Regina. "Please send the donation information to Nadia Webber. Her information's on there." He pointed to the one for Nadia. "And the other card is mine."

Regina wandered off, and I watched her until she disappeared back through the door through which she'd first entered the nave.

I turned to Jack. "That large of a donation to Ava Jett? Does our killer know her? Does she know him?"

"We'll be finding out," Jack said with conviction, his gaze laser focused.

"And is everyone somehow connected to this church? The DUI accident victims and the drivers? Our killer?"

"Not according to Regina, but that's why I want to talk to the priest."

"And if our unsub donated to the Jetts, did he donate to the Coles and the three families affected by West's accident? Either way, our unsub has money. Donating could be a pattern for him." The words were rushing out of me.

Jack's brow arched downward. "Don't get carried away just yet. We know of one donation. But, yes, it's an angle worth looking into."

Footsteps sounded, and Jack and I turned to face the pulpit. A man in his fifties was striding toward us. He was dressed in a black cassock and had a strip of white at his collar. He was maybe five foot nine and balding. Physically unassuming and certainly not intimidating, but here inside the church, the vision of him sent shivers tearing through me.

I must have had a bad experience with a priest as a child. Not in the headline news sort of way, but it had made an impression regardless. I racked my brain, but all I could remember was my mother telling me about my reaction to seeing nuns for the first time. They'd loaded onto an elevator with us, and Mom said I had burrowed into her side and asked if they were witches.

"God's children." The priest had a light, airy voice that was abnormally high-pitched for a man.

Goose bumps.

"Miss Brown said you were interested in a man who gave generously to help a family in need," the priest continued. "That would tell me this man is an angel." He smiled.

An angel of *death*…

Jack's cheek got a tapping pulse. "Angel or not, we are looking for more information about him. Do you recognize him?" Jack pulled out his phone, this time going right to our unsub's picture.

Father Ryan looked at the screen. "I recognize him."

"From where?" Jack stretched his neck, his discomfort hard not to see. I'd wager he was more unsettled by religion than I was.

"From here, I'm sure."

"Have you seen him more than once?" Jack asked.

"It is hard to say."

"Not really," Jack fired back.

Could disrespecting a priest earn Jack eternal damnation? Hopefully, for his sake, belief in such a punishment was necessary for its fulfillment.

"Our congregation is an active one, Agent. This place is packed every Sunday." Father Ryan stretched his arms open, pride sparkling in his eyes.

Though wasn't pride one of the seven deadly sins? Then again, what did I know?

"Our interest is specifically in the funeral services held here," Jack clarified.

"Sadly, I have spoken at too many of them over the years." The priest gestured toward Jack's phone. "Whether that man was here for a funeral or mass, I don't know." He steepled his hands and looked expectedly at Jack, as if seeking dismissal.

Instead, Jack gave the priest time to practice self-control and perseverance. He ran through a series of questions similar to those we had asked Regina and netted the same results. Cole, Jett, and Kelter were connected to this church, and our unsub had been spotted only at the Jett funeral.

"Now, if that will be all…" Father Ryan said drily.

"Thank you for your help." Jack's tone matched the priest's.

"You are very welcome, Child of God." Father Ryan moved his gaze from Jack to me and back again, then turned to leave.

Once we were outside the church, I took a few deep breaths.

"You all right there, kid?" Jack asked.

I faced him, and we locked eyes. He knew I didn't like it when he called me "kid," but it never stopped him from pulling it out from time to time. And no amount of staring him down or stating my grievance with it would make him stop.

"Let's just say I'm not a fan of religion," I admitted. "And from the looks of it, I'd say neither are you."

Jack pulled out his cigarettes, knocked one from the pack, and lit up. He took a couple of long drags and exhaled his polluted smoke upward. "We've got a lot of new avenues to explore," he said, completely disregarding my comment. "We need to pay Jett another visit, see if she knows our unsub."

"And it wouldn't hurt to find out why she lied about quitting her job."

Jack met my gaze. "That, too, but I'm not sure it will crack the case." He gave me the lopsided grin he typically reserved for when he was chiding me.

But I decided to be the bigger person and let it go. "We also need to know if any of the other families affected by the DUI accidents received donations, anonymous or otherwise, in a significant amount."

"Yep." Another drag and exhale. "Also why he gave that money to the Jetts, and by extension, if it is a pattern."

"Well, it would seem he's dishing out punishment on the drivers but taking it one step further by giving money to the families of those who were killed in their accidents. Almost like he's paying for damages. Again, that's assuming he's done so with all of them."

Jack took another puff. "Right now, what does that tell you?"

"That our unsub was *personally* affected by a DUI accident." The conclusion felt good coming from my lips, and I was prepared for an attaboy when Jack's phone rang. Though I had to face it: I probably wasn't going to get one anyhow.

"Agent Harper," he answered. As he listened to his caller, he was watching me. If I was reading the hardening lines of his face right, the news wasn't good.

He hung up, took one more puff and squashed what was left underfoot. "Jenna Kelter's head was just delivered to her lawyer's office."

CHAPTER THIRTY-ONE

Kelter was supposed to have one more day.

It was a crazy thought to be running through my mind as we pulled up to the high-rise that housed Stanton, Sloan & Henderson. *As if killers operated on the principle of what's fair or stuck to an agenda without fail.*

Jack and I had filled in Paige and Zach on the donation to the Jetts, and Zach and Paige had told us about the vomit-inducing results from Banks's autopsy. As if severed heads weren't enough, this unsub had to take things to a whole other level of depravity with necrophilia.

Uniforms were cordoning off the front of the building and requesting that civilians stay back. Marsh moved toward the four of us as we approached.

Slamming doors alerted us to a local news van parked across the street. A cameraman was making haste trying to catch up with a reporter who was already stepping onto the sidewalk and weaving her way through the crowd.

The reporter thrust a microphone in front of Marsh. "Is it true that a decapitated head was delivered to Mr. Henderson?"

"You'll need to direct any questions to the Public Information Unit," Marsh said firmly and waved for the four of us to follow her inside. In the lobby, officers were talking with two men dressed in suits.

"The law offices occupy the top five floors," Marsh began. "I've made it clear that no one is to leave their offices or even the building until you give the say-so." She gestured to the suits. "Those two were just signing in for appointments when we locked down."

"Were their appointments with the law firm?" Jack asked.

Marsh shook her head. "An accounting company on the third floor." She led the way to the elevator bank. She pressed the "up" button, and a car dinged and opened right away. We loaded on, and she selected the twentieth floor.

Marsh continued once the doors shut. "The package came by an intercity delivery service for Mr. Henderson—he was Kelter's lawyer. Now, most packages are routed through the mailroom, but LDS always bypasses them and delivers straight to the recipient. A delivery slip was left, and there was a printed label affixed to the box. I've already called LDS, and they were adamant that this delivery never came from them."

"They'll have to do better than that," Jack said.

"We'll talk to them in person, for sure," Marsh replied. "But it's probably best to go to them armed with the face of the delivery person."

"The law firm has security cameras, then," Paige surmised.

"They do. It's handled by the building's security. I've already talked with them, and they're getting the surveillance video ready for us to view. It's only visual. No audio."

The elevator arrived on the twentieth floor, and we all unloaded. A police officer greeted us, and we signed into the crime scene.

Marsh turned and pointed to a corner of the ceiling to the right of the elevator. "The camera's there." She nodded toward a reception desk with the law firm's name on the wall behind it in raised gold lettering. "And the package was delivered there."

"Was the box the same kind as the ones used for West and Sullivan?" I asked.

"Yes." Marsh took a few steps toward the main desk. "The receptionist, a Donna Olson, signed for the package, and she is beside herself. We've put her in an office with a uni watching over her."

Cop talk for uniformed officer.

"Have you interviewed her yet?" Jack asked.

Marsh shook her head. "Not yet. I didn't get here too long before you. I did call for paramedics to come take a look at her."

"Good thinking," Paige said, and the women made eye contact.

"Did Olson see...the head?" I swallowed roughly.

Marsh's eyes flashed anger. "She did."

That poor woman. I'd seen decapitated heads before and even my heart was racing at the thought of seeing another one. She had done good not passing out.

"From what I gather, Mr. Henderson made her look at it. If that's the case, he's a real piece of shit," Marsh said, explaining the flicker of rage in her gaze. "As I said, Mrs. Olson hasn't been questioned yet, so I'm not sure exactly how it played out. What I do know is that she kept saying the delivery guy seemed so nice and they shared a laugh."

"She's in shock," Zach said.

"Absolutely," Marsh agreed.

Charm and charisma were two of the best weapons in any murderer's arsenal. Sweet, yet sticky like honey. Still, our unsub would have to have brass balls to deliver the head himself, especially after knowing police would be on to him after the restaurant. Though they'd figured their unsub liked to see the impact of his work. It was possible that he made the delivery himself, despite the risk. He could be calling them out, taunting them. Really, he was doing that by having killed Kelter before day three. He was sending them the same message: *I'm in control.*

Jack smacked his hands together. "All right, let's see it." If he had any qualms about viewing the head, he hid it well. Then again, he was a tough old dog, and I don't think much of anything could faze him.

Marsh led us down a hallway to Henderson's office, which had probably cost a small fortune to furnish. Two CSIs, standing with their backs to the door, blocked a mahogany executive desk. From what I could see it was a statement piece, as was the leather furniture in the sitting area. Framed prints of a gray-haired man, likely Henderson, with a younger woman and children of about six and ten adorned a file cabinet that matched the desk.

There was no sign of the lawyer, but the two CSIs turned to look at us. I hadn't seen either of them before, but they lit up at the sight of Paige and Zach.

"We meet again," one of the CSIs said.

"Don't take this the wrong way, but I was hoping to never see you again," Paige said.

"This is Ken Trevors and Alan Bury. They helped us yesterday with the Chrysler 300," Zach explained.

Trevors and Bury dipped their heads at Marsh, and I got the sense they'd met before too.

"I'm SSA Jack Harper," Jack said. "And this is my team. Paige Dawson and Zach Miles, you obviously know, and that is Brandon Fisher."

Trevors and Bury slid their gazes to me.

"We've taken a slew of pictures and processed the box for prints and trace. There will be a more thorough investigation, of course," Trevors began, "but it's ready for the ME at this point."

The CSIs stepped aside, no longer blocking the line of sight to the desk, though it wouldn't hurt my feelings if they'd continued to barricade it.

A white square box was sitting in the middle of Henderson's desk on a plastic sheet. The lid had been lifted, and its contents were already out for all to see. Kelter's head was inside a clear plastic bag and sat on top of tissue paper.

Wooziness twisted my stomach and I swallowed roughly.

"I understand someone lost their head." Lily chuckled and glided into the room.

I was hoping she'd be the ME to get the call. I'd liked her from Banks's crime scene.

Paige was biting her bottom lip, her mouth twitching as if she was about to burst out laughing. Marsh was shaking her head and smiling. Jack seemed completely unaffected by Lily's morgue humor, his face all rigid lines. Zach was grinning, too. Me, I was wincing, though amused.

"Is it ready for me?" Lily pointed to the head.

"It is," Trevors confirmed.

Lily took a pair of gloves out of her bag and slipped them on. She set her bag on the floor next to her feet and lifted Jenna Kelter's head out of the plastic bag.

I wanted to puke, but I forced myself to keep looking.

Like West's and Sullivan's heads, Kelter's had been inside a plastic bag, but her face was bruised and her eyes swollen. Our unsub had worked her over before ending her life. My heart sank with compassion, but I kept my emotions reined in tightly.

Lily proceeded to turn the head in her hands—and my gut along with it. She examined the head from different angles and then held it up a little and crouched down to look at where it had been separated from the neck.

Kelter's long brown hair was matted to her scalp, but it wasn't with blood. Rather, it was likely seeping bodily liquids from decomposition. I winced.

"Her head was cleanly severed," Lily said as she placed it on top of the plastic.

If I were Henderson, I'd be shopping for a new desk. Nah, I'd take matters further than that; I'd purge the entire office and find somewhere else to lease.

The rest of my team stepped closer to Lily and the head. I tried, but my legs didn't want to move. Marsh glanced at me, and my pride forced me to shuffle my feet. It was the best I could manage.

The smell of blood and decomp slapped me in the face. My legs ground to a halt, and bile shot up my esophagus. I covered my mouth and swallowed. Bitterness coated my tongue, making me want to puke even more.

I pulled a piece of gum out of my pocket, hoping to do so discreetly. Paige caught me and smiled. Thankfully, she didn't razz me about it or make a big deal out of it. It was bad enough I'd vomited during a couple of my previous cases.

I chomped down on the gum, the peppermint doing little to calm my nausea, but it helped to freshen my breath and tamped down the smell of death—if only a little. At least it gave me something else to focus on besides the macabre.

Chomp, peppermint, chomp, peppermint, chomp, peppermint…

"It's hard to determine TOD with a head alone," Lily said, and I remembered that the same thing had been said about West and Sullivan, too. "But I am seeing insect activity, namely blowfly eggs." Lily jutted her chin toward the head. "They would have been laid within twenty-four hours or they'd be maggots by this point. Additionally, her head was severed perimortem. The tissues in the area of the decapitation tell me there was acute hemorrhaging."

"We never stood a chance of saving her," I said.

"Not likely," Marsh said solemnly.

Lily pulled the head to her nose and sniffed.

Chomp, peppermint, chomp, peppermint, chomp, peppermint…

"I'm picking up on—" Lily shoved the head under my nose before I could blink. "You smell that?"

I blinked back tears. Oh, fuck yeah, I smelled it.

"The killer used cologne to mask the odor," Lily concluded.

It was hard to get past the offensive combination of odors, but I detected a subtle hint of the cologne.

"It's a male fragrance and it's cheap," Lily added. "I can tell from the sweet overtures."

"How do those two things correlate?" I asked.

"Cheaper colognes usually smell sweeter because generally their market is teenagers," Zach replied. He really did have answers for everything.

"A cheap cologne doesn't fit with our unsub's age range or the fact that he gave away tens of thousands of dollars," I reasoned. "I also don't remember reading anything about cologne being used on West's and Sullivan's heads."

"That's because there wasn't mention of it," Zach confirmed.

"If we can identify the cologne, it could help us find our unsub," Marsh said.

"I still can't see a guy who gives away all that money wearing cheap cologne," I repeated.

"His financial means might not have anything to do with his choice of cologne," Zach said. "It could have meaning to him. Maybe it was one he used as a teen? Then again, our unsub could have intentionally purchased a cologne he doesn't personally use."

"Assuming he bought it just for this," Marsh said, "he could have bought it within the last twenty-four hours. Given what we know about his preferences geographically, he probably picked it up from a store within the blocks we've marked off on the map."

"That's still over thirty square blocks," I said.

Zach shook his head. "Even if you found the store, it probably won't get you anywhere. It's not like he'd be careless enough to pay with a credit card."

"It still doesn't hurt to find out." Jack looked at Marsh.

"I can run it by the brass, see if they'll authorize uniforms to visit stores in the activity radius that sell cologne," she said. "Maybe we'll get lucky."

On a wing and a prayer.

I kept my Debbie Downer thought to myself.

"I'd have them focus on pharmacies," Zach suggested. "They always have cheap cologne."

Marsh gave Zach a thumbs-up from the doorway, where she already had her phone in hand.

"You said that the head looks like it was cut cleanly?" Jack asked, veering off the topic of cologne and back to the ME's findings. "Any idea what could have been used?"

Lily looked at the severed head thoughtfully. I followed her lead. Thankfully, the combination of peppermint and adrenaline were finally working to keep my stomach contents down.

"It's definitely a straight-line cut." Lily pointed to the base of the head. "The instrument used was very sharp, and it would have taken a lot of force to cut this cleanly."

"No hesitation or restraint, either. Two things that mark our unsub," I summarized. This unsub certainly was a cocky bastard, and so far, he was outsmarting us.

"Same could go for the beating. He didn't hold back from hitting her hard." Lily put a gloved fingertip to one of the bruises on Kelter's cheek. "And I'd say given the color of some of the contusions, she was struck within minutes of her death. Others look to be a day or two old."

"So he was beating her from the moment he took her." Paige crossed her arms and rubbed them. "Do you think he used his fists or some sort of tool?"

"I'd say the injuries appear consistent with bare-knuckled punches," Lily responded.

"Do you think he just beat her face?" I asked.

Lily pursed her lips. "Obviously we don't have the rest of her body, but I wouldn't be surprised if it shows signs of battery, as well."

"At this point, nothing this guy does would surprise me," Paige said, shaking her head.

"You'll be doing the autopsy?" Jack asked Lily.

"Yes. Tomorrow morning," she replied. "Eight sharp. Will I see you there?"

He nodded. "You will."

I'd managed to escape Banks's autopsy, but I guess I wouldn't be getting out of this one. Where Jack went, so did I, and his next comment confirmed it.

Jack turned to me. "You and I will go talk to Henderson, and you two—" he addressed Paige and Zach "—will go talk to the receptionist who signed for the package."

"On it, Jack," Paige said.

The four of us headed for the door as Marsh was walking back in. "The request has been approved and officers have been dispatched to check out pharmacies in the area. They'll take along the photo of the man from the Cuban restaurant."

"Good," Jack said.

"Where are you guys going now?" Marsh asked.

"We're going to talk to the lawyer," Jack said. "Where can we find him?"

"Down the hall to the right, third door on the left in a conference room."

"And the receptionist?" Zach asked her.

"I'll take you to her," Marsh offered and looked at Jack and smirked. "Then I'll go hover over the security guy until that video is ready."

CHAPTER THIRTY-TWO

It wasn't even noon yet, and there was a decapitated head. Zach hadn't blinked twice at seeing it and his lack of response stood in stark contrast to the abject horror on Brandon's face. And that was even before Lily had pushed the head under his nose. When she'd done that, Zach had fought not to laugh then and there.

Call it my evil streak.

But what did that really say about him?

He remembered what it was like to be newer to the job, how every disgusting sight would buckle his knees. All that had been a long, long time ago. The job had come to desensitize him—good or bad—just as it would make Brandon callous.

Marsh led Zach and Paige down yet another hallway. "We put Donna Olson in an associate's office, who's off sick today. Hopefully, she's doing a little better." She stopped outside an office door. The sound of sobbing leached into the hall. "Guess not." Marsh took off in the direction they had come from.

Zach entered the office first, Paige following.

Donna, a fiftysomething woman, was sitting at the desk blowing her nose. A uniformed officer was standing next to her. He bobbed his head at Zach and Paige and left the room.

"Mrs. Olson?" Zach broached, moving toward her.

She looked up at him and Paige. Her eyes were bloodshot, and she balled the used tissue in her hand, then gripped the fabric of her shirt over her heart.

While Zach empathized with Donna, he and Paige still had a job to do, and the killer needed to be stopped before there was another victim. Donna just might play a key role in making that happen. But for any chance at that, they might have to push her a bit to draw out relevant information.

Zach glanced around the office, seeking a place for him and Paige to sit, but there were no options. Donna was in the only seat. He hated that it would leave him and Paige standing. Donna was fragile enough without feeling like they were towering over her, possibly intimidating her.

"We're with the FBI. I'm Paige, and this is Zach," Paige said gently.

Donna just stared at them.

"We have a few questions." Zach crouched down next to Donna. Her hand was trembling on the arm of the chair. "Are you okay to talk for a bit?"

She nodded, fresh tears in her eyes. "I thought I was doing him a favor."

"Who's that, Mrs. Olson?" Zach asked.

"Mr. Henderson. But I broke procedure."

Paige stepped forward slowly. "What do you mean?"

"I should have sent the delivery guy to Mr. Henderson's assistant, but she's not scheduled to come in until this afternoon. She had a doctor's appointment," Donna explained. "I actually thought that I was doing *both of them* a favor by signing for the package. Mr. Henderson didn't see it that way." She paused, her eyes glazing over. "He called me into his office when he saw what it was…" She paused, her chin trembling. "He made me look—" she gulped back disgust "—and threatened my job."

"None of this is your fault." Paige came around to Donna's other side and placed a hand on her shoulder.

The receptionist shook her head. "I should have told him to come back later when Gina—that's Mr. Henderson's assistant—returned. But we receive a lot of urgent packages. I didn't want to be responsible for turning it away. It was one of those 'damned if I do, damned if I don't' situations."

"Well, you made the right decision," Zach comforted her. Who knows what would have happened if she'd refused the delivery, regardless of whether it was the unsub himself, an accomplice, or an unwitting scapegoat.

Donna went on. "I should have known better than to sign for it. Mr. Henderson was right. I made an intern move, and I should be fired. What am I going to do if he—"

"We'll speak with him," Paige said, and Zach looked at her. She bugged her eyes at him as if to challenge him to dispute her promise. He knew better.

"Have you worked with the delivery company before," Zach asked, knowing full well what the answer was.

"Yes, LDS comes here all the time. Not this guy, though. I've never seen him before." As long as Donna focused on the specifics of her job itself, she was more at ease.

"What was he like?" Paige asked, taking her hand from Donna's shoulder.

"As I told the officers, he was nice, even witty. He cracked some joke about the weather." Donna took her dirty, bunched-up tissue and proceeded to fold it into squares.

This description was another reason Zach believed their unsub wasn't the delivery guy. Their killer was unraveling, as evidenced by Kelter's rushed murder. No matter how good he typically was at being a chameleon, there'd be a crack in that veneer now. "Tell us about him," Zach requested in a friendly manner. "His looks? Voice? Demeanor? Age? Anything you can remember." They should have the video soon, but they might get something out of Donna that the recording wouldn't show.

"He was in his twenties." Donna continued to toy with the used tissue.

Their unsub was in his thirties. Someone else had likely delivered the package. Though this was not a complete surprise, Zach still asked, "Are you sure?"

"Uh-huh." Her chin quivered, and she dabbed the tissue to her cheeks to wipe up some fresh tears. "I've been a receptionist for thirty years of my life, twenty of them here. I should know how to read people by now. He had me fooled, I tell ya. I've become a gullible old lady."

"Don't say that, Mrs. Olson," Paige cooed.

"Agent Dawson's right," Zach intercepted. "It's quite possible that he wasn't even aware of what he was delivering."

"I didn't read anything off with him." She shook her head. "Maybe I just don't know anything anymore."

"Did the delivery man have an accent? Was his voice high, low, mid-range?" Zach asked.

Donna shrugged. "It was normal."

"So nothing stood out to you about it?" Zach pressed, finding himself getting more impatient, a quality that rarely surfaced for him.

"Not really. I'm sorry." She sniffled.

Paige patted the woman's shoulder. "It's all right. Just try to remember what you can."

Zach nodded at Donna and asked, "Did he have any piercings or tattoos?"

"None that were visible." Donna's eyes glazed over. Zach would guess that her mind was back on what she'd seen in the box. She definitely had a lot of therapy ahead of her.

"Any watches or necklaces?" Paige asked next.

"No."

"Did he take out a phone? Make any calls?" Zach spewed out another possibility that could lead them somewhere.

"Ah—" She rubbed at her neck, her gaze blank.

"Mrs. Olson?" Zach prompted.

"He received a call," she said.

Zach's eyebrows rose in surprise. "Did he take it?"

"Uh-huh. He even excused himself. He answered, 'Hello, this is Ben.'"

What do you know? I netted us a lead.

"That's good, Mrs. Olson. You're doing great," Paige said. "Anything else you can remember?"

"He was wearing a ring on his wedding finger." Donna twisted hers.

"What did he smell like? Was he wearing cologne?" Paige asked.

Donna shook her head. "Not that I can remember."

There was a knock on the door, and Zach turned to see a police officer standing there with a couple of paramedics.

"Mrs. Olson?" one of the paramedics said, coming into the room.

Donna may have been barely holding herself together emotionally, but she'd come through for them and given them two things they likely wouldn't have gotten from the video.

"Thank you for your time, Mrs. Olson. You did really well." Zach handed her his card, and she looked at him with a question in her eyes. "In case you think of anything else."

Out in the hall, Paige said, "The guy's married."

"The guy's named Ben," he said. "What we need to know now is if he's an accomplice or a paid stooge."

CHAPTER THIRTY-THREE

Jack and I stepped into a conference room that was all about impressing visitors, just as Henderson's office was. There was a large table, leather chairs, and floor-to-ceiling views of the downtown core. A credenza in one corner even housed a bottle of 18-year-old Macallan and crystal tumblers.

Two silver-haired attorneys sat side by side, and one of them had bathed in cologne. It was certainly not sweet smelling and was probably sold by the ounce. Regardless, it was potent and had my eyes watering.

The two men stood to greet Jack and me as we walked over to them. One was about six foot two while the other was stretching for five foot six. Both men's suits were tailored to a perfect fit and neither had let himself go around the middle, despite both of them probably pushing sixty. Their body language was rigid—shoulders squared, necks held high. My guess was they were using their posture to cover their true feelings, as the glimmer in their eyes disclosed apprehension and fear.

"I'm Raymond Stanton," Six Two said as he took my hand, then Jack's. "This is my fellow managing partner, Brian Henderson."

Henderson had a killer grip of a handshake when he greeted us next.

"I'm Agent Harper, and this is Agent Fisher." Jack gestured to me. "Will Mr. Sloan be joining us?"

The firm's third partner was nowhere to be seen.

"Unfortunately, Jason Sloan was called away due to a family emergency a few days ago," Henderson said. "We're not sure when he'll be back. If you gentlemen would like to take a seat…" He swept a hand toward the table and twenty chairs.

Jack motioned for me to go first. He sat beside me, and the two lawyers took up position across from us.

"I'm in shock," Stanton confessed.

Meanwhile Henderson was clenching his jaw and appeared to be staring past Jack and me…

I addressed him. "Was it a shock to you, Mr. Henderson?"

The lawyer met my eyes but said nothing.

"Is that a yes or a no?" I pressed.

"*Of course*, I was in shock," Henderson served with heat. "It's not every day a client's head shows up in a box on my desk."

Despite Henderson's attempt at bravado, there was something in his eyes that spoke of weakness.

"Were you aware of any threats to her well-being?" Jack leveled his gaze on Henderson, who paled and looked at Stanton.

"You need to understand that we receive threatening messages directed to our clients all the time," Stanton said.

Henderson sprung to his feet and paced the length of the table. Sweat was beading on his forehead and upper lip.

"We understand, but did you receive any threats directed at Mrs. Kelter?" I asked again.

Neither lawyer said anything.

"If you know something that could help us find Mrs. Kelter's killer, you need to tell us," I said firmly.

Jack looked at me and subtly shook his head.

"I *need* to tell you?" Henderson spat. "I don't *need* to do anything." He gripped the back of a chair with both hands so strongly that his knuckles turned white.

I knew Jack wouldn't like it, but I wasn't going to just sit there while some hoity-toity lawyer gave me attitude. "If you're holding something back, that could be construed as interfering with an investigation."

Henderson looked at me, then slowly let his gaze drift to Jack.

"You know that he's right," Jack stated ever so calmly.

Henderson glared at me again and said, "Ah, so that's how this is going to play out? You threaten me, and I cave? I've been around too long for that tact to work. And I'm not going to be bullied into—"

"What are you afraid of?" Jack fired out.

Henderson snapped his jaw shut, and his eyes darkened. For an attorney, this guy didn't take to being put on the spot.

"Tell us about these threats," I directed.

"I…" Henderson stood up straight and let go of the chair, thrusting it forward. It hit the edge of the table and rolled back toward him. "I received an e-mail after the ruling in Mrs. Kelter's trial. It didn't threaten her, though; it threatened me."

I'd brought up the idea that the lawyers could have received hate mail, but this was the first time we were hearing of it happening. I leaned forward and glanced at Stanton, who was looking over a shoulder at Henderson. "What did it say?"

Henderson met my gaze. "That I was responsible for inflicting chaos and I would suffer the consequences."

The hate mail turned over by Gordon Kelter was still back at the station waiting to be reviewed, but maybe something in Henderson's message could be connected to what we already had.

I said, "We're going to need to see—"

"I didn't really take it seriously." Henderson was peaked and panting. "Not until…" He gestured emphatically toward the doorway, no doubt implying the head in a box but not wanting to say it aloud.

"You must have taken the letter seriously enough," Jack said. "Otherwise, why commit the contents of the letter to memory?"

"As a lawyer, my mind is sharp. Hazard of the job," Henderson stamped out sardonically. "And I don't remember all the details—just the gist." He straightened his tie.

"We'll still need to see it," I said.

Henderson turned to his colleague.

"We never take threats seriously." Stanton must have felt that if this sentiment was reiterated enough times, it would downplay any culpability on behalf of the firm.

"So what are you telling us? Was the message deleted?" I asked with skepticism.

"We get threats all the time, as Mr. Sloan said," Henderson stepped in again. "And we're used to working with criminals, some real deviants too. We digitally archive everything in case it's needed."

"Then dig up that e-mail." Jack's request left no room for negotiation.

"I'll get it to you when we're done here," Henderson said, finally showing a glimmer of compliance.

Jack pulled out one of his cards and pushed it across the table. "Forward the e-mail to me."

What I didn't get was why Henderson was so resistant to talking to us. If he had been threatened, one would think he'd be more forthcoming. Unless…

I recalled the smiling family in the framed photos in Henderson's office. "Did this message also threaten your family?"

Henderson dropped into a chair at the end of the table and gave birth to a long, drawn-out breath.

"Oh no, Brian… Really?" Stanton held out a hand as if he could reach Henderson. "We should have brought in the police sooner."

"No." Henderson's curt reply was like a red-hot poker, and Stanton pulled back. Henderson continued. "The e-mail said it was for my eyes only, and if I showed it to the police, they'd hurt Amy and the kids."

"Did this e-mail give you any reason to believe Jenna Kelter was in danger?" Jack asked Henderson.

"No, I swear to you." Henderson's face knotted up, showcasing wrinkles in his brow that otherwise were not there. "But do you think I'm in danger? My family?"

"You could be," I said calmly.

"Dear God…" Henderson raked his hands through his hair and sank deeper into his chair.

"But we have no reason to believe you are, either," Jack stated.

Henderson blinked rapidly. "No reason to believe…"

"You received that threat four years ago," Jack reasoned, but I wasn't sure why he was putting Henderson through the ringer. Our unsub was capable of anything at this point.

"And I kept quiet about it until now." Henderson wiped his brow. "Look where that got me. Her head on my desk," he exclaimed.

Jack, not swayed by Henderson's emotional outburst, went on. "Was there any other hate mail besides that one e-mail?"

"No." Henderson was trembling, and I found myself feeling for the lawyer.

"Do you remember anyone who showed hostility toward Mrs. Kelter during or after the trial?" I asked.

Stanton was the one to respond. "Whenever there's a lawsuit that gets the public worked up, you have protesters. DUI accidents resulting in fatalities attract a lot of them."

"Do you often see the same people at these protests?" Jack pressed.

"Usually, there are familiar faces," Stanton admitted. "But they are harmless, right? I mean, if they actually followed through on their threats, they wouldn't be free to protest. Then again, they could disappear, serve some time, and return, and I wouldn't know."

"Well, someone could have acted on their threats," Jack said.

Stanton licked his lips. Henderson was still paler than pale.

I pulled up the photo array on my phone and let Stanton study the pictures. Then I walked it to Henderson at the end of the table and showed him, too. "Either of you recognize any of these men?"

"Not me," Stanton replied.

"Me either." Henderson's eyes were glazed over, not seeming to be focused on anything. His mind was probably on his family.

Jack tapped the table and stood. "Send me that e-mail as soon as possible." With that, he headed for the door.

"Wait, aren't you going to do something to protect me and my family?" Henderson cried out. Jack just kept walking.

I picked up my pace and caught up with him in the hallway. I grabbed Jack's arm, and he faced me. "I think we should get some protective detail on the Hendersons, just to be safe."

Jack reached into his shirt pocket and pulled out his pack of cigarettes. He lifted the flap and then put it back into his pocket without taking one out.

"I agree with you," he said.

"But you told him—"

"I know what I told him." Jack had a subtle smirk on his lips when he turned to continue walking.

Leave it to Jack to toy with a shark and walk away without being bitten.

CHAPTER THIRTY-FOUR

Kelly had already paid the building's security office a visit not long after she had arrived on scene. It was located on the first floor and consisted of two tiny, side-by-side offices. Her point of contact was a man by the name of Johnny Cash, who shrunk a little after the introduction. She was used to encountering this response because of the badge, but she guessed his had more to do with his name. She'd wager he wasn't a fan of the country legend. She gravitated more toward pop music herself.

"Got it ready for me?" she asked as she breezed into his office. Based on its size, it may as well have been a cubicle. He just had the benefit of real walls, but that actually made the small space feel even more cramped.

"They're both queued up," Johnny said. He had a laidback manner to him. He marched to the beat of his own drum, as they say, or so it seemed. He was aware of what had transpired up on the twentieth floor, but he struck her as indifferent—not that she thought he was involved in any way. He was probably just hardened by all the news stories and cop dramas on television.

Kelly sat in a chair beside Johnny and the seat dropped a few inches. "Holy shi—"

Johnny winced. "Sorry, I should have warned you."

Yeah, a warning would have been nice.

She smoothed out her pants and caught her breath. Nine monitors were mounted on the wall, laid out in a three-by-three grid. The middle screen and the one to its right were paused. One was a view of the law office and the other was the building's lobby.

"I'm ready when you are," she said.

"Which one first?"

"The law office."

Johnny started the video, and she watched the events play out on-screen. The others would see it later, but she wanted a sneak peek at what they were dealing with.

The video was time-stamped 9:08:15 AM. The camera was facing the front desk. Off to the side—or what she could see of it given the angle—the lobby was empty.

The delivery guy approached the counter, and Donna glanced up at him.

"Can you zoom in more?" Kelly asked.

Johnny did so.

Donna's brow wrinkled as she scrutinized the delivery guy. She clicked a button on her headset and addressed him. There was no audio, but Kelly imagined Donna was asking how she could help him. The man set the box on the counter and held a slip toward Donna.

She waved her hand as if rejecting the delivery, but her movements slowed, then stopped altogether. She started laughing. She then reached for the paper and signed.

Their interaction was casual. He wasn't acting rushed or jittery, looking around. He tapped the top of the box before he turned to leave, and a few frames later, he was at the elevator and looking right at the camera.

"Stop the video," she said.

Johnny did as she said, capturing a still of the delivery guy staring back at them.

He wasn't the man from the restaurant. He was younger—a twentysomething for sure. He probably had no clue what was inside the box. Most likely, he'd been paid in cash to drop it off. If he had given the contents any thought, he could have surmised it was a prank or a gift for someone. Regardless, they needed to find this man.

"Can you print that and send it to—" she reached into a pocket and pulled out the card Jack had given her with Nadia Webber's information on it "—this person." She handed Johnny the card. "If you could just write down her name and e-mail? That's my only card for her."

"Sure." Johnny pulled a notebook and scribbled on the lined paper.

"Also, please send it to my e-mail." She gave him her card. "That one you can keep." She smiled at him.

"Can do." He clicked here, clicked there, and a printer whirred to life.

She returned her attention to the screen. *Who is this guy?*

"Is there anything else I can do?" Johnny asked.

"Ah, yeah. Send a copy of the entire video to Nadia, as well." She wasn't looking at the security guy; she was still fixated on the screen.

"Here you go," Johnny said.

She pulled her eyes away from the monitors, and Johnny had a colored printout extended toward her.

"Thanks." She studied the picture. The kid had scruffy blond hair that stuck out from behind his ears. He was wearing a T-shirt, loose shorts, and a Miami Dolphins baseball cap. Just your average Joe Schmo. Except he wasn't. He could be the key to finding the killer she'd been hunting for years.

She fought the impulse to run from the office before watching the other video. The camera in the lobby covered the front doors, looking out, and that one could help determine which way the delivery guy had gone when he'd left.

She pointed to the screen. "Let's watch the next one."

Johnny hit "play," and just as she'd hoped, it showed the delivery guy going out of the building and heading right.

"Thanks," she called over a shoulder as she hurried out of the security office. "Send that video to Nadia, too."

She heard Johnny call out an affirmative and headed for the first officer she saw in the lobby. The two of them, who had been there when she'd led the FBI through, were still kicking around but were no longer talking to the two men in suits. They were now seated, and given their scowls, they were feeling more than a little pissed at this disruption of their day.

She stopped about two feet away from one of the officers—McGuire, according to his badge. He was good-looking with chiseled features, nicely sculpted biceps, and broad shoulders. The way he was regarding her was with a mix of curiosity and lust. He hooked his thumbs on his waistband.

Keep it in your pants, cowboy…

"This is the man who delivered the package." Kelly handed the photo to McGuire. "I need a bunch of officers canvassing the area to see if they can find out where he went from here, maybe even where he came from. What I do know is that he left through the main entrance and headed right."

"You got it, but—" McGuire's gaze went from the printout to her eyes. "Do you have more copies?"

She pulled out her phone and opened her e-mail app. The message from Johnny, complete with attachments, was there. "Your e-mail, Officer?"

He smiled at her. "If you want to meet up for drinks sometime, just say so."

She stared him down. "I don't know how long you've been on the job, but your behavior isn't appreciated, nor is it professional. A woman is dead. You do realize that?"

His cheeks flushed. "My apologies."

She wasn't sure whether he was being sincere or sarcastic. "E-mail?" she prompted.

McGuire gave his e-mail address to her, and he took out his phone.

"Let me know when you get it." She forwarded the photo of the delivery guy, and a few seconds later, McGuire confirmed receipt. "Share it with the officers canvassing the area," she continued. "But hurry." She glanced at the clock in the lobby, and it showed it was creeping up on eleven thirty. The head was delivered over two hours ago now. "We're already more than a couple of hours behind this guy."

"I'm all over it." McGuire hurried off.

Her phone rang and startled her. She answered. "Marsh."

"Sergeant Ramirez," he said, formal, tight, and pompous—his trademark.

She'd take it over the phone if she had to. It was a small miracle he wasn't there, underfoot. Maybe his embarrassment with the mayor bursting into the conference room had made him reconsider getting in Jack's face again. But that would be assigning the sergeant a conscience and she wasn't sure he had one.

"What's the latest news?" he asked as if they hadn't just spoken about getting officers out on the street to hit up the pharmacies.

"It's still early." She wasn't inclined to share information on the delivery guy unless—or until—she absolutely had to. Technically, the FBI was lead on this so for once she *could* circumvent her boss. If Ramirez got ahold of the guy's picture, that was one thing, but she didn't want to be party to him flapping his gums to the mayor—and who knows who else.

"Give me a little more than that, Detective."

"We have a lead, and we're following it," she said curtly. "I'll update you when we have more."

"Should I come down there?" he asked as if she needed micromanaging.

Her hand squeezed around the phone; it saved her palm from digging fingernails. "Officers are canvassing the area to see if they can find the delivery guy."

"There, now was that so hard?"

Smug, arrogant bastard.

"I really need to go." She didn't wait to see if he was going to say anything else. She hung up and was on the move.

She tucked the printout under an arm, took out Nadia's business card and called her. Jack would either approve of her initiative or be irritated that she didn't run it by him first, but it's said that it's better to beg forgiveness than ask permission.

"Nadia Webber."

"Nadia, this is Kelly Marsh, the detective in Miami working with Jack on the Kelter case."

"Yes. What can I do for you?"

"You'll be getting an e-mail from a Johnny Cash," Marsh told her. "It will include a video and a still of—" Kelly stopped. Nadia might not have been kept up-to-date on the case.

"Of what, Kelly?"

Kelly smiled. Nadia seemed polite and down-to-earth. Kelly gave her a brief recap of the day's events so far.

"Damn. I was hoping…"

"That makes two of us," Kelly said, certain Kelter's husband and the FBI team could be added to that list.

"So the pic coming to me will be the guy who delivered Kelter's head?"

"That's right."

"I'll run it through the databases, see if we can get a hit with facial rec."

"Thanks, Nadia."

"Don't mention it."

Kelly detected the smile in Nadia's voice. Speaking to the analyst had made Kelly's mind go back to what her life could have been if only things hadn't transpired the way they had. With that thought, she remembered Clark West's gratitude for her taking his son's murder case seriously, keeping the perspective that Kent had been a person, not just a file number or a toe tag. If her path hadn't led her to Miami PD, where would she be right now? And if it wasn't here, maybe that would mean this killer would remain free.

CHAPTER THIRTY-FIVE

The first-floor security office was the size of a cubbyhole. I could tell this much just from the doorway. If Jack, Paige, Zach, Marsh, the building employee, and I were all in the room, we'd be packed like sardines in a can.

For now, we were in the hallway where Paige, Zach, and Marsh had been standing when Jack and I approached.

Marsh handed me and Jack a colored printout. "That's the delivery guy."

"His name's Ben," Paige said before going on to share how she and Zach had made out with Donna. Talk about striking gold.

"So what are we looking at? A partner?" I hypothesized.

"Or a patsy," Paige suggested. "You'll see it looks like Ben is married."

I looked closer at the picture and noted the gold band on his finger.

"I'd more readily believe he's a fall guy," Jack said. "This guy—" he shook the photo "—was relaxed. You said he even cracked a joke. And we've pegged our killer as organized, and even though his game has changed a bit, I still see signs of that. That doesn't lend itself to a partnership that could mess with how he wants to do things."

"This younger guy could explain the cheap cologne," I said.

"Nah." Jack dismissed me with a wave of his hand. My temper flared beneath the surface.

"His only role could be to deliver the heads," I said, not giving in just yet.

"He wasn't the guy who dropped off West's head on the courthouse steps," Marsh said.

"You don't know that," I served back. "It wasn't the clearest picture."

"Huh." Marsh angled her head. "Yesterday it was clear enough to determine stature. I remember you saying that you thought it was our unsub. Now you think it's Ben?"

I didn't respond.

"Until we can find this Ben guy and question him, we'll keep our options open as to his relationship—or lack of one—with the unsub," Jack said.

I took his words as a tiny victory: he didn't sound as opposed to a partnership as his initial reaction had indicated. Maybe I'd actually swayed him.

Jack turned to Marsh. "Get officers…" He stopped talking when Marsh started nodding.

Were they reading each other's minds again?

"I have them showing his picture to everyone in the area," Marsh said.

"Next time lead with that." Jack grinned at her and added, "Excellent work."

"How did you and Brandon make out with the lawyer?" Paige asked Jack.

"Apparently, Henderson received an e-mailed threat after Kelter's trial that warned him to keep quiet about its existence or the sender would hurt him and his family."

Marsh's eyes widened. "I'd love to know what it says."

"Same here," Jack said. "I'm waiting on Henderson to send me a copy. Then we'll know more about what we're dealing with there."

"So the guy has it from four years ago, and he said nothing this whole time?" Marsh bit her lip.

"The threat against him and his family," I happily reminded her, but Marsh gave me no reaction again.

"We need to check in with the lawyers for West and Sullivan," Jack began. "See if they received anything similar. We should have the e-mail from Henderson soon."

I looked at Marsh, taking pride in the fact we'd now be exploring an avenue I'd brought up before.

"I'll reach out to the other lawyers," Marsh said. "They know me."

"That works for me," Jack said.

Marsh jacked a thumb over a shoulder to indicate the security office behind her. "The video's queued up for you to watch. I'm going to notify Gordon Kelter—if you're all right with that."

Jack and Marsh fell silent and locked eyes. Eventually, he nodded.

"Thanks, Jack."

I wasn't sure why someone would volunteer for notification duty *and* be grateful for the assignment. It was one of the worst aspects of the job. Much better her than me.

Marsh left, and the remaining four of us squished into the room. The security employee was at a bank of monitors. He swiveled his chair and looked at us. He had a long, narrow face and a scraggly beard. He gave me a pressed-lip smile.

"This is Johnny Cash." Paige put her hands on the back of his chair, a smile tugging at her lips.

I laughed. "Johnny Cash?"

"Yep, lucky me." Johnny's words were thick with sarcasm, anger's ugly cousin. "My parents were big fans. Sadly, I don't share their taste in music or their sense of humor."

I liked this guy. I held out my hand. "Brandon Fisher."

Jack introduced himself, as well, then pointed to the monitors. "Go ahead and play the feed."

"Ah, yeah, sure…" Johnny spun forward and worked the mouse right off the desk onto the floor. "Oops." He bent over and retrieved it. A part of me felt sorry for the guy. Jack could be intimidating for someone who *knew* him, let alone a stranger.

"Here we go." Johnny's tongue curled over his top lip as he clicked the mouse, and the feed started to play.

A heavy energy cloaked the room, and we all fell silent as we watched the video.

"Freeze it there," Jack told Johnny when the delivery guy was facing the camera. "Whoever the hell this is we need to find him." His statement was obvious—we'd just had an entire conversation about it—but it clearly communicated his frustration.

Jack extended a card to Johnny. "Get this still forwarded to Nadia Webber at that e-mail address."

Johnny took the card but said, "Detective Marsh already told me to do that."

Of course, she had… I was going to have to up my game if I was going to knock Marsh off the pedestal Jack no doubt had her bolted to.

Jack nodded and stepped out into the hall. Paige and Zach followed, but I lingered next to Johnny.

"Thanks, Johnny *Quick*," I teased.

He turned, made a finger gun, and pulled the trigger. "Heard it before, but that's a kickass nickname."

His preference to a comic book superhero over a musical legend might have made Johnny some enemies, but I wasn't one of them.

I fist-bumped Johnny and left to find the team waiting for me. Each of my colleagues met me with expectant expressions.

"Brandon and I are going to LDS," Jack said. "See if we can shake anything loose. I want you two to visit Abigail Cole and find out if she received any mysterious donations or if she recognizes the unsub or the delivery guy."

"You got it," Paige said.

"When we're finished with LDS, Brandon and I will go to Ava Jett's again and do the same with her." Jack tapped his shirt pocket. "We'll see where the day takes us from there. We should visit the three families affected by West's accident, too."

The laundry list of things to do was getting longer by the second, but that was a good thing. We'd be narrowing in on our killer sooner rather than later.

CHAPTER THIRTY-SIX

One moment here. The next gone. To think that just two days ago Jenna Kelter had been alive, and today, her husband would be receiving word of her murder.

Zach and Paige were waiting at a red light. There were cars in front of them, cars behind them. At this rate, they'd be lucky to reach Abigail Cole's place by dinnertime. The dash clock already read one in the afternoon.

He looked over at Paige. "When we wrap up this case, I won't miss Miami traffic."

"It is crazy." Paige smiled at him, but her mind seemed to be somewhere else.

"You okay?" The fact he was asking her that question when she'd asked him the same thing yesterday just proved how life could change. Nothing was predictable or guaranteed. Why should they ever fall into the trap of believing the killers they hunted were?

"I'll be all right," she told him, though she lacked conviction.

The light turned green.

"This is me you're talking to," Zach said as he drove through the intersection. "I know something's bothering you."

"Honestly?" She turned toward him. "This job gets easier in some ways, but not in others. Maybe part of this is your fault. Your talk about leaving the BAU has me thinking about my future." She sounded somewhat melancholy.

"You're going to leave—"

"Never," she shot out. "I wouldn't know who I am without this job."

"Then what's going on?"

"I see something that horrific and…" Her gaze snared his as if seeking understanding.

He nodded. "I get exactly what you're saying without you saying it. I was thinking the same earlier."

"Right? My stomach didn't even clench at the sight of it." Contrasting her serious confession, her face brightened, and she laughed. "Did you catch the look on Brandon's face?"

"How could I have missed it?" He snickered, and realized that he and Paige weren't laughing as much at Brandon as they were envying his wide-eyed innocence.

That thought morphed, the innocence suddenly representing his unborn child. Every day, he'd be witness to their curiosity and growing passion as they explored the world around them. But if he stayed with the BAU, how much of that would he miss? Wouldn't it be better for his child, for Sheri, for him, if he had a job that allowed him to be around more often?

Zach pulled into the lot for Cole's apartment building. It was located in Overtown, just north of the downtown core.

They parked and then rang up to the seventh floor where Cole's unit was. She buzzed them inside.

A couple of minutes later, Zach had his hand raised to knock on her apartment door when it opened and cold air rushed out into the hall. A thirtysomething woman stood there in flannel pajamas and fuzzy slippers. She smelled of cigarette smoke and whiskey. Her hair was greasy and plastered to her skull, her eyes red rimmed. She looked much better in her DMV photo, but this was unmistakably Abigail Cole.

"Who are you?" she asked gruffly as if they were intruding. Which he guessed they sort of were.

Zach held up his badge. "We're agents with the FBI, and we'd like to talk with you about Justin Cole."

The woman pointed a finger at Zach and swayed. "He's dead."

"We realize that, ma'am," he said.

"Did you really just call me *ma'am* when you're older than I am?" She screwed up her brow.

Zach wasn't going to argue semantics. Besides, he never understood why women took issue with being called *ma'am* in the first place. He gestured to her apartment. "May we come in?"

Abigail hesitated but eventually stepped back, sweeping out an extended arm as an invite. Once the three of them were inside, Abigail locked the dead bolt and slid the chain across. "It's not the best building, but it's what I can afford. Follow me." Abigail sashayed toward a living room where she plopped down onto a couch. "And never mind that old clunker." She turned her head toward a window where an air conditioner rumbled, kicking out cold air and dripping water onto a towel on the carpet beneath it. "It's noisy but it works."

That was a matter of opinion. The water should have been routed outside...

"Sit wherever you'd like," Abigail told them, but the options were limited. They could join her on the couch or...

A nearby kitchen table had four chairs around it. Zach grabbed one for himself and one for Paige and set them across from the couch.

"My name's Zach Miles, and this is Paige Dawson," he said.

Abigail's face was blank, and she reached for a glass next to her that held two fingers' worth of amber liquid. She took a large mouthful that had her cheeks bulging before she swallowed. She swiped a hand across her mouth. "Why do you want to talk about Justin?" Her eyes were dead when they met Zach's. If it was possible grief had broken the woman.

"We're sorry for your loss, Mrs. Cole," Paige offered, seeming to have picked up on the same thing Zach had.

Abigail blinked slowly. "Do you know how many times I've been told that over the last seven years? More than I can count. And you know what? It never makes it easier." Her mouth twitched as if she was about to burst into tears, but she held herself together.

Zach nodded sympathetically. "We can only imagine how difficult—"

"Can you?" Abigail barked. "You know that I lost his baby, too? Just from the stress of losing Justin. My body…" Abigail's chin quivered. "I've relived that day so many times in the last seven years. And each time I wake up hoping that it was all a bad dream, but then I realize it wasn't. This is my life now. No husband and no baby."

The heavy weight of her grief was its own entity in the room. It stabbed Zach in the heart, the resulting pain blinding and suffocating. He could never put Sheri through this. Sure, Justin had died in some random accident, only testifying to the fact life could end at any time, but being a field agent was like tempting fate.

Paige glanced at him and took over. She pulled out her phone. "We'd like to know if you've ever seen any of these men?"

Zach was there in body—his ears hearing Paige and Abigail talking, and Abigail's swearing she'd never seen any of the men in the photo array—but his imagination had already taken over. He envisioned Sheri suffering years after his death, her life flipped upside down because of him, her drinking heavily in the afternoon in a crappy apartment… Their child who knows where, doing who knows what.

"We understand you used to be an active member of St. John's Catholic Church on Northeast Second Street and Northeast First Avenue." Paige's voice made it to his ears as if she were speaking from a great distance.

"Yes." Abigail took another draw on her drink. "What about it?"

"One of the men that Paige showed you was seen at your church," Zach said, forcing himself back to the moment, back to reality.

Paige held up her screen and the photo of the unsub.

Abigail shook her head. "I've never seen him. I told you that."

"Around the time of Justin's funeral, did you receive any monetary donations?" Zach asked.

Abigail indicated her surroundings.

Zach and Paige said nothing.

Abigail rolled her eyes. "Yes, okay, I did."

Zach could have questioned her hesitancy to respond or asked why she had said it that way, but instead, he remained quiet and leaned forward, his elbows on his knees.

Abigail slid her gaze to him. "My cousin, Agatha…"

Zach nodded to encourage her to continue, but when she didn't do so of her own accord, he asked, "She gave you money?"

"She gave some to me, but Agatha doesn't have much money sitting a— Oh, is that why you're here? Something to do with the money? Am I in trouble for something?"

Paige held up a hand. "Not at all. How much money were you given?"

"I tell you, it helped a lot in the beginning. Justin didn't have life insurance," she started, dancing around what Zach wanted to know; he was just waiting for her to say thirty thousand. "You'd think twenty thousand would go far, but it doesn't," she said.

"That's still a lot of money," Paige pointed out.

It wasn't the number he'd wanted to hear, but as Paige had said, it was a large sum. What was more interesting was the fact that Abigail didn't believe her cousin had that kind of money. So where did she get it? "Did you ever ask your cousin where she got all that money?" Zach asked.

"She told me not to worry about it. To see it as a gift from God, but I will never forgive Him for what He took away from me." Tears fell down her cheeks while rage stormed in her eyes. Not only had she lost her husband and unborn baby, but she'd lost her faith in God.

"Have you ever considered grief counseling?" he asked gently.

"No thanks," Abigail spat. "Agatha tried to get me to go to some support group for grieving family members." Abigail was shaking her head adamantly. "That's not for me."

"There are other people out there who are trained to help others work through their grief," Paige said.

"Yeah, and they all cost money. I don't have any left." Abigail drained the rest of her drink. "Mark would have been seven this year. If I hadn't wanted that dumb ice cream, then none of this would have happened. Both of them would still be here."

Zach figured Mark was the baby she'd lost. As he listened to Abigail, he observed her tense body language. She viewed healing as a threat to her memories, to the life she'd had. Despite all the time that had passed since the accident, she wasn't ready to heal and move on yet. She'd become comfortable in her pain, likely seeing the walls she'd erected as a cozy cocoon that protected her from opening up and getting hurt again.

"My mom says I should get out and meet someone. She reminds me that I'm still young, but then adds that I won't be forever." Abigail's eyes clouded over. "It's like she expects me to just replace Justin and Mark, pretend they never existed. At least that lady driver ended up getting hers. Not that it brings my husband and baby back." Her eyes cleared, and she locked her gaze on Zach, then Paige. "Why are you really here asking questions, showing me pictures?"

"Have you heard about the missing woman?" Zach asked.

Abigail's eyes widened. "Jenna Kelter, the mayor's niece? Of course I have. It said on the news that she'd just got released from serving a prison sentence for DUI vehicular homicide." Abigail lifted her glass to her mouth but then noticed it was empty and set it back down. "Is someone out there targeting people convicted of drinking and driving?"

It hadn't taken much for Abigail to take that leap. Impressive. "The investigation is still open," Zach said.

"Well, you don't have to say anything. I know that's what brings you *here*." Abigail tapped a hand over her heart. "Wait a minute, you don't think I'm involved with this do you? Or that Agatha is?" Her eyes darted back and forth between them.

Zach squinted. "Why would we think your cousin would be involved in any way?"

"She went crazy when she heard about Marie Sullivan's murder."

"Crazy how?" Paige asked.

Abigail frowned. "Just really shaken up. In shock but giddy, saying she got what she deserved."

Zach wasn't sure what to make of it. They had their eyes on a male unsub and hadn't completely dismissed a partnership. If there was a partner, though, they'd thought it was the delivery guy. But what if it was Agatha, a woman? She'd had quite the reaction to Sullivan's murder from what Abigail had said—and not in a good way. Plus, Agatha hadn't been forthcoming with Abigail about where she had gotten the money...

"How did the news make you feel?" Paige asked.

Abigail looked at her. "I didn't have any feelings about it really."

"So your cousin said Marie Sullivan got what she deserved?" Paige brought up.

"Yes, but so did I." Abigail sniffed again. Her eyes beaded with fresh tears. "I'm the one who sent him out for ice cream." Her chin quivered, and she stood. "I'm sorry, but you have to leave."

Zach and Paige had just cleared the door when it was slammed shut, and Zach heard the bolt lock and the chain slide into place.

"Don't come back!" Abigail wailed through the door.

Paige exhaled deeply. "Why do I feel like shit now?"

"Because we're not completely callous after all." Zach gave her a tight smile, taking some comfort in that conclusion himself.

They loaded onto the elevator and headed back to the lobby. "I think the cousin is worth a visit," Paige said. "Should I update Jack?"

"They do always say to follow the money." He just hoped to hell it would get them somewhere they wanted to go.

CHAPTER THIRTY-SEVEN

Kelly had imagined it several times, and the scenario always played out much the same way: Her doorbell would ring. She'd answer, thinking it was the food delivery guy, Randall, from her favorite mom-and-pop restaurant.

She'd pause the TV show she was watching and prance to the door, eager to dig into a steaming serving of tortilla chips smothered in cheese and piled inches high with ground beef, hot peppers, olives, and diced tomatoes.

But instead of Randall, she'd be facing an officer with a trainee she'd never seen before. They'd both be solemn, the trainee avoiding her eyes. And she'd know why they were there before they said a word. Her breath would catch, her legs would go weak.

"Are you Kelly Marsh?" the lead would ask.

She'd barely nod, invite them inside, and before they'd ask, she'd take a seat. Less of a distance to fall if she passed out from shock. She'd brace herself for the worst pain she could imagine.

They'd introduce themselves, and the training officer would say, "We're sorry to inform you that your mother, Susan Marsh, is dead."

The news would impact Kelly with the crushing weight of a sledgehammer, shattering the pieces of her life she'd tried so hard to gather and assemble.

Kelly's heart was racing as she twisted her hands on the steering wheel of the department car. She was parked in front of the Kelters' residence. She looked at the house, the Mercedes in the driveway, and thought of the man inside. She was about to wield that sledgehammer, but better her than a stranger.

She knocked on the door, and the curtain in the door's window was brushed aside. The dead bolt was undone not long afterward, and the door opened. Gordon Kelter stood there with one hand braced on the handle and one on the frame. Behind him, colored lights flickered from a television, but no sound accompanied them. It must have been muted.

"Detective?" Gordon's eyes clouded over, and his legs buckled beneath him.

Kelly rushed forward to help keep him upright. It was his two hundred pounds against her 125, but she was strong. She guided him inside the house. He started crying, and the primal sound of it stabbed at Kelly's heart.

There were times when words weren't enough, and other times, like this one, when they weren't even needed. She guided him toward the living room. Once he was seated in a sofa chair, she sat on the couch. She perched on the corner of one of its cushions.

She steeled herself. "I'm sorry to have to inform you—"

"She's dead." Gordon met her eyes and nodded. "You can tell me."

"Your wife was murdered," Kelly delivered sympathetically, though there was no real way of softening the blow.

"She's really..." Gordon choked on his sobs. "What? When? How? Do you know who did it?"

His response was typical of the situation. The questions often came fast and furious.

Gordon repeated his last question with added emphasis. "Do you know *who* did this to her?"

"We don't yet—" she shook her head slowly "—but we will do our best to find the person who's responsible for her death."

"And you're sure it was her?" His eyes were glazed over, like two unseeing marbles.

She'd seen this before: waves of denial and shock ebbing with hope that there'd been a mistake. "You'll need to make a positive ID, but yes, we are. I'm sorry."

Gordon made a move to get up. "Take me to her."

"You won't want to see her in her current state," Kelly rushed out.

He went still and asked barely above a whisper, "What did that animal do to her?"

There'd be no good time to tell him that his wife had been decapitated. That part was best left to Lily after the viewing and the legal identification. The lack of a body at that time wouldn't pose a problem. Kelly had been there for West's and Sullivan's presentations to family and knew that with expert placement of pillows and the use of a black sheet, they could create the illusion of a body.

"Let's not dwell on exactly what happened to her right now," Kelly said gingerly.

Gordon sniffled, letting that fight go for now. "You think that whoever killed her did it because she messed up *once…*" He held up an index finger. "Was it one of the men the FBI agents showed me?"

"We don't know for certain." Kelly hated to admit to their limitations. She wished she could offer him closure and justice, not just sympathy. "If you can think of anyone who might have—"

"No." He shot her down before she could finish the thought. "I don't know anyone who hates her that much. I already told you that when I filed the missing person report. Did you even look at those letters I gave the FBI?"

Her answer was silence.

"What have you been doing?" he snarled. "You didn't save my Jenna, and now you're here looking at me to do your job for you."

The verbal lashing stung, and her heart clenched. She pulled the printed photo of the delivery guy out of a pocket to show Gordon when someone banged on the front door. She jumped up without hesitation, stuffing the photo back into a pocket. "I'll get that."

She opened the door to Mayor Conklin. "What are you—"

He brushed past her, as did his two henchmen, Ramirez, a female TV reporter, and a cameraman.

Kelly caught the mayor by the arm. "You can't be here right now."

He spun and glowered at her. "You didn't save my niece."

Kelly let go of him, feeling like the wind had been knocked out of her. First, she'd failed her mother. She'd never been able to find her; she couldn't protect her if she didn't know where she was. She'd failed West and Sullivan. And now she'd failed Kelter. The weight of it was too much to bear. She heaved for breath.

"There have been three decapitations over the span of six years," the reporter said, drawing Kelly's eye. She was flat-chested, all of five feet tall with her pointed three-inch heels.

"Get out of this house," Kelly roared. The last thing she wanted was for Gordon to hear that his wife was decapitated this way.

Stilettos held up a photo of the delivery guy with one hand, and with the other, she pushed a microphone in Kelly's face. "Do you believe this man is behind the murders?"

If rage were a color, it would be a deep shade of red, and that's all Kelly was seeing. She hadn't given Ramirez the photo; he must have gotten it from one of the canvassing officers. She glared at the sergeant. "You share confidential information about open investigations with the media now? Why doesn't that surprise me?"

"I can't reveal my sources, Detective," Stilettos jumped in as if oblivious that Kelly hadn't addressed her.

Kelly ripped the foam topper off the microphone and pushed it into the reporter's chest. "Stuff it."

The reporter's mouth gaped open, and Kelly was about to lay into Ramirez some more when she heard the mayor calling out to Gordon. Conklin was weaving his way through the house. Kelly lunged for him, but Ramirez pulled her back.

"You've done your job here, Marsh," Ramirez said. "Now go catch the killer." The sergeant slipped in a smug smile to the reporter, which curdled Kelly's stomach.

"What man?" Gordon bypassed the mayor, and he was pawing at the air, almost as though he'd just gone blind. His eyes found Kelly's just before Stilettos hustled between them and held up the photo of the delivery guy.

Are you fucking kidding me?

Kelly swiped the photo from the woman, tore it into pieces, and stuffed them into a back pocket.

"Hmph. I can just get another one," the reporter pouted.

Kelly's guess was that the sulky princess was used to getting her way. Kelly stared her down. "I don't recommend that you do."

"Detective?" Gordon called out to her.

"This man, Gordon." The mayor intervened and pulled a photo from his pocket.

What, had they had the photo mass-printed at a copy center?

The reporter jutted out her chin at Kelly, and she was two seconds away from knocking her block off.

Kelly looked at Gordon. "Mr. Kelter, please don't—"

He took the photo from the mayor.

"Mr. Kelter, you don't have to do this right now." She put her hand over Gordon's to prevent him from lifting the photo. She turned to the minions. "Some privacy would be nice." None of them moved. The reporter crossed her arms. She looked back at Gordon, who'd gotten the picture free of her hold. He stared at the photo, eyes wide. The print fell to the floor, and Gordon soon followed.

Kelly tried to catch him but was too late. The reporter gasped, the cameraman kept rolling, and Ramirez called 911.

Kelly balled a fist, tempted to punch something. She got in Conklin's face, figured she'd try to shut this down by appealing to his main interest. "How do you think it looks to the public that you—" Kelly pressed a fingertip into his chest "—the mayor, have a serial killer on the loose in your city?"

Stilettos became animated, gesturing for her camera guy to keep rolling, never mind the poor man lying on the ground.

"And you." Kelly fixed a glare on the news crew. "You air even a one-second clip of this and I will bring you up on charges."

The reporter looked at her cameraman, and he lowered the camera. Kelly sank to her knees to check on Gordon. She could feel the heat of Ramirez's stare on the back of her head. She wished he'd go ahead and fire her. He'd make it a lot easier for her to leave Miami. But one thing was for certain: she'd be finding justice for the Kelters, the Wests, and the Sullivans—with or without a badge.

CHAPTER THIRTY-EIGHT

Jack had taken Zach's update about Abigail Cole in typical Jack fashion—in stride. It was Marsh's call about what had transpired with Gordon Kelter that I'd thought was going to give him a heart attack. His face had turned bright red, and a vein had protruded in his forehead. If Marsh hadn't worked her charm and dished out reassurances that she'd gotten the situation under control, we would have been loaded back into the SUV and on our way to Kelter's by now. Instead, we were making our way up Ava Jett's front walk.

Henderson's e-mailed threat had come through to Jack's phone, and he'd forwarded it to the rest of us, including Nadia so she could hopefully work her magic and trace its origin.

I read the e-mail on my phone:

> *You are responsible for inflicting chaos and shall suffer the consequences. Tell the police about this e-mail and you and your family will suffer the consequences.*

> *Jenna Kelter's disgusting habit made her a murderer. She killed an innocent man and destroyed lives. The aftermath set in motion is irreversible and has destroyed more than just a family.*

I looked over at Jack. "This e-mail specifically mentions Kelter. No wonder he was so quick to remember this one particular threat."

"I thought the same thing," Jack said.

Jack and I went on to pay a visit to LDS and met with a brick wall. The manager had been adamant that she didn't recognize any of the men in the photo array, which had been updated to include the delivery guy. To cement her stance that LDS wasn't involved, she showed us a stack of colored delivery slips. The one the receptionist had signed for had been black-and-white.

Ava answered the door before we had a chance to knock. She'd ventured out of her robe but not too far from comfy clothes. She swam in a T-shirt that was two or three sizes too big, which she had paired with yoga pants. She stepped back to let us inside, not even asking why we were there, and led us through the house as she had yesterday. As we passed the kitchen, I looked in. It had been tidied. And when we reached the living room, there were no past-due notices on the coffee table.

Jack put his hands to his thighs as he took a seat on the couch. "We just have a few more questions for you."

"Sure." A tad hesitant, but Ava sank back into a chair and crossed her legs at the ankles.

I brought up the photo array and handed my phone to Ava. "Scroll through the next few images. Do any of them look familiar?"

Ava's gaze went to the screen. "Am I supposed to know them?"

This wasn't the first time I'd heard this response from someone I was questioning, but it always struck me as an odd reaction. It was funny how most of us were primed to defend ourselves. "Just let us know if you do," I said.

Ava lifted her head and met my eyes briefly before returning her attention to the picture. She scrolled, paused, scrolled, paused. "How many pictures are there?"

"Four total," I replied.

She scrolled once more and held my phone out to me. "I've never seen any of them before."

I studied her body and facial language for any signs of lying, which could include: twitchy head movement; deepened breathing; extreme stillness; fidgeting; hands going to her mouth; covering her throat, chest, or abdomen; feet shuffling; staring or pointing, to name a few. But Ava didn't show any of these common traits associated with deception.

I took my phone back from her and put it away.

"Now answer me this question: who are they?" Ava pressed her brow.

"We've learned that you received money through the church after Lester died," Jack started. "A fairly significant amount, too."

"After he was *murdered*? Yes, I did." She crossed her arms. "Ain't no law against taking money."

"We never said there was," Jack replied coolly.

"One of those men we showed you was at his funeral," I told her. "Are you sure you've never seen any of these men before?"

Ava fixed a blank gaze on me. "You've never lost anyone you loved, have you?"

Her question caught me off guard and put me on the spot. I pulled on my collar and dropped my hand. "I've had people leave my life." Though I doubted, given the context, that Ava would count my divorce.

"Because they *died*?" She thrust her head forward.

Where was the bell to save me?

"No," I admitted.

"Then you haven't a clue. I wasn't in my right mind that day. Still not on some days. There isn't any way that I'd remember some stranger's face unless he gave the money to me directly. Then *maybe*." Her eyes misted. "I hope you never experience loss, Agent, but the odds are you will someday. And you'll find out it's hell on Earth." She turned to Jack. "You've lost people."

"Sure have." I felt Jack's guard going up. He wasn't the type to share emotions, and I certainly didn't expect him to start bearing his soul right now.

"Then you know. It feels like your heart's been ripped out of your chest and stomped on. Life as you knew it is over. You forget who you were before. Things you enjoyed doing, you don't anymore because the one you lost was a part of it somehow."

The front door slammed shut.

"Nathan?" Ava yelled as she got up and hurried toward the entry. "What are you doing home from school already?"

I didn't hear an answer to her question, and Ava returned to the living room, a teenager in tow. The boy eyed Jack and me skeptically. The only thing about him that wasn't dark was his pale skin. Everything else was black—hair, lipstick, eyeshadow, clothing, and satchel. He had piercings in his bottom lip, nose, all around his ears, and eyebrows.

"What's going on, Mom?"

"Don't concern yourself with it," Ava said firmly. "We'll talk later."

Nathan directed his glare at his mother and then let it slide over to me. If his attitude was representative of teens, I'd apparently dodged a bullet not having kids. Though my mom would tell me there was still time for me to have a family. Normally the "wisdom" came on the tail end of too many vodka coolers, and she figured it was okay to overstep.

Nathan stomped off, and in his wake was the smell of something sweet. I sniffed in the fragrance, and the hair on the back of my neck stood up.

"Something's happened." Ava was looking in the direction Nathan had gone. "I should probably go talk to—"

A door slammed.

"Guess I'll leave that for later." Ava returned to her chair. She glanced at Jack, then me. "I really don't remember seeing any of those men."

I looked over at Jack, and he nodded ever so slightly. He'd picked up on the scent, too. Literally.

"Hello? Did either of you hear me?" she asked.

"We did," I said. It was curious that she'd bring the photos up again when that part of the conversation had come to an end before Nathan had come home.

Ava pulled on the bottom of her T-shirt and was fidgeting with the hem.

"You're sure?" I pushed.

"Yes," she hissed.

There was something different about her since her son had shown up. She was uncomfortable, shifty. Why? What was she holding back?

"Losing someone close to you certainly makes it necessary to rediscover yourself," Jack said. He must have sensed the same thing I had and was trying to coax her into opening up again. "I even changed careers before."

Ah, so he wanted to address her lie about being fired.

"You weren't always a waitress," Jack said directly. "You said you quit your job?"

"Yeah." She began to fidget with more vigor. Her fingers swiftly twisted and kneaded the hem now. "You found out I was fired, didn't you?" She averted her gaze from us briefly, then brought it back to me.

"We did," Jack confirmed, taking her attention. "Why did you tell us you quit? People get fired."

"It was just embarrassing. I'd worked there for years. I lose Lester, and they show me the door. Who fires a grieving widow?"

"Sometimes life isn't fair," Jack said matter-of-factly.

"Damn straight it's not fair!"

"Getting fired made you angry," Jack noted aloud, adding another piece of kindling on the fire.

Ava flailed her hands in response.

"So first your husband, then your job," Jack poked. "Talk about being under the mother of all black clouds."

She shot to her feet. "I think it's time for you to leave."

Jack didn't budge from the couch. "I'm just saying, you really got a raw deal. I'd want someone to pay for that."

"I had nothing to do with that woman's murder!"

It was as if time stood still. My breathing halted for a few heartbeats. "What woman?"

"Jenna Kelter, that bitch who killed my husband. I never killed her!" Spittle flew from her mouth.

Then there was silence—the eye of the storm. I felt dizzy, as if someone had just cuffed me alongside the head. The differences in the way Kelter's head had been treated, the changes to the MO…

Ava was clearly angry with Kelter. As she'd said, her heart had been "ripped out and stomped on." She had always referred to her husband's death as a murder, too, and to top it off, Ava was a religious person. Didn't Sunday school teach the Bible's code of justice, an eye for an eye? Of course, her alibis had cleared her, but there were other ways of taking someone out. She worked three jobs, so unless she was extremely irresponsible with money, she shouldn't be in such arrears. And what about life insurance? Surely, she'd have benefited financially from Lester's death. Where had all that money gone? Not to mention the money she'd received with the anonymous donation. I'd be going out on a limb here, but…

"Did you hire someone to take care of Jenna Kelter?" I asked.

Ava's eyes widened, and her mouth gaped open. "As in, a hit man?"

I kept my attention on her, serious with every fiber of my being. "That's what I'm asking."

Ava snorted out a laugh of derision. "With what?"

Jack stood now. "We're going to need you and your son to come with us, Mrs. Jett."

CHAPTER THIRTY-NINE

If you think I'm going to say I'm sorry to hear that woman was murdered, you're wrong." Agatha was Latino and all pointed fingers and loud diatribes. She was certainly an animated character, and her feelings about Marie Sullivan were plain to see.

Zach and Paige had just stepped inside Agatha's apartment, and all it had taken to wind her up was to mention they were there to talk about what had happened to her cousin's husband. While she was certainly charged about the topic, Zach wasn't drawing a conclusion as to what that meant quite yet.

"We can appreciate that you're upset about what happened," Paige said.

"No," she barked. "To say I'm *upset* is an understatement. That woman killed Justin. It was no accident. You drink, you get behind the wheel, you're responsible for what happens."

Zach was sure that if he were to lose a friend or family member that way, he'd be inclined to feel the same.

"My poor cousin even lost her baby," Agatha continued.

"Was that why you were moved to help her financially?" Zach asked.

Agatha blanched. "Oh God. You know?" She looked upward, signed the cross, and walked deeper into the apartment.

Zach glanced at Paige, and she looked as lost as he felt. "Agatha?" Zach said, as he and Paige followed after Agatha. They caught up with her in a modest living room where she was sitting on a chair. He and Paige sat on a couch.

Agatha was mumbling in Spanish.

"Agatha," he repeated louder.

"Ah, *si*." Agatha's legs were bouncing.

"Tell us about the money." Paige tilted her head. "Where did you get it?"

Agatha's eyes teared up. She signed the cross again. "Please forgive me, Father, for I have sinned."

"How did you sin?" Zach asked.

Agatha was staring into space. "I don't have the kind of money I gave Abigail. A man gave it to me."

Zach was still lost on how she'd sinned, but he'd let that part go. "Tell us what he looked like."

"It was a long time ago now."

"Try," Paige said softly.

She thought for a moment. "Brown hair, brown eyes. Good-looking."

"Age?" Zach asked.

"He was probably in his late twenties, early thirties?"

"Accent? Nationality?" Zach kept the questions going.

"He had some kind of Southern accent. Georgia maybe?"

Zach pulled out his phone and brought up the photo array. He held the screen toward her. "I'm going to show you a few pictures. Let me know if you recognize any of these men."

The first picture was the delivery guy, and Agatha shook her head. The second one was their unsub and met with the same reaction. On the third one, Agatha held up an index finger for Zach to stop scrolling.

"Go back one," she told him.

He did as she'd requested, and she pinched two fingers to the screen and stretched them out to enlarge the photo. "That's him. I swear it."

"He's the man who gave you the money?"

"Yeah, that's him."

Zach's lungs expanded. They now knew their unsub had an accent. "How much money did he give you?"

Agatha looked upward again. "Thirty thousand in cash."

He'd jump and click his heels in glee if he were the type to do something like that. Agatha's testimony had confirmed that two out of five families affected by West's, Sullivan's, and Kelter's accidents had received thirty thousand dollars from an unknown male. Twice could be a coincidence, but a pattern was emerging. However, the man who had given money to the Jetts did so through the church, so why not in Abigail's case? Did it have to do with the fact Justin Cole's service was held in a funeral home?

"Where and when did he give you the money?" Zach asked.

"After church the week of Justin's funeral."

"The service was held on a Saturday, correct? So that would have been the day after the funeral?" Zach queried to clarify.

"That's right," Agatha confirmed.

"And what church do you belong to?" Paige asked.

"Same as Abigail, though she doesn't go anymore."

"Which one is that?" Zach needed to hear Agatha say it.

"St. John's," Agatha said.

"So he just came up to you and handed you all that cash?" Paige's voice was ripe with interest.

"Yeah, pretty much."

"Like a miracle," Paige said with a smile.

"That's how I came to see it."

"Did he say anything to you when he gave you the money?" Paige asked.

"He said he was sorry for the family's hardship and to please pass along the money to my cousin and her son. Something to that effect anyhow." Agatha waved her hands. "At first, I thought the guy was some wacko and I didn't want to touch that money. But I've never seen that much cash outside of TV and the movies." She glanced at the carpet.

"And it was right there, ya know? So I took it." She shrugged, looking at Zach. "He seemed nice enough."

A true mark of a skilled sociopath was presenting themself as relatable. In this case, a bleeding heart. But Zach noted something else—the familiarity. "He knew about your cousin's pregnancy and that she'd been expecting a boy?"

She nodded. "I figured maybe he knew her somehow but wanted to keep the money anonymous."

"Sure." Paige smiled. "What happened after you took the money?"

"I fanned it. Sniffed it. Like I said, I'd never seen that much money." Agatha blushed, seemingly embarrassed. "I looked up to ask his name and thank him, but he was gone."

"Gone? Just like that?" Zach snapped his fingers.

"Yeah, like an angel."

More like the Grim Reaper.

"I know I did wrong by my cousin, that's how I sinned, but I had credit card debt. Now I don't."

Zach pieced her reaction together. "I can understand it would have been very tempting to take some."

"I agree," Paige sympathized. "You have any of the cash left?"

Agatha shook her head.

Zach thought Paige's question had been a reach. It had been seven years ago! But if they were able to get their hands on even one of the bills, they might have been able to track the serial number.

"Did you mention the man to Abigail?" Zach asked, curious if Abigail had withheld that information when they'd spoken to her.

"Not in so many words." Agatha paused and crossed herself again. "I'm going to Hell. I told her I'd collected the money. Thankfully she didn't press me on how or I would have had to come up with some story."

Agatha could work on her morals, but Zach was pretty sure she was telling the truth.

"You're not going to tell my cousin, are you?" Agatha tugged on Paige's arm. "Please don't tell her."

"We have no reason to, but don't go anywhere in case we need to talk to you again." Paige handed Agatha her card.

Agatha studied it. "The BAU?" Her brows rose in perfectly shaped arches. "Like from that TV show *Criminal Minds*?" Her face fell. "Did those guys you showed me kill someone?" She gulped. "Marie Sullivan?"

"We can't answer that," Zach replied calmly.

Agatha was blinking rapidly and panting lightly. "Am I in danger?"

"We have no reason to believe so." Paige put a reassuring hand on Agatha's arm before leaving with Zach.

When they were back at the SUV, Paige grabbed the door handle on the passenger side. "She's terrified, and I don't blame her."

"He won't be coming for her." Zach started the SUV.

"We know that, but she doesn't."

They both strapped in when Zach's phone rang over the onboard system. He answered, and Jack's voice came through the speakers. "Get back to the station. The kid and I just brought in Ava Jett and her son."

"See you in five." Zach barely had gotten the words out before the line went dead. He put the SUV into drive, contemplating how the lead they'd received from Agatha would tie into this new twist in the case.

CHAPTER FORTY

I can't believe you think I hired a hit man," Ava spat with enough contempt to anchor a ship.

She sat with her son Nathan across from me and Jack in an interrogation room at Miami PD. Neither of them was under arrest, but we were interested in getting some straightforward answers she didn't seem to be volunteering on "neutral territory." There was something about four cinder block walls and a two-way mirror that could loosen lips as well as seal them. With the Jetts, I was betting on the former.

Nathan was staring at the table; one would think it was as entertaining as his cell phone that we'd asked him to put away.

"Your bank records will tell us what we need to know," I said, completely bluffing as we didn't have enough to subpoena them.

"Good. Then let us go," Ava said coolly.

"You know we can't do that yet." I relaxed, sinking back into the chair. "Why all the past-due bills?"

Ava's cheeks flared red. "Because life sucks!"

Nathan still sat there, his gaze downcast, his mother's outburst not having any visible impact on him whatsoever. Looking at him again brought my mind back to the cologne he used. He told us it was called Swept Away, and a quick online search revealed it was definitely priced for the teenage market. Beyond his fragrance choice, we had nothing connecting Nathan to Kelter's murder.

"Nathan, have you always used Swept Away?" I asked.

Ava crossed her arms in a huff. "I really wish you'd leave my son out of this."

"*This* being what specifically?" I countered.

I'd had empathy for Ava when I'd first met her. I understood why she thought of her husband as murdered. I sort of *got* her. But if she was innocent of anything regarding Kelter's disappearance, I was having a hard time understanding why she was being difficult. Generally, the guilty become defensive while the innocent keep their cools. Ava Jett definitely was withholding something. We just needed to figure out whether it had to do with Kelter or not. Maybe she was even keeping a secret for her son.

She glared at me. "You really think I killed that woman? Or that my son did?"

"We never said she was dead," I told her again. We'd been through this, first at her house, and since here in this room, and were still playing that game.

"It was a logical conclusion, the way the two of you came at me. You've checked my alibis?"

"For Sunday." I leaned forward across the table and mustered a menacing look to level on Nathan. "We'll need his—and yours—for last night, too."

"I swear to you," Ava pleaded.

"If you weren't involved, then it should be easy. Tell us where you were," I said.

Ava's chin quivered, and a tear fell down her cheek. "I work at Quincy's Diner until ten on Mondays, so I did that, then went home to bed." She turned to her son.

"I was hanging out in my room from the time I got home from school at about three."

"Can anyone verify that?" I asked.

"Seriously?" Ava said with derision. She was like a Chihuahua yapping at a bullmastiff—all bark, no bite. "My son wouldn't harm anyone."

I sat back, studying mother and son. Desperation was clear in her eyes. Nathan shifted in his chair as if anxious to leave. Was it due to discomfort and guilt? I noticed that Ava hadn't testified to being home with her son later in the evening.

"Nathan?" I pressed.

"I don't think so," Nathan mumbled. He was a different guy in this room than he'd been at home with his mother. The attitude and brash edge were gone.

I was starting to think he'd just had the bad luck of wearing the cologne used on the decapitated head. If I was really convinced that Nathan was guilty, I would push him harder and make him crack. That had to be my next step, just to find out for sure. I glanced at Ava, then back at Nathan. She was hiding something. Maybe if I summoned the instincts of the mother bear…

"If you can't tell us where you really were, we'll need to hold you," I threatened Nathan.

"I told you I was at home." Nathan glanced at his mother, but Ava said nothing and was avoiding eye contact. So much for momma bear stepping in. She must have been finished lying.

I shrugged my shoulders. "I don't think you were."

"Maybe our neighbors saw me come home?" Nathan sounded desperate.

"Are you friends with your neighbors?" I noticed he didn't refer to any by name so I figured I knew what his answer would be, but his response would help me break him.

Nathan gulped. "No."

"But you think they have been paying close enough attention to you to know when you came home?" I served back and winced. "Not sure I buy that, either. Unfortunately, we need more than what you're—"

"Mom," Nathan burst out, panic gripping his features as he turned to Ava, "say something."

"Just leave him alone," Ava snarled. "He doesn't know anything."

I withheld the smile I so badly wanted to show. "Are you ready to talk, then?"

"Yes," she hissed. "I recognized one of those men you showed me. I lied about it."

"Seems you have an issue with telling the truth," Jack interjected. Apparently, he was assuming the strong, mostly silent role for this interview.

I slapped the printouts of the men down on the table. When the one of the unsub looked up at Ava, she sucked in air.

I looked at Nathan. "Do you know him?"

"I've never seen him," Nathan mumbled and went back to staring at the table.

Ava blinked, tears wetting her lashes.

"Who is he?" I demanded, and it had her flinching.

"I might have seen him around. I don't know where."

"Really? That's how you're going to play this." I moved to get up. "We'll have no choice but to take Nathan into—"

"No!" she cried out. "Stop."

"Sure," Jack said coolly. "We have all night to wait for your memory to come back."

I snuck in a glance at my watch and realized we'd already been talking with them for a few hours. It was going on five thirty in the evening.

"I don't want any trouble." Her chin trembled subtly as if she was about to cry.

"Seems to me you already have that," Jack replied.

"A worse kind of trouble." Her gaze darted to the photo.

I put my hand on the corner of the printout. "You're afraid of him?"

Ava nodded.

"How do you know him?" I asked, projecting a slightly calmer demeanor than a moment ago.

"I've seen him at the supermarket before."

"And you're afraid of him," I scoffed. "Why?"

"You're showing me his picture for one! The damn FBI! He must have done something wrong—horrible even." She flailed her arms emphatically.

Neither Jack nor I responded.

Ava's face became serious. "What did he do?"

"We can't tell you that," Jack deadpanned.

Ava looked at me. "I don't know him from seeing him in a supermarket," she confessed.

"Why doesn't that surprise me," I replied drily.

She rolled her eyes. "It's not like I know his name or anything."

"Tell us what you *do* know." I was running out of patience—and fast. I wasn't a huge fan of liars, and yes, I realized I was in the wrong industry as being lied to was par for the course.

"He gave us money," Ava said. "You said you already knew that, though. At the house."

Nathan looked over at his mom. Jack remained still. I leaned forward. The woman at the church had said the money had been routed through the church's account to the Jetts and donated anonymously. We thought Ava may have seen him at her husband's funeral, but she was making it sound like—

"Did he give you money directly?" I asked.

"Uh-huh." Ava wrung the hem of her T-shirt.

"How much and when?" I asked.

"You know about the thirty thousand through the church?" Ava paused, and I nodded. She continued. "Well, he came into one of the diners where I work. He ordered a coffee and left a hundred-dollar tip."

"A hundred dollars?" I don't know what surprised me more: the amount or the fact that it didn't include the number three.

"Yeah. I thought he'd made a mistake and went after him."

"Did you catch up with him?" Jack asked.

"Uh-huh. He told me he'd left the money for me and my son. He didn't say as much, but I knew then he'd been the one to donate to us through the church."

So the unsub gave anonymously but then decided to follow up to make sure the Jetts received the money...

Nathan lifted his head. "How did this stranger know about me?" he asked his mother, then turned to me and Jack.

"It's probably best we don't get into all of that," I said. "Is there anything else you can remember about this man that might help us find him? How he spoke? What he smelled like? Any tattoos?"

Ava shook her head. "He smelled nice enough that I remember, but I couldn't say what he was wearing."

"Sweet smelling or…?" I prompted.

Ava hitched her shoulders. "Smelled expensive."

A few seconds of silence passed.

"Oh." Ava's eyes widened. "He was wearing one of those keychains that attach to a belt."

My brows pressed downward as I wasn't quite sure what she meant.

"You know, they…" Ava put her hands together and drew them apart and repeated the process as if she were stretching an invisible band between them. Then again, I was never good at charades.

"The kind that retract?" Jack asked. "The keys stay in a pocket, for example, and when the person needs them just the keys themselves can be pulled out."

"Yes, like that, but it had a keycard attached."

Maybe our unsub worked somewhere he needed to bypass security. "Did you see what it looked like? Any writing or logos on it?"

Ava shook her head. "Just that it was white."

Jack's phone rang, and he got up and answered. "Uh-huh. Okay. We'll be there." He pocketed his phone and looked at me. "We've got to go."

"What about us? Can we leave now?" Ava asked. "I told you everything I know."

Jack nodded, and Ava sighed in relief. She patted her son on the back and broke the seemingly hypnotizing effect the table had on him.

Both of them left, and Jack turned to me. "Kelter's phone just went live."

Well what do you know? An actual break in the case.

CHAPTER FORTY-ONE

Kelly's trigger finger was itchy again, and it was taking all her willpower and self-control not to act. Killing Ramirez wouldn't solve her problems, even if he was her problem. She'd end up going to prison, her life over. He wasn't worth it. She just needed to get the hell out of Miami PD.

Paramedics had picked up Gordon at his house and had taken him to the hospital, where they fussed over him some more, despite his protests. She stood by and made calls to West's and Sullivan's lawyers, and neither of them had a record of receiving hate mail related to Kelter. After that, she managed to squeeze in to talk to Gordon while he was waiting on a doctor. He'd told her that he recognized the delivery guy from a bakery he and Jenna used to go to sometimes.

She opened the door for Sweet Tooth Bakery and was immediately enveloped in a heavenly assortment of smells: croissants, cheesecake, sugar cookies, icing, icing, and more icing. She could lick the tops off the red velvet cupcakes in the display case. Icing was right up there with loaded nachos. Yum.

A woman about the same age as Kelly was smiling at her from behind the counter. "What can I get you?"

A tub of icing... Followed immediately by the thought, *A moment on the lips, forever on the hips.*

She pulled out her badge, and the woman shrank back.

"It's okay. I just need to speak to the manager." Kelly smiled at the woman and she nodded, then retreated into the back.

Kelly took in all the goodies, her stomach growling. It was after five and she'd hardly eaten today. Surely, she could justify a cookie, maybe two. Hey, it could be her dinner. But she knew she'd be hungry again in an hour. Pouring sugar down her throat wasn't a solution. Not that she was a health nut, but she watched what she ate, even if it was just before it went into her mouth. Those cookies were probably about three hundred and fifty calories a piece, which would mean she'd have to spend somewhere in the neighborhood of an extra hour running. Not worth it, especially when her time was such a hot commodity. Her regular hour a day was hard enough to work into her schedule, but it was also her savior—both physically and mentally.

"Can I help you?" A woman in her fifties approached, her gray hair tied back into a tight bun, her hands clasped in front of her. Nothing about her fit the image of what Kelly had expected for a manager of a bakery.

Kelly held up her badge again. "I'm Detective Marsh with Miami PD."

"Connie Baxter. I'm the owner here." She crossed her arms and tilted her head, clearly impatient.

Some people really didn't like cops—some outright hated them—and it was possible that Connie was in their ranks.

Kelly brought up the photo array that included the delivery guy and the unsub on her phone. She held out the screen to Connie, who moved closer to the counter, albeit reluctantly.

"Now, what am I looking at?" Connie asked snidely.

"I need to know if any of these people look familiar to you."

Connie regarded Kelly with suspicion. "Why?"

"Unfortunately, I can't—"

"Let me guess. It's an open investigation or some such thing." Connie loosened her arms and lowered them when a female patron stepped up to the counter beside Kelly.

Connie smiled at the woman, but when she looked back at Kelly, she was scowling. "I'd love to help you, but I'm not sorry I can't."

"You can't, or you won't?" Kelly served back with some heat.

"Both."

Wow, there was nothing sweet about the owner… Kelly put her phone away. She couldn't force Connie to do as she asked, and she didn't have a legitimate reason to take her down to the station. Kelly glanced at the customer next to her, who smiled back. At least there was one friendly face in the crowd.

Kelly was turning to leave when she locked eyes with the cashier who had gotten Connie for her. She was watching Kelly and something about the look in her eyes expressed a desire to help.

Connie asked, "Will you be leaving or are you getting anything to—"

"I'll have a cookie," Kelly interrupted, taking only a modicum of pleasure from repaying the favor. *Three hundred and fifty calories.* "And a large coffee—black." *Zero.*

Connie turned up her nose. "Christine will help you." With that, the owner rode her broomstick back to where she'd come from.

Christine finished up with the customer, bagged Kelly's cookie, and poured her coffee. She collected the money and said, "Just give me a minute." She disappeared into the back before Kelly could respond. When she returned, she was untying her half apron and proceeded to set it on a counter. She pointed toward a side door and went outside, Kelly close behind.

The door opened into a small alleyway, and Christine shuffled away from the door about twenty feet.

Kelly stopped across from her. The women were about a foot apart and facing each other.

"Connie doesn't like cops," Christine said, as if that were necessary.

"I take it you do?" Kelly concluded. It wasn't like Christine knew exactly what Kelly wanted. She would have seen Kelly show her phone and ask Connie if she recognized anyone. It was doubtful that Christine could have seen the faces from where she had been.

"Let me see those pictures you were showing Connie." Christine held her hand out. "I take it you're trying to track down a customer."

This woman was smart, Kelly gave her that, and intuitive. But Christine had also made a large assumption. How could she know the pictures were about a customer? "How do you know—"

"Well, it wasn't personal to Connie or you would have asked for her by name. And you followed me out here, so it's something you figure I might be able to help with." Christine's gaze softened, becoming apologetic. "I'm sorry for interrupting you. It's just that I don't have much time."

Kelly put the bagged cookie in the pocket of her light jacket and exchanged it for her phone. She balanced the coffee in one hand and worked to bring up the pictures with her other one. She put her phone in Christine's hand. "There are a few photos. Just scroll through them and let me know if you recognize anyone."

"Okay." Christine glanced at Kelly, almost hesitant before looking at the screen. She squinted and moved it at different angles. "Ugh, the sunlight," was all Christine said. She settled on an angle, and her eyes widened if only marginally as she swiped the screen.

Kelly felt a rise of excitement in her chest. "You recognize someone?"

"Uh-huh. This guy." Christine turned the phone and pressed a finger to the screen.

Kelly understood what she was saying about the sunlight as a glare was cutting right over the face Christine was indicating. Kelly took Christine's hand and maneuvered it so she could see clearly. She expected to see the delivery guy; instead their unsub's face was staring back at her.

She wanted to scream and celebrate, but caution reined her back. "You're sure?"

"Definitely. He's been coming here for a while."

The white boxes the heads were placed in were pegged as confection boxes, like the kind one gets from a bakery. Kelly gulped. Her heart was pounding in her ears now, an infusion of adrenaline racing through her veins. "He's a regular?" They could set up surveillance, see if he returned, catch him, put an end to the killings. Finally.

"He comes in probably about once a week."

Okay, keep your cool, Kelly coaxed herself. "The same day every week?"

"Not that predictable."

And there it was: a piercing needle taken to her balloon of hope. Some air hissed out.

Christine added, "His name's John Doe, if that helps."

"John Doe?" Kelly was taken aback. "If this is some sort of joke—"

"I know how it sounds. My first reaction to hearing it was the same as yours, but I swear I'm telling you the truth. He said his parents had a stupid sense of humor."

If someone actually named their kid John Doe, they had bigger problems than a warped sense of humor. Kelly studied Christine's eyes and, satisfied she was being honest, took her phone back. "What else can you tell me about—?"

The side door opened behind Kelly, and she glanced over a shoulder. It was Connie.

"Christine, your five minutes are up," the owner snarled.

"I'll be right there," Christine said.

"Now," Connie ordered and retreated back inside.

"I've got to go. Obviously." Christine rolled her eyes. "Otherwise she'll hop on her broomstick. I'll save you from seeing that."

Kelly laughed. She knew there was something she'd liked about Christine.

Christine took a few steps and said, "Come back tomorrow morning. Eight o'clock. It's Connie's day off."

"I'll be here," Kelly said. "Thanks."

"You should know that John Doe wasn't the only man I recognized from your pictures."

"Who—"

The door opened again.

"Christine!"

Christine leaned in toward Kelly as she walked by. "The one who was wearing a Miami Dolphins hat."

Kelly stood there for a few minutes after the door opened and closed behind the cashier. The Miami Dolphins hat belonged to the delivery guy. Although she was at the bakery because Gordon recognized him from there, it felt great to hear someone else did, too. Someone who might have something to offer as to his identity.

She pulled out her phone and dialed Nadia Webber. She figured what she was going to ask was a reach, but if she called anyone at Miami PD, it would get back to Ramirez. She wanted to keep him in the dark for as long as possible.

Nadia answered on the second ring.

"It's Detective Marsh."

"Kelly? I haven't received any hits on the delivery guy with facial rec yet."

"Thanks, but that's not why I'm calling," Kelly said. "Could you do me a quick favor?"

"Anything."

"I just had someone ID our unsub."

"That's great," Nadia exclaimed.

"Hold off on getting too excited just yet. The name I was given was John Doe."

"Are you joking?" Nadia let out a bark of laughter. "You have to be."

"I know this is a crazy long shot, but would you run the name through the database, see if anything pops in Miami or surrounding area. From there, see if any match our unsub." The second her verbal request hit her own ears, it only confirmed what an improbability this was, but she couldn't just disregard the fact she'd gotten a name, whatever it was.

"John Doe? Okay." Nadia sounded skeptical, not that Kelly blamed her. Regardless of how Nadia felt, if the keystrokes coming across the line were any indication, she was doing what Kelly had asked.

"There are a few John Does actually," Nadia confirmed.

"Among the living?" Kelly teased, attempting to remain light and unattached to the outcome.

Nadia laughed. "Yeah."

"Those poor men."

"You can say that again." At the tail end of that short sentence, Nadia sounded more serious. "But none of these John Does match the picture we have of the unsub."

Kelly sighed. She couldn't say she was surprised. She thanked Nadia and ended the call.

John Doe was a name that would taunt and ridicule her until she had this unsub in custody. This guy sure as hell had a sense of a humor, just like the parents who actually *did* name their sons John Doe, but she wasn't amused.

Her phone rang, and she answered quickly. As she listened to the caller, that balloon of hope was filling with air again. Kelter's phone had just been traced.

CHAPTER FORTY-TWO

It was six o'clock when the four of us and Marsh moved in on the customer counter at Bob's Wireless on West Flagler Street.

Jack held out his credentials to an acne-faced teen wearing a name tag that read *Kurt*. "A phone of interest to our investigation was tracked back to here," he said. "It would have been a new phone purchase that required that an old SIM card be installed."

Kurt blinked quickly and cleared his throat. "I've activated a few since I started my shift at four o'clock." His eyes were darting over the group of us.

"It would have been within the hour," Jack specified.

Kurt stepped away from the counter and looked toward the back of the store. The kid was nervous as hell.

I leaned casually on the counter. "I'm Brandon. We just need your help, Kurt." Using his name would go a long way toward making the conversation more personable.

Still, Kurt's body language was guarded. "I'll do what I can."

"Hey, that's all we can ask," I said in a laid-back tone. "We think the person who came in would have had a smashed-up phone they wanted replaced. Does that ring any bells?"

Kurt stepped closer to the counter now and nodded.

I angled my head. "It does?"

"Yeah, and she was real pretty and nice."

I gave him a cocky smile. "*Nice.* What else can you tell us about her?"

"Long legs. Shoulder-length blond hair."

That sounded like our unsub's girlfriend from the Cuban restaurant surveillance video. "Anything else?"

"She had a baggie of phone pieces with her. Told her all I needed was the SIM card."

"Sounds like the phone we're interested in," I said. "And how old do you think she was?" It never hurt to have more than enough information.

"In her thirties?"

"Okay, very good. That's a big help."

Kurt's shoulders relaxed, and he leaned on the counter, mirroring my pose.

I pulled out my phone and brought up a picture of the woman from the Cuban restaurant. "Was this her?"

Kurt nodded. "Yep."

"Do you remember how she paid for the phone?"

"Credit card."

"Oh, great." I reined in my excitement so as not to freak him out, but a credit card was a welcome break in the case. "Do you think you could bring up a copy of her receipt—"

"What's going on here?" A woman in her forties came barreling over to us.

It had to be the manager. We'd all have known we took that risk from the moment we approached poor Kurt here, but we wanted to see what we could get out of him first.

The woman seared Kurt with a heated glare, then focused it on Jack. She'd obviously pegged him as the one in charge, even though I had been talking to Kurt. I stood up straight.

Jack held up his credentials. "FBI, ma'am. We have some quest—"

"Then you talk to me and leave Kurt alone. I'm Betty-Lou, the manager here."

She didn't seem like a Betty-Lou. I shrugged off the silly thought. What did a Betty-Lou look like?

"We need to see a receipt," Jack told her.

Betty-Lou pursed her lips and tilted her head. Seconds ticked off. If she insisted on a warrant, that would set us back at least until morning, if not longer. As it was, once we had a receipt in hand, we'd have to get a signed subpoena. That was a job in and of itself. It would involve testifying to a judge about how we came into possession of the receipt and showing how the identification of the cardholder was relevant to our investigation. Easy enough to do with the woman activating a murder victim's SIM card, but this alone would take time, not to mention paperwork.

"I'd love to help. Warrant?" She held out her hand toward Jack.

"We could get one, but the woman we're trying to track down could be in danger." Jack was likely trying to appeal to her humanity. Betty-Lou didn't have to know that the woman could be romantically involved with a serial killer.

Betty-Lou chewed on her bottom lip and addressed her employee. "What receipt do they need?"

Kurt told her the approximate time and that the customer had paid with plastic.

Betty-Lou looked at Jack and moved behind the counter next to Kurt. "I'll get it for you," she said. "It shouldn't take too long to reprint the receipt."

A few seconds later, Betty-Lou extended a printout to Jack. "You can take that with you."

He nodded his thanks, and the five of us gathered on the sidewalk outside the store.

"The receipt shows five thirty," Jack said and pulled out his cigarette pack. "We didn't miss her by much."

"She could have come here after a day job," I bounced out, seeing if it would stick.

"If so, I'd say she works close by," Zach said. "Traffic isn't the fastest-moving around here."

Marsh smiled at him. "You get used to it."

"I'll take your word for it." He smiled back.

Marsh continued. "It's worthy to note that La Casa de Jose is only one block west of here."

"It seems clear this blond woman and the unsub are mostly tied to blocks in this part of Miami," Jack began. "But between them, there has to be a vehicle for abduction and disposal."

"Though we know Dominick was killed for his vehicle," I said.

"No, he was killed for his *job*," Marsh corrected.

Damn her and the technicality.

"I can handle the subpoena," Marsh offered. "Oh, and I got ahold of West's and Sullivan's lawyers. None of them received hate mail related to Kelter."

Jack nodded. "I thought you might get that response, but now we know." He took a picture of the receipt with his phone and gave the hard copy to Marsh. "Hold off on the subpoena until we bring one another up to speed." Jack fished out a cigarette, lit up, and took a deep drag.

My stomach rumbled so loud, I might as well have had a megaphone up to it.

Marsh laughed. "Brandon?"

"What?" I tried to play coy. "Any chance we can eat while we catch up?"

"The kid's stomach has a good idea." The cigarette between Jack's lips bobbed as he spoke. He smirked that lopsided smirk of his.

"I could eat," Marsh said, smiling at me.

After her, Paige and Zach chimed in their agreement. Thank God, because I'd missed lunch.

CHAPTER FORTY-THREE

Zach's first choice for dinner wouldn't have been the pizza the rest of the team and Marsh had opted to bring back to the station, but it was food. They all caught one another up, and Zach turned his attention to the hate mail delivered to the Kelters. He'd already pored over the threat sent to Henderson.

"I can't imagine what it must have been like at Gordon's this afternoon. And how you didn't hit anyone, especially Ramirez." Paige clapped. "Bravo."

Kelly smiled. "It was questionable there for a minute."

"Well, good for you. You're stronger than I would have been." Paige laughed.

Paige underestimated herself. She wouldn't have lost her cool, either. She was far too professional to do otherwise. Zach could imagine the two women being friends if they lived in the same area.

"Let's just say Ramirez can be a handful." Kelly slid her gaze to Jack, who was watching her thoughtfully. "He said he'd have Henderson covered for the night, but tomorrow will present another battle." Kelly balanced on the back legs of her chair. "He just doesn't seem to care that the man's life could be in danger. Though he's never been a fan of lawyers, so maybe he has a biased viewpoint." She met Jack's eyes and smiled.

"It seems you might have gotten the impression that *I* don't like lawyers." Jack turned to Brandon—some inside joke, Zach surmised. Though there wasn't anything unspoken about Jack's dislike for suits. *Skip impression, skip the fine print.*

Zach's eyes went from Jack to the whiteboard to the faces of the victims. A crime scene photo of Jenna Kelter had been added to the board. Another graphic reminder of the man they were hunting. A man with a face and an accent, of flesh and blood, but he may as well have been an apparition.

"What did you find with Kelter's hate mail?" Jack asked him.

"The gist of many of the messages was the same," Zach said. "Many struck me as coming from activists against drunk driving. The senders hold Jenna Kelter responsible for the death of Lester Jett. They all use the words *murder, murdered, murderer,* or *killer*." In his mind, Zach had cataloged every piece of mail from its envelope, to the handwriting, to the messages.

Brandon turned to Jack. "That's how Ava Jett termed her husband's death several times."

"And Agatha," Paige added.

"Getting back to the letters," Zach said, "most were mailed. Gordon had told me and Paige that someone had shown up to the house in person and banged on the door. Can't say that the same person hand-delivered hate mail, but some pieces weren't put through the postal system."

"We know our unsub isn't shy about being seen," Brandon began.

"Again, we haven't been able to conclude that our unsub dropped off West's head," Kelly said.

"It wouldn't surprise me if he did," Brandon served back. "We're talking about a guy who showed up at the church to give the money in person. He went to where Ava Jett worked and gave her money there, too."

And there's the redheaded dog with a bone...

Zach smiled to himself. "Yes, Brandon, he could have been the one who banged on the Kelters' door, though I doubt it. Right now, that's neither here nor there," Zach said. "There is a handwritten letter that makes me think of the one Henderson received via e-mail. This particular letter wasn't sent—electronically or snail-mail—but the word *chaos* pops up again as it does in Henderson's threat. And so does the word *aftermath*. I find the use of the two words together interesting. The meaning of the words have a similar effect, and while both can have a negative connotation, that's not necessarily the case." The others' eyes were glazing over. "Let's start with *aftermath*. It's the result of a negative event that can have long-lasting and far-reaching consequences. But in farming, *aftermath* is the term used for grass that grows after mowing—essentially, creation. And chaos? Well, everything is created from it. In the Sunday school version of the beginning of the world, everything here was chaos and formless."

"First the church connection, now the word choice," Kelly started. "Hard to believe that's a coincidence."

"Agreed. So we need to find out what affected our unsub both negatively and positively," Zach said.

"And does it have anything to do with St. John's, or the Catholic religion in general?" Brandon asked.

"Too soon to know," Jack started. "But we know that the Jetts and Coles were connected to St. John's. Regina didn't know the three families affected by West's accident, but maybe there's a less obvious connection between them and the church. We also need to know if they received any money. From there, we pinpoint what might have triggered our unsub," Jack concluded. "For now, Zach, read the handwritten letter you said reminded you of the one Henderson received."

"'She is a killer and deserves far beyond any sentence this life has to offer for murder. The chaos she set in motion is unforgivable, the aftermath undeniable.'" Zach rattled it off from memory.

"'Far beyond any sentence'? He could be speaking out against the judicial system. By killing West, Sullivan, and Kelter, he's setting himself up to be judge, jury, and executioner," Brandon reasoned.

"I think that's entirely possible," Zach replied.

"And the part about being unforgivable hints at a religious mentality," Paige surmised. "I remember from church that the Bible speaks of an unforgivable sin."

"Blasphemy," Zach said.

"Not sure how that would fit our situation." Paige grabbed a fresh water bottle from the middle of the table, twisted off the lid, and took a sip.

Zach was chewing on her question, and even his computer of a brain was working hard to pull up and sift through dictionary definitions of the word *blasphemy* and cross-reference them. "Actually, blasphemy is to speak or act sacrilegiously against God or sacred things. *Sacrilegious* is defined as a 'violation or misuse of what's regarded as sacred.' That's straight from Google."

"And your brain." Brandon raised his brows.

Kelly looked at him and angled her head.

"I swear." Zach was smiling.

"What's regarded as sacred?" Brandon mused. "Could it be life itself?"

"Exactly what I thought," Zach admitted. "Now, we all know what Henderson's e-mail said. It too mentioned chaos and aftermath."

"I also thought it sounded quite personal," Paige started. "It had said something about the aftermath Kelter set in motion being irreversible and destroying more than a family. Our unsub must have lost a loved one to a drunk driver."

Brandon said, "Hate to play devil's advocate here, but—"

"Since when?" Zach said with a smirk.

"Since when, *what*?" Brandon countered.

"Since when do you hate to play devil's advocate? You do it a lot." Zach was toying with him and having a lot of fun doing so.

"Anyway," Brandon dragged out. "I think whoever *sent* that e-mail and the others were personally affected by drunk driving. I think we're rushing to assume it's our unsub."

"I agree," Jack said, and Brandon smiled.

"What was the sender's name?" Kelly asked.

"Voice in the Crowd," Zach answered.

"Huh," Kelly said.

"Now, I never said the hate mail came definitively from our unsub," Zach clarified, "but I do find them interesting enough that I think we should consider strongly that they might."

Paige was nodding. "We need to revisit digging into families who were affected by DUI fatalities. This time from a fresh perspective. What if we narrowed the criteria to DUI victims' funerals held at St. John's Catholic Church?" Paige suggested. "He seems to be drawn there for some reason. From there, we could look into the families, see if our unsub pops out."

"Okay, I'll have Nadia take care of all that," Jack said as his phone rang. He glanced at the screen and answered on speaker. "Talk to us, Nadia."

"I've got some updates for you," she started. "The threat sent to that lawyer, Henderson, came from a free online account. I tracked down the IP address, and from there I can get a physical one, but I have to wait until the morning to reach the owner of the IP."

Zach perched on the edge of his chair, surprised. One didn't need to be tech savvy to utilize an open-source router that hides IP addresses and provides fake ones. "You got an IP?"

"I did, but it's too early to get excited about it."

"I agree," Zach said. Just as Brandon had pointed out, following the hate mail might not even take them to the killer.

"I'm still working on compiling a list of people whose names popped in relation to all the victims from the accidents and the ones who were murdered. I've just scratched the surface," Nadia said. "I've found three names so far that are the same—one female doctor, a male nurse, and a female paramedic. Given their clean backgrounds, I'd say none are worth further scrutiny."

"Let us be the judge of that," Jack told her. "Send their information over to us, just in case."

"You got it."

"And what about the delivery guy?" Jack started. His phone pinged with notification of a message. "Tell me he was in the system."

"No can do, but I wish I could. I ran his pic through facial recognition databases. Nada."

Jack went on and requested what Paige had suggested, then added, "Did you get the deposit information from the church about the unsub's payment to Ava Jett?"

"Not yet."

"Let me know the moment you do." He hung up. "Let's carry on. Find out if the families affected by West's accident received donations. See if they recognize our supposed unsub or delivery guy." Jack sighed and pulled out his cigarettes. "We'll talk to those families, then get a fresh start tomorrow."

"I realize there are three families," Kelly started, "but do you want me to go to one of them or get the signed subpoena for the cardholder information?"

"Stick with the latter. The team will divvy up the three families." With that, Jack was out the door.

Zach was too tired to move. If he kept his job with the BAU, even if he did come home alive, would he have any energy left for his wife and child? He yawned, not too sure that he would.

CHAPTER FORTY-FOUR

The Night burned within him, and it was becoming next to impossible to ignore. It spoke to him, taunted him, lured him with memories of how glorious it felt to have the power of life and death within his grasp.

He gripped his head, willing the Night to disappear into the darkness, even if just for a little while. "You don't want to get caught, do you?" he mumbled to himself and shivered at the realization that he'd said it aloud.

His hands were shaking, and when he looked at them it was as if they were no longer his own. He tucked them into his pants pockets, letting the tremor of the Night lace through him.

As he felt it calm, he slipped the key into the door of Roxanne's apartment building.

Kill her tonight.

He stopped, glanced around, but no one was there. Now he could hear the Night talking to him?

He gulped. Each step he took inside the building was tentative. He had to slow the killings. And this was Roxanne. Harmless Roxanne. Unless she'd talked to the police... But she'd told him she hadn't, and she hadn't pressed his interest in the police any further. Her birdbrain had likely thought he was concerned about getting in trouble for breaking a paper towel dispenser.

He picked up his speed, opting to take the stairs to her fifth-floor apartment instead of the elevator. A part of him defended Roxanne's life. She was of more use to him alive. It's why he'd apologized for running out on her at the restaurant and for choking her. Sometimes the words *I'm sorry* were necessary, whether true or not. It kept her compliant, submissive.

He stopped outside her apartment door and took a deep breath, not fully trusting the Night to stay concealed. He lifted his hand to knock, but the door opened before he could. She was standing there staring at him, a scowl on her face.

Ah, so she wants to play hard to get...

"I thought we were good, baby." He reached for her hand and she recoiled under his touch, though she didn't step out of reach. She wanted him to work for her forgiveness.

"I can understand you being angry." Though it was about as laughable as an ant raging at a tromping shoe.

"You left me there, all alone," she whined. If she was trying to put up a brave front, she was failing bitterly. She had no backbone. In fact, he smiled as he caught a whiff of fried ground beef, onions, and mashed potatoes.

"You made my favorite meal," he said and tossed out a smile. He'd almost killed her, yet she was making things up to *him*.

"Doesn't mean I'm not still mad at you." She pointed a finger at him.

He pulled her arm down, smooshed his body against hers and captured her mouth. He kept pressing, backing her into the apartment. He closed the door with his foot, his hands running over her body. She melted against him, the embers of her supposed contempt already turning to ash.

He pulled back, ran a hand over her head, and tucked a strand of hair behind her ear. "Am I forgiven?"

She tilted up her chin, being harder to appease than normal. But even so, her performance was lacking; weakness was in her eyes.

He took her mouth and this time it stirred awake the Night. He pulled back panting and pushed away from her.

"Hey," she cried out. Her eyelids were lowered seductively.

He turned his back to her, clenched his fists and closed his eyes. He stuffed the Night deep down inside and faced her again. "I wouldn't want dinner to get cold. You have worked so hard on it."

Her snarled expression relaxed, and she smiled. "Guess I can't be mad at you forever, and shepherd's pie is a little work."

He inhaled, this time for show, though he did savor the smells associated with the dish. They were homey and comforting, like life before it had darkened.

"When's it going to be ready?" he asked.

"I put it in the oven just a bit ago. It has more than thirty minutes to go. Come, I have a surprise for you." She hooked her finger and moved toward the living room.

He followed. "A surprise?"

"Here." She picked up a package from her coffee table, one of the few pieces of furniture in this room. And like the rest, it would have been picked up at IKEA.

The box was wrapped in silver paper and red ribbon—likely leftover from Christmastime. He recalled her wrapping his gift with the same paper back then. Only the box from the holidays was much bigger than this one. He struggled to stamp down his amusement. He messes up, and she makes up for it—in spades.

He pointed to the gift. "What's that?"

"You can open it before dinner if you'd like." She handed it to him and sat on the couch. She patted the cushion beside her.

The package was light. Two pounds at the most. "You didn't have to get me anything."

"I really wanted to." She smiled, naive and *pathetic*.

"I'm the luckiest man alive," he said, humoring her without her even knowing it.

"You are." She was still smiling. "Go ahead and open it. I hope it makes you happy."

I hope so, too...

He looked at her, baited by her words. He took hold of the ribbon, tugged an end, and slid the bow apart. He then tore the paper, without care or precision.

"Oh." Roxanne clapped her hands and was grinning like a baboon.

He glanced over at her but went back to attacking the paper. It ripped away to reveal the box for a cell phone. The blood in his veins went cold.

"To replace the one you broke." She was still smiling at him. "I thought I'd surprise you. Turns out all they needed was the SIM card, but I did pick up all the pieces—" She stopped talking, frozen under his glare.

His insides darkened and swirled. His heartbeat sped up, and he could hear its thumping in the back of his neck. The Night clawed up his spine. This phone now had Jenna's SIM card in it. The police could be tracking it right now.

"You shouldn't have done this," he said, struggling to keep the Night's rage tamped down.

"I know I didn't have to, but I wanted to. The salesman said all your contacts should be in there."

All of Jenna's *contacts...*

Again, he said, "You shouldn't have done this." Heat blanketed him even as shivers danced across his skin. The Night was stalking in. It would do whatever was necessary to protect itself.

He stood, grabbing the phone from the box, the packaging falling to the floor. He pressed a button on the phone and the screen remained dark. Yet, it did little to reassure him. "Did you turn it on?"

"No, no, of course not. The guy at the store had to turn it on to add the SIM card—just to make sure it was working—but I swear I didn't violate your privacy, if that's what you're worried about."

Furthest thing from my mind...

The cops tracking the damn thing was foremost. He had no doubt they'd be watching the phone, and they'd have known the second it was reactivated. But maybe there was a chance they wouldn't find their way here.

He got down on his knees in front of Roxanne and gripped her shoulders, his face mere inches from hers. "How did you pay for this?"

"I… I…" Her eyes were full of tears, and he could feel her trembling beneath his hands.

He took a few deep breaths in through his nose, exhaled through his mouth. He should have just taken her with him when he'd left the restaurant. He could have prevented all this…

He held the phone up in her face. "How. Did. You. Pay. For. It?"

She swallowed loudly. "Credit card."

He didn't know how fast the cops worked, but they could be moving in on the building now. He got up and paced in a circle. "When was this?" Regardless of her answer, he had to be running out of time.

"Just after work today," she said between clipped breaths. "I got to the store at about five thirty."

Kill her!

The Night screamed for her blood. He pinched his eyes shut for a few seconds. Opened them. "Which store?"

"Bob's Wireless—"

He stopped moving. "The one we've gone to together before?"

She nodded.

Kill her!

He took another breath in through the nose, out through the mouth. What the hell was he going to do?

He pinched his eyes shut again. Surely it would take the cops some time to track Roxanne's apartment down through her credit card. Everything might be okay—for now. As long as she hadn't turned the phone on. As long as she had told him the truth. He opened his eyes. "You swear to me you didn't turn the phone on since you left the store?"

"I promise I didn't."

He lunged across the room, closing the distance between them again, and gripped her throat in his hands and squeezed. Her eyes bulged. "Did you—"

"No, no," she croaked. Tears ran down her face. "Please…" She clawed at his hands. All he'd have to do was squeeze and squeeze until he watched the life drain from her eyes, give release to the Night. An offering.

But when will the killing stop?

He loosened his hold incrementally, forcing himself to release her, and seconds later, he stepped back from her. He took another deep, centering breath. He was barely keeping the Night at bay.

She touched her neck, and her entire body was shaking as she heaved for breath.

"Thank you for the phone," he forced out through gritted teeth.

"If you…don't…like it…I can…just take it…back." The sentence fragmented as she continued to fight for air.

"It was a lovely thought," he said, using every morsel of willpower inside of him to come across as calm and collected. It appeared to be working, as she was palming her cheeks and no new tears were falling.

"So you like it?" She sounded hopeful but fragile, though she always came across as fragile. And it was just the way he liked her. Fragile things broke easily.

CHAPTER FORTY-FIVE

I'm going to hold it together. I'm going to hold it together.

I was armed with peppermint gum and chomping down on it like a nicotine addict trying to shake smoking.

Kelter's severed head was on the gurney in front of me. The team was with me, but Marsh had an appointment at the bakery this morning. Lucky her. Better scenery. Better smells.

We were waiting for Lily to start the autopsy, and I had to put my mind elsewhere for a bit. At least we were finally starting to get some traction with this case. Before we had come to the morgue, we'd briefed one another on how we'd made out with the three sets of parents affected by West's accident. Each of them had confirmed receiving donations of thirty thousand dollars apiece. So we knew now that our unsub had a generous heart—as cold and ironic as that seemed. Especially considering Exhibit A in front of me.

Chomp, peppermint, chomp, peppermint, chomp, peppermint.

"I had some time to look over the remains before you got here," Lily began. "And I'm pretty sure you're going to be interested in what I found." She snapped on a pair of gloves and traced around the base of the neck where it had been severed. "If you look closely, you'll notice faint bruising. At first, I thought it had to do with the beating inflicted on the head, but that's not what it's from."

Tingles ran down my spine. I had a feeling I knew what she was about to say. "She was strangled?"

Lily simpered. "You stole my thunder, boy."

I winced. "Sorry. I'll keep quiet."

Lily looked at me with a cross between a smirk and scowl. "She was strangled—"

"That's the cause of death, then? She wasn't decapitated when she was alive?" I asked.

"She *was* decapitated alive, of that I have no doubt, but before that she was also strangled," Lily said. "She likely lost consciousness if the bruising is any indication. But a lot of people are into that sexual asphyxia crap these days. Why anyone wants to see the white light to orgasm beats me, but to each their own, I suppose." Her last sentence was riddled with judgment.

"Strangulation is intimate, and even if sexual assault isn't involved, it can be a sort of sexual release," Zach explained. "We've already surmised that the sexual element is very important to our unsub."

My stomach tossed. Severed heads approached the scale of being bearable compared with necrophilia. I didn't want to give the matter too much thought—or any actually. Whether our unsub sexually violated the corpse or the unconscious Kelter—or both—I really didn't want to know.

"Is it possible that West and Sullivan were strangled, as well, and the MEs could have just missed it?" I asked.

"Oh, absolutely," Lily said. "It could have easily been overlooked. And I'd wager the deceased—" she gestured to the severed head "—was strangled within just hours of decapitation."

"There was more decomp with Kelter, as well," Paige said, "than there was with West and Sullivan. It's possible the bruising hadn't shown up by the time the MEs did their thing."

"Possible, but it's more likely there would have been some," Lily said. "Though the contusions would have been fainter. I will request autopsy photos from the previous victims and see if I can spot signs of strangulation. Don't hold your breath. Like I said, they might be harder to see, and depending on the quality of the photographs and the lighting…" Lily pressed her lips. "What I can confirm is I stand by my original estimated TOD, which I know isn't a very narrow window, but I might have something for you." Lily smiled, and I looked at her sideways. Her eyes spoke of a secret. "I was able to do what I did with Banks's contusions and estimate the person who killed this victim was also six three or roundabouts. I have even more for you. I have fingerprints." Lily was grinning like the cat who ate the canary now. "They were pulled from her neck and were a match in the system to ones pulled from the restroom at La Casa de Jose."

Now the entire team was grinning, myself included. We could finally link our unsub to a murder.

CHAPTER FORTY-SIX

Kelly had hardly slept last night. How could she have when she'd been so busy tossing and turning, wondering what else Christine from Sweet Tooth Bakery had to share? Or maybe it was the sugar intake after eight at night when she finally had eaten the cookie she'd bought.

She shook that notion aside. It had definitely been about Christine. Kelly wished she'd made arrangements to meet Christine when her shift ended. But there had been the call about Bob's Wireless... That had sent her off on another path for a signed subpoena.

She'd already run this morning, had eaten, and was fully caffeinated when she set out for the bakery at seven thirty.

Christine greeted her with a serious expression and gestured for her to bypass the line that went from the doors to the counter. Some customers grumbled as Kelly brushed past them. They didn't want to hear her pardons or apologies. When she got to the front, Kelly saw that Christine was working with three other women. Kelly stepped to the right of where Christine was posted.

Christine finished up with the man she'd been helping and directed the next person in line to wait on one of the other cashiers. That garnered her nasty glares from the coworker positioned beside her. If Christine noticed, she didn't seem to care. She approached Kelly. "It's crazier than normal in here this morning. I can't talk long. Can I see that picture of that younger guy again?"

Kelly figured Christine meant the delivery guy and pulled it up on her phone. She held it out for Christine to see.

"His name is Ben Cummings," Christine started. "He used to work here."

That got the skin tightening at the back of her neck. "Do you know his address?"

Christine pressed her lips together and shook her head. "I can't give you that."

Kelly nodded. "Phone number?" she tried.

"I'm sorry, but his name's all I can give you. I better get back to work." With that, Christine returned to her register and called for the next in line.

Ben Cummings. Kelly had a name, but she'd resist the urge to celebrate until she had Cummings in custody. It didn't stop her from grinning like the Cheshire cat as she made her way to the door. A man stepped to the side of the line, and she bumped right into him.

She held up her hands, half-annoyed, half-apologetic. The man was built like a truck. Then she took notice of his face, and his name came right to her. "Marcus Mayfield?"

He looked at her quizzically, as though trying to place her. Kelly was sure he'd tried to put her from his mind years ago. He had been the prime suspect in an old murder case, one that she was only privy to through her mentor, Harvey Barkhouse. All that had been about six months before she became a detective. Mayfield had been cleared of all suspicion, and the case had gone cold.

"Excuse me." She brushed past him and could feel his eyes on her back as she left the bakery.

She got into her department car and requested an APB be issued for Cummings, then fired off a text to Jack to let him know about the lead.

Her phone beeped with a reply from Jack that read, *Follow it through. Keep me posted.*

Will do, she keyed back.

She glanced at the bakery again and could see Mayfield looking back at her through the window, his face still furrowed in uncertainty. The woman Mayfield had been suspected of killing had been strangled, but she had regained consciousness before dying. First responders had rushed to save her life so there weren't any photos of the crime scene before the victim was removed. But if Kelly remembered correctly, she had been found naked in her living room. Her mind slipped to Banks's murder scene—how he was positioned and how the scene had looked overall. It was imaginable that's how that woman would have looked when emergency services arrived. But surely, she was reaching to think that the unsolved murder had any connection to this current investigation.

Strangulation and decapitation were two very different MOs, though their unsub had no qualms about using both. Maybe Mayfield did factor in somehow... She'd never even thought of him with the West or Sullivan cases, but then again, she hadn't had a full body or a clear indication of strangulation.

A seed of doubt started to germinate in her gut as she recalled why Mayfield had been a suspect in the first place. If she remembered correctly, his parents and three children had all been wiped out in one fell swoop by a drunk driver.

She got out of the car, intent on racing back inside and dragging Mayfield in for questioning when her phone rang. She looked at the caller ID.

Speak of the devil...

"Detective Harvey Barkhouse," she answered with a smile. "I was just thinking about you."

"I'd say great minds," he said, then rushed on. "But I'm pretty sure I've got a DB you'll be interested in."

Another dead body?

"Hit me," was all she said.

"Name's Ben Cummings. He was strangled and found next to a dumpster downtown."

She felt herself go cold, and she pinched her eyes shut. So close, but so far away. Another lead slipped through her fingers.

Harvey went on. "I just saw the APB."

That had to be the fastest turnaround on an APB yet. "Cummings was a person of interest in a serial murder investigation," she informed him.

"The case you're working with the Feds?"

She didn't know why his knowing bothered her, but she felt a pang of guilt as if even her thinking of leaving Miami PD would somehow be viewed by him as a betrayal. She should know him better than that; he'd always wanted what was best for her. Twenty years older than her, he was like her work dad, looking out for her where he could. They'd stayed in touch over the years, despite their jobs keeping them so busy. They'd meet for beers and catch up. He was married to his high school sweetheart, a doll of a woman, and they had three kids. All of whom grew up to be spoiled brats in Kelly's opinion, but that she kept to herself.

"You heard about that?" she asked.

"Everyone's heard. Loose lips around here, Kel, you should know that," he said lightheartedly.

She smiled, realizing she was being paranoid. "True enough." Her mind switched back to the news that Harvey had called to deliver. "When was Cummings found?"

"Yesterday afternoon."

Damn. "So the autopsy's been conducted?"

"Just heading there now actually," he said. "I thought you might want to join."

"You bet." Kelly ended the call and jogged to the department car.

An ME by the name of Anita Barnes was charged with conducting the autopsy on Ben Cummings. Kelly had sent Jack another quick update to let him know about the turn of events and that she was going to Cummings's autopsy with Harvey.

She met up with him outside the morgue.

"You're looking a little frazzled," he told her.

She smirked at him. "Oh, don't hold back. Tell me what you really think." Harvey tended to state the obvious, flattering or not. She had been up and at it early this morning, and her thoughts were all over the place, as was her hair. For those two reasons, it was back in a ponytail and probably what Harvey's observation had hinged on. She only put her hair up when she was concentrating deeply on something. She wished she could counter with some smart comment on his appearance, but it appeared life was agreeing with him—as it always had. No matter his caseload, Harvey had a knack for separating business from his personal life. For that, he didn't have the deep wrinkles so many cops had by the time they were in their fifties. He hadn't let himself become hardened over the years but had managed to find a balance of caring enough to get the job done but not so much as to upset his health. In addition to her granddad and Jack, Harvey was her hero.

Ever the gentleman, Harvey got the door for her, and they entered the morgue. Barnes greeted them with a dip of her head. She wasn't as talkative as Lily, but her work ethic was the perfect blend of efficiency and thoroughness. And she got right down to business.

The Y-incision was made, the organs weighed and measured, everything was verbalized for an audio recording Barnes was making, and it would all be catalogued.

Kelly's gaze rarely left Cummings—or the pale, bluish version of him that remained. She wondered what secrets he was taking with him to the grave and if she could wrestle them back to life somehow. It was the *how* that lingered overhead like a dark cloud. Really, there was only one possible way that she could think of to get more information: she needed to talk to Cummings's wife.

When Barnes finished up with Cummings's body, Kelly didn't feel any further ahead than when she'd arrived, save one thing. The COD hadn't changed from what Harvey had told her on the phone, but there was trace under Cummings's fingernails and he had some defensive wounds. He'd fought back, which meant that their unsub hadn't struck in a surprise attack this time.

They had found trace under Banks's nails, too, but nothing had come back definitively on what it was yet. There was no evidence that he'd fought back. He'd been caught off guard. Why was the approach different with Cummings, then? It was possible that someone else had killed Cummings, but the time and the cause of death were awfully convenient and coincidental. His murder lent itself to Cummings being used by the unsub to deliver the head, and once that was done and his usefulness ran out, the unsub had killed him. That made sense. But it was also possible that the two had been in a partnership and there was a falling out. That might explain the defensive wounds.

Harvey turned to Kelly once they were out on the sidewalk. "I'm going to need you to share what you know with me."

"I'm going to need to take charge of this case," she said.

He put his hands on his hips. "I've started this, and I'm finishing it. You know how I work."

"I know that's how you'd like it to go, but the FBI—"

Harvey's brow furrowed. "It's not how I'd like it, Kelly; it's how it's going to be. Whether the FBI's interested in the DB or not, I caught this case."

Kelly knew Harvey well enough to know that once he started a case, he was committed to seeing it all the way through. She supposed there was no reason to bench him altogether. In fact, his participation could be useful. She needed to speak with Cummings's wife, and Harvey was no doubt already acquainted with her from when he gave the notification. "I'd like to speak with Cummings's wife."

"If I come with you," Harvey stated as a requirement.

"That should be fine."

"Fine?" He raised an eyebrow. "That's the way it is, kid."

There was no point arguing with him; he'd win. She'd always let him win. Life was easier that way, and often, he was right. "Let's go. I'll drive."

Her phone rang as she got behind the wheel, and she answered. By the time the call ended, she had another lead and was making yet another call.

"What is it?" Harvey sounded concerned.

Given the level of worry he expressed in just those three words, it was a miracle he didn't have wrinkles.

Jack answered her call on the second ring. "The cardholder information came back from Bob's Wireless," she told him. "Her name is Roxanne Cabot."

"Address, phone number, place of employment?" Jack fired at her.

"I should be getting an e-mail with all of that shortly, which I'll forward to you. I just received the call." Kelly looked over at Harvey. "Do you need me on this, Jack? If you can spare me, I'm following another lead." *Or two…* She wasn't sure if Mayfield could be considered a lead, but she was definitely going to look into him.

"Well, were there any noteworthy findings at Cummings's autopsy?" Jack asked.

"The ME concluded that he'd fought back, and she got some trace from under his nails. She's having it run." Kelly looked over at Harvey. "Detective Barkhouse and I are headed to talk to Cummings's wife now."

Jack was quiet for a few seconds. "You stick with that. The rest of us will take care of following up this lead on Cabot."

"Thanks."

Jack hung up without saying goodbye, but she'd detected pride when he'd told her to keep going with her lead. It warmed her up inside.

"Jack?" Harvey asked when she set down her phone.

"Yeah." She dragged out the word and hitched a brow.

"I'm guessing that was the FBI agent in charge of the serial murder investigation you're on?" Harvey scanned her eyes.

"You'd be right."

"Is this Jack *Harper* by chance?"

Kelly may have mentioned the FBI Academy and Jack once or twice—or a million times. "The one and only."

"Interesting…"

"What?" She couldn't read what was going on in that mind of his.

"It's just interesting that of all the FBI agents to come down here—"

She'd save Harvey some time. "I called him."

"Ah." Harvey smiled, and his eyes sparkled.

"What, Harvey?" she asked.

"It's just that I know you haven't been happy at Miami PD for a while now. Maybe this is a sign that it's time for you to move on?"

Harvey was more into signs than she was, and they'd had many a debate on the subject. He was a firm believer in everyone being here for a purpose. Her faith wasn't as strong in that regard. It failed to explain some larger-scale problems with the world. If we were all here for a reason, if we all had control over our lives, why would anyone choose to be a victim or to live in a third-world country where life expectancy was short and the likelihood of catching a life-threatening disease from drinking water or starving to death was as daily an occurrence as a cup of morning java for most Americans?

"Not sure about that." She wasn't going to lie or say that she hadn't been entertaining thoughts of running back to Virginia and becoming FBI.

Harvey circled a finger in front of her face. "I can read you. You know that, so why are you trying to hide the truth from me?"

Guilt saddled her.

"Only you can make this decision, but it might be time for you to move on. Do what makes Kelly happy. And I know that's not continuing to work under Ramirez."

Another strain of guilt snaked through her. "But my mother—"

"I'll be here. We both know I'm not leaving." He smiled at her, and she felt a deep sense of peace nestle into her chest. "And I'll always have your back," he added.

She reached over and put a hand on his forearm. "I know you will, and I thank you for that."

They said that family wasn't always blood, and having Harvey in her life truly made her believe that.

CHAPTER FORTY-SEVEN

If the visit to the morgue hadn't paid off enough, at least we now had the name of our unsub's girlfriend. The team split up, with Paige and Zach heading to Roxanne Cabot's apartment and me and Jack paying a visit to Cabot's place of employment.

It was noon when Jack and I entered into the lobby of the building that housed Herringbone Trust, an investment company. The information kiosk directed us to the fifth floor and once there, we faced a large reception desk. A trim brunette was posted there and watched us unload from the elevator.

"Welcome to Herringbone Trust. How can I help you?" The woman greeted us by rote and pasted on a smile that *almost* touched her eyes.

A+ for effort.

"We're with the FBI." Jack held up his credentials. "We're here to speak to Roxanne Cabot."

The receptionist's eyes sparked to life now. We were probably the most excitement she'd ever seen around here. Personally, I'd pluck my eyes out if I had to sit inside an office all day. She didn't even have a window to look out.

The receptionist clicked some keys on her computer and looked at Jack. "That's strange…" She bit her bottom lip. "Roxanne's not in today."

"Should she be?" I asked.

"Yeah. If she called in sick or had a personal appointment, it would be noted here." The brunette pointed to her monitor. "But nothing's showing."

I wasn't liking where this was headed. Our unsub's girlfriend might be missing. Was it just coincidence or was there a reason to worry?

"Her supervisor, then," Jack said, wasting no time.

"Let me try her office." She pressed a button on her earpiece and was speaking into it a few seconds later. "The FBI are here to see you." The receptionist hung up a moment later. "She'll be out in a minute if you want to take a seat."

"Who is *she*?" I asked.

"Caroline Burgess."

"Thank you."

"Uh-huh." The receptionist went back to whatever she'd been doing before Jack and I had interrupted her.

Jack didn't move but stayed directly in front of the receptionist, despite the small grouping of chairs for waiting guests. I'd hate to have someone hovering over me like that, but the receptionist didn't give any impression that she cared.

"Hello?" A single word, but it carried an impatience. It came from a woman who was close to six feet tall in flats. "I believe you're looking for me." She held out a wafer-thin hand speckled with age spots toward Jack. She was in her midfifties, easy. "I'm Caroline Burgess."

Jack shook her hand. "Agent Jack Harper."

Caroline looked at me and kept her hand out for me to shake.

"Agent Brandon Fisher," I said.

"We need to speak with you about an employee of yours," Jack said. "Do you have someplace private we could talk?"

The receptionist was watching us now, her eyes brimming with curiosity.

Caroline nodded. "Follow me." She led me and Jack down a hall and stopped outside the third door on the right, gesturing for us to enter.

The office was not even close to as extravagant as Henderson's at the law firm, but it was nice enough.

She closed the door and directed Jack and me to two chairs that faced her desk. She sat down in her seat. "I'll be happy to help you however I can, but some things are strictly confidential."

Jack nodded. "Of course. Now, we understand that Roxanne Cabot reports to you."

"That's right." Caroline clasped her hands on her desk. "Has she done something wrong?"

"Is she supposed to be at work today?" he replied, answering her question with a question.

Her features softened somewhat. "I haven't heard from her."

"Is it normal for her not to show up for work?" I asked.

"She's never done it before." Caroline angled her head, her gaze on Jack. "Should I be worried about her?"

"Worrying never does any good," he deadpanned.

Her jaw tightened at Jack's blasé rebuttal. "Can you give me anything?"

"We're working an investigation, and Roxanne Cabot is a person of interest," he told her.

"Oh, so she *did* do something wrong." Caroline was missing the mark altogether.

I brought up the photo array that included the unsub and the delivery guy. We already knew the latter was in the city morgue, but I ran with what I had at the ready. I handed my phone to her. "Do you recognize any of these men?"

Caroline looked and considered. "No." There was confusion in her eyes, but she didn't push Jack for any more information, likely because she'd finally realized that he wasn't going to give her anything.

I put my phone away. "Roxanne has a boyfriend. Do you know him?" She hadn't identified him from the photos, but I thought I'd take a stab at it from another direction.

Caroline winced. "We don't exactly talk outside of work. And at work, we talk *about* work. I'm sure you can appreciate that." She looked right at Jack.

"I do," he responded.

"Maybe if you talked to her coworker Amber Smith. She sits in the cubicle right next to Roxanne. The two of them gab far more often than they should. Mind you, it's often Amber's fault; she feels that everyone should know about the minutiae of her life. What she had for breakfast and why, who she's dating, who her sister's dating—it goes on and on and on." Caroline rolled her eyes. "I'd fire her if she didn't get her work done, but somehow she manages to pull off jabberwocking and her job."

Jack raised both brows. "Jabberwocking?"

"What I call running off at the mouth."

All right, then…

"We'd like to speak to Amber," Jack said, though given the warning we'd just received, I wasn't in too much of a hurry. We'd have to keep Amber's talking to a minimum so we could move on finding Roxanne Cabot.

Caroline nodded. "I'll get her for you and set you up in a conference room. That okay?"

"Sounds good," Jack said.

The next half hour passed with me and Jack doing all we could to deflect Amber's attempts at banter and her rambling on about things that didn't matter. She didn't know the name of Roxanne's boyfriend, only that she had one, and that he "didn't treat her well." Amber made it clear that was her feeling on the matter and not something that Roxanne had ever said.

We spoke briefly to Caroline again before we left the office and thanked her for her help. We told her we might be back with a warrant to search Cabot's computer. She told us she wasn't going anywhere.

Jack had Nadia on speaker the moment we got back in the SUV. "I need you to run a phone trace." He proceeded to give her Cabot's cell number, and a few moments later, we had a location and were on the move. I just hoped we weren't too late.

CHAPTER FORTY-EIGHT

It's very important that you let us inside Roxanne Cabot's apartment." Zach tried to feed a sense of urgency to the landlord, a man by the name of Howard Mann. He was pleasant enough, but he was worried about infringing on his tenant's right to privacy. Zach and Paige had tried knocking on Roxanne's door several times, but that hadn't gotten them anywhere. Yes, it was possible she wasn't home, but there was another, much uglier possibility.

"I can't just do that… Do you have a warrant?" Howard asked, slipping his gaze from Zach to Paige. The two of them were in the hallway outside Howard's apartment.

"We don't have a war—" Zach's phone rang, and he turned his back to the landlord and answered. As he listened to Jack, he also heard Howard prattling on to Paige about how he couldn't just make an exception and let them in, not without a court order or strong evidence that suggested Roxanne was involved in criminal activity.

Zach hung up, having received Jack's message loud and clear, and faced Howard.

"She isn't suspected of a crime, is she?" Howard's eyes widened as he slid his gaze to Paige.

She shook her head and glanced at Zach.

"It might be worse than that," Zach said in all seriousness.

"What do you—" Howard swallowed audibly.

"We need to get in her apartment. Now." Zach delivered the directive while looking at Paige. Redirecting his gaze back to Howard, he said, "I can get a warrant if need be, but she might not have that sort of time." Jack had called to let him know that Roxanne hadn't shown up at work and her phone had been tracked back to her apartment. It was possible that her cell was in there and she wasn't, but Zach's optimism was rather shaky at the moment.

"She might not have that sort of time?" Howard parroted, his eyes widening even more. "She could be hurt in there?"

"It's possible." Zach glanced at Paige.

The landlord nodded. "Let me go get the key."

Howard retreated into his apartment, and Zach updated Paige on the call. She didn't say anything, but her eyes said it all. She wasn't feeling too optimistic about Roxanne's fate, either.

"Okay, let's go." Howard stepped into the hall, fiddling with a keyring. He closed his door behind him and led the way to Roxanne's apartment.

Howard slipped a key into the lock and twisted the handle. He opened the door and made like he was going to go inside.

Zach touched the man's shoulder. "You should probably wait in the hall."

Howard didn't say anything, but given his deer-in-the-headlights look, Zach wagered that Howard was starting to piece together that it might not just be a matter of his tenant being *hurt*.

"Just stay here," Zach reiterated, and Howard nodded.

Zach and Paige entered the apartment.

"Miss Cabot, it's the FBI," Zach called out. "Are you home?"

No response. Just complete silence.

The feeling of dread crept over his skin and raised the hairs on the back of his neck. He hoped what it was telling him was wrong. There'd been enough death already.

Upon entering the apartment, one could go right into an open living space or go straight down a small hallway. He and Paige both chose the latter.

No doorways came off the right-side of the hall, but there was one to the left and it was a galley kitchen. In a sweeping assessment, the counters and stovetop were clean and bare except for a coffeemaker, a toaster, and a spinning spice rack.

"Miss Cabot? FBI!" he called out again as they continued to move deeper into the apartment. "Are you home?"

"Should we call her phone?" Paige asked, but she already had hers to an ear.

The trill was coming from ahead of them. They hurried to the end of the hall. As he moved, Zach strained to hear anything that would fill him with hope: a whimper, a cry for help, a sign of life. Nothing, but the ringing phone.

The hallway opened into a dining area, but there was no table, and then it veered right for a continuation of an L-shaped living room. Sparse furnishings, simplistic furniture, a modest couch, a matching chair, a coffee table, and an entertainment stand with a thirty-two-inch flat screen atop it. Zach observed all this in the milliseconds before he let the rest of the scene hit him. There was a good—and obvious—reason why Roxanne wasn't answering her phone or responding to his callouts.

Zach drew back and pinched his eyes shut.

"I'll call Jack and let him know," Paige said. Roxanne's phone stopped ringing when Paige dropped the call and made one to Jack.

Zach dialed Crime Scene and scanned Roxanne's living room as he waited for them to answer. There was a phone wedged between two couch pillows. He'd leave it there for the CSIs to process. What *he* was trying to process was the level of failure he was feeling right now. They were too late. Again.

CHAPTER FORTY-NINE

Cummings's body had been found next to a dumpster as if the man had been meaningless. Harvey had shown Kelly the crime scene photos, and they were fresh in her mind when she walked into Cummings's apartment building. The images would probably stick with her for some time to come. It had less to do with the graphic nature of the scene and more to do with the fact that it resembled how she imagined finding her mother one day. Cast aside, as if forgotten. What pained Kelly almost as much as the thought of her mother being dead, was that her mother had lived with the pain of being alone. Then again, maybe she was off somewhere with her life rebuilt and had forgotten all about Kelly and her brother. She swallowed roughly at the stab of heartache the thought caused. In contrast, imagining her mother turning up dead may have been easier. Though, any time she got called out for a DB in an alley, she'd break out in a cold sweat. Her heart would race, her breathing becoming labored.

"Remember that case you mentored me on?" Kelly began as they sauntered up the front walk.

Harvey looked over at her and squinted against the sunlight. "More specifically...?"

"The one with the woman who was strangled and left for dead. She didn't die until a couple of days later?" Kelly wished she could remember all the details.

"Pamela Moore," Harvey rushed out. His mind was like a steel trap. "She was an Op-Ed columnist. It had looked like a home invasion gone south, but nothing was confirmed stolen."

"Right." The pieces were now coming back to Kelly. "And Moore wrote an article on that guy Mayfield's family."

"The prime suspect? That's right," Harvey confirmed.

"He was cleared, if I remember correctly."

"He was."

"And the case went cold."

Harvey got the door to the building for Kelly. "Yep."

While many a detective would let the cold cases eat them alive, Harvey had a way of letting them go. He had told her from the start that sometimes justice wasn't going to be found. She wished that she could adapt his perspective. She'd certainly sleep more peacefully that way.

Harvey held a finger over the number pad for the intercom. "I'd appreciate it if you'd let me take the lead in there. Tessa's familiar with me."

Kelly nodded. Harvey taking the reins would put the wife more at ease, and that was what she wanted. Harvey punched in Cummings's apartment number, and they were buzzed in.

On the way up to the apartment, Harvey said, "She was a real mess when I told her—gasping for breath, tears everywhere."

"It's probably the first real loss she's had in her life," Kelly said, feeling stupid for saying such a thing. As if experience with death made it easier to take. While accepted as the ending of a natural course of life, nothing felt natural about the way loss ripped one's heart out.

"It was."

Harvey knocked on the door to apartment 203.

A lanky brunette in her late twenties answered. This wouldn't be Tessa, who Harvey described as twenty-two, blond, and petite.

"Detective Barkhouse," Harvey said, "and Detective Marsh."

The brunette stepped back, weariness dragging down features that would otherwise have been quite beautiful: a small, turned-up nose, a dusting of freckles, green eyes. "Tessa's not in a good place. Please be gentle with her." The brunette's gaze went from Harvey to Kelly.

"We will be," Kelly told her. "You're a friend of Tessa's?"

"Older sister. Name's Linda."

She led them into the heart of the apartment, which was a small living room. A petite blonde, who Kelly assumed was Tessa, was curled up under a blanket. Her eyes were bloodshot and puffy. She put her feet down when Kelly and Harvey entered the room.

"Tessa, these two detectives want to talk with you," Linda said gently.

Tessa moved the blanket aside. "Did you catch his killer?" Her attention was first on Harvey, the familiar face, but then transferred to Kelly.

"I'm Detective Kelly Marsh," she felt the urge to say.

Tessa nodded, although it was barely perceptible that she had.

"We're still looking into the matter," Harvey answered Tessa's question. "But Detective Marsh here might have a lead."

"Oh?" Tessa looked at her with wide eyes.

"Do you recognize any of these men?" Kelly made sure that Cummings's photo wasn't in the array before handing over her phone.

Tessa looked at the screen and shook her head. "I don't. Did one of them kill Ben?"

"I'm not comfortable confirming that right now." Kelly sat on a chair so as not to tower over Tessa anymore. The next few things she had to ask wouldn't be easy for Tessa. "I'm sure Detective Barkhouse has been through this with you, but do you know of anyone who could have done this to your husband?" Kelly thought it best to ease into the direction she wanted to go.

"Not at all." Tessa glanced at Barkhouse.

"It's just a few questions," he assured her and looked at Kelly.

Harvey had filled Kelly in a bit on Cummings's background. No criminal record, but one thing stood out from the briefing more than anything else. "Your husband was unemployed, is that correct?" Kelly asked.

"He was between jobs." Tessa smiled, her eyes glazing over. The expression lent itself to her being swept up in a memory.

"That's what he'd say?" Kelly prompted gently.

Tessa met Kelly's gaze. "Yeah. He was the most positive person I've ever known."

Kelly hated to broach the possibility that Tessa's husband had been knowingly involved with a killer, and she preferred to approach things as if he was innocent and had been used by the unsub. Sometimes a direct route was the best way to go. While Cummings might not have a record, it could simply be he hadn't been caught.

Kelly leaned forward, her elbows on her knees. "The next question I have to ask won't be easy to hear, but we're just trying to figure out why your husband was killed."

Tessa eventually nodded.

"Was Ben friends with any questionable people or involved in anything illegal?" Kelly asked.

Tessa drew back and gasped. "No! He was the sweetest man. He'd never do anything that broke the law."

"Even if it meant getting his hands on some cash?" Kelly hated to apply more pressure, but she had no choice.

"Not even then," Tessa hissed.

Kelly got to her feet and extended her card to Tessa. "Thank you for your help. If you need any—"

"I won't be calling." Tessa jutted out her chin. "He didn't do anything wrong, and I hate that you're implying otherwise."

"I'm sorry, ma'am." Kelly saw herself out of the apartment, and once she was in the hallway, she leaned up against the wall.

"You all right?" Harvey asked.

"If I had a dime for every time you've asked me that…" Kelly peeled herself from the wall and left the building with Harvey. "It was worth a try."

"Guessing you didn't hear what you wanted to in there."

"You'd be guessing right."

Harvey locked eyes with her. "You think one of the pictures you showed her on your phone was of her husband's killer? The one you're hunting with the FBI?"

"Quite positive of that fact."

"Then all you can do is keep doing what you're doing and catch the bastard."

"Why does it feel like that will never happen?" she spat, frustrated at the situation, not at Harvey.

Harvey's phone rang, and he was still talking on it as they got back to the department car they'd driven there.

She merged onto the street and was headed back to the station to drop Harvey off by the time he hung up. She looked over at him, and he was pale. "My turn," she said. "Are *you* all right?"

"Well, Forensics has looked at Cummings's phone, and it seems there was a message left for you and the FBI."

She slowed their speed, tempted to pull over. "What did it say?"

"'This one's on you.'"

"Son of a bitch." She smacked the steering wheel and gunned the gas. She had to get Harvey back to the station and meet up with Jack immediately.

"I know this goes without saying, but you better watch yourself with this one," Harvey said, speaking like a concerned parent.

"I always watch myself," she said, certain it came out with more heat than she'd intended.

"What can I do?"

She looked over at him. "You're not going to like my answer."

He sighed. "You're taking point on the case."

She nodded. "I have no other choice."

"I'll let it go this time, but just because it's you," Harvey teased.

"I'll update you once the killer's caught. You can take care of following through with Tessa Cummings, if you'd like."

"I'd appreciate that." Harvey's eyes lit as if he'd smiled.

Kelly dialed Jack on speaker. "Just stay quiet, okay?" she said to Harvey while the line was ringing.

He mimed zipping his lips.

Jack answered, and Kelly blurted out, "Jack, it's Kelly. I have news, but it's not what you might be expecting. The wife didn't recognize our unsub, but the killer left a message for us on Cummings's phone. It said, 'This one's on you.'"

"Okay." Jack gave her no reaction. "Meet me and the rest of the team at Cabot's apartment. There's news on that front, too. Roxanne Cabot is dead."

CHAPTER FIFTY

The BAU team and Marsh gathered at the edge of Roxanne Cabot's living room. Two CSIs were processing the scene around her body. Like Banks, Cabot was naked and supine on the floor, and her eyes were shut. I'd wager that they'd be glued as well, but we'd have to wait for the ME to determine that. Unlike Banks, however, bruises marred Cabot's face, arms, and legs, as well as her neck. A pool of blood haloed her head, and on the floor about three feet away from her, there was a twenty-inch-tall Buddha statue, its corners bloody. An iPhone also sat on her abdomen.

I was instantly curious who it belonged to. If I were a gambling man, I'd go with it being Kelter's. We'd found Roxanne's Android between two couch cushions already. Then my breath hitched, my mind shifting to what Marsh had said about the Cummings crime scene. My heart raced at the thought of what message this phone might contain for us. I took a deep, patient breath. I couldn't do anything now; the scene needed to be processed before we could touch anything.

"He beat her face like he did Kelter's," Marsh said slowly.

"Then he strangled her like he did Banks." I pointed to the bruising on her neck.

If only we'd gotten here sooner, put the pieces together faster...

Marsh shook her head. "He must have found out that she'd reactivated Kelter's phone, then panicked and killed her." She tilted her head toward the phone on Cabot's belly. "That's probably it."

"Given the message left on Ben Cummings's phone," Jack said, "I'd be more surprised if it wasn't."

I waved a hand toward Cabot. "He's obviously making a statement."

"Yeah, and blaming us again without saying a word." Jack tapped the pocket where he kept his smokes.

"He has a problem with accepting responsibility for his actions," Zach theorized. "It could explain gluing their eyes shut. It's not just that he wants to be the last one they see, but rather, he may regret that he's taken life and doesn't want to see it staring back at him."

"Could be. Though I'm not seeing remorse," Paige said. "He's killing more frequently. I just hope he messes up."

Zach nodded. "He's certainly acting on impulse more than usual, so there's a good chance of that happening soon."

"Whatever his motive is," Jack cut in, "he's always one step ahead of us, and that has to stop."

The five of us fell silent. I looked over at Marsh, and she was staring at Cabot's body, clearly deep in thought.

"What are you thinking about?" I asked her. She didn't respond. "Detective Marsh?"

"Oh, sorry," she said. "It's just that…" She pulled her bottom lip between her teeth. "I wished I'd picked up on it right away with Banks. Maybe because he was a man…"

"A previous case you worked?" Jack asked her.

Marsh nodded. "Well, yes and no. Detective Barkhouse was mentoring me at the time. This was his case, and he shared a lot of it with me."

"Is the scene here exactly the same?" Jack asked.

"Not *exactly*, but the level of violence, the layout…" She gazed at the body again. "The case I'm referring to was a home invasion, though robbery couldn't be confirmed as a motive. Barkhouse looked at people in the victim's personal life."

"What was the cause of death?" Jack asked.

"Here's the thing," Marsh said. "She was found naked and she'd been strangled, but she'd regained consciousness and called nine-one-one. She didn't even get a word out to the dispatcher, but officers were sent. They found her breathing but in obvious distress, barely clinging to life. She died a couple days later in the hospital. The fact that she made it that long was a miracle. Heck, it was surprising she even came to. Her hyoid bone was fractured."

"He tried to kill her," I said.

"If you ask me, he ultimately succeeded," Kelly countered.

"This woman could have been our unsub's first kill," Jack ground out. "Who was she?"

"Pamela Moore," Marsh answered. "She was an Op-Ed columnist."

"Hmm," Jack moaned.

Marsh regarded Jack curiously.

"When was this?" he asked.

"Six years ago. About six months before I made detective."

"Six years ago?" I blurted out and added, "And West was killed six years ago?" How many other victims were we potentially looking at?

"Was the case ever solved?" Paige asked.

"It went cold. All leads were exhausted, and everyone in her personal life was cleared," Marsh told us.

Jack pursed his lips. "Who was the prime suspect?"

"Marcus Mayfield." Marsh massaged one of her temples. "Moore had written a piece on Mayfield's family after he'd lost his three children and his parents to a drunk driver. The grandparents had taken the kids to the zoo, and they were returning home when they were struck. He was cleared, though." Marsh sounded like she was trying to convince herself.

Jack pointed a finger toward the door. "Go. Do some digging on Mayfield and Moore."

But Marsh didn't move other than licking her lips.

"Detective," Jack prompted.

Marsh took such a deep breath, it was as if she were sucking the life from the room. "I ran into him at Sweet Tooth Bakery this morning. Literally, I—"

"Go," Jack said gruffly. "Now."

Marsh nodded and left. For the second time since we had arrived in Miami, Jack seemed to question the detective. The first time she'd pulled through, and though she and I often butted heads like two ramming mountain goats fighting for territory, I hoped she would again.

CHAPTER FIFTY-ONE

Zach was hoping for some big lead to close this investigation. He hated feeling as though they were racing to stop a killer who would always be just out of reach. As it was, there was another body to their killer's credit now, and they'd been powerless to prevent it. Sadly, reality didn't mirror law enforcement as presented in most crime dramas. There were cases that went cold, and the ones that didn't certainly weren't solved within an hour. And the job certainly wasn't as glamorous. Solving murders was a hard task that entailed a lot of tedious hours mulling over reports and questioning people, just in the hopes of catching insights into their killer. But, hell, he'd miss it. Almost as much as he'd miss the team.

The CSIs had worked around Roxanne's body, collecting evidence and snapping photos. But the phone remained on Roxanne's abdomen, taunting them. Everyone had to be asking themselves whose it was, but until an ME got here and had a first look at the scene, they'd go on not knowing.

"Beating his victims may be something he's been doing all along," Brandon noted. "West's and Sullivan's heads didn't show bruising, but that doesn't mean their bodies weren't beaten. Cabot's body clearly showed signs of physical abuse, and Kelter, well, her head showed it. Does he usually keep the beatings beneath the neck?"

"We don't have them, so we don't know," Paige said with a subtle smile.

"Another lovely thought," Brandon responded with sarcasm.

Jack's phone chimed a message notification and he pulled it out.

"Strangulation could be his signature," Brandon suggested. "It certainly would give our unsub a pattern. Even Kelter has signs of it on her neck…or what was left of it." His Adam's apple bulged, and a paleness washed over him but quickly disappeared.

"It's quite possible that West and Sullivan were strangled, too," Zach agreed. "It easily could have been missed. Lily barely noticed it on Kelter."

"Whatever the case, it seems that even though our killer has an efficient way of killing people, he derives some pleasure from using his own hands," Jack jumped in, his eyes still on his phone.

"He derives pleasure *in taking life*," Zach added. "His self-restraint may seem low, but he's very much in control of his actions. It seems he may be getting more of a lust for killing. And if that's the case, we could be looking at more victims before this is all over."

"Don't even say that," Paige lamented.

"I'm just calling it how I see it." As sick as that all was, and as much as Zach didn't want to admit it, it was true. "He might not even bother worrying about if the people he chooses are connected to DUI accidents anymore. He could come unhinged to the point that anyone he views as a threat to his way of life needs to be eliminated."

"Possibly, but—" Jack lifted his phone "—I was just scanning the background on Cabot that Nadia sent me. Roxanne doesn't have a vehicle now, but she had a Honda registered to her years ago. It was written off four years ago—after a car accident demolished it."

"Don't tell me. Let me guess," Paige said. "The accident was caused by a drunk driver."

"It was," Jack affirmed, "but they died."

"So Roxanne wasn't at fault," Brandon stated the obvious. "Maybe the killer could relate to her and that's how they bonded."

"That's assuming he knew about it," Paige said.

"I think it's fair to assume that he did," Jack cut in. "I'll have Nadia look into when and where Roxanne was treated for any injuries from the accident. See if anything matches up with our other DUI accident victims."

Jack was about to touch the screen to e-mail Nadia when a man called out. "Anyone going to talk to me?"

Zach peeked through the living room doorway and saw the landlord. An officer was struggling to hold him back from entering the apartment.

"You!" the landlord called to Zach. "Agent Miles? Talk to me."

Jack asked, "Who is that, Zach?"

"Howard Mann. The landlord." Zach glanced back at the door, and the officer was looking over a shoulder, begging for respite.

"He wants to speak with whoever is in charge," the officer said.

Jack dipped his head. Projecting his voice, he said, "I'll be right out." To Brandon, speaking at regular volume, he added, "You're with me. We'll talk to Mann and then Cabot's neighbors. Paige and Zach, you two check with the CSIs, see if they've found a laptop, desktop, or tablet yet. We know the unsub left Cabot's phone, which was either a stupid move or he's not concerned about it leading us to him. But there has to be a digital footprint somewhere for us to follow, communication between him and Cabot. Make sure the phone's rushed for analysis." Jack headed for the door, waving for Brandon to follow.

Paige flagged down a CSI and told him how important it was to get Cabot's phone processed ASAP, and he promised to make that happen.

"Did either of you find a laptop?" Zach asked the CSIs.

"Not yet. Glove up and feel free to take a look around," one of them said. "Just call us to photograph it if you find anything. And don't touch it, of course."

"You got it." Zach was pleasantly surprised by the accommodating tech. No need for a turf war.

Zach snapped on a pair of gloves, and Paige did the same. She stepped toward the entertainment credenza, and she was dipping into drawers before he even left the living room. He took off down a short hall and came to a bedroom. It looked like a cyclone had struck. Clothes covered the floor and dresser drawers were open with shirts and pants hanging out of them. The closet doors were open, too, as was the drawer in the nightstand. The comforter was bunched up on the floor at the foot of the bed. It was hard to say if the place had been ransacked or always looked this way.

He skipped the room, not wanting to potentially contaminate the scene. He heard Lily's voice coming from the living room and smiled. The woman may work with the dead and have morgue humor down pat, but she made the living happier just by her presence.

Zach went back down the hall and found a bathroom of modest size. Nothing fancy, just functional, much like the rest of the place. The toilet and vanity were to the right, and there was a tub-and-shower combo on the left. Directly across from the toilet was a shelving unit with a bunch of folded towels. And on one of the shelves, a laptop sat, positioned at a height almost equal to the toilet seat. Seeing that made him think of Sheri instantly. She loved to rig up her laptop on a chair next to the tub. She'd Netflix and soak until her fingers pruned.

He called a CSI in to photograph the location and discovery of the laptop. After the CSI finished, Zach picked up the laptop. Hopefully, it had battery life or he'd be on another hunt. His gaze fell, drawn to the woven tote on the bottom shelf, and he pulled it out. There was a mess of wires inside, most belonging to various hair appliances, but he saw the one he'd been after—the laptop charger. He grabbed it and set out for the kitchen.

He set up at the counter and opened it. Thankfully, it was on and Roxanne was logged in. There was no security or password required. That was rather unusual these days, but it would make his job go faster.

Paige rounded the corner into the kitchen. "Oh, looks like you had luck."

"Yep. I'm not complaining." He looked at the battery icon in the bottom corner: 75 percent remaining. "And it's got juice."

He opened Cabot's e-mail program. Seven new e-mails filtered in as he read through the subject lines and senders of the ones already in her inbox. Most were newsletters. Lots saved from IKEA. Her inbox was overflowing; it showed six hundred e-mails. He pointed the number out to Paige. "There's where the luck runs out. There are just a few we have to wade through."

Paige held up her hands, backed up, and smiled. "You mean *you* have to wade through."

"Come on. Be a team player," he teased.

He proceeded to open some messages, Paige watching over his shoulder, but it wasn't long until he spotted a name that made his blood run cold: John Doe. Zach double-clicked the first one he saw from that sender. It popped open, and Paige gasped. A graphic filled the screen, but there was nothing funny about what it was portraying or what was captioned.

He closed it, and Paige turned away, putting a hand to her stomach. "Necrophilia cartoons? It's official. I've now seen everything."

Zach proceeded to sort the inbox by sender and cringed at the number of e-mails from John Doe.

Another 235 to go.

No paycheck could compensate for this. These images would not only be burned into his retinas but forever seared into his memory.

CHAPTER FIFTY-TWO

Jack and I just hit the hallway, and the landlord started gesturing wildly in the direction of Cabot's apartment.

"What's going on? No one's updated me since I was asked to stay in the hall." Howard's face was getting redder as he spoke, but I had a feeling he was just amping up. "Is she okay? You need to tell me." He put a hand on the top of his head and bit down on his bottom lip. Sweat was glistening on his brow. His breathing was rushed, and he appeared one jolt away from screaming.

"Maybe we should talk in your apartment," I suggested. "Someplace where you can sit down."

The landlord waved me off. "That's all right. I'll be fine." He leaned against the wall.

"We're sorry to inform you that Ms. Cabot was murdered," Jack said.

"She was—" He clamped a hand over his mouth and looked at the officer stationed outside Cabot's apartment. "I should have known she was dead... I did on some level. But *murdered*? Wow." His eyes were wide and wet.

Jack squinted. "Why should you have known?"

"Oh, just all the activity around here."

Jack and I watched the man, but he didn't seem to have anything else to offer on the subject of the murder.

"What was your relationship with Ms. Cabot?" Jack asked.

"Landlord and tenant. Nothing more." He lifted up his left ring finger and tapped the gold band with his right hand.

"Is there anything you can tell us about Ms. Cabot that might help us find her killer?" I asked.

"Guess that would depend." Howard paused and shook his head. "I still can't believe this happened to her."

"Just be patient with yourself," I started. "This must all come as quite a shock to you."

His eyes latched on to mine. "It sure does. She always pays— Um, she always *paid* her rent on time. Nice lady."

If only her credit or good deeds could have saved her from dying.

"Did you ever see her with a man?" I asked.

Howard looked at me. "Are you talking about her boyfriend?"

"Sure." I leaned in closer to him. "Do you know him?"

"Well, I could point him out in a lineup, but I'm horrible with names. I want to say his name starts with a *J*," Howard continued, "but I could be out to lunch on that."

John Doe, perhaps.

Jack took out his phone and brought up the photo array. He held the screen for Howard to see. "Do you recognize anyone here?"

"Guess I'm being tested on what I just said, huh?" Howard softly laughed it off, but no light hit his eyes. He focused on the pictures and pointed to our unsub. "That's her boyfriend." Howard looked at Jack and stepped back. "Did he do this to her?"

"What did you say his name was?" Jack asked.

"I didn't say. I can't remember it." Howard was unapologetic, and it was plain to see that he really couldn't remember the guy's name.

Jack nodded. "How did the guy seem to you?"

I understood why Jack kept the questions rolling about our unsub. It was possible that the more Howard talked, the more he would remember.

"I met him a couple times, and both times, he seemed like a really nice guy. Before him, Roxanne would bring home…" Howard's eyes went blank.

"Would bring home…?" I repeated, nudging him along.

His gaze met mine. "She'd bring home losers… Oh god… He *did* kill her, didn't he?" His face paled, and his knees buckled. I reached for him, but he rejected my help with a wave of his hand.

"Spouses and lovers are always looked at first," Jack told him with the ease of an experienced agent who'd been through this a million times.

"Right. I should have known that. The wife and I love those crime shows." He looked at me. "Which one's your favorite? I bet it's—"

"I don't watch any of them, actually," I said, shutting him down quickly. "Please answer Agent Harper's question."

Howard looked at Jack. "As I said, he always seemed like a really nice guy. One day I opened my door as he and Roxanne had just walked past, and there was a flyer on the carpet. It must be someone in the building who leaves them, and when I find out who, there will be hell to pay."

A vein throbbed in Jack's forehead at Howard's detour.

"Anyway," Howard said, "he picked it up for me. Saved me from bending over. He even told me to have a good day."

"When was this?" I asked.

He blew breath out his mouth. "Awhile ago now. Easily months ago."

"When did you see him last?" I asked.

The color drained out of Howard's face. "Actually, I think I saw him out in the hall last night."

"And what time was this?" Jack inquired.

Howard squinted as he thought. "About nine thirty? Yeah, that sounds about right."

Jack and I thanked Howard for his help and told him we might be in touch. We left him, knocked on a few doors to do more interviews, and returned to Cabot's apartment about two hours after we'd left it. Apparently, we'd missed Lily, who'd already come and gone.

"She said TOD's looking like last night between six and ten," Zach told us.

"The landlord saw the unsub in the hall around nine thirty," I said.

"Good, so we can place him here," Paige said, then added, "Lily's leaning toward strangulation as cause of death."

"Just as we thought." Jack went on to fill them in on how we'd made out with other tenants in the building, which hadn't netted anything close to what we had gotten from the landlord.

"Lily also told us that she had a look at the autopsy photos for West and Sullivan. She could make out faint contusions on their necks above where they'd been severed from the rest of the body," Zach started. "She's not definitive that they were strangled but said it was a possibility."

"Can't say I'm surprised. The more we keep going with this case, strangulation seems to fit our unsub's MO," I said. "As does sexual assault and, obviously, decapitation."

We really need to get this sick bastard off the streets.

"Speaking of sexual assault." Paige curled her lips in disgust. "Lily thinks Cabot was sexually assaulted after death."

My stomach turned, and the others looked just as peaked as I was feeling. After a few seconds, Paige said, "Cabot's eyes were glued shut, too. Her phone was taken to the lab for rushed analysis as was the one on the body."

"I take it that one was Kelter's?" I asked.

"It was," Zach stated soberly. It then struck me how serious he'd been most of this investigation and how uncharacteristic that was for him. Usually he was a goofball who cracked jokes, often at my expense. It could have been the case itself, but maybe there was more to it.

"I hesitate to ask," I began, "but are there any messages on it for us?"

"Oh yeah," Paige replied. "It said, 'The chaos you've caused is unforgivable.'"

Our unsub wasn't just calling us out. Those words sounded like a threat.

CHAPTER FIFTY-THREE

Chaos, aftermath, and being unforgivable could be three things that marked our unsub and motivated him in some way. I was with the team back at the station, and there was an unsettled quality to the air, like we all just wanted this case to end—preferably before another body turned up. Marsh was still off researching the cold case with the murdered columnist while Zach was updating us on the e-mails to Cabot from John Doe.

"All the e-mails were jokes of a sexual nature, the bulk of them focused on necrophilia," Zach said, his laptop in front of him. "One showed a cartoon of a woman lying on her back, her head lolled to the side and blood coming out of her mouth. The caption was *I told you to play dead*. That was a very mild one compared with some others."

"We all know it's not uncommon for serial killers to have these types of fantasies," I commented, not that saying it aloud made it easier to accept. It still twisted the stomach. "We know our unsub took his girlfriend into a public restroom and had sex with her. Obviously, we have no way to know if he made her 'play dead,' but the thrill of doing it in a public place would have fed a sexual perversion."

"We know Dominick Banks was sexually assaulted," Paige added. "Lily thought it looked like Roxanne Cabot was, as well. So we can surmise that he probably treated the bodies of West, Sullivan, and Kelter the same way."

"Seems like sexual violation may be a part of his signature," Jack surmised.

Zach nodded. "So while we've been considering his motives rather mission-oriented with taking a stand against drunk drivers who have caused fatalities, he also shows signs of having hedonistic motives."

"I agree," I started. "He sees his victims as dispensable and at his service. He derives both sexual release and a high from killing," I concluded. "It's for lust *and* the thrill."

"One thing I can't stop wondering is why he chose the victims he did? Why West, Sullivan, and Kelter? There are a lot of drunk drivers out there whose bad choices resulted in the deaths of innocent people." Jack cut right to the heart of it. "We've been looking at it from the standpoint of the drivers, but maybe it's time to flip things and look at it from the perspective of the accident victims. He must have resonated with them on some level. After all, he had donated thirty thousand to each of their families. Why?"

We all took a moment to think. Jett had lost her job and had a pile of past-due notices on her living room table. Abigail Cole had lost her baby and had become an alcoholic. The families affected by West's accident had to bury their young adult children and suffered marital problems. None of their situations were identical.

"Kent West killed three of his friends, all college age. Marie Sullivan and Jenna Kelter each killed a husband and father." Paige shook her head. "The accident victimology isn't completely lining up."

"There's something we're missing," Jack said.

Everyone fell silent again, this time for a few minutes, all of us trying to piece together this puzzle somehow—even though pieces seemed to be missing.

My mind went back to my earlier thought process about the hardships suffered by those left behind. "Okay, for Sullivan and Kelter, their accidents would have affected two children: Nathan Jett and potentially Cole's unborn baby, Mark. Both boys."

Zach was on his laptop, clicking around like a mad man. "The three students that West killed also left behind brothers."

"Speaking of *three*, what's his attachment to that number?" I asked. "The victims were all abducted *three* days after release and killed *three* days later."

"Might be something we'll need to ask him once we get our hands on him," Jack said.

Marsh burst into the room with a folder in her hand. "I know what triggered our unsub. It was Marcus Mayfield... Well, in a roundabout way anyhow."

My brow furrowed. "I thought he was the prime suspect in Moore's murder?"

"Yeah, he was. But Mayfield's *story* was the trigger for the real killer—our unsub," Marsh explained. "When Moore wrote that article on what had happened to Mayfield's family, she put a positive spin on his situation. The article came out less than a week before Moore's murder."

"A positive spin?" Paige raised an eyebrow. "You told us that his three kids and his parents died in a DUI accident. How could Moore spin that positively?"

"The article was entitled 'Light in the Face of Tragedy,'" Marsh said.

"You've got to be kidding me," I grumbled.

"Wish I were," Marsh admitted. "Moore commented on how grandparents and grandchildren had spent their last day together being happy."

"I'm still failing to see how this triggered our unsub," I said, genuinely unconvinced.

"Let me back up a bit first," Marsh said. "Moore was found naked, strangled and left for dead in what looked like a violent home invasion. That part you know. What I'd obviously wanted to forget was Moore had been sexually assaulted with an object from her home office. Just as Banks had been."

I clenched my jaw. I was about to tread into territory I really didn't want to venture through. At least I didn't need specifics to get to a conclusion. "The perp used something from Moore's office," I reiterated. "I'd definitely say that something she wrote attracted our unsub's attention." I was hanging tight on how this all tied into West and Sullivan.

Marsh snapped her fingers and pointed at me. "What I discovered was, twenty-one years ago, fifteen years before the article on the Mayfield family, Moore wrote a piece on another family for the local paper where she lived in Georgia."

"The unsub was said to have a Georgia accent," Jack said, hope threading into his voice.

"That's right." Marsh pulled printouts from her folder and handed them to Zach to pass around. "That's the article. It was also an opinion piece about a family who was affected by a DUI accident." She pointed to the handout. "Meet the Kensington family from Warner Robins, Georgia."

"'*Chaos Creates a Family*,'" Zach read, holding the article at an angle. "There's that word again."

I looked at my copy, at the black-and-white photo of a family with two boys.

"The Kensingtons adopted their nephew when his parents were killed in a drunk driving accident," Marsh told us. "The article focused on how loving the family was taking in their nephew. What wasn't mentioned in the article was that the Kensingtons—a family of three who had a son—didn't have a lot of money... And that they had even less after adopting their nephew, Michael Hughes."

"So we're thinking our unsub is..." I prompted Marsh.

Marsh put a printout of an enlarged DMV photo on the table. "Jason Kensington."

"The son?" I asked.

"Uh-huh."

Everything our unsub had done so far involved both money—or lack thereof—and death by DUI. "It was the chaos, the burden of not having as much money anymore, that snapped the kid?" I tossed out the theory with incredulity.

"Yeah, really?" Paige started. "He's not happy with the gifts under the tree at Christmas so he becomes a serial killer?"

"Oh, it was worse than just tight times," Marsh said. "It became a devastation. Mr. Kensington lost his job not long after taking in his wife's nephew and turned to the bottle. The wife left him after the first year and ended up marrying another man."

"And the boys?" I asked. "What happened to them?"

"They stayed with Mr. Kensington," Marsh responded.

"I'm starting to see how Moore's story about Mayfield could have triggered our unsub to kill Moore," I said. "She'd downplayed the severity of what happened to the Mayfield family just as she had the Kensington family. It could have brought everything back to Jason's mind, and I see how that could anger him."

"Exactly." Marsh said. "Now Jason was sixteen when the article hit on his family, and he would have been thirty-one when he killed Moore. What's more, within six months of her murder, an article on West's release from prison was published in the same paper Moore had freelanced for."

"The same paper? That can't be a coincidence," I chimed in. "The fact that West had served time obviously mattered little to Kensington, either. He'd killed once and now he had reason to kill again," I concluded, satisfied to now know the connection between Kensington and West. Though there wasn't a direct line to Sullivan or Kelter yet. "Were Sullivan's and Kelter's accidents or release from prison covered in the paper?"

"Uh-huh." Marsh smiled. "And Kensington lives in an apartment within the activity radius."

Jack's phone rang, and I jumped. He answered on speaker. "What do you have, Nadia?"

"Jason Kensington." Nadia sounded so proud of herself. No one said anything. "Aw, you beat me to it, didn't you?"

"Detective Marsh did," Jack told her. "What did you find out?"

"You know about the cousin?"

"Uh-huh."

"His parents?"

"Uh-huh."

"Did you know that Kensington's cousin, Michael Hughes, has been in a long-term care facility for the last twenty years from a boating accident that took away his quality of life?"

For twenty years? "How old is this Michael?" I asked.

"Oh, so I take it this is new information?" Nadia sounded pleased, and I imagined her eagerly rubbing her hands together. "Michael's thirty-four and Jason Kensington is thirty-seven."

"Why do I have the feeling it wasn't an accident?" I asked, not sure I wanted to know the answer.

Nadia continued. "I was of the same mind as you, Brandon. It seemed hinky to me. Though there's no way to prove it was intentional."

"What happened?" Paige asked.

"Jason and Michael were pulling into a slip at a marina. Jason was behind the wheel. Michael had his arm out of the boat to prevent it from hitting the dock, but the boat accelerated and smacked into the dock. Michael was standing at the time, and he was expelled from the boat. He broke his neck and was paralyzed."

"Jason hit the gas on purpose?" Paige asked.

"Like I said, *hinky*. Doesn't help that there was nothing mechanically wrong with the boat that would have caused the engine to rev like it did."

"When was the accident?" Jack asked.

"Jason would have been seventeen at the time, Michael fourteen. It was only a few months after the boys started living with only the father."

"He could have been acting out because the mother left," I suggested.

"You said a *few*, Nadia," Zach pointed out. "As in three or four?"

"Three," Nadia said.

"Okay, that can't be a coincidence," I said.

"And there is a three-year difference between the two boys' ages, too," Zach pointed out. "Michael would have been thirteen when he moved in with his aunt, uncle, and cousin, as well. The occurrence of the number three again. We were also just saying that the families affected by the DUI accidents included sons and/or brothers. Jason could have seen himself as the brother left to deal with the repercussions and aftermath of the accident that claimed his aunt and uncle's lives."

"Where are Jason's parents now?" Paige asked.

"Both are dead," Marsh replied. "As I mentioned earlier, though, the mother had remarried. Her husband's net worth is fifty-eight million. He's still alive."

"Wow. Nice," I said.

Marsh went on. "You'll also find it interesting that the mother left money in her will to a Catholic church back in Warner Robins, and she set up a trust that will keep Michael in good care for the rest of his life. She also left a sizable amount to Jason."

"What's a sizable amount?" I asked.

"A few million."

That explained the donations. "Does Jason have a job?" I asked, thinking he must have latched on to his victims someplace we failed to see.

"He does, and that's how I found him," Nadia said. "He works part-time transporting bodies from the hospital to the morgue. All the DUI accident victims were transported by him."

I raised an eyebrow at Jack. Surprisingly, he did the same. Ava Jett had told us that our unsub had a keycard. I'd thought at the time that he might work somewhere that required security clearance. Maybe Jack had also.

"You'd asked me to look into doctors, EMTs, etcetera," Nadia went on. "It was by tracing the e-mailed threat to Henderson that led me to the hospital. And by the way, Roxanne Cabot was treated at the same hospital."

I nodded. "So our unsub works transporting DBs, but he's also roaming the hospital from the sounds of it. Was there any way our unsub could have found out if the DUI victims were Catholic?" I asked, my mind going to the possible religious connection.

"Well, he got into the hospital system to send the e-mail to Henderson, so who knows what other things he accessed," Nadia reasoned.

"Are you able to determine who he logged in as or on what workstation?" Jack asked.

"I'm working on that," Nadia told him.

"Does Kensington still work for the same transport company?" Jack asked.

"He does. I'm sending you his info now."

"We already have his address," Jack said, glancing at Marsh. "It's an apartment, though. I doubt he's doing the beheadings there. Are there any other properties tied to him?"

"Actually, yes."

I held my breath, and it felt like time had stopped before Nadia said, "Michael owns a cabin just outside of Miami, near the Everglades. And the place has electricity."

"Meaning someone's using it," I said. I'd wager that was where the rest of West's, Sullivan's, and Kelter's bodies had been dumped—and who knew who else's.

CHAPTER FIFTY-FOUR

There was nothing like approaching a cabin in twilight that made my skin crawl. Complete darkness would have been worse, though. Still, out there, removed from civilization, there weren't streetlights overhead, so nine o'clock at night may as well have been midnight.

It had taken a few hours to secure warrants, but we now had them in hand for Kensington's apartment and Michael's cabin. One SWAT team went to the apartment and another accompanied us along with Marsh and some local uniforms at the cabin. Other officers were at Kensington's place of work.

The structure was a good twenty-five yards from the road, and the nearest house was a couple of miles away. The property butted up against a canal and was flanked by woods. Trees towered overhead, creaking and groaning as they swayed in the breeze. *Eerie.* And likely just a precursor to what we were going to discover out there.

Besides the cabin, there was a sizable drive shed, but an officer had radioed in that there was no sign of Kensington's vehicle there.

Jack, Paige, Zach, and I were preparing to go inside to clear the cabin. All police vehicles and our SUVs were parked on a road that ran parallel to the one where the cabin was located. We'd approach with caution and as covertly as possible. We had to do whatever possible not to tip off Kensington if he was home or scare him away if he returned.

"You two take the back," Jack directed Paige and Zach. "Brandon and I will take the front."

The cabin was all of five hundred square feet, if that, so thankfully, there wasn't a lot of space to cover.

Jack banged on the door. "FBI! Open up!"

Silence except for birds and bullfrogs.

Jack knocked again, repeated his announcement, and still nothing. Ten seconds later I had picked the lock.

The door opened to the living room, and there was a dining space and kitchen beyond that. To the left were two doorways—probably a bedroom and a bathroom. Everything was cypress—the walls, trim, ceilings, and furniture.

Straight through the cabin was the rear door, and we could easily see Paige and Zach. Jack gestured for them to take the room toward the back while we took the one at the front.

Ours was a bathroom.

"Clear," Zach said from their room.

"Clear," I reciprocated. I holstered my gun as I came back into the living area. "There's no place for a hidden room in here. What you see is what you get."

It wasn't like there'd be a cellar beneath the property. The elevation was too low.

My gaze cut across the room and out the back window. I couldn't see the canal because of the trees, but it was there. I walked toward the window, and one of the floorboards gave a bit under my weight. I retraced my steps. Either a floorboard was loose or— I hunched down and lifted the corner of a carpet.

"I think I found something…" The skin on the back of my neck was tightening. I played my fingers over the plank and, sure enough it lifted. I pulled my flashlight and cast the beam inside the hole. It revealed a stack of VHS tapes. I thought those had gone the way of the dodo. "I've got a bad feeling about this."

The others were looking over my shoulder as I took a photo with my phone and put on a pair of gloves. The first tape I removed had a sticker on the side that read *Pamela*

Moore. "Snuff tapes?" My stomach soured at the thought; the last thing I wanted to watch was someone's head being severed from its body.

Jack took the tape from me with gloved hands and stuck it into a VCR that was under the TV. Paige got the TV and the volume.

"Op-Ed columnist Pamela Moore passed away today after a violent home invasion left her for dead…"

I let out a breath at the sight of a news report. It sure beat what I'd had in mind.

"He taped the media coverage of her murder," Zach confirmed. "We were right about him wanting to see people's reactions to his handiwork. Given the wear on the tape, he's probably watched it more times than even he can count."

"So if that's Pamela Moore's tape, whose are the others? There are more tapes than the six victims we know about. And are they all news reports?" I asked the question, not really wanting to find out the answer.

Jack stopped the video and ejected the tape. "They'll be brought in and examined." He switched gears abruptly and said over his comm, "We're clear in here."

My gaze went back to the window and to the canal that would exist behind the copse of trees. This location was ideal for holding a victim hostage for three days and disposing of a body. No one would know. No one would hear their screams. But where the hell was he holding them and killing them? The two buildings we were aware of had been checked and cleared. Also, if he killed them out here, where were his victims' personal effects—their clothing, their jewelry, etcetera?

"There has to be something we're missing," I said. "The property's seventeen acres. Maybe there's another outbuilding besides the drive shed."

"We have a satellite image of the property and nothing showed," Zach said.

I turned to him. "You see all those trees, right? Isn't it possible that an outbuilding is hidden from view?"

"Hmm." This came from Jack.

"We need to scour the entire property," I said.

"We'll alert the others, split up, and cover as much ground as we can as quickly as we can," Jack directed.

Moments later, we were in the woods with some of the other members of law enforcement. Some officers still remained at the tree line watching the cabin and shed in case Kensington showed up. The same went for the perimeter of the property.

"We move in pairs, keep communication open, and stay alert," Jack directed. "Be as quiet as possible."

The group of us headed out, spreading along the canal and working in a grid pattern with a few hundred yards between each team. The trees made it impossible to have a sightline to one another, but we were close enough that we could hear if any of us found ourselves in trouble and come running. Zach and I headed north toward the canal.

Remaining quiet was tough as twigs crunched underfoot. And every time, my breath would hitch, fearing I was alerting Kensington to our location. It felt like he was in the woods with us, just lying in wait.

I moved with purpose and hesitation. Somewhere out there, Kensington held and beheaded his victims.

I had my gun at the ready and was making wide arcs with my flashlight. The closer I came to the canal, the thicker the sense of isolation became, like a dense fog. The hairs rose on the back of my neck at the sound of splashing in the water ahead of us.

Alligators?

I looked over at Zach, who was intently scanning the area, seemingly unfazed. I gulped. We were on alligator turf and the closer we got to the water, the more aware of it I was.

The ground became spongier the farther from the cabin we went, and my feet sank into the wet earth, but I stayed focused and cognizant of my surroundings. In the distance, I could hear faint crunching noises carrying through the woods, most likely from the others walking.

Sweat trickled down my back, and the collar on my shirt tightened around my neck—or that's how it felt anyhow. I wiped the back of my hand across my brow.

A loud crack sounded, and I ground to a halt. Before I could apprise the team, an officer came over the comms. He'd heard it, too, and confirmed in a near-whisper that he was working the grid just east of me and Zach.

The noise could have been pretty much anything, but my mind was churning around the possibilities with ease. What if it was Kensington and he was ready to pounce the second one of us let our guard down?

I could see the canal from where I stood now. The moonlight cut through the trees, making the surface of the water sparkle like diamonds. I could discern the outline of a dock and a motorboat.

I made my way toward it. Given the heavy, humid air, sound traveled easily as my footsteps thudded a staccato beat as I walked across the planks. The boat wasn't much to look at: a ten-footer with a pile of blankets at one end. I got into the boat and lifted up the corners of a few of them. Nothing.

I got off the boat, and Zach and I stood at the end of the dock, shining our lights over the water. I hesitated to look down, imagining bodies staring back at me from the water. I ignored the thought and followed the beam of my flashlight. I breathed a little easier, though I was comforted little with how murky and thick with algae the water was. The bodies could be weighted down or tied beneath the dock, or the water could be deeper than I thought.

I turned to find a long stick I could use to jab into the water. Only a few seconds later, Zach yelped, and the motorboat revved to life.

CHAPTER FIFTY-FIVE

Zach felt as though he'd been hit on the head with a baseball bat. A throbbing sensation blanketed his neck and the back of his skull. His head was foggy and spinning, and he was having a hard time piecing together his thoughts. In his mind, he saw Sheri's face smiling at him. He reached for her but couldn't move his arms. They felt weighted down. He tried again, but they were restrained somehow. He panicked, trying to open his eyes but they remained closed. His eyelids felt like they had been glued—

Shit!

Were his eyes really glued shut? Kensington had done that to his victims, though they'd assumed it was after death.

"Help!" Zach screamed, but the words came back to his ears as a whisper. He had to get free; he needed to get back to Sheri.

"Now, now. Don't you know that snooping around another man's property is rude?" The guy spoke in a singsong manner, all light and airy as though he was having a grand old time. He had a Southern accent, too.

Definitely Jason Kensington.

Zach willed his eyes open, and his eyelids twitched as they tried to comply. His heart was racing and his mind still a blur, but maybe if he could get Kensington talking, he could buy time for someone to rescue him. Surely the others couldn't be too far behind. Brandon had been right there with him after all.

Zach coaxed his heartbeat to slow, his thoughts to gel, and his breath to steady. He tried to remember what had happened. There had been a thumping noise followed abruptly by a strike on the back of his head. Everything had gone black. His mind was so hazy he wondered if he'd been drugged, but he probably only had a concussion. From what they knew, Kensington didn't resort to drugging his victims.

"Jason Kensington," Zach managed to say.

"Yes, Special Agent Zach Miles of the FBI?"

So Kensington had helped himself to his credentials. "The others will be looking for me," Zach said, reaching, hoping beyond hope he'd get out of there alive.

"Ah, yes, they'll be looking…"

Movement created shadows through Zach's closed eyelids, and he could feel Kensington move closer to him. Then came a subtle waft of a familiar, cheap-smelling fragrance.

Where the hell am I?

Images started to surface: the canal, the dock…

His stomach sank. *The motorboat.*

"How did you figure it all out, Agent Miles?" More moving shadows. He was pacing around in front of Zach.

Why can't I open my eyes? Please don't tell me they're glued shut!

"Do you hear me?" Kensington pressed.

Where am I?

His thoughts were scurrying around like mice, making them hard to catch, though he knew that Kensington awaited a reply. Maybe if Zach could just figure out what restrained him, he could figure out a way to break free. He spread out his hands, his fingertips in search of something to hold on to, something that would provide him with a clue. All he felt was wood. He moved his hands as much as possible, but he didn't have much range of motion. It felt as if he'd been locked into some medieval torture device or something.

Her head was cleanly severed…

Zach's breath started to come in gasps. He had a very bad feeling… He tried to lift his head but quickly met with resistance. He nudged his head left and right. His neck, like his hands, seemed to be fixed into a hole. Then it hit him: he was in a guillotine.

Zach's heart thumped in his ears, and his eyes shot open. He cried out in pain as flesh tore and eyelashes ripped.

Kensington was standing less than two feet from him. "Agent?" It sounded like he was smiling.

Zach's vision was hazy, as if he were looking through gauze, but he forced himself to set that fact aside and push through. As it was, he had to pull his head back against the wood and up as high as possible to see Kensington at all. And even then, he could only make him out to about his waist. He couldn't make out much beyond Kensington, either, besides the base of cabinets—all cypress like the cabin had been. The floor, too, was cypress, but if this was his regular killing ground, there was no sign that people had been murdered here from what Zach was seeing. He looked to his right and determined that another line of cabinets ran behind him as well. There was a window above the cabinets, its curtains pulled closed. Zach glanced left and could make out more shadows. But he thought he also saw a door.

"There's no way out of here for you," Kensington told him, sounding pleased.

And there won't be for you, either!

Oh, how Zach wanted to retort, but he had to play his hand carefully. There was only one way to prolong his life and that was to get Kensington talking. It had to be a topic that would center around him, of course. He was an obvious narcissist who took pride in his work, finding sadistic pleasure in watching his victims helpless and at his twisted mercy. The more fear Zach showed, the happier Kensington would be. And refusing to show any would anger Kensington.

"You weren't easy to figure out," Zach said, his breath hitching as he tried to will his pain and panic away. "We still have questions."

Kensington remained silent; all Zach could hear was his own breathing.

"You'll be my greatest achievement. I've never killed an FBI agent before." Kensington chuckled and rubbed his hands together. "If I time things just right, you might even be able to see them before you die."

Zach's blood ran cold, and his chest became heavy. It was possible Kensington could make good on his promise. He pinched his eyes shut. He had to pull from someplace deep inside and get out of here. He needed to get back to Sheri. He'd already made a commitment in his heart when he'd asked her to marry him.

"You can't imagine how happy this makes me." Sheri grins, her eyes pooling with tears as she holds up her left hand and looks at the ring. "I have something I need to tell you."

The way she says it so quickly, so infused with excitement, sparks my imagination, but I have no idea what she is about to say. I certainly don't expect…

"I'm pregnant." Tears fall down her cheeks, but she is radiating joy.

My chest squeezes, and my breathing stops.

"Zach?" She reaches for my hand. "Are you okay? You're as white as a ghost."

"Yeah…" I shake my head as if willing away a dizzy spell. "Yes, of course, I am." I smile at her, hoping the expression touches my eyes and is convincing. I kiss her, offering up my heart.

Warm tears slid down his cheeks, and he opened his eyes to watch some drip to the floor.

A part of him was giving up hope, but he couldn't do that to Sheri, to their child. He had to be strong. He had to get through this, finish off this case, and leave the BAU. He would. He'd make the pledge to God Himself if he survived.

"I think I understand why you killed those people," Zach said, relying on flattery to continue working while downplaying his own intelligence.

"I don't think you do." Kensington's response was dry and unamused. He stepped out of view, and Zach could hear him pacing the room.

"I wouldn't blame you, anyway," Zach said, pretending to align himself as an ally. "They killed people, took loved ones away from their fam—"

Kensington closed the distance between him and Zach and bent over. Zach turned to look at him, their faces now mere inches apart.

"That is not why I killed them." There was anger in Kensington's eyes, along with a spark of fire.

"Then tell me why." Submissiveness also went a long way.

He lifted a finger, wagged it, and smiled. He stepped back and stood upright again. "You don't get off that easily."

Apparently, Kensington wanted to toy with Zach's mind, but it was woozy enough already. His thoughts were scattered, and he had to struggle to pin them down and make sense of them. If Kensington didn't kill West, Sullivan, and Kelter because of their DUI crashes, then why did he?

There was something in the back of Zach's brain, something that held the answer, but he couldn't get it to come forward. Kensington had also killed Banks, Cummings, and Cabot. And Moore, of course, long before any of them. She was believed to have been his first attempt, her article on Mayfield was his trigger.

Then the hardships the families of the accident victims had undergone, as well. There had to be something there. He could feel it, but he couldn't form a cohesive thought.

"You look like you're thinking too hard, Agent," Kensington sneered.

A connection between Kensington and the hate mail sent to Kelter hadn't yet been confirmed, but the e-mail sent to Henderson had traced back to the hospital where Kensington could have accessed the system. "It's because of all the *chaos* and *aftermath* the accidents caused."

Kensington clapped his hands.

So this had to do with *rebirth* and *growth* after tragedy. As he'd concluded earlier, Kensington had been affected both negatively and positively by what had transpired in his life. Kensington's hardships must have been mirrored in the plights of the families left behind due to West's, Sullivan's, and Kelter's accidents.

Things had changed when his cousin had moved in, and it wouldn't seem for the better. Kensington tended to assign blame to others, rather than assume it himself, too. It was a trait he could have learned from those around him.

"You know about my cousin," Kensington said, piercing the otherwise silence.

"Michael? We do. That's what led us here."

"Michael came and changed everything," he seethed.

"It would have been hard going from being the only child to having a sibling of sorts."

"Do you have brothers and sisters?" Kensington asked.

"No," Zach lied, not about to admit to a serial killer that he had a sister.

"Then you can imagine how hard it was to share after all those years alone."

Zach wondered if there was more to the man's hatred for his cousin than just the fact that he'd moved in with his family. Did it have something to do with his mother leaving? And why had she? Was it just the fact that her husband fell on bad luck, or was there something far more sinister that had occurred in the Kensington home? Zach's thoughts were starting to pull together now, and he recalled how love maps were made at an early age. They often became distorted due to sexual abuse. It might have been a leap, but were the father's affections shifted from Jason to the cousin? It wasn't unheard of for the abused to become hurt and envious when the adult abuser turns their attention elsewhere.

"Your cousin moved in and things changed. You weren't treated the same," Zach said displaying empathy. "That would have been hard."

"You have no idea," he spat.

"Every child deserves to know how special they are, to be loved and given attention," Zach said softly.

"They do, but things were never the same once—"

"Once Michael started living with you."

Kensington said nothing.

"Life changed at that point." Zach didn't think it was a good idea to come right out with his suspicions about the father.

Kensington kicked the toe of his right boot against the floor. "What would you know?"

"Your father lost his job, started drinking. Your parents ended up divorced. Your mother remarried. Your dad—"

"I know what happened in my life," Kensington seethed.

"My apologies," Zach said genuinely.

After a few seconds, Kensington said, "I used to get anything I wanted. Dad even took us to Disney World and—"

There was a rumbling in the distance. Kensington ran out of view, and Zach heard curtains sliding back.

Oh, dear God. Tell me help's coming!

If only Zach could do something to use the distraction to his advantage. He suddenly became aware that the only parts of him that were free were his legs and feet. There was no way he could just pull himself out. He couldn't risk shaking his way out of the guillotine, either. With the suspended blade, he'd likely be decapitated before he got loose. Bile rose in his throat, but he swallowed it down.

There was no way he could get out of here on his own. This was literally a case of having his hands tied. And the thing Zach feared more than anything was going to happen to him unless—

Everything fell silent. Zach closed his eyes briefly, calling on a higher power he wasn't sure existed. Silence meant someone was about to make a move. He could be saved. Then again, he might not be. If there ever was a time for it, now was the time to pray.

CHAPTER FIFTY-SIX

My heart was pounding. Whatever happened to Zach was on me. I'd only turned away for a second, but I should have removed all the blankets on the boat and done a thorough search. Kensington had to have been hiding there all along. I wasn't allowing myself any forgiveness, not until I got Zach back safe and sound.

Marsh and I had led the pack and obtained a boat from a neighbor, but they were a couple miles out. The clock was ticking, and time for Zach surely had to be running out. I wasn't wired to think positively as it was, and the odds against him weren't helping turn that around.

"We'll get him," Marsh said, as if she could read my mind. I knew she was trying to help, but her words only highlighted the fact that we didn't really know what the future held. I said nothing.

She was driving the boat, and we were cutting through the water at a fast clip. Others would be following us, but it was going to be Marsh and me who took this son of a bitch down. We'd spent much of the last few days butting heads, but Jack trusted her. That would have to be enough for now. She had proven herself to be an asset to the team, too, and I could admit that much.

"There!" I pointed to a small shed set in from the shoreline about twenty yards.

Marsh slowed the boat and steered us toward a small dock where the unsub's motorboat was tied. I gave the others the update over the comms as she pulled in.

The boat finally in place, Marsh and I looked at each other. "We're going to have to work as a team," she said. It almost sounded as if it was as painful a thought to her as it was to me. When we'd jumped into the boat together, it had been on impulse, nothing more. It didn't even really hit me that I was with Marsh until we'd set out.

"I can do that. Can you?" I asked.

She nodded. "Zach's life depends on it."

"I know this," I said, a touch irritated that she felt she had to point that out to me.

Both of us turned to study the shed. It was about twenty feet by twenty feet with a window facing the water. A curtain was across it, not allowing us to see inside. I took a few steps to get a view of sides two and three. Side two had a door and side three another window. It was also covered.

"Heat-sensing equipment could come in handy right about now," I grumbled.

"We'll have to make do with these." Marsh pulled her gun and brought it up to the ready.

There was something about seeing that bright nail polish wrapped around a Glock that was sexy—and intimidating as hell.

I drew my gun and said, "I'm FBI. I'll take the lead."

"Whatever you wish, *Agent*, but let's make a move."

I brushed past her, my gun aimed toward the shed. I was prepared for Kensington to come out of the shed, armed with firepower of his own, but there were no sounds except for the whispers of reeds blowing in a breeze and the sucking noise of our footsteps in the soft ground.

When we made it to the door, we each braced against the side of the shed. I was next to the door with Marsh tucked into my side.

"On the count of three, we'll go in," I said.

"Going with the surprise attack. Risky," she replied.

"But also effective."

"We don't even know where they're positioned in there."

"We're about to find out," I countered stubbornly. "One, two, three."

I grabbed the door and swung it open. Both Marsh and I entered the shed, guns at the ready. But I wasn't ready for what was in front of me.

Zach was secured into a guillotine. That must have been what made the cuts so clean… Bile rose in the back of my throat.

Kensington jumped back when we entered. He was standing within a few feet of Zach now, and my eyes traced the chain that held the blade suspended down to where it was wrapped around a dock tie-down, screwed to the side of the guillotine.

Kensington lunged toward the chain, but Marsh came out of nowhere and tackled him to the ground. The two of them were rolling around on the floor at Zach's feet—too close for me to squeeze between them to free Zach. I had to help Marsh fend off Kensington first.

She was on top of him, but he torqued his body and positioned himself above her. His hands went for her neck, and I went for his. I put him in a chokehold and yanked back. He continued to squeeze Marsh as she bucked wildly beneath him.

With my free hand, I pressed my gun to his forehead and constricted his throat more. "Let go of her. Now."

I felt his grip weaken, and he let go of Marsh. I yanked him to his feet.

He stood to his full height, his back to me, while Marsh was still lying on her side, gulping for breath.

"Arms behind your back," I directed him.

He put one arm back. I reached for the other, but he swung out and decked me in the head. The force was like a freight train and had me seeing white.

That's it. Gloves off.

I gave him an uppercut to his nose, palm meeting cartilage, and he cried out. I hit him again and again until he fell to his knees. I holstered my gun and went to lift him to his feet to cuff him. He kicked out his leg and brought me down with a hard thump. He was clawing to get to my gun. I pulled it, and he knocked it out of my hand. It went skittering across the floor, and I lunged for it. So did he.

My fingers grazed the barrel, and so did his. Neither of us got a grip on it.

He reached out to punch me, but I ducked out of the way. My reciprocated blow met his nose again. He clambered across the floor and managed to pin me down. His frame looming over mine.

I couldn't hear Marsh's breathing anymore, and I'd worked with Zach long enough to know he was staying quiet so as not to add to the stress of the situation. Or at least I hoped that's all it was.

I bucked and tried to get on top, but Kensington was strong. His hands reached out for my neck. Suddenly, he fell limp and collapsed onto me.

Marsh's face came into view over Kensington's shoulder.

I pushed Kensington off me and to the side, and Marsh held out one hand to help me up. In the other one, she had my gun. She thrust it down, implying she'd smacked him on the head with the butt of it. "Made do with this just fine." The way she was smiling reinforced that I would never want to be on her bad side. Come to think of it, she was all right. She handed me back my gun.

Kensington was moaning on the floor, and Marsh swooped over and cuffed him. He didn't put up a fight. She read off his Miranda rights while I informed the other officers, including Jack and Paige, over the comms that we had secured Kensington, as I went over to free Zach from the guillotine.

Kensington cackled.

It was then that I noticed a padlock secured the pieces that restrained Zach's neck. I spun to face Kensington.

"You'll never find the key," he chortled.

Marsh had her gun pressed to Kensington's head in a flash. "Tell us where it is."

Kensington laughed. The sound was eerie as hell given the situation.

I went over to him where he was still on the floor but now in a seated position. I shook him. "Key. Now."

He stared at me, smugness saturating his features.

The key had to be in this shed. Somewhere. Or on Kensington's person. "Get up." I pulled him to his feet and started patting him down. Feeling safe that Marsh had cuffed his hands behind his back.

I emptied his front and back pockets. No key.

"It has to be here somewhere." I looked at Zach. "Do you know where he might have put it, Zach?"

Kensington laughed again. The man was certifiably insane.

"Don't know. I came to in this thing," Zach said. Hearing him speak brought mixed emotions. It told me he was alive, but there was something so pained in there as well.

I eyed the half-cabinets that lined two walls of the room. Above them were countertops. None of them had keyholes. I opened one door after another until I found something that might get me closer to that key. It was a small safe with a numerical keypad.

Kensington wasn't laughing now. "You'll never guess the password."

Wanna bet?

It had to involve the number three. I keyed in the code 0-3-3-3 and hit the "unlock" button. Denied.

I straightened out and got in Kensington's face. "What's the password?"

"And why would I tell you?"

"Because you know what's best for you."

"Oooh, is that supposed to scare me?" Kensington mimicked quakes running through him.

Marsh thrust a knee into the back of his leg, which had him buckling. I was starting to like her more with every passing second.

"What are you looking at, Brandon?" Zach asked.

"One of those small safes. Usually they require a four-digit password," I told him.

"It probably has to do with the number three," Zach said.

They say great minds think alike…

"I tried zero-three-three-three," I told him.

Kensington laughed again, and Marsh brought him to his knees. He stopped laughing. She bent over and leaned in close to his ear. "Tell us the passcode," she demanded.

"It has to be something important to him—a number, a date, a birthday," Zach said.

A date… What about the year everything had changed for him? We figured he had been triggered by Moore's article on the Mayfield family.

"Marsh, what was the year of that article on Mayfield?" I looked over at her to see that I was interrupting her "fun time" with Kensington. She had her fingers digging into his scalp, and his head was arched backward.

Marsh told me the year. I typed it in and nada. "Didn't work."

"Another monumental time," Zach prompted. "When—" His head fell forward, limp.

Shit!

I hurried to him and supported his head. His eyes were closed and fluttering rapidly behind his lids. "We've got to get him to a doctor."

"Zach, stay with me," I said, even though I knew that he was slipping away already. "Zach," I repeated louder, and he jolted awake. "Stick with me. I'll have you out of here soon. Just keep your eyes open."

Another monumental time…

It had to be when the cousin moved in with his family. I keyed in that year and nothing. "Argh."

Kensington started to chuckle, but it turned into a whimper. I didn't look, but I assumed Marsh was behind the change in Kensington's tune.

Maybe it was just the month and day. "The date of the accident," I blurted out to Marsh. "The one that killed Michael's parents," I clarified.

"March twenty—" Marsh stopped talking as Kensington tried to pull from her grasp. She yanked him back. "March twenty-six."

I keyed the numbers in quickly, though it felt as if I were moving in slow motion. *Zero, three, two, six.* I squeezed my eyes shut briefly before hitting the "unlock" button. If this didn't work, I didn't know what else to try. Then I heard the soft click.

"See that, asshole? We're in," Marsh said.

Kensington snarled.

I opened the safe and found more than a key. There were pendants, necklaces, watches, bracelets, and earrings. They had probably all belonged to his victims. I grabbed the key and hurried to Zach, whose head had gone limp.

"All's clear, but we need paramedics immediately," I communicated over the comms.

Communication came back that Jack and Paige were moving in, along with some local officers.

I held up my hand holding the key, praying this was the one we needed. I slipped it into the hole and it was a perfect fit. I worked to free Zach.

Moments later, Jack, Paige, and some officers entered the shed.

I helped Zach to his feet. He was in pretty rough shape, and I had to support most of his weight. Kensington was hauled off by a couple of Miami police officers.

Marsh and I helped Zach to one of the boats and got him aboard.

"Jack, I'd like to go with him," Paige said.

He nodded. He hadn't said a word since he'd entered the shed, and his expression was dark. He was certainly deep in thought.

"You all right?" I asked him.

He turned his head slowly to look at me. "I should be asking you two that."

"We're fine, Jack. Tough birds." Marsh was smiling as she put a hand on my shoulder. "Good work in there."

"You too." I smiled at her, though the expression was tempered over concern for Zach. I sure as hell hoped he was going to be okay.

CHAPTER FIFTY-SEVEN

Lights were brought in, as were more officers. The area surrounding the cabin and the cabin itself were teeming with law enforcement personnel of all shapes, sizes, ranks, and expertise. K-9 cadaver dogs were brought in and they uncovered the burial site of three bodies in what I would think was record time. It would take longer to identify them. Forensics was working over the shed, collecting all they could.

Kelly—that's how I thought of Marsh now that we had saved the day together—had handed over a diamond that she'd found when wrestling with Kensington. Its cut, clarity, and color hinted at it being expensive—far more so than any of the other pieces of jewelry found in the safe. And none of them were missing a diamond. So whoever this belonged to was still a mystery.

Jack's phone rang, and he put it on speaker. It was Nadia.

"I was finally able to track down the workstation at the hospital, and I know whose log-in was used."

"You're not going to make me ask, are you?" Jack said, rather abruptly.

"Stella Bridges's," was all Nadia said.

The three of us fell silent. My guess was that the other two were just as blindsided as I was. "Stella Bridges?" I repeated.

"That's right. And what's more, I've been able to connect Bridges and Kensington." Nadia paused just a few seconds to draw in a breath. "Bridges's supervisor at the hospital ordered her to complete an anger management course when she hit a fellow doctor, who was also her ex-lover. I got ahold of the records for that course and found that Jason Kensington was there, too."

I wasn't even going to ask how Nadia found this out at—I looked at my watch—close to midnight.

"Why was Kensington there?" Kelly asked.

"I couldn't find any reason that he had to be," Nadia replied. "I'd say that he chose to be."

"So they hit it off, became friends, and decided to become a serial killing duo?" I theorized. As crazy as it sounded, it was plausible.

"Not sure if it's that simple, or even of the extent of Bridges's involvement in the murders, for that matter," Nadia said, "but I wouldn't be surprised if she's had some idea of what Kensington's been up to."

"Well, at least it seems likely she's either behind the hate mail to Henderson or facilitated things so Kensington could send it," Jack said. "We don't know if they were conspiring together, but we need to find out. We can at least bring her in for suspicions of uttering threats to Henderson."

"Ah, Jack? There's more," Nadia said. "Bridges also lost her mother to a drunk driver. The defense attorney got the charges dropped on a technicality."

I thought there was an element to the killings that spoke to a disapproval of sentencing. It could have been Bridges's influence on Kensington, assuming they were buddies. "Can we even put Bridges and Kensington in contact after the course?"

"Uh-huh. I took the initiative and got ahold of Bridges's phone records. She talked to Kensington for twenty minutes the day of Kelter's release."

I turned to Jack, who thanked Nadia and ended the call.

"Let's go bring her in," Jack said, and I wasn't about to argue.

...

Two hours later, we were at Bridges's front gate, an arrest warrant in hand. She buzzed us in and answered the door with a serene look on her face.

"You found her killer?" There was the hint of a smile on her face, but it faded when Jack told her to turn around and put her hands behind her back.

"What?" she spat. "Why?"

Kelly snapped on the cuffs. "You were an accessory to the murder of Jenna Kelter."

"That is ludicrous. I was no such thing," she argued. "We were lovers!"

"You were also friends with this man." Jack held up a color photo of Jason Kensington.

Kelly and I corralled Bridges to the door, and she fought us the entire way.

"You don't understand, you..." She stopped talking, and she stopped bucking. "I have the right to freedom of speech, to speak out when people do horrible things."

"So you admit to sending threatening hate mail to Brian Henderson, Jenna's lawyer?" I ground out.

"I...I plead the fifth."

"Let's go." I shoved her forward to get her moving again, and as I did, I tightened my grip on her wrist. My fingertip dipped into an indent on the tennis bracelet she wore. "Just a second, Detective."

Kelly stopped all movement, and I bent over to take a closer look at Bridges's bracelet.

"Like the view back there?" Bridges asked.

I ignored her and turned the bracelet. At a quarter turn, I saw it. "You're missing a diamond."

"I'm what?" Bridges snapped.

"You're missing a diamond," I repeated, "from your tennis bracelet."

"I can't..." Bridges's eyes widened, and I glanced at Kelly.

"You were there with Jenna when the killer had her," Kelly accused before I could. "Does the Hippocratic oath mean nothing to you? And you claimed to have loved—"

"Please," Bridges hissed. "Love only takes a person so far. She *killed* someone," she uttered with contempt.

"Then you *let* someone kill her," Jack rebuked.

"I didn't…" Bridges went reflective.

"Still, you could have helped her, but you didn't," I said. "You even called Jason the day Jenna was released. You were probably talking about how to arrange the abduction."

"You can't—" Bridges clamped her jaw shut. "I demand a lawyer."

No surprise there. The bitch was guilty as hell. Whether she was also involved in West's and Sullivan's murders or not, I didn't know. But the coolness that emanated from Bridges and blanketed the foyer of her house had told me she wouldn't have shed a tear even if she had.

CHAPTER FIFTY-EIGHT

Zach had hardly slept, but his REM cycle had a lot working against it. The hospital wanted to hold him overnight, and whenever he closed his eyes, he was transported back to the guillotine. The sun coming through the window told him it was morning, and the clock on the wall confirmed it was nine. Thoughts of being held in a guillotine had given him night sweats.

Being strapped up in that contraption had really been a matter of being too close. He'd thought he was going to die, and he now viewed still being alive as an opportunity to change his life. It had certainly provided him with clarity; he knew exactly what he was going to do about the BAU. He'd even made a call to Sheri last night—or early this morning, rather—and bared his soul. He told her about the promise he'd made to himself years ago—*after* he shared with her what he'd just been through. It would give her more insight into the dangers that were possible if he stayed with the BAU. She'd sounded relieved when he told her he'd made up his mind and that his decision was final. She didn't put up any resistance.

"Oh, look who's up." Paige came into the room, a huge smile on her face. Jack and Brandon followed her.

"Good morning," he said to them.

"I should have known you were a morning person, Sleeping Beauty," Brandon teased, tossing out a smirk.

The nurses had told Zach he'd passed out on the way to the hospital and that in cases of severe trauma, the reaction was quite normal. As if he didn't know...

"How are you feeling?" Jack asked.

"Like I was hit on the head with a bat." Zach laughed, despite the fact it made his head pound. The doctors had confirmed he had a concussion, and the Tylenols he'd taken were only helping so much. And his eyes also hurt. As it turned out, Kensington had glued them shut.

"It was a plank of wood," Paige said. "But pretty much the same thing."

"Oh. Just talking about it hurts." Zach rubbed his head, but it was more for show as he didn't press hard. He didn't dare. "Where's Kelly?"

"She's at the station briefing Sergeant Ramirez." Paige rolled her eyes.

The man was certainly a tool, and it was easy to see just from a first impression. What he'd pulled at Gordon's house with the mayor and the news crew was something else altogether.

The three of them fell silent, and their expressions all became serious.

"Is everything all right?" Zach asked warily.

"Some things occurred after you were taken to the hospital," Jack began, and he went on to fill Zach in about Bridges.

"Incredible." With the word, Zach's memory sparked, his mind clearing enough to let through a ray of recollection. "Unforgivable." He groaned and shifted. "Bridges used that word when talking about the patient she'd lost. Remember, Paige? I should have pieced it together."

"We had no reason to suspect her," Jack assured him.

"When Paige and I went to see Bridges on Monday, to see if she recognized the unsub, she mentioned 'unforgivable.' I should have caught it right away."

"And if you're to blame for missing it, so am I, Zach." Paige touched his arm. "Besides, there wasn't any reason it should have stood out to us. It was just a word, even if it was used in the hate mail."

"But it's not one that is used a lot in everyday speech," Zach said.

"We were focused on the hate mail coming from the unsub," Jack said. "We'd all lost perspective."

Paige rubbed Zach's arms. "And you've had a lot on your mind." She withdrew her hand as if she'd said something she shouldn't have. Zach knew she'd been referring to his thinking about leaving the BAU.

"I'd like to think I would have eventually figured it out, but—" Zach pointed a finger at Brandon "—Marsh came in and saved my ass."

"It was mostly me, but we can give Kelly some credit." Brandon teased. "We also could have left you there...you know...to *figure it out.*"

"Ha-ha, Brandon," Paige said, grinning.

Zach picked up on how Brandon had finally called the detective by her first name, and something about hearing that made him quite happy.

"So you know how Nadia was looking into funerals held at St. John's Catholic Church for DUI victims?" Brandon started, and Zach nodded. "Well, Nadia didn't turn up any more than the Jett and Cole funerals that we knew about already."

"It seems that our unsub was more interested in who the paper wrote about," Paige interjected. "Kelly ended up confirming that West, Sullivan, and Kelter were mentioned in it—"

"The paper never reported on other DUI accidents causing fatalities?" Zach asked, not convinced.

"Oh, there were others," Paige replied, "but the deceased didn't leave brothers or sons behind or meet with financial burdens like West's, Sullivan's, and Kelter's accident victims had."

"Talk about being very selective," Zach said.

"Absolutely," Brandon began. "And do you remember the VHS tapes we found under the floorboards in the cabin?"

"Do *I* remember?" Zach attempted a smile, but for some reason it felt like someone was stabbing a knife into his forehead. He winced. Paige stepped forward, but Zach held up a hand. "I'm fine." He looked at Brandon. "What about the tapes?"

"We were right about suspecting that Kensington met with sexual abuse. So did his cousin. Both boys were abused by Kensington's father," Brandon stated matter-of-factly.

"This was on the tapes?" Zach asked. There was more of that "ugly" he faced with being a field agent with the BAU.

"On some of them," Brandon confirmed. "There were also snuff tapes—not of his victims—and news stories on his victims."

"On one tape of his cousin being abused, it showed Jason Kensington as the cameraman," Paige said, her face scrunching up in disgust.

Zach's stomach clenched. "He taped his own father sexually assaulting his cousin?"

"Yeah," Brandon said. "And you'll never guess what he said at the beginning of each of his recordings."

The spark hit Zach immediately. "Just a guess but… 'On the count of three'?"

Brandon pouted and shot Zach with a finger gun.

"That was how the number three came to define him," Zach summarized. "Kensington didn't stand much of a chance." Oddly, Zach found himself feeling some empathy for Jason Kensington. If things in his life had been different, would the man have been? The answer was definite and absolute: people were all byproducts of their experiences. It's what each person chooses to do with those experiences that comes to define them.

Speaking of, Zach had something quite important to discuss with the team, but he owed it to Jack to tell him first. "Jack, can I talk to you for a moment?" Even just laying out the question made his heart beat in his ears, almost as loud as it had been when he'd thought he was going to die. *Almost.* Verbalizing his decision was going to be much harder than it had been to make. It would present a finality.

"We'll be in the hall," Paige said, and she waved for Brandon to follow. She closed the door behind them. Now Zach was face-to-face with Jack.

The moment of truth.

The thought of leaving the team cut Zach to the core. His hands were sweating, and his heart ached. He cracked his knuckles, hesitating. "I don't know how to say this."

"You want to leave the team?"

Jack's intuitive response stunned Zach, and he looked his boss in the eye.

"You didn't think you'd be surprising me with this, did you?"

"I… Yeah, I guess I did."

"You should have known better."

"I should have *known*," Zach parroted and smiled.

Jack smiled, too. "As soon as I heard about your engagement, I figured it was only a matter of time before you'd be coming to me." He tapped his shirt pocket, then let his hand fall. "Is your plan to stay with the FBI but move to a desk job?"

"Yeah." Zach's voice was in there somewhere, but he was having a hard time finding it. "I'm not leaving because I'm engaged, though."

Jack squinted, studying Zach's face. "Why then?"

He took a deep breath. "Sheri's pregnant." Zach found himself smiling as he relayed the news. The enormous responsibility that a baby entailed had been cast aside. He couldn't wait to meet his child, to teach him or her what he knew, to experience life through a child's eyes.

"Congratulations." Jack's sentiment was sincere, but Zach read disappointment in his eyes, maybe even sadness.

"I can stay on awhile longer," Zach rushed out. "I wouldn't want to leave you shorthanded or anything. She's just a couple of months along."

"We'll figure it out." Jack took out his pack of cigarettes and pulled one out of the sleeve.

"I'll get you an official letter of resignation." Zach was rambling now, his nerves working him over.

"I don't want you to concern yourself with how I'm going to handle your leaving. We'll all be fine." He stuck the unlit cigarette in his mouth and spoke with it bobbing there. "Not to say we aren't going to miss you. And you better say your goodbyes to them."

"Why don't you bring them back in?" Zach's heart was tearing apart; that was the awful thing about goodbyes.

"I'll go get them." Jack opened the door and told them that Zach had news to share. Paige and Brandon filtered into the room.

It was seeing the look on Paige's face, one of pain that had her chin quivering slightly, that was making this the most difficult. No one had died, and that's why they all owed it to themselves to live life to the fullest.

"You've made up your mind," Paige stated solemnly, and Brandon looked at her, his brows pinched together.

"I did," Zach said.

Jack nodded for Zach to just go ahead and tell them. The strength in Jack's presence bolstered him, and Zach met Paige's gaze. "I'm leaving the BAU." He slid a glance to Brandon.

"You're—" Brandon stopped speaking, his mouth opened slightly, then he smiled.

"You happy about this, Pending?" Zach asked, pulling out the nickname he'd given Brandon when he'd joined the team. He'd only bring it out now and then after he became a full-fledged agent eight months ago.

"Well." Brandon tilted his head side to side.

Paige bumped him in the elbow.

Brandon's expression turned serious. "Is this because of what happened to you? You could take some time off. I'm sure Jack would be okay with that."

Jack grimaced, but then the corners of his mouth lifted.

"I just need a change of pace."

"Ah." Brandon was smiling again and bobbing his head. "You're getting too old to keep up."

Paige narrowed her eyes at Brandon. "Would you cut it out and be serious?" There was the hint of sadness in her tone and she palmed her cheek.

"Now none of that." Zach pointed at Paige.

Paige ran to him and threw her arms around his neck. "I'll miss you."

Zach hugged her back, soaking up the friendship she offered. "I'll miss you, too."

She pulled away, and Zach was left staring at Brandon.

Brandon held up his hands. "Don't expect me to hug you."

"Just cut it out." Paige shook her head, laughing while wiping her cheeks of freshly fallen tears.

"So if it's not bad joints getting to you, what is it?" Brandon asked.

"You know I'm getting married?"

Brandon nodded.

"Sheri's also pregnant."

"Oh, so you're going to be the stay-at-home parent. Nice. Very modern." Brandon was smirking.

Zach shook his head. "Not exactly. I just want to get a desk job."

"Playing it safe and reliable in your old age. I get it."

"You're unbelievable, you know that, Pending?"

Brandon growled but laughed quickly and came over to hug Zach. He pulled back after a brief embrace. "In all seriousness, *Paige*—" Brandon glanced briefly over a shoulder at her, then turned to Zach again "—Zach, you've been like an older brother to me."

Zach wasn't about to get all soft in front of everyone, but he gave Brandon a slight bob of his head. Then he turned his attention to Paige. "Be sure to call Brandon Pending every now and then for me."

"I can do—"

"That's really not necessary," Brandon interrupted. "Nor is it accurate anymore."

Zach laughed, and the rest of them joined in.

Maybe he'd built up resigning as something far worse than it actually was. He'd always be friends with Jack, Paige, and even Brandon. It wasn't as if he was disappearing altogether or moving to another country. He'd be looking for placement at Quantico still. But the assurances started to dim as reality sank in. Things changed, and that was a fact of life. And they never went back to the way they had been before. Time would put space between them, and eventually, they'd all go about their separate lives.

But just as Kensington's relationships and experiences had formed the man he'd become, so too had the three people in this room shaped Zach. And no matter what happened from here, they'd always remain a part of him. No need to get emotional or regretful. The future was full of possibilities, and he had so much to look forward to.

CHAPTER FIFTY-NINE

Kelly didn't want Jack to leave. Scratch that. She didn't want any of them to leave, but they'd be headed out today anyway. Zach had also been released and was on the mend. She'd gotten over to see him yesterday afternoon, but given what she'd found out, she was glad that she'd decided to give the team some time alone.

Zach is leaving the BAU.

She'd repeated it to herself probably a million times since she'd heard the news. Even now, as she sat at her desk working on paperwork and the team tore down the conference room, she couldn't get over the fact that there was an opening on Jack's team out of her mind. But she had to be crazy to seriously consider a move from Miami PD. Despite it requiring her to give up year-round summer to contend with some cold weather and snow—*ick*—the thought of a career change fired her up inside.

It felt amazing to bring down a killer who had claimed at least six lives. There was a rush to it that was indescribable, a sensation that made her feel whole, as if she mattered and had made a real difference. She'd swallowed the flipside—that she'd failed to save those lives—but it was a tough thing for her to do. She was a perfectionist after all.

Jack was the same way—and so much more than that. Being around him these last few days brought her grandfather back to life. Instead of Jack's presence stirring up painful memories, it had been healing. Beyond the personal, she respected him as a member of law enforcement. She aspired to be like him, to see things through without imbuing them with too much emotion. That's really the way she preferred to work.

She remembered a training officer from the FBI Academy once saying that people are only as good as their leaders. Not an original thought to be sure, but a poignant one nonetheless, and something she believed to be true. It wasn't too promising if she stuck around here.

Ramirez was no leader and certainly no mentor. He'd seen no issue in showing up at a grieving widower's house with the mayor and a news crew in tow. He'd thought nothing of violating the boundaries and confidences that went with the job. Even at a basic level, his thinking was different from hers, as were his motivations. She was all about uncovering the truth, while Ramirez was just about lapping up attaboys. He'd made a good display of that by soaking up the lights at the news conference to update the public on the case. He had told everyone that Miami was safer now—the implication plainly being that it was because of him, his leadership, his people, and his executive decisions. He'd spoken as if bringing in the FBI had been his idea and that Jack and the BAU had been his puppets. Mayor Conklin had stood beside him, not even objecting. Then again, Conklin had made his own plays for the camera as he had talked about how tragic the murder of his niece was and lamented that the city had lost a bright light.

Kelly glanced at her hands, half-expecting to still see nail impressions in her palms from clenching her hands yesterday when she'd heard his little speech. She'd wager the man had hardly known Jenna.

Neither Ramirez nor the mayor had ever mentioned Kelly by name, just that one of Miami's own contributed to bringing down the killer. All that was fine by Kelly. She preferred her name out of the headlines.

She sighed. How could she stay here in good conscience?

She tapped her foot. Clearly, law enforcement wasn't for everyone, but it came with its own rewards. They'd never be able to save every victim, but she was committed to finding justice for those she could. It just wasn't for Miami PD anymore. It was time that she let her mother go, move beyond her past, and embrace her future—no matter how daunting it was. But as Kelly thought about it now, nothing about it scared her. Rather, she was excited. It was time to take a bold step. She needed to go after what she wanted, and after working so closely with the BAU these last few days, she knew what that was. She shot up from her chair.

"Hey." It was Paige. Zach, Brandon, and Jack stood behind her. "We thought we'd drop by to let you know we're headed home."

"Well, they are anyway," Brandon said with a smile. "I'm starting vacation the moment I walk out those doors." He pointed to the exit.

"Nice place to take some time," Kelly said.

"I'm actually headed to Sarasota," Brandon told her.

"Still. Beautiful weather." She smiled at him. When he smiled back, something ached in her chest. She'd miss all of them—even Brandon. Though that wouldn't be necessary if she joined the team... Kelly glanced at Jack.

"Thanks for all your help with the case. And for saving my head—literally," Zach added with a chuckle. He held his hand out for her to shake.

"Hey, I was there, too," Brandon whined in jest.

They all laughed.

"Well, anytime you guys find yourselves back this way..." She rubbed her hands on her pants, her eyes darting to Jack again.

Paige pulled her into a hug.

"Oh," Kelly said, caught by surprise.

Paige stepped back. "We'll definitely have to share a bottle of wine sometime."

"It's a date." Kelly turned her attention to Brandon and held out her hand to him. He took it. Their relationship had a more than rocky start, but it landed on solid ground.

Jack was the only one left to say goodbye to, and it was ripping her apart. She couldn't let him go for a couple of reasons, but she definitely couldn't let him walk away without at least talking to him about joining his team. Plus, seeing him go would somehow make her feel like she was losing her grandfather again. She had to give her dream a shot. "Jack—"

"If you guys go on ahead, I'll catch up," Jack said, inadvertently cutting her off.

Paige, Zach, and Brandon took off down the hall.

Kelly angled her head, a smile curving her lips. "Jack, I—"

He pulled out a card and handed it to her. "You decide you want to become FBI, you've got a spot on my team."

Her heart bumped off rhythm. Had she heard him correctly or were her ears playing tricks on her?

Jack pressed on. "You were too good to have left after the Academy. But your grandad, he had to come down here."

"I couldn't let him come alone, and then when he got sick…"

"I understand. But he'd want you to have a job you love. And you're not happy here."

Tears stung her eyes. Was her misery really that obvious?

"He would," she admitted, her insides whirling with excitement.

"You'll have to jump through some hoops, but if you do that, I'll get you on my team."

On his *team*.

He had said it before, and now he'd said it again. This was getting real.

"Think about it." Jack gestured to the card she still held and extended his hand.

"There's nothing to think about." She hated that tears sprung to her eyes again—and a couple actually fell—when she threw her arms around his shoulders and hugged him.

He even hugged her back.

CHAPTER SIXTY

ONE WEEK LATER...

I snapped the cap off the beer bottle and took a long, satisfying draw. There was something about a sunny day in Florida, lying back in a lounge chair next to a pool enjoying the salty breeze—even if it was on Mom and Pops's patio.

Seeing them had actually been a welcome relief from the job. Our relationship was mostly stitched together by blood and Skype since I'd joined the BAU. Jack had been understanding when I'd asked for some time off, not that my parents had asked how I'd swung the vacation time. All they'd cared about was that their son was home. They never needed to know what I'd recently faced or how close Zach had come to being decapitated. I viewed holding this back a courtesy. Mom worried enough about the dangers that came with my being in law enforcement without giving her something solid to stand on.

But I had changed from this investigation. I appreciated the fragile nature of life more. None of us knew when our time would come to a screeching halt. Zach's life had almost ended right in front of me. *Intense* didn't even begin to describe it, and the fact that all this had been a week ago did little to dull the memory.

We all had to die someday. It's a fact of life, like taxes. There would be no escaping it when the Grim Reaper came, but I was far from ready for that.

Zach had spoken to Sheri on speaker when the team and Kelly were hanging out in his hospital room. Listening to him and Sheri talk, feeling the love that existed between the two of them, had only stressed to me how life was meant to be lived. And lived fully. That meant continually morphing and evolving.

What could I say? With everything I had gone through recently, I was feeling a little philosophical. A part of me even wondered if there was something bigger than us that determined the course of our lives. But if so, wasn't that like living life as a marionette being willed this way and that by a greater being? I needed to believe that I had some say—and control—over my own destiny. In the least, I'd be happy to live out my life doing what I loved, surrounded by the people I loved.

I looked over and took Becky's hand. I did love her, and we'd had *the* talk. I still wanted her in my life, but I wanted to slow things down. She'd taken it a lot better than I had thought she would. And that's what had gotten her invited down here.

I drained some more beer, hoping to quiet my existential mini-crisis. Still, the thoughts crowded in.

This case had tested—and stretched—my limits. I'd made peace with Kelly and that felt great, even if I never saw her again. I had faced a personal fear head-on—no pun intended—and I wished I could've said that I was now able to handle decapitations, but I wasn't. It was just one of those things that would always stick with me. Sometimes we just had to accept things about ourselves, whether they made us appear weak or not. Maybe the judgment should stop with us judging ourselves.

Furthermore, just being in Florida had forced me to think about the relationship I had with my parents. No one was getting any younger, and I had a lot to be thankful for with them. So what if Pops and I didn't see eye-to-eye much of the time? He was still my old man.

"You shouldn't just sit around all day," came my Mom's voice.

I turned to see her and Pops walking toward us. I gulped another mouthful of beer.

Becky nudged my elbow. "Your mother—" She smiled when she noticed I was grinning. "You heard her."

"Maybe," I teased and let my gaze linger over Becky in her pink string bikini. Yes, it had been a brilliant epiphany to invite her to join me down here. And Mom and Pops had been accommodating. Mom was happy to see me so happy, especially since my marriage had ended.

Sun, sand, and surf were taking their toll on my fair skin, and my freckles were out in full force. But Becky's skin was silky and smooth, and—

"Brandon," Mom said a little louder.

"I heard you, Mom." I laughed.

"Brandon." Becky shoved my shoulder and had me nearly upending the beer bottle I was holding.

"What is it with you men? I swear, he never hears a word I say." Mom looked daggers at Pops. I loved how he was on the receiving end when I'd been the one to get her riled up.

Pops put one hand over his heart and held up the other one. "I swear it's a scientific fact that once a couple passes twenty years of marriage, a man doesn't hear his wife's—"

"That's something you just made up." Mom pretended to be irate, but her eyes sparkled. "Besides, if there was some study, it was probably conducted by a man," Mom said and added, "Your father and I are going down to the beach to watch the waves. Do you want to join us?"

"I thought you just said that I shouldn't sit around all day," I countered.

"That's *you*, baby, not us." Mom laughed. "I know how you need to keep busy to be happy." She passed a smile to Becky.

Mom did know me pretty well. At least that was normally the case. But sitting around here was serving me well for the time being.

"You could cook dinner for us," Pops suggested, hearing Mom when it served him. "It doesn't have to be fancy. Just throw something on the barbecue."

"Oh, I don't—"

"Brandon Robert Fisher," Mom cut in.

I held up my hand and chuckled. "I will figure something out."

My mother smiled, pleased to have gotten her way.

They wandered off across the patio to the side gate. Their car started not long after.

"You didn't tell them anything about the case..." Becky shook her head and sighed.

"No way."

She shifted, sitting up straighter. "Not even about what happened to Zach? You facing off with a serial killer?"

When I'd invited her, I'd filled her in. She was in law enforcement. She could handle the truth. I swung my legs over the side of my lounge chair and faced her. Tried giving her smoldering eyes. "That's part of the job."

Becky mirrored my position. "What, do you think you're some type of James Bond?"

"Of course not. He's MI6, answering to her Majesty; I'm proudly American and FBI. Plus, I'm much better looking and far more charming than Bond, James Bond." I put on my best British accent and smiled at her, but she wasn't smiling in return. "Come on, that was good."

"You could have been killed."

I screwed up my face. "Technically, Zach had a better chance of that happening."

"This time around, maybe," she said. "Be serious, Brandon."

The truth was, I couldn't allow myself to sink too deep into thinking that things could have gone a whole lot differently. It wouldn't lead anywhere good. "You know the job, Beck."

"I know..."

"And you go after the bad guys, too. You're a cop. It's not like that's the safest job."

Becky shifted her gaze away from me.

"Eh?" I touched her chin, and she peered into my eyes. I leaned in and kissed her.

"Fine, you got me," she said.

"Good." I smiled. "Now could you maybe rub me down?"

"That's right where your mind goes? To bed?"

I touched my arm. It was glowing red through my shades. I'd been referring to applying sunscreen, but I liked her dirty mind a whole lot better. "Sure. You rub me. I'll rub you."

Becky pursed her lips and narrowed her eyes seductively. "I think that sounds like a terrific idea."

As we paraded across the hot stones toward the house, my thoughts were on both Becky and my job. This case had definitely taught me to look for the positives in the seeming negatives. Chaos and aftermath didn't have to be viewed as horrible. Light came from darkness.

For instance, Zach leaving the BAU. My first thought had been how the team would go on without him. But nothing was guaranteed. Not tomorrow. Not the day after. And things always had a way of working out. Maybe not how we'd like; sometimes it ended up being better. I didn't know what the future looked like for the team, but I did know that if all went according to plan, in five days, sixteen hours, and—I glanced at the clock on the kitchen on the way to the guest room—twenty-five minutes, I'd be back on the trail of another serial killer.

ACKNOWLEDGMENTS

It's been said that it takes a village to raise a child. Well the same could be said of bringing a book to publication. I am so thankful to my team and my friends and family who have helped me through the process of completing this book. The first shout of gratitude goes out to my husband, George, who is by my side always. He reads every one of my books, and he is always there for me along the way. He encourages me and keeps me balanced emotionally through the process.

A thank-you goes out to those in law enforcement who tirelessly answer any procedural questions I have. To a Florida homicide detective, who shall remain nameless so as not to upset the brass, for his valuable insights into drinking-and-driving offenses and punishment, as well as crime scene processing. Also, I thank Ed Adach of Toronto Police Forensics for answering my many e-mails. Thank you to Yvonne Bradley, a former coroner, for being there for me again and responding so quickly to questions I had about time of death, etcetera. Thank you to former detective Samantha Harper for always being just one direct message away.

Congratulations to Angela Jett in winning a character naming and becoming Ava Jett in this book. I hope you enjoyed seeing your name in print and were happy with the character you became.

And last, but not least, thank you to my editing team for their contribution to this project.

Catch the next book in the
Brandon Fisher FBI series!

Sign up at the weblink listed below
to be notified when new Brandon Fisher titles are available
for pre-order:

CarolynArnold.net/BFupdates

By joining this newsletter, you will also receive exclusive
first looks at the following:

Updates pertaining to upcoming releases in the series, such
as cover reveals, book descriptions, and firm release dates

Sneak peeks of teasers and special content

Behind-the-Tape™ insights that give you an inside look at
Carolyn's research and creative process

There is no getting around it: reviews are important and so is word of mouth.

With all the books on the market today, readers need to know what's worth their time and what's not. This is where you come into play.

If you enjoyed *On the Count of Three*, please help others find it by posting a brief, honest review on the retailer site where you purchased this book and recommend it to family and friends.

Also, Carolyn loves to hear from her readers, and you can reach her at Carolyn@CarolynArnold.net.

Upon receipt of your e-mail, you will be added to her newsletter mailing unless you express your desire otherwise.

Keep on reading for a sample of *Past Deeds*, book 8 in the Brandon Fisher FBI series.

CHAPTER ONE

The sun was just coming up, and the sniper's hands were sweaty as she looked through the rifle's scope to the streets eight stories below and point eight miles away. In mere minutes, the target would be dead, and she would walk away. Scot-free. But a lot of variables needed to be accounted for to pull off the shot, including the vehicle and pedestrian traffic that was picking up and the wind coming out of the west at two miles an hour. None of this was a challenge to her, given that she was a skilled sniper, but her nerves threatened to upset the entire operation. She wasn't a killer by nature, but she was good at it—and maybe that meant she was supposed to do it.

She'd do as she was taught and remove emotion from the equation, focus on her purpose, and the end result. Her target certainly deserved to die—and he was one of many.

She checked the time on her watch. *5:56 AM.*

"*Fortuna favet fortibus*," she chanted. Fortune favors the strong.

She readjusted the rifle's stock, letting it sink comfortably into the meat of her shoulder, pocketed there. The rifle was like an extension of her body, another appendage. Peering through the scope again, she took a few grounding breaths.

The terrain was different from her past. In place of desert was concrete jungle. Instead of emptiness, people scurried along sidewalks, rushing to get to wherever they needed to go. They had no idea what was about to take place just outside Wilson Place, a few blocks to the south.

Her mark was currently inside the building, but he'd be emerging in mere minutes. His routine was boring and predictable, which made it easy for her. She knew that every Tuesday, Thursday, and Saturday morning, he'd leave the condo structure at six o'clock in the morning and head to his office.

She was homed in on the front door and watched as the doorman, who had been standing sentinel to the right of it, sprang into action. She held a breath, prepared to take the shot when a thirtysomething woman stepped outside and headed east.

The doorman closed the door after her and returned to his post, but quickly hurried back to open the door again.

This is it!

The sniper took another calming breath, intensifying focus through the scope.

The door was opened, and the target emerged.

Right on time.

The sniper slowly squeezed the trigger and watched the bullet find its mark.

CHAPTER TWO

A sniping took place in Arlington, Virginia, in the Clarendon District about an hour ago, at oh-six-hundred hours, outside of a condo building called Wilson Place."

FBI Supervisory Special Agent in Charge Jack Harper started his briefing with one heck of a punch. Jack was my boss and the leader of a team with the Behavioral Analysis Unit, which consisted of myself Brandon Fisher, Paige Dawson, and a new member, Kelly Marsh. Kelly was a former homicide detective with the Miami Police Department and had recently replaced Zach Miles, who took a desk job as an FBI analyst because he was starting a family and wanted to increase his chances of returning home at night. Risk was minimal behind a monitor versus staring down the barrel of a gun held by a psychopath—which we did far more often then I'd like.

The team was in a conference room at the FBI office in Quantico, Virginia, and I was seated directly across the table from Jack. Arlington was essentially our neighbor, but I wasn't overly familiar with the city's segments. "Clarendon? What kind of neighborhood is that?"

"Clarendon is in the downtown area, near the Courthouse District. Lots of condo buildings, upper-class." Jack responded without enthusiasm, proof he wasn't too thrilled that I'd cut in with questions before he'd finished laying out the situation. He continued. "Several civilians have been taken to the hospital for stress-induced illnesses. Panic attacks and the like, but there is only one reported casualty. A prosecuting attorney by the name of Darrell Reid."

I'd keep my thoughts to myself for now, but prosecutors, by the very nature of their jobs, attracted enemies—though revenge usually took the form of a bullet from a handgun or a stabbing, maybe strangulation. So why had he been taken out so dramatically?

"We've been asked to look at the evidence, establish a profile on the sniper, and conduct a threat analysis," Jack said. "We need to know what we're dealing with here. Was this an isolated incident, or are more attacks planned?"

I looked at Kelly, her shoulder-length brown hair, brown eyes, and…neon-green nail polish? *To each her own*, but I also couldn't help but think that for her first case with the BAU, she'd netted an anomaly. Our team was normally assigned to profile and track down serial killers, but a shooting like the one in Arlington, given its vicinity to Washington, DC, needed to be handled swiftly.

"My guess is the area's busy this time of day," Paige started. "The fact there was only one death makes it seem like Reid was targeted."

"I thought the same," I admitted, "but why such a drastic means for taking him out? Regardless, we're looking for a skilled sniper. Someone who is former military or law enforcement? Someone who still is?"

Jack looked at me with a serious expression.

"The sniper might be skilled, but not necessarily intelligent." Kelly tossed out, and we all looked at her.

"We're listening," I said, challenging her to continue. When Kelly and I had first met during an investigation this past spring, we hadn't exactly hit it off: we butted heads repeatedly. It had taken facing down a serial killer together to morph the dynamics of our relationship into something congenial.

"Let's say Reid was the target." She gestured, her arm shooting out emphatically, her green polish grabbing my attention again. "Why not shoot several people to throw off the investigation? We wouldn't know who the intended victim was, and it would take longer to hunt down motive."

"We're just getting started. Motive is likely still a long way off," I peacocked. "Besides, it's also possible the sniper could have missed the intended target and hit Reid by mistake."

"Not based on what's come in to us," Jack stated sourly. "Reid was hit directly in the chest. Now each of you has a folder." He laid a hand on his and gestured to the ones in front of each of us on the table. "Nadia prepared them, but there's very little there."

Nadia Webber was our assigned analyst who worked out of Quantico along with us. But while our work mostly took us into the field, she remained holed up in a windowless office.

The three of us opened our folders. As Jack had said, there wasn't much. Only Reid's driver's license photo blown up to letter size, his basic background, and contact information for the building's management.

"Nadia's in communication with officers on the ground and is gathering as much intel as she can," Jack added.

Kelly held Reid's background in one hand and pressed a fingertip to the full-page photo of Reid. "What do we know about him besides he was a prosecutor?"

"Nothing much. Everything we know is in there." Jack nudged his head toward the file. "Keep in mind that the first rule of profiling is never jump to a motive. We do that, and we might as well hand in our badges. Our priority right now is whether or not we can rule out terrorism."

Kelly slid her bottom lip through her teeth, clearly uncomfortable by Jack's mini lecture. But she'd appeared frazzled from the moment she came in the door this morning, as if she were running behind and trying to catch up. She'd come to realize soon enough that this job usually felt like that. After all, we were usually steps behind the unsubs, the unidentified subjects.

Kelly scanned the file. "You mentioned terrorism, Jack, but on the surface, Reid doesn't seem your typical terrorist's target. And don't terrorists like to make a bigger splash? The more blood spilled, the better?"

"It's far too early to rule out Reid's attractiveness to a terrorist. We don't know enough about him," Jack replied and studied his new agent as if he were just getting to know her. But part of why I hadn't liked Kelly at first was because she and Jack seemed to know each other too well. As it turned out, Jack had served in the military with her grandfather and had known Kelly from her days at the FBI Academy.

Kelly's eyes pinched with concentration. "As a prosecutor, sure, he'd make enemies, but given how he was killed, maybe we're looking at a hired gun."

"Which would also imply he was targeted, but it's too soon." Jack's tone was cool, correcting, and one I recognized well from my days as a rookie agent—days that were only two years behind me. Any concern I had that Kelly would receive special treatment due to her past connection with Jack was eroding with his rebukes.

"Let's move." Jack stood, and the rest of us followed and headed toward the door. "Brandon, you'll be with Paige, and Kelly, you'll come with me. We'll meet at ground zero. When you get there, ask for Captain Anthony Herrera from the Homeland Security Division of the Arlington Police Department."

My heart paused in dread: *I am paired with Paige.* Guess I should have seen it coming. Jack had mentored me as a new agent, and now it was Kelly's turn. I put on a smile for Paige's benefit, and she returned it, but her expression faded as quickly as mine. Let's just say we had a past, which held no place in the present.

I'd been a student at the FBI Academy, and she, a teacher. In a moment of weakness, I'd ignored the fact I was married, and we fell into bed together—more than once. Big mistake, and nothing to be proud of. That might have happened four years ago, but our efforts to bury the past were thwarted when we'd both ended up on Jack's team. And it didn't help that a lingering attraction and unexplored feelings were still there.

"That's not a problem, is it?" Jack had his gaze set on me. He had found out about Paige and me, but he let us sort things out, making it clear it wasn't an option for us to fraternize romantically and remain on his team.

"No, not at all. It's fine." That's what I said, even as sirens were sounding in my head.

I was divorced now, not because of my affair with Paige, but rather just irreconcilable differences. My ex couldn't stand my job with the FBI. Again, nothing to do with Paige being my colleague. Anyway, Paige and I were making the best of it, and I was currently in a relationship with Becky, an officer from a neighboring county.

"Just keep your mind about you out there," Jack cautioned all of us. "The sniper's probably long gone, but there's the chance they've stuck around to peck off some law enforcement. Vests are mandatory."

Before the four of us made it to the door, Nadia entered the room.

"I haven't been able to uncover any other shootings in the DC/Virginia area that are similar to this one," she informed us.

"Expand the geography and keep looking." Jack brushed past her.

The one thing that Kelly would quickly learn about Jack was that he liked answers, not updates for the sake of updates. Sometimes even those of us who had worked with him for years failed to remember that if we weren't providing new information, we were a hindrance.

CHAPTER THREE

Kelly felt like she was starting her life from scratch with a knot in her gut reminiscent of the first day of school after summer break. Jack had meant so much to her grandfather—and her grandfather to her—that she just wanted to impress him. It had taken her six wardrobe changes until she settled on a cream blouse and a black pantsuit devoid of all personality, but it was clean, crisp, professional, and it communicated confidence. She might not be feeling it, but that didn't mean her outfit couldn't say it.

She split her attention between looking at the road and glancing over at Jack in the driver's seat. Sometimes it was hard to believe she was actually here—her dream of becoming an FBI agent finally realized. She'd wanted this since she'd graduated the academy eleven years ago, in her early twenties, but life had other plans for her, and the bumps in the road all started with her mother.

She wasn't exactly the saint of motherhood—who was, really? But Kelly's mom had served time for murder. Self-defense, really, even if the victim had been Kelly's father. Kelly had been six at the time, but in her twenties when her mother was released from prison and ran off. After Kelly's granddad had a heart attack, Kelly left Virginia to live and care for him in Florida. The dream of being FBI had become nothing more than a flickering memory. It wasn't until this past spring, when she'd called Jack to Miami to help with a case, that she realized she still hungered to be FBI. And now that she had the job, she was determined to keep it, and that would mean impressing Jack.

She opened the folder in her lap and eyed…*bright green nails!* She'd meant to go with something more neutral before today and resisted the urge to sit on her hands.

Come on, Marsh, pull yourself together. Get your mind back on the case!

The information packet didn't offer much. On paper, Darrell Reid looked like a regular guy: father, husband, prosecutor. What had he done to get himself killed? Was he even the true target?

Jack's caution that it was too soon to conclude anything, including motive, wasn't far from her mind, but she felt she had to say something useful. She scanned Reid's background, groping.

"Reid's married and has a seventeen-year-old son." The instant the words were out, she felt like a rambling fact giver. Jack could have read that much from the file himself; he probably had. She needed to offer something fresh and intelligent, or Jack might start to rethink bringing her on board. "He's worked for the commonwealth's attorney's office for ten years," she added. "That's certainly enough time to build up enemies…assuming he was the true target." She was starting to feel she couldn't say anything right.

Jack remained silent, lowered his window, and lit up a cigarette. Technically, he shouldn't be smoking in a government vehicle, but who would be brave enough to give Jack grief about it—or anything for that matter?

"You know, smoking isn't good for you." She'd heard the words in her head as carefree banter, but they landed with more weight.

Jack angled his head toward her, and her stomach flopped. She should have kept her mouth shut.

"I shouldn't have—" She scrambled to backpedal.

Jack smiled at her. "You sound like Brandon."

"Ouch. Of all the things for you to say." She returned his smile. It hadn't been much of a secret that she and Brandon hadn't gelled immediately. Sadly, she'd come to realize part of the reason was they were too much alike. "I take it he doesn't care for your habit, either."

"Nope." Jack sucked back on the cigarette and blew the smoke out the window.

The cigarette cartons she'd seen in an airport duty-free shop flashed to mind. The warning was clear, printed in an open-face font about an inch high on a white band: SMOKING KILLS. She spoke the words out loud.

"So does our sniper," Jack countered drily.

She could have smacked herself for letting her guard down. They were headed to the scene of a fatal shooting; it wasn't the time for mindless chitchat. She would also do well to remember that Jack had the reputation of being one of the best FBI agents the Bureau had ever seen, and it would take more than a personal connection to remain part of his team.

She went back to burying her head in the file, wishing for a miraculous epiphany, but none came. Maybe she was stressing too much about impressing Jack and should let things flow naturally. It wasn't like she was a floundering rookie new to law enforcement. She'd solved countless murders during her six years as a homicide detective with the Miami PD.

Jack entered Arlington, and she marveled at the buildings and architecture. *The city is beautiful*, was her thought, just as Jack pulled up to the outskirts of the crime scene.

He parked the SUV and got out, and she wasn't far behind him. He held up his credentials to one of the officers securing the perimeter, and she followed his lead, feeling pride in displaying hers.

"I'm Supervisory Special Agent in Charge Jack Harper with the Behavioral Analysis Unit, and this is Probationary Agent Kelly Marsh. She's with me. We need to speak with Captain Herrera."

Kelly couldn't wait for the "probationary agent" to drop, but she had twenty-four months left before it technically wouldn't apply. She tried to tell herself that the time would go fast—it always did.

The officer studied her while she studied him. The name tag on his uniform read PEREZ.

"Sure, just give me a sec." Perez spoke into his radio, and voices came back telling him where to find Herrera. He went to repeat what was said to Jack, but he was already on the move.

"Thanks," Kelly called over a shoulder to Perez as she hurried to catch up with her boss.

Past the tape, Kelly took in three ambulances and ten police cruisers parked haphazardly, at different angles, lights flashing. Responders were moving about the area at a hustle, stark looks on their faces, each person driven by his or her mission.

She went past one ambulance that had its back doors open; a man in his forties was sitting on the back step, breathing from an oxygen mask. A female paramedic was by his side, and a police officer was standing nearby.

The voices of panicked civilians carried past the barricade—some in hushed tones, others shrill with excitement and fueled by adrenaline. But it was impossible not to feel the tendrils of death clawing in the air, clinging to the skin as gauze.

This "energy" was a reliable companion where there had been a fatality, and it was something Kelly was certain everyone felt—law enforcement and civilians alike. The only exemption would be the inanimate. The buildings that towered overhead, unable to feel anything. If she thought about it for too long, she'd become envious of the edifices, who stood as silent witnesses with no way of telling their stories.

A trim man of just over six feet, with a head of silver hair, was rushing toward them. His face was chiseled with resolve, but years of experience had left weariness lingering in his pale blue eyes and lines etched in his brow. He held out his hand toward Jack. "I'm Captain Anthony Herrera."

"Supervisory Special Agent in Charge Jack Harper and Agent Kelly Marsh."

Agent Marsh. Kelly liked the sound of that much better than *probationary* agent.

Herrera directed Kelly and Jack to follow him to a command trailer that had its front driver's wheel up on the curb. Someone didn't know how to park, but the vehicle was nestled in a pocket of calm surrounded by chaos.

"As you can see, it's still a bit of a gong show," Herrera said, pointing around. "By now, you know the victim was Darrell Reid, a prosecuting attorney. He had his wallet on him and his identification, so that preliminary step was easy. Of course, his wife will need to provide the formal ID. She has yet to be notified, and we're doing our best to keep his identity out of the media until that happens. Sometimes that's easier said than done." Herrera flailed a hand toward the growing crowd of pedestrians. Back to Kelly and Jack, he said, "The other injured are being treated, and the DB is still on the ground."

Dead body.

"Other injured?" Kelly prompted. She recalled Jack mentioning panic attacks and wanted to confirm that's all they were looking at.

"Collateral injures. Just minor stuff...well, mostly." Captain Herrera squinted into the rising sun. "One woman has since been taken to the hospital, complaining of chest pain." Herrera pointed past a crowd of responders to a tall building across the street. "Shall we head that way?"

Jack started in the direction of Wilson Place, Kelly and the police captain in tow.

"The medical examiner on the way?" Jack asked over his shoulder.

The captain and Kelly scurried to catch up with Jack.

"Should be here any minute," Herrera said. "I put the call in just after arriving on scene at six fifteen."

That was only fifteen minutes from the time of the shooting. "Fast response time," she commented.

"We try."

An officer who had been standing in front of the victim stepped to the side as the three of them approached.

The body was supine on the sidewalk. His gray hair was groomed short, and his skin was pale. His brown eyes were large and open, unseeing marbles. His lips were curled in a mask of horror. Blood had poured from the chest wound and pooled to the left of the torso. Kelly kept her eyes on the corpse; she had never been fazed by the sight of death. Maybe it was because she had been exposed to it at such a young age, watching her father shot before her eyes. To her, death was nothing more than the logical progression of life—even when it was aided along.

Kelly hadn't thought of it earlier, but being there and seeing the body, it sank in that only a highly skilled sniper could have pulled off a shot like this one—through a crowd, vehicle traffic, and net no other casualties. A head shot would have been far easier to execute.

Reid was dressed in a black suit, tailored to his fit frame, and a white-collared dress shirt with a tie. He wore a platinum wedding band on his left hand and a gold pinkie ring on his right. Peeking out from beneath his left sleeve was a Bulgari watch. Not that they were within Kelly's price range, but her best friend Brianna back in Miami had one, and it had cost five figures. Everything about the man's wardrobe was high-end, down to his Salvatore Ferragamo shoes, the toes of which pointed upward.

Kelly lifted her gaze, her eye on buildings farther away and her mind on where the sniper may have built a nest.

Another take at the body, she started to make deeper observations. Who had this man been in life, besides a prosecutor? The shoes, watch, and cut of suit didn't testify to someone working on the right side of the law. If Reid had been a defense attorney, the expensive wardrobe would be much easier to reconcile, as criminals paid much better than the government.

"Prosecutors make, what, fifty thousand a year?" she asked.

"Somewhere around there, depending on the office where they work," Herrera said.

Jack faced her, one eyebrow raised in curiosity. Maybe she should take that as a cue to keep quiet, but she felt doing so would be more of a crime than speaking up. Besides, she finally had a contribution worth making.

"The file we have on Reid said he worked out of the commonwealth's attorney's office. He was fifty-five, had seniority, but still, his clothes don't match up with his earnings." Kelly watched Jack as she spoke for any tells that she was displeasing him somehow, but she couldn't see any.

"What do you think that means?" Herrera was studying her, his eyes squinting in the rising sun.

She glanced at Jack, briefly tempted to elaborate on her leanings toward Reid possibly being involved in criminal activity or on the take, but without anything to back up her suspicions, she thought it best to keep quiet. "Too soon to say," she said, pegging that as the safe road and determined to remain there. She recalled Jack telling them this neighborhood was near the Courthouse District. "Do we know why Reid was here this morning?"

"Wish I could tell you," Herrera replied.

"Could be for his job," she tossed out.

"Sure, but we don't know for sure. It's still something we need to figure out. That guy—" he gestured with his head toward the man sucking back on an oxygen mask "—is the building's doorman. He might talk to you, but my men haven't been able to get much out of him."

Kelly was eager to head right over, but Jack remained grounded, his gaze on Reid. As she looked back at the gaping wound in the man's chest, she was pretty sure the bullet had struck his heart. If it had, was that where the sniper had aimed and, if so, was it of any significance?

Also available from
International Bestselling Author
Carolyn Arnold

PAST DEEDS

Book 8 in the Brandon Fisher FBI series

The sun is just coming up, and the sniper's hands are sweaty as she looks through the rifle's scope to the streets below. In mere minutes, her target will be dead.

A prosecuting attorney is murdered in a sniping that takes place in **Arlington, Virginia**, less than fifteen minutes from Washington. **FBI Agent Brandon Fisher** and his team with the Behavioral Analysis Unit are called in to investigate the threat level and to determine if the lawyer was targeted. **The FBI hadn't anticipated previous victims stretching from coast to coast.**

The team splits up across the country, but more than jet lag is getting to Brandon. As their profile on the shooter takes shape, their one theory on motive strikes too close to home and has him battling with regret over a past decision. He comes to discover some choices not only haunt us but can have long- and far-reaching repercussions we couldn't even begin to imagine. **Will Brandon be able to set aside his personal issues for long enough to stop a serial killing spree before there's another victim?**

Available from popular book retailers or
at CarolynArnold.net

CAROLYN ARNOLD is an international bestselling and award-winning author, as well as a speaker, teacher, and inspirational mentor. She has several continuing fiction series and has many published books. Her genre diversity offers her readers everything from cozy to hard-boiled mysteries, and thrillers to action adventures. Her crime fiction series have been praised by those in law enforcement as being accurate and entertaining. This led to her adopting the trademark: POLICE PROCEDURALS RESPECTED BY LAW ENFORCEMENT™.

Carolyn was born in a small town and enjoys spending time outdoors, but she also loves the lights of a big city. Grounded by her roots and lifted by her dreams, her overactive imagination insists that she tell her stories. Her intention is to touch the hearts of millions with her books, to entertain, inspire, and empower.

She currently lives near London, Ontario, Canada with her husband and two beagles.

CONNECT ONLINE
CarolynArnold.net
Facebook.com/AuthorCarolynArnold
Twitter.com/Carolyn_Arnold

And don't forget to sign up for her newsletter for up-to-date information on release and special offers at CarolynArnold.net/Newsletters.